SPIRITUALIZED

SPIRITUALIZED

VICTOR LEVINE

"Spec Time Trilogy" Author's Note

The **"Spec Time Trilogy"** is a series of books about the conflicted path of an aspiring rock musician, Jon Cells. Equal parts entertainment, historical fiction, and social commentary, the stories, based on an actual character, chronicle three distinct phases of the musician's career and the conditions that helped shape his destiny. Lyrics from each period are woven into the narrative, and the music from those times has been released on separate CDs. "Rocky Heights" music relates to **"Spiritualized"**, "Cracked House" music was recorded during **"Vaporized"**, and "Nobody's Fault" has songs related to **"Immortalized"**.

The first book, **"Spiritualized"** (published in 2015), takes place in and around Boulder, Colorado in 1978. It is framed as a story of growth from one state of awareness to another. The second book, **"Vaporized"** (published in 2011), takes place in Manhattan in 1982 and follows the rough road to glory. The third book, **"Immortalized"**, set in Los Angeles in 1986 (due out in 2017), is about embracing destiny.

The books are interconnected with recurring characters and themes, and each has a procedural mystery that drives the action. All the stories take place over consecutive four-day periods, and characters from the periphery, mystical forces, and relevant subplots broaden the stories of a musician's quest for success into twisted tales with unexpected endings. Some of the Trilogy is based on facts, but all people and events are fictionalized versions of the truth. Lyrics to actual songs, most by Jon Cells and available on his commercially released CDs, appear in italics.

Acknowledgements

The author is truly grateful for the unwavering commitment and creative insights of his wife, Kathryn, whose shared karma and love make their lives possible.

The author owes many thanks to his sons, Seth, Daniel, and Drew, who have been instrumental in keeping him and the spirit of the music alive.

The author's mother, JSL Greentree, passed away while this book was being written, so he looks forward to the time when it is technologically possible for her to read in the afterlife.

Special Thanks to Leonard Seigel, for the frontier guidance and source material on Tibet that influenced so much of this story.

The author graciously acknowledges the comments of his editors, Joan Schweighardt, Amy Engle, and Andrew Christopher, whose keen-eyed suggestions improved the story.

Additionally, the author thanks the real people whose lives were the inspiration for many of the characters.

"*It is believed that the first settlers migrated from Asia to the Americas via the Bering Land Bridge … . These first settlers would later be called "Indians" by European explorers.*"
aventalearning

"*When the iron bird flies, the dharma moves west.*"
Tibetan prophesy

"*Bodhisattva, come and take me by the hand.*"
Steely Dan 1973

Chief Niwot's Curse

"People seeing the beauty of this valley (Boulder Valley) will want to stay, and their staying will be the undoing of the beauty."

Chief Niwot was an English-speaking leader of the Southern Arapahos, a Native American tribe that is part of the Sioux Nation. The Aparahos' territory was the Front Range of Colorado, including the land north and south of modern Denver. They were pragmatic people who signed treaties and tried to make peace with the gold-seeking Europeans, but Chief Niwot was killed by the US Cavalry at the Sand Creek Massacre in 1864. His name, and the Anglicized translation of it, Left Hand, now describes a Colorado municipality, numerous land features, and countless commercial enterprises. Somehow, the influence of his people continues to grow.

This book is dedicated to the Native American spirit of living harmoniously with the environment.

Boulder, Colorado
Thursday, October 26, 1978

Chapter 1

Jon Cells never dressed up for Halloween, so seeing all the decorations in the lobby of the Hotel Boulderado where he had a month-to-month lease only made him feel that much more alienated. In the politically charged atmosphere that ended the war in Vietnam and created a culture gap in the American population so distinct that it was epitomized in name by one of the most popular chains of retail clothing stores ever to launch, it was hard for a musician to make a living. The country was deeply split between young and old, the way it was and the way it could be, and it was easy to tell who was dressed – and groomed – for each part. There were still plenty of people stuck in the middle, but Jon always knew which side of the divide he was on. That much had stayed the same. He had been playing guitar, growing his hair long, smoking pot, and traveling on a one-way ticket to an alternative lifestyle since before he was out of high school. It was a journey he hoped would take him far away from the purgatory of suburban New Jersey where he had started out.

And Halloween was so suburbia. That's why he hated it, and that's why he was in a bad mood the minute he saw the orange and black crepe paper threaded through the carved wood railings of the hotel. What was Halloween doing in his house? Shouldn't it be banished from all the cool places? Cool people were already cool, and they didn't need to dress up and become someone else. That's what straight people had to do – become someone else to feel alive. He knew he was going to heaven or hell – and either place was okay with him as long as it wasn't that vacant wasteland of in-between.

Wearing tight jeans, pointy boots, and a partially buttoned nylon shirt, he got off the vintage elevator and walked through the lobby as if he owned the place. At six-foot-two with a tussled mop of dirty blond hair and sculpted Nordic features, his entrance into the elegantly funky Fleur de Lis restaurant on the ground floor did not go unnoticed. A friendly hostess in a black leotard and long floral skirt guided him to his usual table. "This one okay?" Mavis asked rhetorically.

"Swell," Jon sighed and slipped into one side of the two-person booth.

Mavis noticed his sour mood. "Coffee?" she asked delicately.

"Thanks." Jon looked around and was disappointed to see that Halloween decorations had blighted the restaurant's charm. What was it about Halloween that everyone else found so interesting? Colored plastic streamers strung over curtain rods? Tennis balls draped in white napkins hanging from lights? Cardboard cutout black cats in midprance?

Mavis poured his coffee at the serving station and brought it to him. Jon seemed particularly conflicted, so she asked, "Everything okay?"

"Everything's a long word," Jon grumbled. "But these Halloween decorations are … ." He stared at them and shook his head.

"Yeah, they're great, aren't they? I love Samhain!" Mavis enthused. She had changed her name from Michelle when she became a practicing Wiccan. "The veil between the worlds will be thin this weekend," she repeated the myth.

Jon didn't know what she was talking about, so Mavis went to another table. Staring at a giant pumpkin with a hollow smile that was situated directly in his line of sight, he took four packets of raw sugar, ripped all their tops off at the same time, and dumped the contents into his coffee. Sweeping the errant granules onto the floor with a wipe of his sleeve, he glanced around the restaurant to see if any of the other regulars were there.

A waitress arrived with a menu while he was mindlessly stirring his cup with a spoon. Sasha knew he was grumpy even before he said anything. "Good morning, Jon," she said sweetly, hoping a familiar smile would brighten his day. "The usual?"

Jon looked up at her with a twisted grin. "No, I don't think so, it being so close to Halloween and all that. I think I'll try something different. What do you recommend? Orange juice and black toast?"

She assumed he was joking but wasn't sure. "That's what you want? Orange juice and toast well done?"

Sasha was very sexy – something Jon knew from firsthand experience – and Jon delighted in teasing her. "No, not necessarily. They just seem like the right Halloween colors," he said sarcastically. "What do you recommend?"

Sasha was determined to have a nice day and kept her priorities simple. "I usually eat yogurt and fruit for breakfast, but you can get whatever you want."

Jon's hand slithered under the table and gripped her thigh. "What about you? Are you on the menu this morning? Mmm?" He squeezed.

She backed away awkwardly. "Jon! We've been through that. Please just tell me what you want for breakfast," she said, flustered. "There's another table waiting."

"Oh, alright, if you insist. I'll have deviled eggs and ghost soup. If you're all out of that, just bring me the breakfast special."

Marco, Jon's bass player, glided into the restaurant lip-synching "Just the Way You Are" along with the hotel's speaker system. He had a love-hate relationship with the Billy Joel song because it was the soundtrack to his last failed relationship.

Jon didn't like Billy Joel and thought the song was sappy. "I hate you just the way you are," Jon sang as Marco slid into the seat opposite him.

Marco's faded denim jacket was open and his medium-length hair was still drying from the shower. "Hey, man," he greeted, "sleep good?"

Marco never had anything important to say, so Jon didn't bother answering him.

"Well I didn't. Asshole in the next room had a party that didn't stop until I don't know when."

"The room with the famous writer guy? What's his name again?"

"William Burroughs. He's a junky or something," Marco added with disgust.

"I heard that too. The chick I get coke from out in Table Mesa sells to his little lover boy."

For all his rock and roll pretension, Marco was still a white boy from a middle-class family. "Yech! Gay, junky sleazebag – and *he's* the one that's famous!"

Jon stirred his coffee. "I know, man. Whadya gotta do to make it these days? Fuck sheep?"

Marco noticed the decorations. "No man, the new thing is horror. Dare 'em and scare 'em, slice 'em and dice 'em. You hear about that new movie *Halloween*? There's less blood than *Jaws*, but I still want to see it."

Jon didn't really care about movies because he wasn't in them.

Marco waved for coffee and continued, "So what time are we rehearsing today? I've got some things to do this morning; places to go, people to meet."

"The guy at BlueStar said to come by the studio after lunch, so let's meet there at one o'clock. We can rehearse after that. You hear from Frankie?"

"He said he could get off work early if we were ready to jam. I'm picking up my bass from the shop this afternoon." Marco looked around and realized how overdone the Halloween decorations were. "Holy shit. What's happened to this place? I've never seen it so decked out."

"Yeah, I know. So lame."

"I guess they did it for the big Halloween party this weekend."

"Party? Here? I thought Halloween wasn't until next week."

Marco asked Sasha about it when she came to take his order. "We're going to have the party this weekend," she explained, "'cause, well, it's the weekend, and that's when you have parties." She thought it made perfect sense.

"Oh, I just can't wait," Jon deadpanned. "Scaredy-cats and goofy ghosts."

Sasha knew he was being sarcastic. "You should come, Jon, really. It's not going to be just a regular Halloween party."

"Don't tell me – everyone's going to wear a costume."

"Of course, silly, but that's not why it's going to be so special."

"No?"

"No. The movie company is paying for everything. Free drinks and catered food. Everyone's invited."

"What movie?"

"*Halloween.* You guys are so dense! They paid Mavis and me to help them decorate."

"But why are they having a party here?"

"Why not? The Boulderado always has great Halloween parties."

Marco was beginning to like the idea. "I don't usually dress up for Halloween, but this could be cool."

Jon reconsidered. "I might have to peek in on the festivities to see who has the best strumpet outfit on."

Baby don't you tell me no lies,
'Cause I got a little case of Terminal Thighs.

"The posters say there's going to be live music and dancing."

"Dancing? Where?"

As they imagined how it was going to be set up, Simone LeFete, the owner of the downstairs lingerie boutique, strolled into the restaurant and seated himself at the table in the corner. His slinky Asian girlfriend, whose straight black mane was streaked with a shock of blond, trailed him. Covering his well-fed paunch with a loose-fitting jacket and his balding curls with a beret, Simone exerted a secret-keeping, silent influence over the restaurant. He acknowledged Jon, then did the same to several other regulars. Mavis brought him coffee before he asked. A rough-shaven man rose from another table and sat down opposite him. Glancing furtively as they talked, their quiet conversation ended when someone else stopped to say hello. Flatware clinked a porcelain melody over satisfied murmurs, and sweet bacon odors wafted through the posh air of an unhurried Fleur de Lis morning. An assortment of regular customers and overnight guests savored the tasty Eggs Benedict, seasoned potatoes, custom French toast, and whole grain pancakes. The late-night anthem "Hot Blooded" oozed through the timeless atmosphere of the historic hotel that had been welcoming guests since 1909, and the admixture of diners expanded into uncharted territory when a delegation of Naropa Buddhists occupied the large round table near the window. Having successfully transplanted their secretive disciplines in the New World, the Buddhists' roots were much deeper than anyone realized.

Throughout its long history, the brick and limestone Hotel Boulderado had always been a beachhead for the waves of population beating against the eastern shores of the Rocky Mountains. The building's five-story architecture, reminiscent of a luxury cruise ship, placed all the rooms on the outside and left the center for communal experience: The main lobby boasted a white marble drinking fountain whose water came directly from a nearby glacier; the prominent stairway featured ornate wood balusters and a landing that overlooked the lobby's patterned tile floor; framed photos of the miners and pioneers who had settled the area decorated the original panelled walls; and a massive covered entryway supported by Greek columns was designed to withstand the elements and instill the security of European culture into the brave souls who made the Wild West their home.

Still the largest and most imposing building in the downtown area, the elegant hotel with Victorian flourishes was ground zero for Boulder's recent arrivals. Visiting yoga teachers, iconic poets, entrepreneurial drug dealers, and disaffected youth from both coasts descended on the picturesque town tucked into the foothills of the Front Range like a swarm of social insects, and some took advantage of the hotel's efforts to stay booked by becoming long-term residents. They worshipped the area's natural beauty with and without chemically stimulated vision, were reborn in the icy waters of Boulder Creek, communed with the local mountain spirits, made businesses out of the wild herbs they picked, tooled leather goods from the abundant cowhide, panned for gold on lazy Sundays, and fell so much in love with the ten-speed biking lifestyle that many bought houses, got married, had kids, opened stores, and transformed the downtown economy. But they were always the outsiders.

Situated at the base of stunningly scenic rock faces that marked the end of the Great Plains, Boulder was also home to twenty thousand Colorado University students whose Big 12 football team had a real live buffalo for a mascot, and whose cafeteria was named after an unfortunate prospector who resorted to cannibalism for survival. The stately campus grounds, dominated by multistory buildings faced with native sandstone and topped with red adobe tiles, were a magnet for well-heeled matriculates who played Frisbee on the expansive lawns, basked on outdoor blankets, strummed their guitars, frolicked in Hacky Sack circles, and even got some studying done. Not surprisingly, picnicking under the towering cottonwoods and gorging on the pleasures of youth made CU a popular place to get a higher education.

But Boulder was not just a university town. The National Commission on Atmospheric Research (NCAR) called it home, the controversial Rocky Flats nuclear weapon manufacturing facility was located on its southern edge, a massive IBM office complex was located a few miles to the East, and scores of smaller support businesses tied to the scientific, military, and academic communities employed many local residents and occupied warehouses and storefronts throughout Boulder County. The direct descendants of settlers who had driven the Native Americans to the brink of extinction in the gold rush of the last century monopolized the politics, but Boulder was constantly reinventing itself, and the latest incursion of idealistic hippies, drug smugglers, and Tibetan Buddhists was more like a colorful chapter in the history of the area than what defined it.

The idea that independent filmmakers from Hollywood would choose Boulder, and its iconic, centrally located hotel, to launch a national promotion for their groundbreaking movie surprised no one who had spent any time there. In keeping with its business model of conferring its historic gravitas for a price, the Boulderado had recently hosted an international Buddhist convention featuring the Dalai Lama, a well-attended weekend symposium of UFO enthusiasts, and the pre-rush hazing for the most popular fraternity on the CU campus. The owner of the hotel, a reclusive millionaire who rarely left his mountain redoubt, entrusted his manager, Jack Aikens, to make all the arrangements, and although Jack didn't always follow all the rules, he was very good at keeping the hotel full of paying customers and staging elaborate events. Mr. Lawry, the hotel's resident octogenarian, was always invited, but Chief Niwot never was.

CHAPTER 2

The first time he read about it, he thought it was a joke. Mangled cows hanging from the trees? Aliens? They must be kidding. Next thing you know they'll be talking about Sasquatch. Agent William Walker, who had lived in Colorado all his life, was used to tall tales: miners still alive after years of being trapped down below, missing hikers mumbling about alien abductions, Native American ghosts in the forest, wolves who could speak. He put the Denver Post down, took another sip of coffee, and checked his watch. Crisp morning rays sliced through the windows and formed an irregular pattern on his perfectly organized desk. Where was this guy – and more importantly – what was he like in person? He had heard stories about Agent Falin but had to make up his own mind. That's what the bureau paid him to do.

The phone rang, and Agent Walker heard the secretary outside his door talking. He twisted his chair and looked down over the parking lot to see if any new cars were there. Tapping on his open door made him turn around.

Agent Todd Falin stood there, grinning. "Love this weather! As advertised, cool and crisp. October in LA is like a hundred degrees half the time."

"Welcome aboard," Agent Walker answered cautiously.

"Five years in that smog pit and – hey! You can see the mountains from here!" He moved closer to the large plate glass windows. "Nice digs."

"It'll do for a government building."

Six feet tall with square farm-boy shoulders, Agent Falin stood stiff-legged like the law enforcement professional he was supposed to be. "I hope my office has the same view?"

"It's the next one over. Want to see it?"

"Nah," Agent Falin answered watching a high-heeled woman saunter up to the building. "I think I'm going to like it here."

Agent Walker asserted himself. "Good, because we need you. The agent we lost was one of the best we've ever had."

"What was his name?" Agent Falin asked, scanning the area for interesting distractions.

"Mark Dobson. He was with the department for eleven years – a good man and a great pilot." Agent Walker motioned his visitor to a chair on the other side of his desk. "Have a seat and let's talk. Coffee?"

"I've had enough already, thanks." Agent Falin settled into an armed leather chair. "Can't get over this place. It's just so clean and wholesome. Reminds me of where I grew up."

"Where was that?"

"Iowa. Didn't you see my files?"

"Of course I saw them. Just didn't remember that. I was more interested in what you did in 'Nam. Sounds like you've got the kind of experience we're looking for."

Agent Falin sat up straight and cracked his neck. "Did you read the part about when I busted the Chinks in Long Beach Harbor?"

Agent Walker could see that a few of his new-hire's blond hairs were out of place. "We don't use that kind of language around here, Agent Falin. Got to keep it clean."

"Yeah, I know. Bad habits are hard to break."

"So let's talk about what we've got going on here. Anything you want to ask me?"

Agent Falin smirked. "Is the babe outside your door single?"

Agent Walker smiled; rumor confirmed. "I don't know, Agent Falin. You'll have to find that out for yourself. Mind if we talk business?"

"What is it with you bureaucrats? Never have any fun?" Agent Falin got up and walked over to the window again. "That's why I have to work in the field. There's a whole big world out there and –"

"It's our job to keep it safe," Agent Walker interrupted.

"Yeah, yeah. Got to keep the bad guys on the run."

Agent Walker got up and stood next to Agent Falin. They were roughly the same size, but Agent Walker's skin was a few shades darker. "Colorado isn't always so serious. See that mountain over there?" He pointed.

"Which one? They all look bunched together like one big range."

"You'll be able to tell them apart when you've been here awhile. The one I'm pointing to is Mount Morrison."

"Okay. What's so special about that?"

"There used to be a train that took tourists to the top, but that's not what most people know about it. Ever hear of Red Rocks?"

"Sure, that's where they have those outdoor concerts. I think my uncle went to a Beatles concert there. That's where that is?"

"Right there in the foothills."

"I'd like to see it sometime."

"You will; though you may not be able to hear the music."

"Why not?"

"The windows of the plane don't open."

"What plane?"

"The one we'll be flying over it in."

They were still looking out the window when a Boeing 727 on approach to Stapleton Airport banked from base to final. Agent Falin could see the landing gear deploy. "I just can't get over how clear it is here," he remarked.

"You've caught us on a good day," Agent Walker responded. "The air in Denver is dry because the moisture can't make it over the mountains, so there's not much humidity to fog your vision. Unfortunately, we do get some very smoggy days here when the winds are calm. The Indians used to call this place the valley of smoke."

"So what were *they* smoking?" Agent Falin kidded.

"It's not what you think. They smoked a mixture of tobacco, bark, and berries – kinnikinnick."

"That's a tongue twister. Any Injuns still here?"

Agent Walker decided to keep some things to himself. "We don't see a lot of them anymore, but that doesn't mean they're not here. Come on, I'll show you around by air. We've got a Skyhawk ready and a lot of work to do."

"Great! Same bird I flew in 'Nam. When do we take off?"

"Soon, but first you're going to have to get familiar with the territory. Flying around here can be pretty tricky."

"So I hear. Is that what happened to the last guy?"

"We won't know what brought Agent Dobson down until we get some clues from the crash site. Let's get to the maps." Agent Walker brought Agent Falin in front of the 3-D topographic map of the state of Colorado that took up most of one wall of the office. "We're here," he said, pointing the red marker in the middle. "And this is about where we lost track of our plane." He stretched his arm to the ten o'clock position and landed his finger on a dense green valley between peaks.

"No wonder you haven't found it yet; nothing there. Any chance he might have made it?"

"We can hope, but it's been five days and we haven't picked up any signals or seen any movement. We've got a satellite feed looking for traces of smoke, but with all the ground fog and cloud cover, there's not much chance of spotting the wreckage or a campfire."

"So we're just going to assume the worst and leave him out there?"

"Of course not. You know that's not policy. We've got a hiking team on its way there to recover the cameras and any other equipment that might have survived. We're hoping they can find Agent Dobson too."

Agent Falin ran his hand over the area to feel the contours. "No place to land, and I don't see any towns either."

"Nothing up there except rocks and trees," Agent Walker agreed. "Maybe some bears or mountain lions to worry about. Like I said over the phone, this one's not a rescue mission because we don't expect to find anyone alive."

Agent Falin thought it over. "You can't have granted my transfer request just to find the wreckage. You must have other people for that."

"We do. The ground team will be doing the recovery work. You're here to take over Agent Dobson's mission. He was an experienced pilot, trained by the US Air Force and deployed in Vietnam, just like you."

"I never officially flew over 'Nam."

"Yeah, I read the press brief. Our PR people go out of their way to make everybody happy."

"So who was this guy tracking? Bigfoot? What else is out there?"

"There's more to keep an eye on in Colorado than the first-time visitor can imagine. For one thing, we've got abandoned mines all over the place. It was Colorado's first industry."

"What were they after? Gold?"

"Gold, yes, but other minerals too. Lots of folks know about the silver mines up in the mountains, but there's also limestone they use for building, gypsum for wallboard, coal for energy, molybdenum for steel, and even uranium. The Colorado School of Mines in Golden has been going for over a hundred years."

"I've heard of Golden. Isn't that where they make Coors Beer?"

"Sure is. They use the snowmelt for water and say that's what makes it taste so good."

"I've seen their ads. Can't wait to try some."

"We'll get to that, but there're a few other things about Colorado that you should know about."

"Skiing?"

"That's the part everyone knows, but getting to the slopes can be tricky. Most of the roads through the mountains are narrow. They follow rivers through steep canyons, and because of the weather, they need constant upkeep."

"Sounds like a good recipe for traffic jams."

"Chains are required in some places, which doesn't help the pavement, and unprepared vehicles can't always make the climb over the passes."

"How high are the passes?"

"More than half are over ten thousand feet, and the tunnel on Interstate 70 is over eleven thousand."

"Good thing we're flying, not driving."

"We'll be doing some driving too. The mountains may be rugged, but law enforcement still has to have boots on the ground. Some of the mines are still active, so trespassing is always an issue. And besides the weekend panners, we've got squatter hippies living on state land, summer blizzards, stranded hikers, wildlife poachers, illegal timbering, water diversion, tailing pollution, avalanches, floods, rockslides, and golf ball-sized hail – you name it."

Agent Falin let his imagination wander over the map. "Enough problems to keep the good guys busy, but none of that sounds like Customs Bureau work."

"You're right. The FBI has offices right beneath us. They deal with the local authorities on most of that other stuff. We share information and resources, and they count on us to watch for smugglers."

"Are the smugglers trying to get their stuff in or out of the mountains?"

"Mostly in. Our sources spotted another makeshift landing strip a few months ago. We think Agent Dobson was following a smuggler's airplane when he went down. Let's go meet the office coordinator and get you up to speed."

"Alright! Speed is something I like. When do we get to go flying?"

"Today. Didn't you read the transfer papers?"

"Paperwork's never been my strong suit."

Agent Walker made a mental note. "Well it said to dress warm and pack a bag. We're heading to Steamboat Springs this afternoon."

Agent Falin breathed in the fresh air of a new adventure. "Ready for takeoff."

CHAPTER 3

Duke Dunn had flown into Los Angeles the day before. He was downstairs in the outdoor coffee shop of the Santa Monica hotel where he had stayed, preparing for his meeting. The picturesque weather, warm beach climate, and morning joggers showing off their LA-perfect physiques were making it hard to concentrate. Surrounded by plants and pleasantry, he inhaled the jasmine-scented atmosphere, ordered steak and eggs, and cleared enough table space for his reading material.

"Gooood morning!" a casually dressed man at the next table greeted Duke enthusiastically.

Duke nodded politely, not wanting to be detoured into a conversation.

"Doesn't get any better than this!" the man continued without encouragement. "First time in LA?"

Unable to avoid conversation, Duke answered. "No, I've been here a lot." The waitress turned over Duke's cup and filled it with coffee.

The man had a salesman's ear and heard Duke's southern accent. "Business or pleasure?" It was always the same conversation, and he was very skilled at having it.

"A little bit of both," Duke answered cautiously. There were numerous reasons he didn't want to make any new friends at the moment.

The salesman viewed rejection as an invigorating challenge. "Me too. What's your line of work?"

Duke focused on two seagulls frozen in midflight, surfing the onshore updraft without flapping their wings. They bobbed and glided in a relatively small area of sky across the street from the hotel. "Aviation," he answered, sipping his cup, hoping the explanation would suffice.

The salesman followed Duke's gaze to the gulls and then to the beach beyond. "I sell health food," he said, successfully steering the dialog toward the goal of introducing himself. "This is a great market for me. I come here all the time. What's your name? I'm Sandy; Sandy Woods." He waved and grinned hello.

"Nice to meet you, Sandy," Duke said unconvincingly, then tried to stop the interaction by rummaging through in his over-stuffed satchel.

"I've got today's paper, if you want it," Sandy offered with an extended arm. "*LA Weekly* has the best personals, if you know what I mean."

"No thanks. I've got a meeting soon." Duke took out a magazine with a picture of an airplane on the cover.

Sandy saw the picture and continued his connectivity assault. "I love to fly. I go all over. I was in Bali last week and Miami the week before. Ever been either of those places?" He paused as two young women in formfitting clothes strutted by in tandem, rhythmically punching the air with fists. "I tell you they're really into health and fitness out here. Where you from?"

Conversation unavoidable, Duke answered between mouthfuls. "Boulder."

"Boulder, Colorado? Fried Rocky Mountain oysters with barbecue sauce! That's my favorite thing to eat in Colorado – protein straight from the source. Ever go to the Buckhorn Exchange?"

Everyone knew the Denver landmark, but Duke said, "No, never been," as he leafed through the magazine.

"It's the oldest restaurant in Denver. You ought to try it." Sandy got up to leave and put his business card on Duke's table. "Gimme a call sometime if you're looking for a natural high – completely legit!" Then he looked around to see who might be listening and added, "We import herbs from around the world," with a blue-eyed wink. "Good for what ails you!"

Duke tried to be interested in his aviation rag, but he was single, handsome, and horny. The procession of exercisers bounced and strutted along the jogging path across the street as he sipped his coffee, enjoying memories of chatting up and bedding the local talent when he was a gigging musician. How was he ever going to get any work done here with all the beautiful and friendly people? A perfectly maintained, red '66 Malibu convertible with a white interior and buxom blond driver idled at the stoplight on Ocean Boulevard. Behind her, two scruffy-looking beach bums feathered the gas of their vintage Plymouth Woody station wagon with surfboards strapped to the roof, trying to keep it from stalling. The drone of a biplane announced the benefits of Coppertone from the forty-foot banner it was towing over the beach in front of early sun worshippers. Los Angeles was so different from the small town in Mississippi where Duke had grown up, and he couldn't connect. He owned a recording studio in Boulder that kept him in contact with his musician's soul, but he was older now and had too many responsibilities. Maybe there'd be time for some fun if the guys he was supposed to meet at the Santa Monica Airport didn't stay too long. He checked his watch against the clock in the restaurant. It was exactly one hour ahead of local Colorado time.

"More coffee?" the waitress asked cheerfully.

"No thanks; just a check please."

The sound of the surf, rumbling up the bluff from a half-mile away, blended with the roar of street traffic, and a cool morning breeze seasoned the exhaust fumes with the smell of the ocean. Duke stood up before the waitress returned and hoisted his custom leather bag to his shoulder. A low-flying helicopter drifted down to the beach against the wind. Fascinated with all flying machines, he squinted up.

"Thank you," the waitress said as she deposited the bill on the table.

Duke focused in on the helicopter markings. Rescue? Traffic? Police? He couldn't see. Without bothering to look at the bill, he put a saltshaker on top of a twenty-dollar bill and exited onto the sidewalk. His car was parked around the back of the hotel, and he had to pass through the mall to get to the parking garage. The stores weren't open yet, but he planned to come back later to buy a Hawaiian shirt he saw in a window. After backing his Ford Mustang rental car out of the second floor space of the parking garage, he ramped down to the street, channeled through the radio, and joined the flow of the eastbound traffic on Santa Monica Boulevard. Everyone was talking too fast on the AM dial, and the Bee Gees had taken over FM. The soaring harmonies of "Night Fever" whet his appetite for the high life, and the trebly car speakers made him appreciate the JBLs he had recently ordered for the studio. He wished he had more time for music, but there was always the nagging quest for money. That's what had gotten him into this mess. Money! Which credit card could he use to pay the hotel bill? How long would he have to replenish his bank account before the bill came due? How much would the minimum payments be? The numbers bunched into one another like the crumpled receipts in the bottom of his briefcase. How well did his partner Remy know the guys he was meeting, and how much could he trust them? Duke turned off of the main drag, zigzagged through the residential streets that led to the Santa Monica Airport, and parked on a side street next to the fenced runway. He was early, and there weren't many planes using the field on a weekday morning, so he turned up the radio and leafed through a *Billboard* magazine he had bought at the hotel to remind himself that he was in the music business. When Eric Clapton told Sally to *lay down*, he started singing along.

The dull drone of an incoming plane sounded like part of the next song, so Duke didn't realize what it was until it got closer. He got out of the car to look but couldn't see anything in the air. Then, facing the wind and looking over the ocean, he realized that the onshore flow meant that the plane would be approaching from the other way. He turned around and squinted into the morning sun, but the approaching plane was barely visible as it emerged from the inland morning fog. His pulse didn't accelerate until he saw the unmistakable profile of a Beechcraft King Air. With his gaze fixed on the approach, he walked along the chain-link fence toward the hangar as the twin-engine bird made a stately descent. With landing gear splayed from the rounded surface where the low wings tucked into its belly, the aircraft look like a giant three-legged duck nearing the water. Duke's heart skipped as the touchdown chirped the tires. After a perfect landing, the King Air taxied down the runway in front of the assortment of single-engine Cessnas and Piper Cubs, its towering T-tail affirming its claim as the most important plane on the tarmac that morning. It came to a full stop opposite the office, revved one engine to turn, then shut down both props. Duke was standing near the side-mounted steps as they hinged open.

Remy, his cohort since childhood, wearing his usual army fatigues tucked into mud-crusted boots, donned a soft-brimmed swamp hat and bug-eyed sunglasses to protect his eyes from the California sun. Holding on to the rail as he stepped down, he greeted Duke in a slow southern drawl. "Y'all picked a perfect day. We ain't seen a real cloud since San Diego."

"Welcome back," Duke said with an easy-bro handshake.

A stocky man with a bulbous head grasped the handrail as he descended the steps after Remy. Even though his King Air was one of the smoothest rides in the sky, Oswaldo Benitez was very high strung and usually got nauseous when he flew. Once on the ground, he reached into the pocket of his sport coat and separated two more mints from the roll. He deposited them in his mouth before extending his hand. "*Buenos dias*, Señor Duke. Nice to see you again."

"*Buenos dias, mi amigo*," Duke greeted him. "And muchas gracias for making the trip. I know how much you hate to fly."

A loud curse punctuated their reunion. It came from a burly man with a loose-fitting jacket who hadn't ducked low enough while trying to exit the airplane cabin door. Demario's meaty fist, clutching the handle of a briefcase, emerged before his head and shoulders. Rubbing his forehead after clearing the undersized opening, he straightened up and looked around cautiously from the top step.

"Come come, Demario," Oswaldo encouraged him. "Everything is alright."

Demario felt for the revolver he kept in his coat pocket and stared at Duke. Duke gave him a friendly salute as he came down the steps. The pilot, still seated in the cockpit, held up his clipboard and waved through the window at his passengers.

Oswaldo held up one finger and pointed to his watch. "*Regresar uno la hora*," he yelled. The pilot gave the thumbs-up. Oswaldo turned to his host and said, "Okay, Señor Duke, we follow you."

The airfield was too noisy for conversation, so the procession satisfied their aeronautical curiosity with the colorful assortment of small planes that could only be found at a busy private airport. There were Piper Cubs in need of paint, Cessna 152s for training and rent, sleek Mooneys, tail-dragging Stinsons, reclamation projects from Europe, converted crop dusters, gliders, and decommissioned military fighters. Most of the owners worked during the week and only had time to fly on the weekends, but the tinkering and fussing never stopped.

Owning your own airplane and knowing how to fly it was a luxury that very few could afford, and those who were members of that elite cadre felt superior to the earthbound population. Duke, who had owned his own plane for eight years, wasn't alone in believing he was more than physically above the terrestrial population as he soared and swooped through a limitless ocean of possible directions, witnessing the trivialities of human behavior from God's perspective. He didn't really believe in God – not like they taught him in Sunday school when he was a kid in Jackson – but he did believe in the power of the Universe. A convert to the counterculture wisdom of the day, he believed that everyone and everything was connected somehow. He wasn't sure how it all worked, but he was convinced that he was one of the only people to realize it and had felt that way for as long as he could remember.

His journey from the stifling Mississippi heat to the crisp chill of upper altitudes started when his father bought him a Heathkit radio for his twelfth birthday. It took most of the winter of 1959 to assemble, but Duke never forgot the thrill of hearing the first crackles of static coursing through his creation. He didn't realize it at the time, but that sound marked a turning point in his life. All his inchoate ambitions were mysteriously wired inside one small and sturdy wood box with brass fittings. His next do-it-yourself project, a Heathkit amplifier, was similarly encased, but it was when he discovered Heath's connection to the aviation business that his lifelong interests took form and flight. Heath, the original everyman of aviation, sold an affordable assemble-it-yourself airplane kit – The Heath Parasol – back in the 1920s when flying was a completely unregulated hobby for those brave enough to try it. Young Duke idolized him, and waxed nostalgic about the wild, uncharted times when a man's wits and bravado were his ticket to fame and fortune. Heath's flying kits, incredibly crude by modern standards, were no longer available, but do-it-yourselfers like Duke had been home-building versions of them ever since.

Duke led his visitors toward a row of corrugated metal hangars where the more valuable aircraft were coddled and repaired. He stopped at the rear of one building and dialed the combination to the padlock on an eight-foot-wide door. Sliding it open, he ushered his guests inside the space a friend used to store parts and do metal work.

As his boss instructed, Demario put the briefcase he was carrying on the drafting table in the center of the crowded space and stood to the side. Oswaldo opened the briefcase, extracted a large sheaf of heavy paper folded in quarters, and spread the detailed diagram of an airplane, rendered in blue ink, under the light. "This is the final one," he said, smoothing the creases to help it lay flat. "We made all the fixes you asked for, plus a few of our own." Tracing the outline of a high-wing, custom-built fuselage with his finger, he said, "See here, mi amigo, the wheels have special covers now."

Duke touched the technical rendering and nodded.

"We rubbed down all the creases to make it smooth," Oswaldo said proudly.

"Flies like a jitterbug," Remy added, "only not as loud."

"Yes, Señor Remy likes the long pipes." Oswaldo pointed to the extended muffler. "It's so quiet now you'll have to blow the horn to get the cows off the runway. You don't want everyone to know you're coming, no?"

"No, of course not. I can't wait to hear it run. What about the transponder? Can it be tracked?" Duke questioned.

"No, no, Señor Duke. This one is from Oaxaca – all ears and no mouth." Oswaldo clamped his lips together and filled his cheeks with air.

Duke liked a good presentation and smiled as he studied the outline of the modified wings. "What's its payload now, best guess?"

"We know she can carry two hundred kilos with a skinny pilot and full tanks. Only one hundred if he takes his señorita along," Oswaldo joked.

"Top speed?"

Remy answered for him. "I've had it over a hundred twenty-five knots, if you can trust that indicator. It felt like it could go faster, but I didn't want to push it."

"Yes, Señor Remy isn't the only one who likes to go fast. We call that engine *el jaguar* because of how she growls. Oohhrree," Oswaldo imitated the growl and grinned.

Duke inspected the bulging modifications to the cabin that allowed for two front seats. Oswaldo had been working on his plane for three months. "You sure you put this back together right? What kind of safety equipment is there?"

Oswaldo laughed. "Safety? The only safe place is on the ground, mi amigo. Extra equipment weighs too much, and we don't want to slow you down." He cut through the air with a wedged hand. "That's why you have to pay us before we give you the keys," he kidded. "But don't worry, my friend, you haven't heard the best number yet."

"And that is?"

"Fifty meters."

Duke knew what he meant and considered the possibilities. "Up or down?"

"Either way. You could use an empty field for a runway if there're no trees. That's what our *chacarero* do." Oswaldo popped another mint and folded his arms triumphantly. He had been customizing aircraft for agricultural purposes for many years and was proud of his reputation.

"How many times have you flown this thing?" Duke asked Remy.

"Three," Remy reported. "She's as smooth as catfish skin. I was surfing the thermals like a kid on a coaster."

Duke thought for a moment. "How'd she do in weather? Ever fly through rain or snow?"

"Nah, Baja's a desert," Remy reminded him. "The mountains were too far away to test it there, and the only snow I ever saw was on a mirror."

Duke was concerned about altitude because his journey back to Colorado had some very substantial obstacles. "What's my ceiling now? Am I going to be able to make it over the passes?"

Oswaldo thought it was a fair question. "The mechanics – we talked about that. My people stay close to the ground so no one really knows how high she goes. We gave the engine the biggest mouth we had and opened it up all the way. You can control the mix yourself, but you better stick to the valleys if you can."

Duke clenched his teeth. He knew he'd have to make it over the Continental Divide somewhere. "Guess I'll have to take my chances," he said bravely.

"I don't think you'll ice up," Oswaldo assured him. "We covered the wires with fresh *lanolina* from my cousin's farm."

Duke peeled back to the previous drawing. "How's my lift? The air gets pretty thin in the mountains."

Oswaldo took a smaller drawing from the briefcase and placed his thumb and forefinger on the close-up diagram of the wing. "You see the side view, Señor Duke? We improved the angle of attack with extensions."

Duke knew how hard it was to modify the wing and still keep the plane flying right. "That's some good scoop," he admitted, "but these wings look kind of short now." He measured them with his thumb.

"The wings are shorter, yes, but with the new tips, you won't lose any lift. Short and wide, just like me." Oswaldo rubbed his belly. "Good for floating."

Duke kept searching for assurance. "What's the story with the vertical stabilizers? Will she roll on me?"

Oswaldo inflated his stocky torso to bursting. His rotund face reddened, and he let out a long phew of air. "Mi amigo, Duke, my friend. It is only one plane. You cannot have it do everything. That is like asking your wife to tend the *niños* and be your *conchita* too."

Demario grinned foolishly at the only part of the conversation he completely understood. Remy opened the door to the outside

25

to let in some fresh air and make sure no one was eavesdropping. Duke studied the drawings and muttered calculations to himself, straining at the edge of his knowledge. He reached in his bag to reread the notes he had made from his original drawing, but an airplane on the other side of the hangar started its engine while he was trying to concentrate. When the other plane shut down again, he was out of excuses. "Okay," he said. "I guess we'll know what she can do once we get her in the mountains. Top speed looks good, but we're gonna need a tight stick for close-in flying. I guess this will work."

Oswaldo was unmoved by his indecision. "It's all there, my friend. Everything you asked for. She'll do everything you want if you treat her right. Now what about the payment?"

"Payment?" Duke feigned surprise. "Remy didn't pay you yet?"

Oswaldo looked at Remy with surprise. "I thought you wanted to see the drawings first," Remy said, going along with the charade.

Duke answered, "Well, yes, but I left you a message that you could give them the first half before you came."

"I did."

Demario looked uncomfortable and felt for the gun in his pocket.

"So where is the other half, Señor Remy?" Oswaldo asked suspiciously.

"Left it down in Baja with the family," Remy drawled in slick Mississippi.

"He'll give it to you when you get back," Duke promised.

Demario looked concerned. Oswaldo spoke to him in a dialect neither of the gringos understood, and then Oswaldo asked in English, "And what about the money for the samples?"

"Oh, I've got that covered." Duke patted his satchel.

"Good. May we see the cash, Señor?" Oswaldo asked formally.

Duke pulled a tightly bundled pack of bills from his briefcase and fanned the edges as if they were a deck of cards. "Here's ten-thousand for the first one." He handed the bills to Oswaldo. "And the merchandise?"

Without counting, Oswaldo accepted the money and folded it into his pocket. "*Gracias*, amigo. Demario, please show them."

Demario withdrew a zippered bag from a pocket inside his coat. Duke hid his excitement as Oswaldo removed an object the size of a small book and handed it to him. The white brick was double-sealed in quart-sized baggies.

Duke held it up to the light then opened the outer baggie. "You don't mind?" he asked as he removed the second baggie from the first and pulled the pressure seal apart. A frisson of tension connected them to the coruscating cocaine.

"One hundred percent Peruvian flake, my friend," Oswaldo boasted.

Duke stuck a fingernail under the wrapping, touched it, and sampled the residue with the tip of his tongue. There was no taste, only a numbing sensation that spread to the roof of his mouth. "Very pure," he agreed, smacking his lips and savoring the feeling like a connoisseur. "How much is this? Did you bring a scale?"

"We do not travel with our best scale," Oswaldo explained. "It is too sensitive, and the Federales would be suspicious."

Duke noticed that the kilo was perfectly rectangular as if formed by machine.

"I assure you, each one is exactly one thousand grams," Oswaldo said proudly. "You can keep that one and weigh it for yourself. We'll give Remy the rest when he pays us. You still want the other three, no?"

"Absatively."

Oswaldo calculated. "So ten each for the other three, plus the other ten for the airplane." Oswaldo extended his hand. "*Fijaro?*"

Duke shook on it. "Deal." He made telepathic contact with Remy as he repackaged the merchandise and slipped it into his satchel. "Remy will tighten you up tomorrow morning before he takes off."

Demario folded the plans and closed them in his briefcase. Remy slid the door back open and checked the perimeter as they were packing. Duke put on his manners. "You guys staying for a meal? There are some great restaurants not far from here."

"Thank you Señor Duke, but we have to get back." Oswaldo rubbed his roiled stomach. "Bad weather coming and our pilot is waiting."

"Okay, let's get you back in the air." Duke walked his guests back to the tarmac. Deflecting suspicion, he gave a friendly hello to a stranger washing his plane and pointed out a rare Mooney to his guests. The King Air was refueled and idling by the time they reached it. Duke shook Oswaldo's hand. "Thanks for coming, mi amigo," he told Oswaldo. "See you tomorrow!" he yelled to Remy over the engine noise.

"Weather permitting." Remy winked and climbed on board.

Watching them take off, Duke decided that he had to own a King Air someday.

CHAPTER 4

A morning of full sun had warmed the cool mountain air into the fifties as Jon strolled through the Pearl Street Mall on his way to the studio. Lunchtime on the mall was in full swing at restaurants that made use of sidewalk dining: businessmen and office workers flirted with the college coeds serving them beer and burgers, mothers met for salad and small talk while their kids were still in school, and scientists from NCAR, NOAH, and IBM discussed their findings in the relaxed atmosphere of bright skies and coffee. Graduate students, homemakers, and municipal employees circulated through the local shops on errands, avoiding homeless hippies in ragged sweaters who were scrounging for leftovers to share with their dogs. The mall's bustle was decidedly calm because October wasn't a real tourist season, and the city center had settled on the halfhearted holiday of Halloween to amuse itself in between summer and winter commerce. The grounds of the county courthouse were adorned with previously used orange and black ornaments, and other than the ubiquitous pumpkins, most of the street displays were sparse and dispirited. Blending in with the holiday's orange colors, a single Hare Krishna, having exhausted himself performing the bell-ringing chant of his inveterate troupe all morning, relaxed in the grass alongside the promenade. Jon stared into his sucrose-soaked eyes and wondered what had inspired him to cast off all his clothes and put the saffron on. He couldn't understand the attraction of giving up earthly desires and stopped inside

Rocky Mountain Records and Tapes to rate the musical competition. Seeing how many other musicians already had albums out irritated him, so he exited quickly and was waiting impatiently in the alley behind the studio when Marco parked his battered Ford Fairlane at the end of the mall and scuttled toward him.

Hassled and out of breath, Marco declined Jon's offer of a smoke. "No thanks, man. I'm saving my lungs for the good stuff."

Jon flicked his ashes. "I'm saving the good stuff for rehearsal. You pick up your bass?"

Marco jerked his head in the direction of his car. "It's in the trunk." He had spent the morning doing laundry and borrowing money at his parents' house.

"You bring a tape?"

"Got it right here." Marco patted his pocket.

"The one from last night?"

"That and the one of the really good jam we had last week. Which one do you want to play?"

Jon snuffed out his cigarette. "I'm not sure. Let's see how it goes."

Packed anonymously among a row of one-story enterprises whose front doors also faced the alley, BlueStar Studios was an appointment-only business. Its landmark feature, a dark blue tiled wall, was mostly hidden behind a gated six-foot-high wooden fence.

Marco was nervous. "You sure they're expecting us?"

"Lighten up, man. It's all set," Jon said confidently. "They're busy doing construction or something. Dennis said to just come by."

"You know this guy, right?"

"Sort of. We know some of the same people – business people."

Marco knew not to ask Jon too much about business. "That Dennis dude was kind of mean to some friends of mine. He said they sucked and didn't want them in the studio."

Jon knew the friends Marco was talking about and agreed with Dennis's assessment. "Not my problem, man. Let's go." He opened the gate and approached the oak door with an oval BlueStar Studios logo etched into its smoked glass window. He tried the handle, but it was locked, so he pressed the button on the intercom and waited.

"Hello, who's there?" a pleasant woman's voice asked through a wall-mounted speaker.

"Jon Cells and Marco. We're here to see Dennis."

"Jon Cells," she repeated. "Okay, I'll find Dennis. One moment, please."

A few moments later the door starting buzzing. Jon twisted the modern brushed-chrome handle and pulled it open. They entered a highly decorated reception area with soft gray carpeting, stained wood paneling, and dark blue painted walls. The sophisticated decor was shockingly different from the outside, and the receptionist sat behind a wraparound front desk that hid everything below her neck.

"Dennis said he'll be up in a few," she informed them from behind her fortress. "Would you like some coffee or tea or water while you wait?"

Marco wasn't used to people being so polite, but Jon took it in stride. "I'd love some coffee, thanks. Four sugars and some milk, please."

The receptionist stood. Smartly dressed in a tailored yellow blouse with her hair set in a perm, she looked like she was working in a lawyer's office. "And for you?" she asked Marco.

"Uh, some water if you have any. Thanks."

"Plain or sparkling?"

Marco didn't know what she meant by "sparkling," so he said, "Plain, please."

Diane came out from behind the desk. Her skirt, shoes, and belt matched her professional comportment. "I'll just be a minute.

Please make yourselves comfortable," she instructed before disappearing down a darkened hallway.

Jon plopped himself into a sumptuous black leather sofa and stretched out his legs. "Ah, this is the life," he said, enjoying the polished surroundings.

"Yeah, sure is a swell place. I wonder how much it costs to record here. Must be a fortune just to keep the lights on."

"Some really famous people come here. You've got to be rich or famous or both to afford this place. That's why I'm trying to get us some spec time."

Marco noticed a few gold records hanging on the wall and went to take a closer look. He was mesmerized by the concentric lines that ringed the surfaces and tried to imagine how a needle traveling through the labyrinth of microscopic grooves could reproduce sound.

Diane came back with drinks and handed them blue mugs with the BlueStar logo. "Here you go, gentlemen. Dennis said to come on in. First door on the right."

Jon put down the *Billboard* magazine he was reading and led the way down the carpeted corridor. The dim lighting and monotone walls camouflaged the door into the studio so well that they missed it, and it was only when Marco bumped into the giant handle that they discovered where they were supposed to go. Jon jerked the hefty staple-shaped handle toward him and swung the heavy lead-lined door open, only to find another door in front of him. Seeing no handle, he pushed the second door open, and a change of atmospheric pressure sucked them into a large, high-ceilinged room strewn with building materials and recording equipment. Dennis was nowhere in sight, but lying on the floor under a sheet of clear plastic was the first professional recording console either of them had ever seen. It was eight feet long and about four feet wide. Marco bent over and thought about touching it, but there were so many buttons and knobs packed closely together on its surface that he wondered how it would be possible to move one without disturbing the others. The colored ceiling lights reflected off the plastic covering, making it even more difficult to see the tiny white letters and markings on the painted metal surface. He tried to make sense of the anodized lettering. As a musician, he could have understood "louder and softer" or "treble and bass," but "bus," "wet," "lo pass," and "pad" were from a language he didn't know. Small dashes and were arrayed like hour indicators around each knob, and symbols that looked like hieroglyphics appeared in rows between the knobs.

They were both crouched in front of the sleeping giant, attempting to grok the technical cryptography, when Dennis announced himself from behind.

"Hi, guys. I see you've already discovered Mrs. Peabody."

"Hey, man." Jon slapped him five. "Some piece of gear you got here."

Dennis came closer and gave the console a friendly pat. "You don't know the half of it," he boasted. "Mrs. Peabody can fry eggs, talk to the animals, and fly you to the moon."

Jon and Marco had no idea what he meant.

Dennis bent to one knee, lifted a portion of the plastic cover, and began pointing out the console's features. Jon stood with his arms folded because he was more interested in how the machine would make him sound than what each knob did, but Marco knelt reverentially in front of the modern masterpiece of recording technology and studied the profusion of buttons and dials. Years of recording jam sessions on reel-to-reel tape recorders in basements and bedrooms had left him unprepared for the studio experience, but it would be many years before he realized he had been praying to a false God.

"They're all the same, except the ones on the right." Dennis pointed.

They looked to his right and noticed that the density of the knobs was a little less on the right side. Marco checked both sides against the middle and thought he saw some patterns.

"Twenty-four," Dennis continued. "You can use all of them at once, and there're really thirty-six, including the subgroups. These faders are input to tape, and those on the right are the monitor mix. If you want to hear what you've got, you press these." His finger hopped across a row of square buttons positioned along the bottom that seemed to light up as they were pressed.

The numbered squares, which were the largest and most accessible buttons, made a clicking sound each time they were touched, and Marco had the momentary fear that Mrs. Peabody might be carrying a dangerous electrical charge. Not wanting to be shocked, he moved back as Dennis's finger landed on the square marked "sixteen" in front of him. "Why do you need so many?" he asked. "There're usually only four people in the band."

Dennis realized he was talking to complete novices, so he covered the console and stood. "Believe me, you'll want at least twenty-four channels once you get going. Come on in here and I'll show you the control room." Jon and Marco followed him into an adjacent room with an angular ceiling and diagonally patterned wood on the walls. Furniture and equipment were neatly dislocated to the back. Carpentry tools and coils of wire sat on the floor in front of an older six-foot-long console perched in the center of the room on a chipped metal frame. Dennis patted the top of the console like a reliable draft horse. "I can't play you anything right now because we're down. We're going to put the new desk in tomorrow so you can bring a tape by when we're live again."

Jon was disappointed, but Marco was enamored with the equipment. "What's the matter with this one?" he asked, stroking the worn leather bolster.

Dennis thought about explaining the differences but figured they wouldn't understand. "Oh, nothing, really. It's just that the new one does so much more."

Marco touched a dial on the control surface and gently twisted it. His imagination slipped into reverie with the smooth feel of the friendly knob.

Dennis registered Marco's rapture and altered his approach. "Maybe you guys know someone who wants to buy this one?" He pushed one of the faders up and down like a used car salesman. "A bunch of hits made on this baby – Firefall, Tommy Bolin, Zephyr – and she's not done yet."

"I don't know," Marco summed up his knowledge.

Jon saw an opportunity to appear important. "Well, maybe we do."

Marco looked surprised. "Really?"

Dennis started negotiations. "It's coming out of here tomorrow, and we'd rather sell it than put it in storage."

Jon had no idea what it was worth but figured it was valuable and was always interested in making money. "How much do you want for it?"

"I'm not sure, but Duke will probably sell it for around fifteen grand."

Jon pulled up on the frame to assess its weight. It was heavy, but he lifted it a few inches off the floor with one hand. "Fifteen grand for all that?"

Dennis pushed it back down and remembered what Duke had told him about Jon's temper. "Easy, man, it's not totally disconnected."

Jon tipped it again irreverently. "Just checking."

Marco moved one of the prominent dials in the middle. "What does this one do?"

"That's the cue send," Dennis said patiently. "We turn it way down if we don't like the musicians," he added slyly.

Dennis thought he was the only one who got his own joke, but Marco shot Jon a told-you-so glance.

Jon considered himself a musician and took offense. "What if the musicians don't like *you*?"

Dennis asserted himself. "This is a recording studio. The musicians do what we tell them to do. And if they don't, we throw them out."

Jon didn't give an inch. "And then they go somewhere else to make hits where the people are nicer."

Dennis registered the insult and stared. He didn't want to escalate the conflict with Duke's friend and a potential paying customer.

Marco steered the conversation away from confrontation. "So who have you recorded here lately?"

"We did some tracks for Firefall last week," Dennis reported. Firefall was one of the only big name bands that called Boulder home, and they all knew it. "They were the last ones to roll tape before we unplugged."

Jon wasn't ready to stop fighting. "I thought they recorded in LA?"

"They do. They cut their tracks here and go to LA to finish them." Dennis expanded his chest authoritatively. "This is a totally pro studio. Gold records have been made right here." He pointed to the floor.

Jon considered himself an undiscovered rock star. "Yeah, that's what we heard. That's why we're thinking about recording here."

Marco echoed the idea. "So when do you think this place will be all put back together?" It looked a long way off to him.

Dennis gave the standard reply. "About a week, maybe two. When do you think you'll be ready?"

"We're ready when you're ready," Jon assured him.

Marco followed his lead. "Yeah, we're tight. You should hear our set."

Dennis wasn't really interested but asked, "When's your next gig?" assuming they rarely played out.

"In about a month, but we practice all the time at our rehearsal studio out on Valemont."

The fact that they had their own space gave Dennis an idea. "Ever do any recording there?"

"Just with the cassette player," Marco answered. "We could play you something if you want. It doesn't sound that great, but you can hear all the instruments."

Dennis sized them up and became unexpectedly agreeable. "I believe you. I'd like to play your tape now, but the monitors are unplugged." Then, he switched gears. "Do you have room for a recording console out there?" He put his hand on the old console in front of them.

Marco shot Jon a look of surprise. "Er, I'm not sure. Maybe we do. Why do you ask? What do you think, Jon?"

"We might have room, but who's got fifteen grand?"

Dennis nodded. "Maybe you don't need fifteen grand."

Jon blinked. "What do mean, man?"

"It's just an idea, but it just might work." Dennis moved to the front of the console and delivered his pitch leaning over it. "I'll have to talk to Duke of course, but maybe he'll let me park this thing at your place until it gets sold." Then he addressed Jon. "You're a friend of his, right?"

Jon nodded affirmatively but didn't say anything else because he wasn't sure how much Dennis knew about Duke's business.

Marco's eyes lit up at the thought of the impressive piece of equipment in their humble rehearsal space. "Will we be able to use it? I mean until someone buys it."

"Well maybe, but it would have to be wired in and connected to a tape recorder," Dennis explained, still trying to interpret Jon's silence.

Jon surprised them both. "I might know someone who has an extra tape recorder."

"Really? Who?" Marco asked.

"This guy who lives up in the mountains. He came by the rehearsal studio and said he was looking for a place to set up his equipment."

Dennis knew everyone in the state of Colorado with serious recording equipment. "He's got a twenty-four track?" he asked skeptically.

"I'm not sure. He says he does. I know he's got some professional recording equipment that he got because someone owed him money. He doesn't want it and asked me if I wanted to buy it off him." Jon didn't want to share too many details of how he knew the guy.

Dennis thought for a minute. "Well, I'm not sure who you're talking about, but hooking it up to the console won't be a problem if we have the right connectors. I still have to talk to Duke, but if he gives the okay, we can look into storing this at your place. It'll be easier to sell if it's operational."

Marco was getting excited. "When do you think you'll talk to Duke?"

"I talk to him every day. He's out of town right now but always calls in to see what's going on. I need to take this out of here before I can put the new one in."

Marco expedited the arrangements. "We'll be down at the rehearsal studio tonight. Our drummer gets off work at five. Maybe you want to stop by, see the space, hear us play?"

Dennis accepted the invitation. "I don't need to hear you play, but I'd like to see how much room you have."

Jon was slightly offended. "You don't want to hear us? Duke said he wanted you to hear us play before we came in to record."

"Of course I want to hear you," Dennis backtracked. "I was just focused on the equipment. I always work with the band at least once before we roll tape. That's production. That's what separates us pros from the amateurs."

"Cool. Then what time do you think you'll come?" Marco asked.

Dennis looked around at his mess and sighed. "I don't know. There's so much to do around here and the kid from the AV club who was helping me can't work until after school. He usually gets here by four, and then I have to show him what I want him to do. I probably can't get over there until later tonight sometime."

Marco touched the old console. "I used to be in the AV club. You need some more help?"

Dennis was interested. "Where'd you go to school?"

"Right here, man. Good old Boulder High. Walter Hardaway was my teacher."

"Walter was your teacher? Small world! Walter's the one who's helping us do the changeover. Some of the work I've been having the other guy do is prepping for the switching matrix that Walter's building for us. You know how to solder?"

"Sure do. Of course you have to show me exactly what you want me to do."

"Of course. Good, I could use the help." Dennis recalibrated. "We can get a few things settled when I come by tonight. How about seven o'clock?"

"Works for me. Okay by you, Jon?"

"Okay by me."

"Where's your rehearsal place?"

"It's 3117 Valemont; glass door with a Devo poster."

Dennis nodded and said, "See you at seven."

"Awesome." Marco slapped Dennis a hearty five.

Jon kept his distance. "Later," was all he said before they left.

CHAPTER 5

Agents Walker and Falin stopped for lunch at the Buckhorn Exchange on the way to Buckley Air Force Base. They sat near the bar where the television was tuned to the coverage of the Bronco's recent loss to Seattle.

"You follow football?" Agent Walker asked.

"Sure do. Rams are a great team this year," Agent Falin claimed.

Agent Walker had to agree. "You're undefeated, right?"

"Almost. Last week was our first loss. Couldn't do anything right against the Saints."

An indifferent waitress arrived to take their order. Agent Walker went first. "Burger and fries for me, everything on it."

"When in Rome ... same here."

"Drinks? We've got Coors on tap."

"I wish we could, but we've got to go flying soon. I'll have a root beer."

"Coke for me, thanks."

Agent Falin was watching an interview with Randy Gradishaw. "Now there's a player! I wish we had him on our team."

"You want Craig Morton too? You can have him!"

"Who's this guy Haven Moses? What kind of name is that? Who names their kid Haven?"

"Takes all kinds. Maybe his parents were very religious."

"I don't believe in all that God stuff anymore," Agent Falin told his boss. "I used to when I was a kid, but I saw too much over in 'Nam. If there's a God up there, he's got some sick sense of humor."

Agent Walker had never been out of the country. "Well, I don't know what goes on over there, but folks 'round here got plenty to be thankful for."

Agent Falin didn't want to get off to a bad start with his new boss, so he let it go. The weather report indicated sunny skies with a high near sixty. "Looks like we'll have some good weather for flying."

"I know it does, but you can't go by what you see on TV. Things can change real fast in the mountains. What's the highest you've even been?"

"Flying?"

"You know what I mean. We've got peaks over fourteen thousand feet out here."

Agent Falin thought for a moment. "I've never been that high in a prop. That's at the top end of the Skyhawk's range, isn't it?"

"Got that right. Not much room to stay above the ground. A few thick clouds or one good downdraft and it's good-bye Charlie Bravo. If you don't respect the Rocky Mountains, they're going to disrespect you. The guys at the field will fill you in on all the government safety protocols."

Two juicy burgers, teetering with toppings, came steaming to their table. Agent Falin's nostrils flared at the aroma. "Nothing like the smell of flame-grilled beef."

Agent Walker was used to it. "Lots of that around here. It's always fresh so there's no need to overcook it. Bothers some folks, but you can even smell the slaughterhouses when the winds are right."

"Doesn't bother me." Agent Falin sunk his teeth into the moist flesh for a second bite. "My uncle butchered his own, and I helped out when I was old enough. Made me sick the first few times, but you kind of develop a stomach for it."

"Good, 'cause this is cattle country. Every once in a while we get called in to help sort out a problem."

"Like what?"

"Big rig flips over with forty head, accidents at the slaughter-house, cattle rustlers."

"The bureau gets involved in all that?"

"Colorado's a big state and everybody's up to something. We've got farmers and ranchers with big spreads all over the place. There're thousands of miles of barbed-wire fencing, but it's not enough to keep them from having water wars and boundary disputes. Most of the population lives along the Front Range where the mountains start. Colorado Springs, Denver, and Boulder have all the problems every modern city has: crime, traffic, bad neighbors, and pollution. The mountains are dotted with mining ghost towns, and there're hideaway cabins and single-family homesteads scattered everywhere."

"What about the skiing?"

"Skiing has made Colorado an international destination. Everyone knows about Aspen and Vail. Tourism is one of our most important industries."

"More important than gold mining?"

"There're still some active mines, but most of them were abandoned a few years after they were dug. You can see the tailings and rusted equipment right from the road – along with trout fishermen and white-water rafters."

"Colorado's more interesting than I knew."

Agent Walker swelled with pride and showed off his knowledge of local attractions. "Mesa Verde, near the Four Corners, is one of the most important archeological sites in North America. Teddy Roosevelt helped preserve the area, which was the ancestral home of the Native American Anasazi. Archeologists say the biggest concentration of dinosaur bones in North America is in the northwest corner of the state. That site is also federally protected because, besides the constant archeological digging, the Native Americans that used to live there left quite a few petroglyphs. You already know about Red Rocks and Pike's Peak, but it would take a lifetime to visit all the interesting places. The good thing is even though Colorado's been a state for a hundred years, more than third of the one hundred thousand square miles belongs to everyone – everyone except the Native Americans."

"What happened to them? I mean, were they just killed or moved to reservations?"

Agent Walker was used to answering that question. "A few hundred years ago, the Europeans moved into what they saw as the unexplored Western Territories in numbers that amounted to a full-scale invasion: Spanish explorers came from the South searching for El Dorado, French trappers came from the North looking for beavers, and English-speaking prospectors came from the East when gold was discovered and never left. The Native Americans were friendly up to a point, but whenever there was a dispute, the Europeans usually won."

"It sounds like you've done your homework."

"This is my home, and most of us who grew up around here know all these stories. My great-grandfather came to Colorado in 1865. His wife was half French, half Arapahoe, so this story is personal for me."

"Then you're part Indian!"

"I prefer 'Native American.' One-eighth, to be exact."

"Doesn't it upset you, what happened?"

"Of course!" Agent Walker's emotions took over his tongue.

"Some of my ancestors were quick learners, and they put up much more of a fight than the Europeans expected. They had always fought amongst themselves, so when they learned to ride horses and shoot rifles they were able defend their territory. The Natives were brave and accustomed to the climate, but the Europeans had the technology. Winchester rifles and Colt 45 revolvers have been called the guns that won the West. The Indian Wars lasted for two hundred years, but there were a lot more white people than Natives, and you know the rest."

Neither man could find anything nice to say, so the rest of lunch was chewing, swallowing, and draining sodas in front of the TV. Agent Falin found the restroom while his boss settled up the bill. Full of protein, sugar, and carbohydrates, they strolled to their car. Trying to escape history, Agent Walker drove the police-modified Chevrolet Impala on the broad strand of interstate asphalt at eighty miles per hour as if he was already airborne. As they sped past stockyards, silos, and barbed wire pastures toward Buckley Air Force Base, he filled his new man in on the details of the mission. "The first thing we've got to do is get an update on where our search and rescue team is. They were supposed to be at the crash site yesterday so everyone is eager to know what they found out."

"Can't they just call in?"

"They can call, but that doesn't mean anyone will hear them. The mountains block communication. Signals just bounce around the canyons or go into outer space. You have to be really high up to transmit."

"So why don't they climb high enough?"

It had been a long time since Agent Walker had to explain the basics to a new pilot. "Do you have any idea what the weather is like above fourteen thousand feet?"

"Cold?"

"Cold and windy all the time. That's above the tree line, and the highest peaks never lose their snowcaps. It's all just ice and rocks. Walking around up there is treacherous. I can't tell you how many hikers have died from stepping into snow-covered cracks and crevices. They just get stuck and we find them – if we find them – frozen in place. The lucky ones get swept down in avalanches where their bodies can be recovered."

Fresh off his stints in Southeast Asia and Los Angeles, Agent Falin hadn't lived in a winter environment since he joined the military. "Guess I'll have to buy a parka."

"At least one, and some long johns too. We've got a government-issue flight suit for you at the field: boots and gloves and everything. Never know when the Cessna's heater might crap out."

Agent Falin missed the easy living LA climate for the first time. "So why are we going to Steamboat? Is that near the crash site?"

"Near enough. Our field office is there, and we want to follow up on the intel before it gets too old."

The highway exit dedicated to Buckley Airfield funneled all traffic directly to the base. Agent Walker lowered his window at the gate to show his badge to the guard. They drove past a cluster of boxy industrial buildings painted the same tan as the poured concrete road and runways. Clearing the hangars, they came to a row of fierce-looking fighter jets, each one covered by an arc of corrugated steel.

Agent Falin got excited at the sight of military hardware. "*Now* we're talking," he said as they parked in front of the hangar opposite the jets. He jerked open the car door and started walking toward the poised fighters like a hypnotized subject.

Agent Walker had to yell over the sound of jet turbines being tested nearby. "Agent Falin! Over here. We can do some sightseeing another time."

Agent Falin indulged in one more wistful look and turned around. "Now *there's* something worth flying," he muttered to himself.

"Have you ever flown a fighter?" Agent Walker asked as he led them toward the entrance.

"Oh yeah, that was part of my training," Agent Falin said. "Even got to plant some flowers on targets."

"You flew fighters overseas?" Agent Walker asked.

"I wish," Agent Falin said wistfully. "We used some high altitude surveillance planes over there, mostly props, but the Air Force guys always got the stick. Intel had to ride in back."

Agent Walker looked concerned as he opened the door. "So you weren't a pilot over there?"

Agent Falin followed him in. "Oh, I flew, just not jets. They always tried to keep us out of the serious combat areas because we had all the classified equipment. It got real boring buzzing in circles over the jungle like a goddam dragonfly."

A uniformed sergeant approached them. He had a rolled map under his arm and was carrying a military duffel bag. "Afternoon, gentlemen," he said briskly.

Agent Walker shook his hand. "Afternoon, Sergeant Strothers. This is Agent Falin. Thanks for making the arrangements so quickly."

Sergeant Strothers and Agent Falin shook hands. "Welcome aboard. I know you're in a hurry, so let's get down to business," he said, rolling the map out on a table. "I read your flight plan, but we need to familiarize all new personnel with protocols and procedures." The agents followed the sergeant's hand over the map as he spoke. "We're using runway 09-R and standard 236.600 to talk to the tower. Agent Walker knows the local search-and-rescue frequencies for ground comm. When you hit six thousand feet, bank right and take up a heading of one-nine-seven. That's the fastest way out of the restricted area and you'll be heading in the right direction."

"One-nine-seven at six thousand. Got it."

"Here's your flight suit and a few other items we hope you don't find useful." The sergeant handed Agent Falin a duffel bag. "You can change in there." He pointed. "Agent Walker and I will review the flight plan while you're getting ready, and he'll fill you in as needed."

Agent Falin went to change. He unpacked the duffel inside a barren locker room, took off his pants, and pulled the one-piece suit over his legs. After inserting his arms, he zipped himself in and stuffed his civvies back into the duffel bag. The clumsy combat boots they had given him had the usual too-many laces, and Agent Falin's back hurt bending over to restring them. Standing awkwardly, he missed the loafers and regulation khakis that he got away with wearing in Los Angeles.

When he rejoined his boss, Sergeant Strothers drove them to where their Cessna was parked. "It's all gassed and ready to go," the sergeant said as the agents exited. "Keys are in the ignition."

Agent Falin hopped out of the back and petted the struts. "Wow, this one's all shiny and new, not like the swamp boats we had overseas."

"Only the finest wings for the US Air Force," the sergeant confirmed. "This is the new Skyhawk N. It's got a hundred and sixty Lycoming horses running on real aviation fuel, the electrical system has been upgraded to twenty-eight volts, and you've even got rudder trim now. Of course the NavCom is all military."

Agent Walker was troubled. "Is this the same as the one that went down?"

Sergeant Strothers nodded. "Sorry to say, Cessna delivered two at the same time, and this is the other one."

"Thanks for all your help, Sergeant," Agent Walker said as he grabbed his overnight bag from the back of the Jeep. "I think we can take it from here."

Agent Falin looked skeptically at the shifting sky. "What's in the survival kit?" he said, shouldering his bag of concerns. "Not that I think we'll be needing that stuff."

Agent Walker's mood darkened. "Accidents aren't planned. I keep telling you that mountain flying is no picnic, but I guess you'll see for yourself. You take the left seat."

The two agents stuffed their duffels into the back, climbed in through the space between the seats, and squeezed, side-by-side, into the cramped cockpit. Agent Walker read the preflight checklist aloud as Agent Falin followed his directions. "Fuel selector – both, mixture – lean, circuit breakers – in, master switch – on."

Agent Falin yelled, "Ignition. Clear!" as he twisted the key. The gages sprang into action as the engine purred to life.

Agent Walker adjusted the rest of the cockpit equipment as they taxied. "Transponder – on, avionics – on, beacon – on, magneto – check, suction – check, amps – check, flaps – down."

Piloting, Agent Falin wheeled the plane into position and came to a stop at the end of the runway before he called the tower. "This is Xray Zebra 243 requesting permission to take off."

"Xray Zebra cleared for takeoff."

Agent Falin opened the throttle, released his toes from the brakes, and accelerated to fifty-five knots before easing the yoke toward him. The engine noise swelled to a full roar and the nose wheel lifted effortlessly off the ground. Climbing quickly toward the cirrus cloud ceiling, they flew without talking, studying the gages. When the compass and altimeter aligned, Agent Walker spoke to the tower through his headset. "This is Xray Zebra. Leaving Buckley air space now. See you tomorrow night."

Agent Falin was surprised. "Tomorrow night?"

"We won't have enough daylight to make it back here. We'll have to overnight somewhere in the mountains."

"Somewhere?"

"It always depends on ground conditions," Agent Walker explained. "I'd like to put down in Steamboat Springs, but they've had some weather up there lately and the runway's still dirt."

Agent Falin smiled. "Now I feel like we're on an adventure." He pulled back on the stick and followed the exit vector with a sharp right turn.

"One-nine-zero," Agent Walker reminded him.

"Roger, or is it William?"

"I see you've read *some* of your briefing. I don't mind using first names when we're flying, but let's try to keep it all business on the ground."

Agent Falin was disappointed but decided to keep it professional. The engine noise filled the silence, and the flat expanses below drifted away as they climbed. Staying well south of commercial airliners on approach to Stapleton International, they passed over the nearly lifeless trickle of the Platte River, whose boulder-strewn boundaries were interrupted by irregular fields of melons and sugar beets. Houses and barns, surrounded by cottonwoods, were positioned along roads that formed a patchwork of rural infrastructure. Flying west, they could see the distant juts of the Front Range casting shadows as the afternoon sun crossed behind the Continental Divide. Below, the suburban sprawl of Lakewood clustered around Interstate 25 and crept into the foothills south of Denver.

Agent Walker spoke as they flew over Mount Morrison. "That's where Red Rocks Amphitheater is." He pointed beneath them. "We need to climb to ten thousand and take up a heading of three-one-five."

The snowy peaks of the high Rockies loomed ahead like giant white-capped waves of stone. Flashes of light reflected off the shallow water in the river canyons. Clouds, in varying shades of gray, floated over the land masses like a foamy sea. Following the compass, Agent Falin aimed for a wide valley between mountaintops.

Agent Walker pointed in the direction they were heading. "Everything changed when they discovered gold up here."

"How long ago was that?"

"The first gold rush started in 1858. It was called the Pike's Peak Gold Rush, but that's just because everyone knew where Pike's Peak was. The actual mining took place everywhere. They started out panning in the creeks around Denver, but moved into the mountains in search of the veins. The first lode was discovered where the town of Idaho Springs is now, and that's when gold fever really hit. They say a hundred thousand people came over the next few years. It was Colorado's first population boom. Not everyone was a miner though, and towns sprung up wherever there was digging. Nearly all the towns in the Colorado mountains started out like that, but most of the digs were short-lived, and most of the speculators went broke or died."

Agent Falin looked down and saw how rough the terrain was. "I'm guessing those miners were a pretty tough lot."

"Tough, but stupid too. The successful ones had plenty of help spending their profits at the saloons and whorehouses. There're not too many mines still in operation, but there are more holes in the ground – and deeper ones – than most people know about, and the best way to see them is from the air."

Agent Falin was tired of being formal. "So do we have time to land and look for leftover nuggets before heading to Steamboat?"

"You can hike in and nose around if you ever get some time off, but for now I'm just going to show you how to spot the places where there's been digging. Let's get a little lower and slower before it gets too dark."

"Works for me." Agent Falin backed off the throttle, nosed down, and was surprised at how fast the ground rose up to meet them.

"See that little smudge of light brown near the river? That's a tailing – a mine tail – and it's always connected to the body of the dig, which is sticking its head way down a dark hole. Excavations are often right next to the river because there's water to sluice the dirt. My great-grandfather did some prospecting. He found a few nuggets and went broke a couple of times, but one thing he always said was that if you follow the tailings, you'll find out everyone's secrets."

"What secrets? I thought you said the mines were abandoned."

"Just because a mine is no longer producing doesn't mean it's abandoned. If they're near a town, they get used for everything from storing root vegetables in the winter to ice in the summer. Bears, rattlers, coyotes, and bats love them, and the old shafts are the first place the local police look when they're searching for fugitives."

"So they must be a good place to hide contraband too," Agent Falin deduced.

"Welcome to Colorado." Agent Walker pointed ahead to a gap between peaks. "Okay, let's pull up before we wind up in the river. We'll need to climb to thirteen thousand to make that pass."

Agent Falin pulled the stick all the way back and returned to full throttle. They passed a thousand feet over the tree line and entered the elevation where the snow cover and sky met. "Can't say I've ever been this high in a prop before."

"Just let me know if you start to get dizzy. You haven't had time to acclimate to the altitude, and it wouldn't be the first time someone passed out from lack of oxygen."

Agent Falin was an accomplished drinker, and the idea of passing out annoyed him. "You saying I'm not tough enough?"

"This land is going to take every bit of strength you have and make you wish you had more. You didn't know the man that just went down, but let me tell you, no one was more prepared or a better flier than Agent Dobson. I honestly cannot imagine what might have gone wrong." Agent Walker paused to reflect on his friend's fate. "That's enough of a tour for today. The shadows come up fast around here. Let's just head straight for Steamboat Springs while there's enough light to stay VFR."

CHAPTER 6

After his rendezvous banked out of view, Duke stopped by the small airport office and talked shop with the retired pilot who collected rent and logged traffic. The man didn't know of any King Airs for sale but pointed out some other planes that he knew the owners would be happy to be out from under. Although he already had one plane he couldn't afford, Duke feigned interest in a sleek Bonanza with low hours. There was just something about airplanes he found irresistible, so he went outside to look it over. He ran his hand along the distinctive V-tail stabilizers and felt the smooth surfaces where the countersunk screws and rivets held the sturdy aluminum together. He raised up on his toes and looked through the window to see the upholstered interior and well-designed instrument panel before doing a complete walk-around: the booted prop was only missing a few paint chips, the wheel skirts didn't have any scratches, the high-gloss blue paint glowed under a fine layer of dust, and he even liked the call letters because they reminded him of his birthday. Duke added a bonanza to his endless list of future acquisitions as he walked back to his car.

He was parked in a quiet residential neighborhood, so he slipped into the driver's seat as casually as if he lived across the street. Inconspicuously, he placed his carrying bag on the seat next to him and slid his right hand inside. His fingers located and opened Oswaldo's package by feel, and he pried open the seals on the plastic bags while fixing his hair in the visor mirror. No one was watching, so he broke off a shard of the illicit merchandise with his fingernail, jammed the piece into a tiny glass vial, broke it into flakes with a tiny metal spoon attached to the top, and screwed the top back on. The day was unfolding as planned, and he licked the residue off his fingers to celebrate. Resealing the baggies and pocketing his stash bottle, he drove away like any other resident on a Thursday morning errand.

The rented Mustang handled much better than most of the soft-shocked people-movers coming out of Detroit, but compared to flying, racing from intersection to stop sign in residential Bel Air was a disappointing tease for a man whose ambitions were airborne. Once he got out of the heavily populated neighborhood around the airport and onto the narrow roads that twisted around the Riviera Country Club, Duke rolled all the windows down and blasted the radio while apexing the turns. Passing the modern, ocean-view houses of the Pacific Palisades, the Bee Gees reminded him that even if he couldn't afford to live there yet, he was still stayin' alive. Exhilarating in the morning sun with a refreshing ocean breeze in his face and a valuable packet tucked into his bag, he was feeling very LA'ptimistic when he finally arrived at his friend's house nestled into Temescal Canyon.

Marty saw the car pull up through the closed circuit monitor. Duke parked at an angle next to a box van that Marty's clients used for touring, and Marty was waiting in the open doorway of his midcentury modern home as Duke came down the heliotrope-lined flagstone walkway.

"Good morning, mi amigo!" Duke greeted as he approached.

Marty grinned and spread welcoming arms. "Sky King himself! *Mi casa su casa.*" They hugged in a backslapping embrace. "Com'on in, pardner. We're just getting going around here."

Marty's sunken living room opposite the front door was lined with full-length glass panels that made the distant ocean, shimmering over the tops of the eucalyptus trees in the canyon, seem like it was a living wall mural. A sentinel Buddha in the corner enjoyed the same spectacular view as the residents of the pricey homes in the area, and the room was covered with soft gray carpeting. A collection of tastefully understated side tables made of smooth glass and chrome were positioned around the plush leather sofa set, and large illuminated globes, supported by weighty disc-shaped bases, were suspended over the seating area on thin arching arms.

Marty's wife, Marsha, a subtle siren in her thirties, was lounging on one of the off-white sofas in stylish, loose-fitting clothes. "Good morning, Duke," she said in a hoarse morning whisper. "We've been waiting for you. How are you?" She straightened up and brushed her hand through shoulder-length dirty-blond hair. Marsha, daughter of a Hollywood luminary, was every bit as attractive as Duke remembered.

"Nice to see you again, Mrs. Freedman," he said.

"Please excuse the mess," Marty said. "We were up late with one of our artists."

Marsha tidied up the magazines on the coffee table to make room for the next round of socializing while Marty, a balding forty-something dressed in leather loafers, designer jeans, and a logoed pullover, took the used napkins and wine glasses into an adjacent kitchen. "Please make yourself at home," he called from the other room. "Something to drink? Water, coffee, tea, soda, wine?"

Duke hadn't been to the Freedman's house in more than a year. "A little too early for drinking, but I'd love some water, please. Perrier, if you've got it."

"Coming right up."

Duke stepped down into the living room and touched Marsha's shoulder on his way to look through the west-facing plate glass panorama. Tiny bushtits and ruby kinglets percolated through the thick bougainvillea blooms around the small back yard two stories below him. A long-haired man with a hairy chest and bikini-clad girl in dark glasses were sunning themselves on recliners next to a small, irregularly shaped swimming pool.

"When did you get into town?" Marsha asked languorously.

Duke answered without turning around. "Just last night."

"Long flight?"

"No, I flew commercial. They did all the work." Duke stretched his arms and studied the horizon. "How are things around here? Business good?"

Marsha could tell he was jerked up. "Well, we're *busy*, if that means anything."

Marty brought Duke his drink and invited him to sit. "Sooo?"

Duke took a sip of water. "Sooo what?"

"So what's the news from on high?"

Duke was still looking out the window at the sunbathers. "Beautiful day around here."

Marty realized some transactional foreplay was necessary and indulged him with small talk. "Yeah, everybody around here likes the weather. That's why we live here. What was the weather in Colorado like when you left?"

"They got a dusting of snow in the mountains, but it was in the fifties down in Boulder."

"We had a freak snowstorm here last year. It was very surreal for a few hours, but everything melted by the afternoon."

"Speaking of snow," Marsha insinuated. "Did you run into any on the way over?"

Duke still wasn't ready to get down to business. "Who's that girl by the pool?" he asked on his way to the sofa.

Marsha pretended she was insulted. "I'm not good enough for you?" She primped in jest.

"Oh, stop teasing him, babe," Marty said. "Everybody wants you. They're just scared of me." They all chuckled. Marty looked more like an accountant than a street tough, and everyone knew he was a softy. "I'm a green belt now, so you better stop laughing or I'll ... ." Marty angled his arms in a martial arts position and chopped the air.

Duke laughed. "Okay, I surrender, mi amigo."

"Duke," Marsha asked suggestively, "don't we have some other business to discuss?"

Marty got up and looked out the window to make sure his guests were still by the pool. "Right. What's the story? How's it going?" he asked, still facing the window.

"The studio's cooking. New console should be on line by the time I get back."

Marty was getting impatient. "Glad to hear it. And the other matter? The white matter? How does that look?"

"Well," Duke hesitated for effect, "in a word, incredible."

Marsha perked up. "Incredible? In what way?"

Duke removed the brick from his satchel and laid it on a sunlit coffee table. It sparkled brightly through layers of plastic. There was a collective gasp. "In that way," he said emphatically.

Marty poked at the baggie with his finger and felt how hard it was. Then held the brick up to his face for a closer look. "Holy shit! How much is in here?" he asked excitedly, feeling its density. "Is there more? What is this stuff?"

"One hundred percent Peruvian flake," Duke said proudly. "I told you we were onto something good. Take a taste, then you'll really believe me."

Marty unsealed the baggies and carefully scraped a pocket knife against the hardened formation. Marsha moved closer and held out her tongue. "Me first," she said from her knees.

"Ladies first, of course." Marty tapped a few flakes onto her tongue. Marsha had a reputation as a connoisseur, so they studied her reaction as she settled onto her haunches with her eyes closed. Enjoying the attention, she heaved a sigh that showed off her chest and smacked her lips sensuously.

"Sooo?" Marty asked.

Marsha opened her eyes widely. "Sooo … . It's fucking incredible! Maybe the best ever."

"Coming from you, that says a lot." Marty deposited a few flakes on his own tongue and sampled it himself. After a brief pause he reported, "You're right! This stuff is so pure we'll be able to cut into a thousand pieces." He started calculating. "How much for this brick?"

Duke had already prepared his answer. "That's a full kilo. I need twenty for it, and I'm going to get three more tomorrow when my partner gets back."

Marty wasn't a successful artist manager because he let his guard down easily. "You trust these guys? It's not some sort of setup? I don't want to get busted. We've got a lot to lose here." He motioned toward his posh surroundings.

"I've got some other people lined up if you can't handle the quantity," Duke said gamely. "You can just tighten me up for this one now, and I'll see you next time," he proposed.

Marty and Marsha looked at each other. "Mind if we talk in private?"

"No, sure." Duke got up.

"No, you stay here," Marty told him. "We'll be right back. Make yourself comfortable."

Duke moved back over to the window. He could see the seagulls swarming where the cliffs met the beach and the outline of a cargo ship on the horizon. A TWA jet on its way down from San Francisco descended toward LAX with full flaps. Duke checked his watch and figured that the King Air must be in Mexican airspace by now, and his stomach twitched when he thought about the scam he and Remy were trying to pull off. Oswaldo was more intense than he had expected, and his bodyguard Demario wasn't as dumb as Remy had told him he was. Timing was going to be critical.

A trio of Bluejays came squawking past the window in pursuit of a crow that dove into the treetops of the canyon. Duke looked down and saw Marsha talking to the sunbathers next to the pool. The long-haired man was sitting up smoking a cigarette and listening to her. Duke could see him nod and shake his head, but the sight of his female companion, who had rolled onto her side without her top, was much more interesting. The house phone rang, and he heard Marty downstairs talking. Marsha disappeared from view, and a few minutes later, they both came back upstairs to the living room.

"We've got a proposal," Marty began. "We'll give you ten now, and thirty when you bring us another one."

"So you only want two?"

"I think that's all we can handle right now, unless we get a call later today."

Duke thought for a minute. How could he make this work? He needed to deposit twelve thousand in the bank by Monday to keep the checks from bouncing, and he didn't have any other cash. He came up with a solution. "Okay, how 'bout this, you give me fifteen now and twenty for the next one tomorrow?"

Marty was surprised when he calculated the discount. "That's a generous offer. You sure you can afford to do that?" he asked.

"You guys are so good to me, and this stuff is so good we'll all make money. I'm really rolling right now, so consider it a favor."

"I don't know if we have that much cash," Marsha said. "Let me go count what we have again." She went to an adjacent room.

"You're a dangerous man to owe favors to," Marty said, winking, "but if we have the cash here, I think we've got a deal."

Duke went back to the window to see if the half-naked girl was still visible. She was – and Marty knew what he was looking at. "Maybe you want to come by the studio tonight? Could be fun. I'll introduce you to her friends.

"Where are you working?"

"Shangri La, out in Zuma."

Marsha came back with an envelope of cash. "We only have fourteen now, but we can give you the rest tonight." She handed the money to Duke. "I hope that works."

Duke grasped her hand and kissed it valiantly. "From you my dear, a promise is worth at least a thousand dollars."

"You saying my old lady is only worth a grand?" Marty teased.

"I said *at least!*"

"Who are you calling old?" Marsha complained.

Duke left the baggie of drugs on the table. "Alright friends, I need to get going. You know where to reach me."

"You're at the Miramar?"

"Room 303."

"Marsha will run the rest of the money over to you later," Marty said. "What time tomorrow should we expect you?"

"Not sure. Maybe late afternoon or early evening. We'll see how things go. I'll ring you before I come, okay?"

"Okay." They bro-shook, and Marty walked him to the door. "Adios, amigo. Fly high. See you mañana."

Duke took the more direct route back to Santa Monica by way of the PCH. The traffic thinned to one lane in a spot where a dusty cliff had crumbled onto the road, and he slowed down for a detour and merged with his surroundings. Pricey condos, perched closely together on stilts along the beach, allowed passersby only slivers of liberating ocean views. Inner-city bathers in search of parking spaces and seaside refreshment peered impatiently out the windows of overloaded cars. Sunglassed studs and bathing beauties in gleaming metal-flake convertibles crawled along behind smoky delivery vans that hadn't passed inspection for a decade, and sweat-stained workers in pickup trucks brimming with building materials, ladders, and tools blighted anything magical or pleasant. At less than five miles per hour, Duke's mood descended to the grinding pace of reality, and he mentally sorted through the maze of half-truths, presumptions, and deceptions that supported his lifestyle.

After he finally parked in the hotel lot, he stopped at a rock-and-roll-themed store that sold reprinted psychedelic posters and tee shirts along with a full assortment of drug paraphernalia. He tried on an Hawaiian shirt, then sized up his image in the mirror.

The shirt fit, but the short sleeves didn't hide his the pasty-white skin. He found a wide-brimmed straw hat that covered most of his unkempt red curls, but on the brown-skinned beach he would have to cover all his arms and legs to avoid standing out like a black man in a snowstorm. That's how he saw it. He was originally from Mississippi, and the racially insensitive imagery just stuck in his mind like a birthmark. It wasn't prejudice. He had lots of black friends. They had toured and drank and partied together, and many people said his music often sounded more black than white. But no one could know all that just by looking, so he had to find a way to blend in. He finally settled on a gauzy, long-sleeved Indian shirt, white muslin guru pants, bamboo-surfaced flip-flops, and the floppy straw hat. It was only one o'clock by the time he got back to his room, and he didn't have to be anywhere until seven, so he ordered room service and planned on getting some sun.

CHAPTER 7

After leaving the studio, Jon strolled back to the Boulderado through the Pearl Street Mall with his rockstar dreams closer than ever. The open air space was designed by a local firm, Communication Arts, and created when the city blocked off and cobblestoned six blocks of Boulder's widest downtown thoroughfare. With tasteful benches, brick pathways, and iron light fixtures, the large, pedestrian-only expanse invited shoppers, exercisers, and random citizens to linger. The stately grounds of the Boulder Courthouse in the middle of the mall were decorated with large pumpkins on each of the wide limestone steps leading to the front door, and orange-and-black rope had been twisted through the iron railing around the fountain. Outside the subdued headquarters of Naropa Institute, Jon heard the Hare Krishnas' endless chant, watched an STP family member furiously strumming a John Denver song on an out-of-tune guitar, and stopped to read the coming attractions posters in the windows of the Boulder Theatre before going back to his place at the hotel. He wasn't interested in a friend's invitation to spend the afternoon in the mountains, but he popped his head in the lingerie shop to see if the proprietor was there.

Simone, the unofficial guardian of hotel secrets, was behind the counter, looking through a magazine and humming along to "Another Green World" by Brian Eno. "*Bonjour, monsieur*," Simone greeted him without fanfare.

Jon looked around to see if anyone else was in the store before talking. "Hey, man, how's it going?"

Simone was from Baltimore, but because his favorite grandmother was born in France, he liked to pretend he was French. "*Tres bien, et vous?*"

Jon imitated Simone's phony accent. "*Tres bien, merci, oui oui.*"

"*Ca ca, pee pee,*" Simone teased back.

Jon came closer and whispered. "Hear anything?"

"Mmm hmm," Simone answered while thumbing through *Penthouse* magazine. "She's breathing hard, but I can't make out the words. It sounds like *mon dieu!*"

Getting a straight answer out of Simone was always difficult, so Jon leaned over the counter for a peek. The nude model was exhilarating, but Jon said, "That's not what I'm talking about."

"Too bad," Simone mumbled, then reached into his vest and slipped Jon an ultra-thin joint.

"What's this for?" Jon asked, surprised.

"Tell me what you think of this later," Simone said in suddenly perfect English. "I don't know about the bees, but I heard the birds are on the wing."

Jon didn't know what he meant but quickly palmed the reefer into his back pocket. "*Merci, monsieur, merci.* Let me know when the little birdies land."

"You'll know soon enough," Simone said cryptically, salivating over his magazine again.

Jon looked around for clues but didn't see any. "I will? How will I know? What are you talking about, man?"

Simone didn't answer, and Brian Eno was droning on, promising to tie someone's shoes, and Jon knew it was useless trying to establish the facts. He muttered, "Okay then, *reservoir* to you too, Mr. Mysterioso," on his way out.

The Fleur De Lis was closed for the lunch-to-dinner changeover, and Mr. Lawry, the aged military veteran whose entire life consisted of sitting in the lobby, was in his chair by the front door, staring blankly at memories only he could see. After checking for messages at the front desk, Jon went back to his room on the fourth floor and settled into his afternoon routine: he sat on the edge of his bed, sampled the lethal pot Simone had given him, and played his electric guitar without plugging it in. The lack of amplification led to long strums, and the marijuana liberation inspired introspective musings.

Stuck her head in the Lion's den
And she said, "Hey babe, there you are."
Searched the world 'round for you
Now I'm leavin' on a star.

Many times in many ways,
You tell me who you are.
All alone and back again,
You've traveled very far.

It's the rise and the fall
Of nothing at all.

It was five o'clock before he knew it, so Jon returned his sunburst Strat to its hardshell case with purple fuzz lining. Then he put on his worn leather bomber jacket with the faux fur collar and drove out to the practice space in his aging Peugeot 404.

Marco was already at the rehearsal space, measuring the room to see where the new console might best fit by the time Jon got there. The brown and yellow linoleum tile floor of the former furniture showroom glowed like a faded color photograph beneath the neon lights of a white panel ceiling. Pieces of remnant carpeting had been nailed to the walls to deaden the sound, and the band used the elevated platform where the sofas used to be displayed as their stage. Jon walked in as Marco was making diagrams of how the recording equipment could be arranged.

"Hey, man," Jon greeted him. "Wassup?"

Marco answered, "Hey, man," while continuing to sketch. Then he extended his retractable tape and made calculations on a yellow writing tablet. Organized thinking and simple math came naturally to him – often at the expense of imagination.

Jon put his guitar case down, threw his jacket on the sofa, and came closer. "What're you drawing?"

"Making plans. I think I've got it figured out. Let me show you. We can put the console in that office. We've already got a control room window and the outlets in there work. There's enough room for two or three people, and we can put the tape recorder in that small closet."

Jon was more interested in making music than messing with equipment. He tried to imagine what Marco saw but couldn't. "Interesting, but I don't know if I can get the tape recorder."

"Well, if you do, we've got a place for it." Marco pointed to his diagram. "And if not, I can bring my Revox from home."

Jon unpacked his guitar and started tuning. "That's a great idea," he said absently.

Lost in calculations, Marco continued to do his feasibility study. Jon's broken amp hummed when he turned it on, and the sharp crackle it made when he plugged in made them both cringe.

Marco complained. "Turn down the volume *before* you plug in, man! That's how you busted the speaker in the first place."

"Okay, Mom," Jon answered, actually excited by the electrical jolt. He strangled a two-note lick on the seventh fret as Marco tried to say something else, and drowned him out completely with a distorted power chord swimming in a sea of reverb. "Get your axe, man. I didn't come here to build a fucking studio. You can do that on your own time."

"Yeah, right, just like always. I take care of the gear while you jack off with your guitar. Don't you get it? Having a console would be huge for us. We can make our own record right here!" Marco put down his pad and fetched his bass.

Jon demonstrated his dexterity with an arpeggiated progression. "You wanna play music or what?"

"Of course I want to play," Marco answered while unpacking his instrument. "I'm just excited about the possibility of making a studio out of this place. I thought you were into this."

"I am. Who do you think set this up? Me, that's who. I'm the one who knows who Duke – or did you forget that?" Jon plowed through the opening chords of a song he was formulating.

Done talking, Marco strapped on the white Fender Precision bass that was too big for him and asked, "What key is that in?"

"G. It pedals on the suspension then goes to D minor." Jon played the figure again.

Marco tried to come up with an intricate part that didn't fit. "You sure that's a D minor and not some kind of F major?"

"Just play a G, man," Jon said impatiently.

Marco played an obnoxiously loud G and said, "Whatever," as he thumped it again.

Jon turned up louder and stuck his tongue out as if he were tasting the air. Feeling the sass, Marco cranked up his treble and slapped eight-beat Gs on the bottom string. Jon locked into his rhythmic slaps with muted right hand chunks, then moved down two frets to an F. Marco followed, and they stayed on F for two measures before returning to G. Jon changed the G to G minor and turned up the distortion on his amp.

Frankie came in while they were in a full-tilt groove, alternating between F and G minor. He waved his arm in a circle and mouthed, "Keep going," then threw his coat on a chair and sat behind the drums. Starting with four-on-the-floor, Frankie copped the tempo, then cut it in half with snare hits.

They were several minutes into stomping back and forth between the two chords as a power trio when Dennis got tired of knocking and let himself in. Dennis had been to enough rehearsals that he knew when not to interrupt. The band saw him watching, sparsed it up, and turned on the theatrics. Jon leaned into a microphone and tried some vocals.

Oooh, nowhere
And nothing stays the same
Shop a lot of windows
Along the coast of pain

The music paused between lines, and after he had run out of lyrics, Jon rode the volume pot with his pinky and worked a simple melody between the chord changes.

Dennis liked what he heard. "Tight," was all he said when they finally stopped.

"Hey, man," Marco said. "Thanks for coming down." He saw Dennis looking around at the space. "I've got some measurements and a sketch if you want to see them."

Frankie thunked the kick-drum, demanding an introduction.

"Don't mind him. He's just the drummer," Jon said derisively.

Frankie expressed his indignity by launching into a mini drum-solo that pummeled all other potential insults into submission.

Marco was the first one to speak when voices could be heard again. "Sorry," he addressed Dennis. "This is Frankie, our drummer."

All smiles, Frankie got up from behind the kit and approached Dennis. "Pleased to meet you, man. Can't wait to get in the studio to record." He pumped Dennis's handshake vigorously. "I think you know my brother, Kevin. He's the guitar player in Weed Whackers."

"Yeah, I remember them," Dennis politicked. "You guys been together long?"

"Long enough," Jon answered confidently.

Unable to resist filling in details, Marco added, "Jon and I have been off-and-on-again for a couple of years. Frankie and I know each other from high school."

Dennis steered the conversation back toward his true interest. "You've got some sketches?"

Marco put down his instrument and laid his drawings on a low table where they could be seen. "I took some measurements," he said, pointing at the pictures. "I'm pretty sure we've got enough room for the console."

Dennis bent over for a closer look. "You're thinking of putting the desk in there? Let's go see." Jon and Frankie stayed behind while Marco showed Dennis the space. The manager's office was an empty rectangle sixteen feet long and twelve feet deep with the same linoleum floor and drop ceiling as the rest of the showroom. Dennis looked out the six-foot glass separator window at the rehearsal space and imagined it as a studio. "I think this will work."

Jon and Frankie had started playing again, and there wasn't enough isolation for a discussion, so Marco and Dennis returned to the main room. Dennis went to inspect a Moog synthesizer sitting on its own table while Marco strapped his bass back on and joined the jam. Jon had modulated the riff up a step, so it took Marco a few bars to lock into the A minor to G pattern. While they were playing, Dennis turned the synthesizer on and found a swarm of bees oscillating around four-forty. Jon liked the noise and yelled for him to turn it up, then stopped playing so he could hear how the bass, drums, and synth sounded by themselves. Dennis shifted the long-tone synth swells between A and G in step with Marco's bass, and Frankie accented with his toms. It was the first time the trio had ever heard the synthesizer fit with their rock-and-roll attitude. Jon cranged whole note chords over the undulating bed and tried his lyrics again.

Oooh, nowhere.
And nothing stays the same.
Shop a lot of windows
Along the coast of pain.

It worked much better than he had ever heard it – and that confused him. Upset, he undid his strap, rested his guitar on his shoe, and abruptly turned off his amp. Everyone was surprised and stopped playing.

"What's the matter?" Marco asked. "I thought we sounded great. Why'd you stop?"

Frankie smashed a cymbal and complained, "What the fuck? We were all over that! What're you doin', man?"

Jon lit a cigarette and stared at the synthesizer, then at Dennis. Dennis twisted an oversized filter knob and the instrument emitted a prolonged fart that reverberated through the PA system's internal spring echo. Even Jon laughed at the tension-killing sound, so Dennis twisted the waveform knob and turned the flatulence into intermittent explosions.

Marco leaned his bass against his amp and joined Dennis at the table where the synth was set up. "You know how to work this thing?" he asked Dennis rhetorically. "I just traded my old bass for it. Maybe you can show me a few things."

Dennis held down a key and adjusted the feedback loop until it sounded like a helicopter was about to land. "Sure, man. We've got one like this at the studio. Guys are using them on finished tracks now."

Frankie was not impressed. "Yeah, I like the way it sounds. There're a ton of popular songs with farting and helicopters these days." He cracked his snare and went around the toms to emphasize his point.

"You're such and idiot," Marco scolded. "When are you ever going to graduate from marching band?"

Jon came over to the synthesizer and listened as Dennis explained a few of the functions. "The oscillator is what actually generates the signal. You can make it fast or slow, change the shape of the wave, and send it through the filter banks. The symbols around each knob indicate what they do to the signal." He held down one note on the small keyboard and twisted a sequence of knobs to demonstrate. The sounds morphed from gale-force winds to noisy sea gulls to baying cattle to screeching tires.

"What happens if you press two keys at the same time?" Marco asked.

"Ah-ha. Good question. This is only monophonic. You can only use one key at a time. That's probably why they traded it to you. All the new ones are polyphonic. And they have presets so you don't have to turn all these dials to get a sound."

Marco pecked around on the keyboard and altered some settings. "Do people use these in the studio?"

"You bet. There're some amazing recordings coming out of Berlin right now. The new Kraftwerk record will blow your minds. The whole thing was made with analog synthesizers like this."

Jon touched the keys and the synthesizer made some squishy sounds. "Wow, a whole record of sounds like that," he scoffed. "Good thing I know how to play a real instrument."

Dennis was surprised. "What do you mean, man? You think this doesn't play music?"

"Not unless you consider chirping birds and humming motors music."

Dennis defended technology. "I thought you liked what I was playing before. Wait 'til you hear some of the cool shit you do with these things. You'll change your mind just like the rest of us."

"Okay, you're on," Jon challenged him. "Let's go over to the studio right now and listen."

Marco liked the idea. "Yeah, I want to see your synth. We can take some measurements for the console too. When do you think we'll get it over here?"

"Whoa, man, I still have to firm that up with Duke." Dennis sensed the urgency and captured it with a plan. "He's supposed to call the studio tonight. I have to go back so maybe you guys should follow me. I hooked the speakers up after you left so we can listen to some stuff."

"And you can hear our tape too," Marco enthused.

Frankie was the only one not excited. "I'll stay here. I need some time to practice by myself, and I don't care what instruments are in the band so long as they play something cool and on the beat."

"Okay, you stay here. We'll be back in an hour."

Marco and Jon followed Dennis over to the studio in Jon's Peugeot. It was only a few minutes ride. Dennis parked his old blue pickup in the studio space and waited for them to find a spot on the street.

The evening receptionist saw them in the monitor and buzzed the door open. "Just in time," she said as they came through the door. "I've got Duke on hold. He wants to talk to you." Dennis went into the front office and closed the door. "He'll probably be a while," she told Jon and Marco. "You might as well get comfortable." She motioned to the waiting room sofa. "Can I get you something to drink?"

Jon wasn't in the mood to be patient and said, "No thanks. I'll wait outside and have a smoke."

Marco liked the way she looked and stayed inside. "Yes, please! What kind of tea do you have?"

"We have several choices," Cynthia responded. "Why don't you come back to the kitchen and pick out one you like?"

Marco accepted the invitation and followed her sandalwood-scented saunter down the darkened corridor. The tiny kitchen area was well lit. An assortment of herbal teas was featured. "This one's my favorite," Cynthia said, holding a box of kava. "They say it's an aphrodisiac."

Marco's eyes widened. "Sounds good to me."

"Stay here and I'll make us a cup. It'll only take a minute." She filled the electric pot with fresh water and turned it on, then plucked two clean mugs from the cabinet and put a tea bag in each of them. "I have to stay late tonight, and this helps keep me up," she explained. Cynthia's auburn waves hung loosely around her shoulders. Her long peasant shirt was cinched with a braided rope belt. Painted toenails peeked out from her open-toed sandals. She knew Marco was interested.

Marco pretended to read a studio magazine, and she excused herself for a trip to the ladies room. While he was waiting for the water to boil, Dennis and Jon intruded.

"There you are!" Dennis said. "I was hoping you hadn't given in to sin yet."

Marco didn't know what he was talking about. "Sin?"

"Sin, as in Cynthia," Dennis explained in a conspiratorial tone.

Marco made a guilty smile.

"See what I mean?" Dennis cajoled. "She makes a man think sinful things." He winked. "Come on back to the control room. We've got some business to discuss."

Marco and Jon followed him down the hallway. "It looks a little different from earlier today," Dennis said, opening the door. "I finally got a little bit done." All the construction materials had been neatly arranged at the back of the room. The floor had been vacuumed and the lights were so bright it made them squint. Dennis held the throat of a thick gray cable whose head was a heavy rectangular connector. "See this?" He turned the connector over to show ninety-six tiny holes perforating the molded green plastic housing. "You wouldn't believe how long it takes to solder one of these together."

Marco extended his hand. "May I?" Dennis handed him the connector. It was attached to a heavy bundle of wires that disappeared into the floor, and was one of several snakes nesting in the wide channel. "How long did it take to do all this?"

"Two days short of forever," Dennis answered. "We've had to run new wires to prep for the new board. That Elko you're holding took at least a half-day for each end. And don't forget that's only the female side. The male coupling takes just as long. The good news is I had a little help – not enough – but we'll talk about that later. The other good news is we didn't have to change everything. More than half of those snakes are the same ones we've been using. They go to the outboard gear, monitors, and fax panels. The big multi-pins only connect the new desk to noise reduction and tape decks."

Jon started to fidget. "I thought we had some business to discuss. I didn't come here for a lesson in studio construction. I want to hear some of this new synthesizer stuff."

"Okay, I'll put on tape in a minute, but first, I want you to do something. Jon, you go over to the other side of the console. Marco, you're in the middle. When I say three, we're going to pick this up and move it toward the window."

Marco was skeptical. "We are? What about all the wires?"

"Don't worry about that. They're all disconnected now. Get a firm grip on the bottom of the frame."

Jon elevated his end with very little effort. "Not as heavy as I thought," he boasted.

"Good. How're you doing, Marco?" Dennis asked.

Marco barely got the rear feet off the floor. "Okay, I guess."

Dennis picked up his end easily. "Alright, toward the window on one, two, three." Dennis and Jon held all the weight as they lifted the old mixing desk six inches in the air and set it down four feet in front of where it had been. "Not so bad, eh?"

"Piece of cake," Jon agreed. "Now what?"

"Now we're going to flip it on its side so we can remove the legs."

"I thought we were going to listen to music."

"Right, give me a minute." Dennis found the tape he was looking for and cued it in a cassette player lying in the corner. He set the level low enough that they could talk over it. As the music started, they rested the console gently on its back. Eerie pulsing sounds, sharp clanks, and whiny bursts of grinding that could only have be made by a machine marched through the speakers in a herky-jerky pattern that sounded like an automated assembly line.

The spasms of electronic monotony tested the limits of Jon's patience. "What is this crap?"

"Kraftwerk. They'll start singing soon," Dennis answered. "We can listen while we work." He used a screwdriver to tighten the belly panels that had been undone for the changeover.

"Work? What else do you want us to do?"

"It'll only take a few minutes to get the legs off. We can't take it out of here with them on." He handed Marco a socket wrench and pointed out the bolts he wanted removed.

Kraftwerk started singing, "We are the robots. We are the robots." Their voices had been synthesized by a vocorder, so it sounded as though they were talking machines. They repeated the phrase several times before filling in some of the gaps between the vocals with an ultra-simple, five-note, synthesizer melody. Despite his aversion to anything he hadn't thought of first, Jon kind of liked it. He started imitating the vocals halfway through, moving his lanky arms in time to the music as if they were part of the Kraftwerk machine. Marco joined in when the only lyrics, "We are the robots," repeated for the umpteenth time.

Dennis interrupted their amusement. "I told you you'd dig it. Jon, come here and hold this please."

Jon went around to the front of the console and steadied it as Dennis and Marco pulled the legs all the way off and moved them out of the way. He was balancing it on its thin side when he asked, "Where are we going to put it?"

"In my truck," Dennis told him.

Marco guessed the plan. "And where is it going."

"Your place," Dennis said as he helped control the teetering weight. "I cleared it with Duke."

Jon knew Duke and was suspicious. "What do we have to do for him? I ain't got no fifteen grand."

"He doesn't need any money right now. We just need a place to park it. I need it out of here, and Duke said it'd be okay to hook it up at your place. It'll be easier to sell if someone can test it out."

Marco thought it was a good idea. "That sounds way cool," he confirmed. "But is that all? What's the catch?"

"That's basically it, except that I need you to help me move the new one in here. I told Duke you knew how to solder so I hope you do."

"No problem. When do we start?" Marco asked.

"We already have. You guys stay here while I go put some blankets on the truck."

Kraftwerk's dreamy "Neon Lights" entertained Marco and Jon as they balanced the console on its side and waited. Cynthia came in and brought Marco his tea. The studio ventilation system blew a lukewarm breeze into the airtight chamber. The messy array of unterminated cables emanating from the floor connected to the unsettled atmosphere like the organs of a transplant patient awaiting a new heart. Dennis came back with a four-wheel dolly and organized the transport of the old console down the hall and out to his truck. The back of the pickup had to be left open to accommodate the size, and they slid it into the bed on top of packing blankets.

Dennis offered them a choice while they were tying it down. "We can cover this with plastic now, or we can bring this over to your place first and move the new one in after."

Jon didn't want to do either. He lit a cigarette in protest. "We're supposed to be rehearsing tonight. I don't want to move anything anywhere."

Marco didn't want the offer rescinded and made a pitch. "Let's deliver this now. It'll only take a few minutes to get it in the room and set it down. We can come back over to the studio after rehearsal and help you move the new desk in. Agreed?"

Dennis said, "I'm okay with that."

"I guess so," Jon relented, "but let's make this quick 'cause I've got plans later."

They went back inside, and Marco's energy powered the operation. "It'll go fast if Frankie helps. He'll come back over with us, and then you can go see Donna or whatever." He sipped his tea, hoping the desired effect would manifest by the time he returned.

"Sounds like a plan," Dennis concurred.

Jon and Marco followed the pickup back to the rehearsal space, and with Frankie's help, they unloaded the console, reattached the legs, and set it up in the office of the rehearsal space. Then, they caravanned over to the studio and helped Dennis lift the new desk onto a dolly. It took all four of them to wheel it into the control room and set it on its preassembled metal frame. Jon and Frankie left immediately, but Marco took off his coat and began his studio apprenticeship. Cynthia came in and watched them work for a while but fell asleep on the sofa in the lounge after sharing the pizza that had been delivered.

CHAPTER 8

It was early dusk, and the first lights of town twinkled below as Agent Falin cleared Rabbit Ears Pass and piloted the smooth descent through the broad valley where Bob Adams Field stretched out. Steamboat Springs, located just west of the Continental Divide at seven thousand feet, owed its existence to the easy ski slopes at the edge of town and the natural hot springs that kept the flow of visitors moving through the seasons. The agents touched down on the partially frozen ground and taxied to a stop in front of the field office. The lights were on, but no one was there to greet them, so Agent Walker called an old friend from the outside pay phone. His family had been coming to the area since he was born, and the huge open spaces where he had spent many summer nights camping out with his uncle and cousins excited his Native blood. The outline of the surrounding peaks was barely visible against the darkening sky as the agents stomped their feet and blew on their hands, waiting in the evening chill for a ride into town. Twenty minutes later, a haze of headlights and a dull roar of snow tires on the gravel road announced its arrival.

The Chevy Blazer that Farah was driving was not a standard-issue government vehicle, and the veil of mud that covered its hood and fenders hid most of the original red, white, and chrome. Farah left the motor running as she lowered the powered passenger window. "Good to see you William. Back for more?" she teased.

"Never get enough of this place," Agent Walker admitted. "Thanks for coming to get us. Sorry I didn't have time to make other arrangements. I guess you better take us to the hotel."

"Okay, hop in. Bags in back," Farah said cheerfully.

The agents tossed their luggage behind the back seat, and Agent Walker got in front. "Thanks for the rescue." He leaned over and pecked Farah on the cheek.

Farah glinted with satisfaction. Dressed for mountain living, her rough edges didn't obscure her charm. "No problem. I owe you at least one." The wipers had cleared perfect archways through the otherwise opaque windshield. She looked at Agent Falin through the rearview mirror as she started driving. "So who's the all-American quarterback?"

"Agent Todd Falin, this is Farah. I worked with her aunt when I graduated college."

"Worked? Is that what it's called now?" Farah kidded him.

"Come on, Farah, let's keep personal business out of this. This is Agent Falin's first day."

"First day? And you bring him all the way up here? Must be something special going on."

"You know we're not allowed to discuss agency business."

"Yeah, yeah, I know the drill. You ask questions, and I do the guessing. Is dinner considered agency business – or is that too tough a question?"

"Well, that depends on who's at dinner. You and who else?"

"Still mad at me?" Farah pitched them sideways with a sharp turn. "That guy's history, if that's what you're asking."

"And good riddance to him. You're still teaching?"

"How else can a girl make a living up here? I'll get you a lift ticket if you want to try the slalom again."

"I won't have time this trip, but maybe next time."

"Maybe next time. Story of your life, according to my aunt."

"C'mon, be nice. We've got company."

"Well, *he* might be company," she said, smiling at Agent Falin, "but *you* come up here unannounced and call that company? I call that a taxi service." Farah wasn't burdened with city manners. "What's the matter, Mr. Big Shot Government Man, all your so-called friends too busy for you tonight?"

Agent Walker was slightly embarrassed. "It's not like that, and you know it. We were in a hurry, and I haven't been up here for a long time."

"Got that right," Farah said as she exceeded the speed limit along the road into town.

Agent Falin was entertained by their bickering. "Well, this sounds like it's going to be an interesting stay. How long have you two known each other?"

Farah answered first. "Pretty much forever."

Agent Walker's manners prevented him from disclosing too much. "We grew up in the same neighborhood."

Farah was more revealing. "Our fathers worked together for the government. My family is from Iran, and the Walkers were our only friends at first. They're the ones who got us to join the church."

Agent Walker reprieved his older-cousin persona. "You're still going on Sundays?"

"Hell no! I had enough of that stuck-between-gods stuff. That's one of the reasons I moved up here. No one cares what you believe so long as you don't try to force it on someone else."

"But you still go on Easter, don't you?"

"Hell no! The only time I hear God's name around here is when someone breaks their leg skiing – and they're usually not thanking Him for it."

"Sounds like miss ski instructor has seen a little too much snow. What are you going to do when it all melts?"

"Same thing you're going to do when all the bad guys are in jail. Take up skydiving." Farah pushed play on her cassette and sang along with Bruce Springsteen, changing the words slightly, *"Blinded by the white."*

Agent Falin got the joke and laughed, but Agent Walker felt like they were getting too close to the edge of sanctioned behavior. "Yes, we all know what goes on around here, but come on, Farah, be serious for once."

Farah liked a good spat. "Serious? Like the serious you were when you dumped my aunt?" She stepped on the brakes at the stoplight hard enough to jerk them all forward. "Have a nice dinner and call a taxi next time," she baited them.

Agent Falin liked her spunk. "Oh, come on you two. Farah, why don't you join us for dinner? *I'd* like to hear more of your story. It's the least we can do to thank you for the ride."

"Why thank you, sir. I'd love to – if that's okay with the boss."

"Of course. I was going to invite you to dinner anyway," Agent Walker assured her.

Farah stopped the Blazer in front of the Bristol Hotel and got out to open up the back. "Welcome to Steamboat Springs," she said, "where's there's always a little hot water to dip your feet in." Standing in a bulbous nylon parka, she looked like a Russian doll. Agent Falin was surprised at how small she was. She extended a very feminine hand and said, "See you later, gents," with outsized confidence.

"Thanks for the ride," Agent Walker said with a one-armed hug. "Downstairs in an hour?"

"I've got a few errands and the dogs need to be fed, so that should give me enough time. Start drinking without me if I'm a little late." She climbed back into her car and started the engine.

"Well, that was more entertaining than I expected," Agent Falin remarked as she was driving away. "Seems like we've run into a little history here. I think we're clearly off the clock now."

"Okay, but don't get too distracted. We've got a lot of ground to cover tomorrow." They approached the register at the quaint,

Western-style inn. "This is my favorite place to stay in Steamboat. The owner knows everybody in town."

The check-in was routine, and it was less than a minute before the desk clerk said, "Welcome, Mr. Walker. Here are your keys. Two-oh-three and two-oh-four, up the stairs and on your right."

"Where are we heading tomorrow?" Agent Falin asked in the hallway before entering his room.

"First the crash site area, then we're going to try to retrace the flight plan. We still don't know what happened and I can't file another report until we've got some possible explanations." Agent Walker unlocked his door and said, "See you downstairs at the bar," before going inside.

Agent Falin's room was a far cry from the relatively modern Holiday Inns he was used to. There was no TV and the ancient black phone didn't have any buttons or dials. A faded watercolor picture of cowboys on horseback took up most of the space above a bed with a bouncy mattress. A carved wood lamp in the shape of a rifle-toting trapper supported a beaver-skin shade decorated with paw prints. The dull, faded insulating curtains hanging over single-pane windows were as thick as blankets, and there was a matted trail in the shag rug around the bed. The whole room smelled musty from the lack of circulating air, so Agent Falin changed back into his street clothes and left as quickly as he could.

He was downstairs at the bar sipping his first Coors draft when Agent Walker joined him. The television was tuned to the Aspen station weather forecast. "Good news for all you early skiers, snow is on the way." A cheery reporter pointed to a weather map. "There's a big storm system approaching from the northwest. We're expecting just a few inches in the valleys, but the higher elevations could see as much as a foot of fresh powder."

"Are they talking about here?" Agent Falin asked.

Agent Walker took a swig. "Yep, looks like it'll cover the whole state west of the Front Range. Pretty unusual for snow this early."

"How are we supposed to fly in that?"

"We're not, but the storms move quickly up here. It could snow all morning, and we could still get half a day in the air if the field gets plowed."

Agent Falin looked at his watch. "So if we're not flying until noon, we can drink 'til midnight and still have twelve hours bottle-to-throttle." He raised his glass and toasted the television.

"That's only if you believe everything they say on TV."

The weather dominated the news, interspersed with local interest stories and politicians talking about the upcoming election. At the end of a segment on the serial killer Ted Bundy's recent escape and recapture, Halloween images started crawling along the bottom of the screen. Then an innocent-looking female reporter in a black witch's hat appeared to read a special report. "The annual Strawberry Springs haunted house in Steamboat will be open Friday and Saturday, five to nine, so you can take all your little ghosts and goblins there before or after their parties. Every child under the age of ten who is wearing a costume gets in for half price." The silhouette of a black cat slunk across the screen. "And for all you spooky adults up there, the party at the Ghost Ranch Saloon on River Road will be featuring one of the area's favorite bands, Split Personality. Admission is ten bucks and the party goes until 2:00 a.m. – or whenever you manage to get to sleep."

The TV screen faded to a swirl of stars spinning slowly like a hypnotist's wheel. Melodramatic organ music borrowed from a Vincent Price film accompanied the rotating visual. The image cut to the reporter again, who was now standing in front of a green-screen backdrop of an abandoned mine entrance. She spoke in a conspiratorial hush. "And isn't this fitting. We had multiple reports of strange lights in the sky last night. And while we can't say they're related, the remains of another one of the Carter family's herd was found hanging from the upper branches of a tree out near Craig." A prerecorded ghoulish scream and the momentary image of a severed cow's head with blood dripping from it ended the segment.

Agent Falin wasn't sure what to believe. "Strange place you got here," he muttered into the bottom of his mug.

"This ain't LA, that's for sure."

"What was that last bit with the cow's head all about?"

"That's just another one of those things they show on TV to keep everyone watching," Agent Walker said dismissively.

"So there was no dead cow in a tree?"

"Might have been. The mountain lions like to drag their food up on a limb to eat sometimes. I guess they can keep an eye out from up there."

"What about that bit with the lights in the sky? You've got your share of UFOers up here too?"

Agent Walker nodded in agreement. "Another round over here, please."

Farah came up from behind while their order was being poured. "And one for me too," she said, settling on the barstool next to Agent Walker. "Sorry I'm late. The dogs just wouldn't settle down. Must've seen those aliens again."

Agent Falin looked at her squarely. "Aliens?"

Farah returned his scrutiny over the lip of her beer glass. Her flushed cheeks were offset by sparkling hazel eyes. "What? You don't have any aliens where you come from?" she asked, cocking her head quizzically.

"Yeah, we've got aliens in LA, but most of them come across the border from Mexico. Where are *yours* from?"

Farah loved these kinds of confrontations. "Well, that's a very good question. Some say Mars and some say the Pleiades, but I reckon no one knows for sure." She took a very long swig of beer and wiped her mouth with the back of her sleeve.

Agent Falin liked her pluck. "But you're certain they're not from Earth?"

"Well, certain is certainly uncertain," Farah recited her clever reply, "but there's been so much UFO activity around here most folks are convinced we've got visitors. And with all this cattle mutilation business going on, some of those who weren't convinced last year have come over to our camp."

"Cattle mutilations?"

"Didn't you see the lady on the television? She was talking all about it when I first came in the door."

Agent Walker reentered the conversation. "There's some strange stuff going on around here, no doubt." He winked at Agent Falin.

Farah pressed her case. "I'll say. What about that plane crash near Sheep Mountain? What do think caused that?"

"Told you, can't talk business." Agent Walker ended his response with a swig.

Farah's curiosity was aroused. "Sooo, maybe ... ." The truth circulated up her spine like a jack-in-the-box spring and erupted in a toothy grin. "Well now we really have something to talk about!"

A man with a cowboy hat stared as Farah strained to hide the joy of discovery. A couple behind them were whispering, and Agent Falin got concerned. "Maybe we should go sit at a table and have some dinner," he suggested. "I don't know if it's the altitude or the beer or both, but I'm a little light-headed."

"Good idea," Agent Walker agreed. "I'm hungry myself, and a nice juicy steak will settle us both down. That good with you?" he asked Farah.

"You can keep on lying as long as you're buying," she accepted with a wink and stopped to talk to the man with the hat before joining them at a corner table.

When she sat down, Agent Walker questioned her. "I hope you didn't tell that guy anything you weren't supposed to."

Farah smirked mischievously. "Like what? You didn't tell me any secrets. I don't know if you guys have come up here to investigate the plane crash; see if maybe it was the aliens." She batted her eyes innocently.

Agent Falin's taste in women had expanded over time. Farah's dark hair, smooth skin, and rounded features – along with disproportionately large bosoms squished beneath her flannel shirt – belonged to no body type he was familiar with. "Where did you say your family was from?" he asked indelicately.

Farah remained coy. Agent Falin wasn't her type, but she did like male attention. "Does that really matter? Where's your family from, farm boy?"

Agent Walker laughed. "Good guess. Agent Falin is from Iowa. He's a real cornhusker."

Agent Falin corrected him. "It's true we grow miles of corn in Iowa, but Nebraska's the cornhusker state. We're the Hawkeyes. I thought you would have known that. Didn't you go to CU, Buffalo boy?"

"Sorry, Hawkeye, I can't keep track of all the teams the Buffalos trample," Agent Walker parried. "And just for the record, Farah comes from a prominent family whose roots stretch back to ancient Persia. Her father is a highly respected member of the military intelligence community."

Agent Falin saw her in a new light. "Well, that does explain a few things, but what's a smart girl like you –."

"Please don't say it," Farah interrupted. "I'll tell you the whole story if I ever see you again," she added snidely. Then she redirected. "Did you know that William's family is part Indian?" She put her hand over her mouth and made a silent whoop.

"So I heard."

Agent Walker raised his glass. "Okay, now that we all know each other a little better, a drink among friends!"

They clinked and retreated to their menus. "What's good here?" Agent Falin asked.

"You're in Colorado now. Beef's always the freshest thing on the menu."

"Yeah," Farah agreed, "and they're running a special on 'alien fried steak' tonight. Can't beat it unless you've got your own ray gun."

Agent Falin laughed and said, "I just hope they bring something quick before I pass out."

The sizzling steaks came and consumed everyone's appetite. Farah took the meaty bones to her dogs, Agent Walker was asleep by ten, and the last thing Agent Falin remembered before he got in bed was seeing huge flakes of snow fall through the gap in the smelly curtains.

CHAPTER 9

Duke's afternoon stroll on the beach was disappointing. Buzzed and self-conscious, he felt uncomfortable in the loose-fitting guru clothes he had bought, and his displeasure was only heightened by the fact that attractive women saw him as a perverted tourist with a stupid hat. He wandered down to the water's edge where the ebb tide had deposited an ugly straggle of dead kelp, food wrappers, and soda bottles, and the only people that seemed to be having fun there were inner-city kids who scurried in and out of the waves screaming with the joy of unconfinement. Duke climbed the rickety stairs of the adjacent pier to check out the amusement park, but the quaint carousel with the painted horses was deserted, dirty, and falling apart, and the splintery boards at the end of the pier were littered with the pungent bait of cigarette-smoking fishermen who had nothing better to do on a Thursday afternoon than catch undersized mackerel whose audible protests had earned them the misnomer of "holy". Repulsed and agitated, with his straw hat shoved firmly down over his ears to keep it from blowing off again and his sandals sticking to discarded gum, he barely made it back over the busy bike and jogging path without being run over by self-indulgent exercisers. Once he got back to the safety of his room, he threw his new outfit on the floor, escaped to the shower to wash off the salty residue, and sat naked on the bed in a fresh towel. The light on his phone was blinking, so he called the front desk and retrieved the messages left for him on their answering system.

The first message was from Remy. "Hey, man, back down in Bah-ha," he said, exaggerating the phrase. "Nasty hot – as usual," he drawled. "Ain't seen a day this bad since I's in 'Nam, or maybe that time we got lost in the bayou. Whatever. I tell you what though, that hombre Oswaldo is some kind of pain in my ass, all fidgety and nervous, askin' me about the money like he knows sumpthin's up, then he tosses his cookies in a special bag and the whole plane stinks like crocodile guts all the way back. Could not *wait* to land! Sheeeet! What I don't do for us! You'll owe me big time for this one. Anyway, we're all set up, I guess. I paid the girl half of what we said, told her she'd get the other half after I took off. I figure I'll be back up to you by one o'clock, give or take. You can leave a message at the hotel if you need to, but I won't get it 'til the morning. Might as well get soaked my last night down here. Later."

"Hi, Duke," a distinctive woman's voice he didn't recognize started the next message. "This is Stacy. I'm a friend of Marty and Marsha. They gave me your number and said it would be okay to call you. We're having a little party tonight in Beverly Hills and – well, if you're not doing anything funner, maybe you'd like to come." The throaty tone of her invite got Duke's attention. "It's at the house of one of the guys from the FrontRow Management office – Patrick, you may know him. Some of the guys from the band are coming over because they're mixing the record right now and the engineer wants them out of the room – you know how it is. Anyhow, it's all music and studio people, so you'll fit right in," she decided for him. There was a pregnant pause, and then she spoke in code. "Marsha said you've got some great tracks. I thought maybe we could listen to them and see if they're the kind of songs we're looking for. I won't be able to hear the phone, so just call Marsha for the address. Hope to see you later," she added emphatically.

Duke had to get up and look in the mirror while he replayed the sultry invitation. Stacy's sexy voice refueled his confidence, and the prospect of customers salivated his scam gland. He tapped out a small pile of blow next to the bathroom sink and dabbed it with his finger. Then he rubbed it in his nostril and washed it in with a snort of water. Blinking and swallowing, he ran the Norelco electric razor over his chin for the second time that day and primped his hair in the mirror with a blow-dryer like a runway model. Moving back for a three-quarter view, he put his hand on his hip and practiced a thin-lipped pout, hoping to be mistaken for David Bowie again. Reconnected to his natural persona, Duke pranced naked around the hotel room, muttering, "He was a young American," as he fussed through his luggage looking for the perfect evening outfit.

Marty called while he was trying on clothes. "Amigo! Glad I caught you. Have a nice relaxing day at the beach?"

Reinspired, he answered, "*Si, señor, fantastico!* I was going to call you."

"Oh yeah? Did Marsha's little friend call you?"

"Mmm-hmm! Thank you. Stacy, I think she said her name was."

"Yeah, Stacy. That voice!"

Duke repositioned his genitals in his boxers. "I'll say!"

"And she looks even better than she sounds. What a story. One of the musicians she was fucking had her make moaning sounds in the background of his record, and now she gets calls to do it for money – background vocals, I mean. It's a crazy business man. Marsha just signed her and we already got a call back from the movie audition we sent her on."

"Not surprising, based on what I heard."

"I want you to meet her. That's why we had her call you. Her family's from Colorado, so it's a natural. Plus she knows some people who might be interested in your other business."

"She said there was some guy from FrontRow I might know."

"FrontRow? She didn't tell me that. They manage Ronstadt. I wonder if it's Patrick. Wait a minute, there's someone at the door."

Duke cradled the phone against his ear as he pulled on a pair of pleated poplin pants and threaded a tooled-leather belt through the loops. The phone cord was long enough for him to slip his favorite black leather loafers over his bare feet, and by the time Marty got back on the line, he was buttoning a billowy blue shirt splattered with silver stars. He tucked it in, making sure enough buttons were open to show off his shiny good-luck pendant.

"You still there?" Marty checked.

"Mmm-hmm," Duke answered, admiring his image in the bureau mirror.

"Sorry that took so long. One of the neighbors found a stray dog and wanted to know if I knew who it belonged to. What were we talking about?"

"Stacy. Racy Stacy," Duke fantasized.

"Oh yeah, but there was something else. I know, FrontRow! That's Benzi's company. You know who that is?"

"Yeah? I've heard of him – but nothing good."

"He gets a bad rap from jealous people. I've done some business with him, and it's always worked out fine. I didn't know Stacy knew anybody over there. That girl really gets around."

"So you think it's okay for me to go to the party?"

"Party? I don't know anything about that."

"She called to invite me to a party. Said to call Marsha for the address. You're not going?"

"Not that I know of. Just a minute." Duke heard him call out for Marsha. A moment later, he came back on the phone. "Let me call you back. You going to be there for a bit?"

"For a while, but I'm supposed to meet someone at seven."

"Okay, I'll talk to you later."

Duke's next call was home. Cynthia answered the phone, "Good evening, BlueStar Studios."

"Hi Cyn. This is Duke. Diane left?"

"A little while ago. Want your messages?"

"Yeah, sure. Let me get a pen."

"Okay, but there's not much going on around here except construction. Remy called because he forgot your number at the hotel, and the guy you're supposed to meet with at seven – Roland something – asked if you could come by at ten tomorrow instead."

"Did he leave a number?"

"No, he said you had it. I asked him just in case you didn't, but he wouldn't give it to me. He sounded hassled."

"Okay, thanks for trying. I've got his number here somewhere. Anything else going on?"

"Diane said that guy Cells came by with his friend this afternoon and talked with Dennis. Walter was in for a couple of hours doing something. He left you a note. I don't see anything else in your box."

"Is Dennis there?"

"No, he went over to Cells' rehearsal studio with the old board. Want me to have him call you when he gets back?"

"No, I'll talk to him later. Anything else?"

"Well," Cynthia wasn't sure where the boundaries were. "I don't know if I should ask."

"It's okay Cyn. Remember what we said; trust."

"Well it's not such a big deal really. It's just that there's going to be an awesome Halloween party at the Boulderado on Saturday night, and I was wondering if it was okay if – "

"Of course you can go. Just get someone to fill in, or maybe we'll close early or whatever. Nobody's scheduled, right?"

"No. Dennis said we won't be up by then. Diane told the guys from Nashville they can't load in 'til sometime next week. So seeing that there's nothing else happening, can we do some kind of Halloween thing here too?"

"Huh? What do you mean?"

"Oh, I don't know, but Diane and I were talking, and it's been real quiet down here lately, and we thought maybe some of the people from the other party might want to come by and see the studio while they're out partying, and if they did, we should do something fun so it doesn't look like we've got nothing going on, and even though Dennis didn't like the idea, he said we could clean the studio room so it looked presentable," Cynthia rambled on excitedly. "And we thought maybe some decorations might help, and maybe some of the people who came might want to record here someday so it would be good for business besides being fun. What do you think? – Pleeease."

Duke thought about a studio full of potential customers. "Hmm, interesting." The sunset over the ocean lit up the sky in shades of orange and black. "Decorations might be a good idea."

"Yippee! That means okay? I knew you would like the idea. Diane thought you'd never go for it so she made me ask. When are you getting back?"

"Tomorrow night or maybe Saturday afternoon; depends."

"So you'll be here! Cool. I'll make some calls tonight."

"Who're you going to call?"

"Everybody. Everybody loves a party. I'll tell them to be here around eight on Saturday. Okay?"

"Wait a minute. I thought the party was going to be at the Boulderado."

"It is. Here, the Boulderado, the mall, campus, everywhere. It's Halloween weekend! The weather's supposed to be great, and who doesn't like to party? Is it okay if we use a few bucks from petty cash for food? I know these cool chicks who do catering, so all we really need is some wine and –."

"Whoa, girl. How much are you planning on spending?"

"Is like five hundred bucks, okay? Diane said the bank approved you for another twenty-five thousand, so it doesn't seem like a lot."

"The bank called? Approved? You didn't tell me that!"

"I thought Diane told you."

"No, that's great news!" Duke recalculated. "Okay then, party's officially on. Spend a thousand if you need to, but keep the guest list tight. We don't want the wrong kind of people showing up, if you know what I mean."

"Of course. No narcs, no sharks, no snarks. I'll have Dennis call you when he gets back."

Duke found Roland's number in his daybook and dialed it. An answering machine picked up. "This is Roland Sizemore," a man's voice announced stiffly. "I am too busy to answer the phone, but if you want to leave a message for Pandora Productions, you may do so when you hear the beep tone. Good-bye."

"Good evening, Roland. This is Duke Dunn. I understand you want to reschedule our meeting for ten tomorrow. That may work, but I have a party to go to tonight, so that might be a little early. I'll be in town for most of the day tomorrow so I'll try to reschedule. Peace."

Duke was watching the ocean swallow a giant orange fireball, half-expecting the process to make steam, when Marty called back.

"Amigo. You're still there, good. Change of plans. I have to go to the studio tonight, but Marsha can swing by the hotel and take you to Stacy's party. Sound good?"

"Okay, I guess; if it's not too much trouble. My seven o'clock cancelled, so I'm actually free tonight. What time is she thinking?"

"She's over at a friend's in the Palisades now. They're, well, you know. She'll pick you up when she's done there. You guys go have a good time tonight. Not too good – she's still married you know," Marty joked. "I'll be at the studio late tonight so it all works out."

Duke was duded up, reading the paper in the lobby of the hotel when Marsha drove up in a black Jaguar XJ6. She got out of the car dressed for a night out, and was hassling with the parking valet when Duke came out to rescue her. "Good evening, Mrs.

Freedman." he greeted her. "I'm ready to go," he said loud enough to inform the valet.

Marsha clicked around to his side of the car in four-inch spikes and collected herself.

Duke pecked her on the cheek. "Looking sharp as usual."

She rose up on her toes and gave him a warm, full-bodied hug. "Looking good yourself." Handing him the keys, she whispered, "You drive. I've had a little too much of a good thing."

"Okay," Duke agreed, hugging her back, "but I'm a little buzzed myself, so maybe we should let the valet park the car and sober up at the bar before we go."

Their body heat convected, and neither of them let go. "Good idea. Those parties don't really get going 'til much later," she said, stepping back and snugging her low-cut sequined top over her C cups. A shiny Chanel belt snaked through the loops of her designer jeans as she balanced on glossy red toes.

Duke got close enough to peck her on the cheek again. "What's that perfume you're wearing?"

Marsha returned the flirtation. "Princess Mist. You still like it?"

"You know I do."

She put one hand on his shoulder and the other on his hip. "We could hang out here for a while and *then* go to the party. I mean, if you don't have any other plans."

Duke's put his arm around her and collected the energy. "Let's cool off at the bar before we go."

She felt his excitement and held on for support.

"Valet!" he said, waving the keys.

Friday, October 27, 1978

Chapter 10

The birds in Donna's backyard were making so much noise that they woke Jon up. He wandered into the kitchen in his underwear and saw her feeding them breadcrumbs. Chickadees, sparrows, juncos, and jays hopped and tweeted through the shrubs around Donna's feet as she dribbled treats from her hand. The stray cat she had adopted crouched in the bushes along the fence that separated her yard from her neighbor's. He was used to her bird-feeding ritual and mostly came to watch. The tea water was still warm, the oven timer was clicking, and the odor of fresh bread whet Jon's appetite. Donna was dressed in a full-length dress she had made from a Mexican blanket, and as he reheated the kettle and listened to her chatting with the birds, he could barely remember the complicated sex positions they had tried the night before. He had been with several different girls over the years, but he always came back to Donna. A gusty breeze rustled the wind chimes hanging like metal fruit from the crabapple tree in the backyard. Clanks and tinkles and tones rose to a chaotic pitch, and the birds, spooked by the noisy movement, scattered just as Donna ran out of food. The cat followed her to the door and waited outside when she went in to fetch his bowl. Jon was standing by the kitchen counter in his underwear with a blanket wrapped around his shoulders when she came in. He said, "Gooood morning, Mrs. Audubon," in a singsong voice while holding a mug of hot tea with both hands.

"You're up!" Donna greeted him with a good morning kiss. "Sleep well, hmm?" She opened the fridge and prepared the cat's food. "A new record this morning," she voiced her thoughts. "Thirty-one birds. Mostly sparrows, but there were two thrushes I never saw before and the doves came back again. Must have been the lovemaking."

Jon was familiar with Donna's associative logic. "Must have been," he acknowledged, knowing the explanation would follow.

"See, the thrushes represent cunnilingus because they live in the bushes. I had three orgasms, and that's why there were three doves," Donna concluded matter-of-factly.

"Mmm-hmm."

Donna was experimental in all phases of life. Since coming to Boulder, she had taken up yoga, learned how to make her own clothing, and developed an interest in cooking organic foods that had blossomed into a livelihood. With lots of friends and the vigor of youth, she rarely thought about leaving her mountain paradise. The cat meowed loudly. "He's just like you," she said, placing the cat's food dish outside the back door. "Only you get to eat inside."

"Speaking of food, what's that I smell?"

"Zucchini bread." Donna opened the oven and peeked. "It's ready now." She picked up the hot pan with a folded towel and placed it on top of the stove. "I need to let it cool."

Jon sipped his tea and watched as she put away the dishes. They had met one cold February afternoon during their freshman year at Adelphi University on a cigarette break from a boring lecture on citizenship, but the initial arc of their relationship lasted only a little longer than one semester because Donna had to go back home to Baltimore when school was over. During school, they smoked pot on campus with members of SDS, drank homemade beer with foreign exchange students, took mescaline together out on Long Island, and even attended a few classes. "Need some help?" he offered, seeing her struggling with heavy pots.

"If you don't mind."

He got up, took the oven pan from her, and rearranged the contents of the upper cabinet to make room for it.

Jon was easily the tallest and best-looking boyfriend she had ever been with, and she clung to poignant memories of reading poetry while he played guitar. "Aren't you cold?" she teased. "Better get some pants on before I... ." Neither of them had brushed their teeth, and their natural beauty was still drying on tissues in the bedroom wastebasket. "Breakfast will be ready by the time you get back."

Jon accepted the slap-on-the-ass message and followed instructions.

Donna pressed play on the kitchen cassette player, and the moaning tones of her meditation tape filled the void. She hummed her mantra while slicing and buttering the fresh loaf.

Jon came back dressed and carrying his guitar. He sat on the arm of a chair and tried to play along with the ambient sounds of her tape.

"Please don't do that," Donna said. "Not now."

Jon played some harmonics that he thought blended in perfectly.

"I said please. You know how important my morning meditation is." Donna put his plate in front of him. "This is a new recipe so tell me if you like it."

Jon sampled the bread. It didn't taste any different from usual. "Mmm-mmm," he complimented with stuffed cheeks. "What did you put in here this time? It's great."

"You're such a bad liar. I tricked you. It's the same recipe I always make."

"Why'd you try to trick me? You mad at me because of last night?"

"Last night was last night. Now it's today. We'll never be close unless we are completely honest with one another."

Jon gulped. "Completely?"

Donna held her hands in a concentration mudra and bellowed, "Ohhhmmmm," in her lowest voice.

Jon chomped his breakfast irreverently, washing down the masticated pulp with a long swig of herbal tea. "Completely, eh? Well, maybe you should tell me what really happens on those retreats you've been going on."

"What do you mean? We sit and meditate; that's all."

"Really? Then why did you come back with crabs last time?"

Donna continued her meditative stance. "I told you, everyone got them. It's not like there's a cleaning service in the mountains."

"Cleanliness is not part of the program?"

"Oh Jon, you'll never understand spirituality. The body is just a vehicle for the soul. Monks don't waste their time washing their hands and brushing their teeth three times a day."

Jon itched his crotch under the table and said, "Well, I guess I'll never be a monk because I feel like brushing my teeth now." He headed to the bathroom.

Donna's phone interrupted her contemplation. "Hi, Doh-na," her coworker at the restaurant addressed her with the Tibetan pronunciation of her name. "This is Tara. We had a big pastry order called in last night and we need you to come early today. Can you?"

"What time?"

Tara was agitated. "I don't know, as soon as you can. We need a thousand pieces for tomorrow night."

"That's forty trays! What's going on? Another big party on campus?"

"Well, Delta Zeta wants two hundred and fifty, but there's a big Halloween party at the Boulderado and they want five hundred."

"That's a lot of baking! What kinds do they want?"

"All sorts, whatever we have ingredients for. They just want to say it came from here 'cause they know people want organic food."

"Who are the rest for?"

"I don't know. The recording studio next door is having a party, and the restaurant needs some for the weekend. What time can you come in? Joel and Nancy are freaking out."

"Tell them I'll be in soon."

When she came back Jon asked, "Who were you talking to?"

"The restaurant. They want me to come in right away."

"How come? Somebody call in sick?"

"No, we've got a huge amount of baking to do for the weekend."

"Bummer. I thought we were going to hang out together for a while. Can't you just go in a little early?"

"We only have so much oven space, so I have to get started soon." Donna came closer and petted Jon's head. He buried his face in her robe and inhaled the patchouli. "I'll try to get out in time for the show tonight. When are you supposed to go on?"

"It starts at eight, but I don't know when it'll be my turn."

"How much is first prize?"

"Three hundred. I'll talk to the MC and tell him to put me last. That's the best spot, and besides, the headliner always goes on last."

Donna ran her hand down his stomach and rubbed the front of his pants. "Feeling a bit cocky, are we?"

"I thought you had to go to work."

"I do. Just want to give you something to look forward to tonight."

Donna went to her room and got dressed. Jon turned the meditation tape off, picked up his guitar, and started rehearsing his set. He looked so serious with his eyes closed, methodically practicing a Travis picking pattern that Donna didn't want to disturb him before she left. She was about to leave him a note when the cat howled to come in. Jon opened his eyes and saw her standing by the door with a floppy wide-brim hat and one of her homemade serapes hanging over billowy bloomers.

He raked an open G and sang, *"You've got a strange fascination with style."*

Donna feigned innocence and struck a playful pose.

"Yeah you! Got a strange fascination with style."

"See you tonight, minstrel man."

CHAPTER 11

It was still snowing when Agent Falin woke up on Friday morning. He followed his nose to the smell of coffee and found Agent Walker downstairs with the local liaison for US Customs and Immigration.

"Good morning, Agent Falin," Agent Walker greeted him from worn leather seating adjacent to the lobby. "Sleep well?"

Agent Falin sized up Agent Walker's companion. He was a serious-looking man with short hair and piercing eyes, so he kept it official. "Yes, sir, just fine."

"Good. I'd like you to meet the man we go to 'round these parts, Officer Greg McKnight. We were just discussing the rescue operation, but I'll let you get some coffee before we bring you up to speed."

The thin air wasn't supplying enough oxygen to wake him up, and it seemed like everything about the hotel tread the fine line between charmingly historic and economically depressed. Agent Falin turned over a white ceramic mug and released a dark trickle of brown fluid from the stainless steel coffeemaker. His usual two packets of sugar weren't enough to mask the burnt flavor, curdles of overripe milk floated around the edges of his cup, and the breakfast rolls were so hard that the Danish would have been embarrassed. Missing Los Angeles, he settled into a vintage western chair with torn upholstery and sipped his mud while Agent Walker explained the game plan.

"Officer McKnight was just telling me that the hiking team found the crash site yesterday."

Agent Falin nodded.

"They couldn't do a full search due to the weather."

Officer McKnight took up the narrative. "We're expecting less than a foot of snow in the valley – which around here is considered a dusting – but there could be some real accumulation up where the plane went down."

"Any chance the pilot survived?" Agent Falin asked.

"Well I guess it's possible he survived the crash. We didn't find a body yet, if that's what you're asking, but it's unlikely he could last for more than a day or two in those conditions. They located the fuselage and some of the wing at about eighty-five hundred feet. It's pretty cold up there, and given the probable injuries – let's just say we're not optimistic."

Agent Walker took over again. "Thanks, Officer McKnight. Now let's discuss the reason for our visit."

They checked to see if anyone else was in earshot. A quartet of excited skiers in snow pants and wool sweaters were chatting amongst themselves near the front door, the doorman was helping an elderly couple check out, and the bewildered town drunk who the hotel took pity on was slumped in a chair by the window talking to himself. Satisfied with the privacy, Officer McKnight continued quietly, "Okay, here's where we're at. We think Agent Dobson was tracking a signal that was moving. He squawked his position four times the day we lost him, and when we plotted the coordinates with where he went down, it's a straight line, more or less."

"Did anyone actually speak with him?"

"No, unfortunately it was just a transponder signal."

"So we don't know if he ever made visual contact with the target?"

Agent Walker explained, "He had been working the area for several weeks, following up on everything that moves. The report he filed the night before said he was monitoring activity near a private landing strip he had spotted. We're theorizing that he saw something and gave chase."

Agent Falin started to sense the mission. "Like what? Smugglers?"

Officer McKnight answered, "We're not sure; maybe. I'm a third-generation ranger, and we've been investigating all kinds of weird sightings since the first Christians got here."

Agent Walker filled in. "These mountains can play tricks on you – sort of like seeing mirages in the desert. I've seen some strange optical affects while flying, and there are always shadows in the woods."

Officer McKnight jerked his head in agreement. "I don't want to you to think we're just making things up. There are some real nuts up here, and while we can't believe everything they say, we can't ignore them either. We've got our share of mysteries, just like everywhere, but let's just say the Rockies are particularly good at keeping secrets."

Agent Falin was starting to get annoyed. "I keep hearing that, but so far, all I know is that a plane crashed, which – excuse me – is not so unusual."

"You're right, Agent Falin. I guess we should go down to the station and show you some maps."

"All I've seen since I got here is maps – unless you count abandoned mines as evidence. You guys got anything else?"

Officer McKnight smiled confidently. "We'll start with the maps, then we'll show you the evidence."

"Evidence? Real facts?" Agent Falin's mood improved. "Now we're getting somewhere. Mind if I ask you a question?"

"Shoot."

"Is there a place we can get a real breakfast on the way to the station?"

"I'm sorry," Officer McKnight apologized. "Not used to our mountain cuisine, Mr. LA?"

"I like the food just fine – when they serve it hot and cooked. Dinner was great last night."

Agent Walker spoke to Officer McKnight. "We'll try to find something on the way over to the office. Is Nancy's place still open?"

"No, she moved down to Boulder last year."

Agent Walker asked Agent Falin, "How soon can you be ready to go? I'm not sure where we'll be staying tonight so better pack everything."

"Ten minutes okay?"

"See you soon."

Agent Walker and Officer McKnight talked in private while Agent Falin went to pack.

"How much does he know?" Officer McKnight asked.

"Not everything."

"Why not? Doesn't he work in the same department as you?"

"He does, but I only just met him face-to-face for the first time yesterday, and I'm not sure how much I want him to know."

"Why not? He's one of us, isn't he?"

"He is, but from what I've heard, he doesn't always play by the rules."

Officer McKnight thought before asking the next question. "Whose rules?"

"That's the problem. He follows the law as close as most intel guys who operate on the edge. It's just the other rules that he's not too good at." Officer McKnight looked confused, so Agent Walker continued, "He won't tell the citizens what he's not supposed to, if that's what you're thinking. Problem is, he won't tell anyone everything. He likes to keep a few cards in the hole, and that makes me nervous."

Officer McKnight disagreed. "Sounds like a good detective to me. Let me know if he doesn't work out in Denver, and I'll put him to work up here. I could use a guy that doesn't need his hand held."

Agent Falin came back down with his bag, and Agent Walker settled their bill before Officer McKnight took them to headquarters. A blanket of snow muted the sound of his sure-footed International Travelall effortlessly crunching through the six inches of fresh powder with deep-tread tires. The smell of exhaust fumes trapped against the low-pressure ceiling dulled their appetite, but they stopped at a small convenience store and bought some slightly fresher coffee and few of yesterday's pastries. When they got to Officer McKnight's office, the Denver agents left their bags in his truck and followed him into the basement of the municipal building that housed the Steamboat area office. The door was open, but Margaret Strothers, the only full-time employee, wasn't at her desk. Officer McKnight read the note she'd left on the door and ushered Agents Walker and Falin into his private office.

Agent Falin blurted out, "So where's the evidence?" before they had even sat down.

"I guess the reports are true," Officer McKnight said as he hung up his parka. "Nobody waits in LA."

Agent Falin defended his turf. "Not really. We've got lots of waiters there – only they all think they're actors."

"Well we don't have much theater around here," Officer McKnight parried. "Most folks just look out the window at the weather for entertainment."

Agent Walker interrupted. "Can we please get back to business? Officer McKnight, would you show Agent Falin the aerials?"

Officer McKnight opened the thin drawer of a wide file cabinet that was used to lay maps and pictures flat. He selected a series of grayscale satellite images with remarkable resolution and put them on a table. "Here's where we are now." He pointed. "And here's the crash site area."

Agent Falin studied the aerials. "I've seen my share of these," he commented, "but what's this?" He traced a line of dots that had been drawn on the second photograph.

"That's the squawk line. Each dot is where Agent Dobson was when he reported his position over the past few days," Officer McKnight explained. "We think he was heading straight for this spot." His finger landed on a thin line near the top of a mountain.

Agent Walker was surprised. "Isn't that on the other side of the divide? I thought he went down on this side."

"He did. We think the reason may be related to altitude. The high peaks are all at the top end of the Cessna's range. There're a few narrow passes at lower elevations, but you'd need perfect weather to make it over the top."

"So you're saying he might have stalled?" Agent Falin questioned.

"We're thinking maybe conditions got rough, or he was low on fuel and he circled back toward the valley looking for a place to put down. The wreckage does indicate he was going in the opposite direction at the very end."

Officer McKnight spread out photographs from different angles, and the men studied them silently, formulating opinions. Agent Falin saw one with curious ink marks and asked, "What are these?"

Officer McKnight looked at Agent Walker for permission to explain. "Oh, those have nothing to do with this case. They're locations of … ."

Agent Walker shrugged. "Might as well tell him."

"Those are reports of supposed cattle mutilations. You've heard about them?"

"First time I heard about them was yesterday. It was part of the Halloween report so I figured they were joking around." He looked at the map again. There were at least twenty markings on it. Some of the markings were empty circles, but some of the circles had been filled in with Xs. "What's the difference between the two?"

"The ones with the Xs have been verified."

Agent Falin thought for a moment. "Verified? By who?"

"By us. My brother is a cop over in Granby, and we've got eyes all over," Agent Walker told him. "Might as well show him the pictures," he said, giving permission. "You're not squeamish, are you?"

"Nah, left all my squeams in 'Nam."

Officer McKnight retrieved the folder with the eight-by-ten glossies of bovine crime scenes. In some, full-grown cows lay dead on barren soil with their bones exposed. "You can't tell from the pictures, but all of these animals have been sliced open by very sharp instruments. Some have had their guts removed, others, their brains or heart or liver, and some of the poor critters have lost their sex organs."

"Who did this?"

"We really don't know. There've been investigators from Washington looking into all the possibilities. Most folks around here think there are natural explanations, but not everyone is convinced."

"Why not?"

"The evidence around the bodies leaves too many questions unanswered. Besides the obvious question of why someone would do this, there're often no footprints or blood at the scene."

"And people really think it may be aliens?" Agent Falin was incredulous.

"People make up all kinds of stories to explain what they don't understand. Here, let me show you some other pictures. They're not pretty, but they make more sense."

The photos were much more graphic and disgusting than Agent Falin expected: a half-eaten cow face stared down from a branch with one eye, a headless carcass dripped blood from its neck, and most disturbingly, the entrails of another victim oozed from where it had been sliced open.

Agent Falin thought he had seen it all, but then Officer McKnight showed him the most shocking photo. "What the hell is that?"

"We're not sure. What does it look like to you?"

They all stared at the picture of a creature that could not possibly have met a natural end. Its legs were bound together by rope as it hung upside down from a broken limb at least thirty feet in the air. A zoomed-in version of the photo showed a pattern of slashes on its neck that looked like someone had been writing with a penknife. A huge, lifeless tongue drooped from the mouth.

"How did it get up there?" was the first question Agent Falin asked. "That thing must weight a thousand pounds!"

"Someone would have had to go through an awful lot of trouble to hoist it up there with a winch," Officer McKnight pointed out. "Maybe someone drove a truck up to where this supposedly happened and hoisted it up there with a winch, but here's the bad news; we didn't take the pictures."

Agent Falin thought for a moment. "Why's that bad? They could just be fake pictures. Isn't that the best explanation you could hope for?"

"Well yes, they might be fake, but whoever took them didn't only send them to us."

"You don't know who took them? Can't you find out?"

"We have some theories, some leads. I think we'll eventually find out, but I don't know how long it will take or what damage it'll do in the meantime."

"Damage? The cow's already dead."

Agent Walker answered. "You saw the report last night. Everyone in Colorado is talking about the damn cattle mutilations. That's bad for the tourism business, but *The Denver Post* is in the business of selling papers. They've been printing pictures and running stories on this stuff for months. Some people think the aliens are experimenting with surgery, others say the Native Americans are bent on revenge. Average folks believe it's just wild animals having a meal or maybe the slaughterhouses doing something with diseased carcasses. It could just be some crazy sickos, but no one really knows who's behind it – or why. Aspen's seen a spike in cancellations, and the Cattleman's Convention has been moved back to Dallas this year. Camping permits have been way down and even Steamboat has felt the pinch."

The men shuffled through the array of photos, pointing out interesting land features near the incident sites, and speculating on the possibilities. Margaret Strothers was back at her desk helping a Mexican domestic fill out her immigration paperwork when the law enforcement officers left for lunch.

CHAPTER 12

Duke got up late on Friday. He was sobering up in the steam of the hotel shower when Remy left a message. "Can't talk," the message said. "I should be out of here in a few minutes. Weather looks good and the plan seems to be working, sort of. See you in a while, I hope."

Duke peered out the window to check the local conditions. The regular morning fog had lifted and the sea was calm, but he was still nervous. He stuffed Marsha's torn pantyhose in the garbage and covered them with room-service trash. What would Marty do if he found out? He couldn't tell if the pain in his stomach was from hunger or fear. Did Remy get the rest of the bricks – and was he going to be able to take off before Oswaldo discovered their ruse? How much would he have to kick back to the banker who arranged his line of credit? With so many plans up in the air, the ground started rotating underneath him. He sat back on the bed and tried to stop the room from spinning. The hotel phone warbled in a tone that was both soothing and portentous. He forced a pleasant, "Good morning."

"Good morning, Mr. Dunn. This is Roland Sizemore. I hope I'm not calling you too early."

Duke was relieved. Roland was the only appointment he had in LA that was strictly studio business. He checked the bedside clock. It was almost eleven. "No, no; I've been awake for hours. I just came back to the room before heading out for the day. I was going to call you."

"Well, I'm glad I got ahold of you. Our next session isn't starting until two today, so we still have time if you still want to come by and see the Aphex."

"That sounds good. You have the new Exciter hooked up, right?"

"Yes, you'll be able to hear what it does. They're also letting me demo their new piece, the Dominator, so you can play around with that too."

"Good. I'm looking forward to giving them a listen. I have to pick someone up at the airport around three, so how 'bout I come to you at one?"

"One o'clock is perfect. You have the address?"

"Better give it to me again."

"It's 6620 Selma. We're right around the corner from Cherokee."

"See you in a while."

His agenda reset, Duke ordered room-service breakfast and began packing. While he was waiting for it to be delivered, he fished a pair of clean underwear and socks out from his suitcase, put on his traveling jeans, and checked the room for incriminating evidence. There were still some traces of powder on the glossy "Welcome to Los Angeles" foldout he and Marsha had used the night before, so he licked it off with his finger, crumbled it, and threw it in the trash. The stash bottle was almost empty, but he took a few good-morning sniffs and zipped it into the side pocket of his shoulder bag. The thought of Marsha's intimacy made saliva under his tongue. It had been several years since their last one-nighter, and she seemed to have improved with age. She was so smooth in all the right places, and much more experienced than the young floozies he usually bedded. It pained him to know that he could never possess a woman like that while he was living out of suitcases and scamming to stay alive. Room service came, and he nibbled at breakfast while watching a television show that featured the houses, cars, and personal luxuries of Los Angeles's high-profile residents. He knew he had to make a lot of money – that was the only solution.

When he finished packing and eating, Duke left his room for good and made his way down the hall. A strange thought shadowed his mind like a fast-moving cloud. He wasn't sure if it was some kind of premonition or the overly stimulated tissues in his brain malfunctioning, but when he got off the elevator, the whole lobby seemed to come to a standstill. The voices he heard were slowed down to a low warble – as if someone had set the turntable on the wrong speed. "Oohhrree oohhrree oohhrree," they murmured slowly. Looking around, he saw a spotlight of sun on two poorly dressed Buddhist monks sitting peacefully in the lobby. He thought one of the monks smiled at him, and thinking it was a good omen, Duke smiled back. With the eerie sound still mumbling in his subconscious, he went to the checkout desk. The sound submerged while the clerk spoke, and after he paid, Duke picked up his suitcase and meandered to the sunny seating area where he had seen the monks. He was surprised they weren't there, and puzzled by the fact that in their place sat two scraggly Native Americans. One was very large, and the other was very old. They stared at him silently, looking very uncomfortable and completely out of place. The "oohhrree oohhrree" sound swelled inside Duke's head and he wondered why the other people in the lobby didn't seem to hear it. Images of Colorado's snowcapped peaks and rolling foothills flickered in his mind. Restless Native American spirits in buffalo robes chanted by an imaginary fire. "Oohhrree oohhrree oohhrree, thump!" Trying to distance himself from the unnerving dirge, Duke sought out the peaceful Buddhist monks. Maybe they belonged to Naropa Institute in Boulder and had recognized him? He liked Naropa, even tried meditating sometimes to relieve the stress, but most of his interest in spirituality was interwoven with drug use and withdrawal. Maybe the monks knew that? Duke went outside to the passenger drop-off, thinking the monks might be there waiting for a ride. They weren't, but the sea air was pleasant and the disquieting chant in his head blended into the rumble of the surf. He sat on the bench by the front door and filled his lungs with the mild breeze of morning in LA. The never-ending parade of exercisers moved alongside the wheeled traffic on Ocean Avenue and it seemed as though everyone's weeklong hustle had hit the weekend planning wall. The same seagulls as yesterday were surfing the updrafts, calling to each other in long caws that reminded Duke of the squawks that pilots hear through the NavCom, and he barely noticed when the Freedmans' Jaguar stopped right in front of him.

Marsha interrupted his meditation through the rolled down passenger window. "Good afternoon, handsome."

"*Buenos dias*, mi amigo," Marty called from the driver's seat. "Come on in."

Already disoriented, Duke hesitated. He had no idea what Marsha might have told him about the night before. Marty was usually very even-tempered, but Duke knew he owned a gun.

"Oh come on, man," Marty urged. "We're not going to bite. You look a little lost. Didn't you get our message?"

"Er, no. What message?"

"Marsha called you a while ago and left a message saying we were on our way over. I guess you were on the phone and it kicked over to the answering machine."

Duke wasn't sure about either of their intentions. "I wasn't planning on seeing you until later – after Remy gets here." Duke got up and held his luggage. "I already checked out."

"We figured that, but it's such a nice day, and you're only in town for a little while longer so Marsha thought it would be fun to drive you around and spend some time together. Talk about the old times."

"Thanks, but I have to meet someone in Hollywood at one and return the rental car."

"Perfect. We love Hollywood. I have an act recording at Sunset Sound right now. Maybe we can stop in. I know you love studios. Ever been to Sunset?"

"No, can't say as I have."

"Sunset's the place, man. Best records in the world coming out of there. There and Abbey Road, of course."

The valet interrupted their conversation by asking Marty to park or move.

"Where are you parked?" Marty asked. "I'll take you to your car and follow you to the rental return. Then we'll give you a ride into town."

Duke reviewed the logistics. "I wasn't planning on returning the car until later. I have to meet Remy at the airport. We were going to return the car after seeing you and take a cab back to the airport."

"Well, let's make a new plan. We're both feeling particularly energetic – and I think you know why – so we'll be your chauffeurs for the day. Sound good?"

"That's not too much trouble?" Duke searched Marsha's face for signs of conflict, but all the clues were hidden by sunglasses and a headscarf. "Okay, thanks," he agreed tentatively. "One less cab ride. I'm parked in the lot around back. The rental car place in on Lincoln."

Duke put his luggage in the trunk and got in the back. Marty drove him to the parking garage, and Marsha got out with him. "There's construction on Lincoln, so I'll ride with you and show the back way," she said.

Eager to use his latest gadget, a newly installed car-phone, Marty said, "I have some calls to make. I'll wait here and follow you over."

Marsha walked in front of Duke on their way to the car, mesmerizing him with her sexy saunter up the stairs, but neither of them said anything about the night before until they were on the second level of the parking structure with the door to his Mustang closed. That's when she reached over the bucket seat console and put her hand on the inside of his thigh.

Duke wasn't sure what to do. "Marty's waiting," he said nervously as she moved her fingers.

She leaned over and kissed his neck, allowing the power of her perfume to cloud his mind. "Let him wait."

Trapped behind the wheel, he left the keys in the ignition and reached his arm around her. "You sure this is a good idea?"

Her touch extended to his private parts. "I had such a good time last night," she cooed mischievously, encouraging his hard-on. "How fast can you come?" she asked, unzipping his fly.

His defenses weakened and his judgment drained, Duke lowered the seat back and twisted toward her. Expertly, she extracted his penis and met his erection with her lips. Spreading his fingers on the back of her head to keep her out of sight, his blood pressure rose with each head bob. Marsha finished him off in under a minute, and his heart was still racing as she sat up with a wide-eyed smile. Undoing her headscarf, she wiped her mouth with the designer silk before wrapping it around Duke's shrinking member. "I'm sorry, I just couldn't help myself," she said, helping him zip back in. "Don't be mad. I don't think we got any on your pants."

Still in shock, Duke looked at her in disbelief as she casually straightened her hair and reapplied lipstick in the vanity mirror.

She feigned innocence. "What?"

"Why'd you do that? Not that I'm complaining."

"I knew you didn't finish last night – and neither did I."

"What about Marty? What did he say when you came home at one o'clock looking like – "

"I got back before he did. I was showered and in bed thinking about you by the time he got home. He was probably having his dick sucked by the night girl at the studio again, so why should I behave? He thinks I don't know, but a woman can always tell."

Duke didn't understand the dynamics of their marriage so he just readjusted his seat, put the car in reverse, and circled down the ramps while Marsha tidied up. Marty was on his car phone and waved as they passed. They wound through Venice's warren of one-way side streets to the cheap rental car lot in Venice. After he turned in his car, Duke accepted Marty's invitation to ride in the passenger seat as they drove into Hollywood. Using the mirror on the passenger visor to comb his hair, he saw Marsha mouthing the words to the Commodores song "Three Times a Lady" on the radio. Duke didn't really like ballads, but hummed the chorus of the next song, "I Go Crazy," as Marty steered them across Doheny and east on Fountain. Marsha was content to file her nails and entertain fantasies in the back seat.

"So where exactly are we heading?" Marty asked when they crossed La Brea.

"Six Six Two Zero Selma. It's right around the corner from Cherokee."

"Cherokee Studios?"

"Yeah, on Cherokee Street. You friends with them?"

"Friends? Not exactly. One of my artists has done some sessions there. He likes the vibe, but Sunset has better equipment. What's the name of the place you're going to?"

"Pandora. They're a beta test site for Aphex. You ever try one?"

"Yeah, they brought one out to Shangri-La a while ago. We passed."

"Why? You didn't like it?"

"Well, to be honest, it was kind of hard to tell what it did. The engineer said he could hear the difference in the vocal, but no one else was really sure. Plus, as a businessman, their deal is really weird if you ask me."

"How so?"

"They won't sell you a unit. You can use it all you want, but they only charge you for how many seconds it's on the final mix."

"That's crazy! How do they know?"

"Beats me, but they say what it does to the signal is so distinct that they'll know what to charge you when they put the music through their reader."

"What about the mixes that you use it on that they never hear? How are they going to know everything you did?"

"They say they only charge for what is released, but what are they going to do, check every record released? They make you sign a contract before they'll ship you a unit, so if you try to get away with something their lawyers could sue you. I guess they're relying on the honor system, sort of."

Duke had heard enough to make him change his mind. "That's ridiculous. Mind if I use your car phone?"

"Sure, go ahead, but I only have a local plan, so it won't call long distance. We're coming up to Cherokee and Selma now."

"Just park anywhere. This won't take long." Duke opened his date book and found Roland's number.

"Pandora Productions, Roland Sizemore speaking."

"Hi, Roland, this is Duke Dunn. I'm very sorry, but something's come up and I won't be able to make it in today."

"Oh? Is there a better time? I just found out we won't be starting right on time and the studio will be available until five."

"No, thanks for the offer, but I have to get to the airport. Please tell Aphex thank you. I'll try to come over for a listen next time I'm in town."

Roland paused before answering, "Okay, Mr. Dunn, I'll let them know. See you next time."

Duke hung up and said, "Thanks."

"Smart move," Marty said. "That's what I would have done."

Marsha asked, "So does that mean we have some time to kill?"

Duke checked his watch. "I don't have to be to the airport until two or three."

"What'd you have in mind, babe?" Marty asked.

Marsha saw the flashing sign for the Pussycat Theatre. "Well, you're going to think I'm crazy – maybe we shouldn't."

"I already know you're crazy. What is it this time?"

"Well, we're in Hollywood, so why don't we all go see a movie? I know it's the middle of the day but – "

"What do you want to see?" Marty noticed the Pussycat sign but didn't want to mention it. "We don't even know what's playing around here."

Duke saw the sign too and caught Marsha's Cheshire grin in the mirror. "I don't really care what we see," she said, "as long as it's dark in there."

"You want to get high?" Marty guessed. "Is that what this is about?" he asked. "Maybe we should just take a drive along Mulholland and show Duke our favorite spot. We could pick up some wine on the way and hang out there for a while. You can see all of LA from there, if the weather's good. What do you say, mi amigo, what would you like to do?"

Duke felt conflicted. One part of him regretted losing his independence by accepting their offer to drive him around, while another entertained fantasies of a popcorn handjob in a dark theater, but all he really wanted was to meet Remy at the airport, finish his transaction with Marty, and get out of LA with some cash and a few bricks before Oswaldo came looking for him. "Let's just take Sunset out to the airport," he suggested. "I don't get here often enough and I like to see who's on the billboards. I'll buy us some lunch if we see a place on the way. I don't know exactly when Remy's going to land, but I'd like to be there when he does."

"I think we can do that. What about you, babe? That sound okay?"

"Well, it's not as fun as what I was thinking, but it'll do. I haven't seen the strip in the daytime for a while. We can see who's playing at the Whiskey and Rainbow Room tonight in case we want to get out."

Marty started driving. "I'm back in the studio tonight, but maybe you can take Stacy out to see a show, meet and greet, be seen."

"You don't want to come with us? Make the scene on a Friday night? All work, no joy makes Marty a dull boy," she teased.

"I would, but all the crazies will be dressed up for Halloween weekend. You go have some fun and I'll worry about paying for it."

Marsha kneed the back of Duke's seat. "What time are you and Remy taking off tonight? You never did get to meet Stacy."

Marty was surprised. "You didn't? I thought that's where you were last night."

Marsha realized she had said too much and tried to cover her tracks. "We went there, but Stacy had already gone. I think she must've met someone interesting."

"Were any of our other friends there? What about the guy from FrontRow? How long did you stay? Who did you hang out with?" Marty questioned her.

Duke tried to redirect. "What's that?" He pointed to a mechanically animated billboard blowing smoke.

Marty didn't bother slowing down. "Don't have many of those in Colorado I guess," he said derisively. "Seeing as my wife won't tell me, did *you* have a good time at the party last night?"

Duke was an expert at lying. "It was okay, but we only stayed a little while because your girl Stacy had already split. We drove down the Miracle Mile and then Marsha took me back to the hotel. We had some drinks at the bar and I was asleep by eleven."

Marsha went on the offensive. "Yeah, Mr. Stay-Out-Late. I was in bed before midnight. What time did you get in – 2:00 a.m.?"

"We didn't finish mixing until two. I had to drop off one of the guys on the way home and I crawled in around three. You said hello, but I guess you forgot."

"Up late with *the guys* again?" Marsha sassed.

Marty adjusted the rearview mirror so he could see her. "We can talk about this later," he said sternly. "Duke doesn't need to hear our squabbles."

Duke was happy to be out of the conflict. "Doesn't bother me. Squabble away."

Marty dragged him back into the fray. "You ever been married, Duke?"

"Once, a long time ago," Duke admitted.

"A long time ago? You must've been pretty young."

"I was. We were."

Marsha was interested in the story. "You never told me about this. What happened?"

"I really don't like talking about it. It was all about the pregnancy."

"You have a kid? I never knew! How old is he or she?"

"The kid would have been fourteen by now."

"What happened?"

"He got sick; spinal meningitis."

"That's horrible!"

"Can we talk about something else now?"

Marty took the cue. "I forgot to tell you, we have some good news. We put some samples out yesterday. They were very well received, of course. We've got the cash we talked about in the trunk."

Duke was relieved to be talking business again. "Fantastic! I knew everyone would like this product."

"There's real demand out here. We have almost enough cash for a third brick if you haven't promised it to anyone else."

Duke remained coy. "How much cash have you got?"

"We've got thirty-five thousand now; twenty for the second one and – "

Marsha made her pitch. "And we wanted to know if we could give you fifteen for the third? Sort of a package deal for friends." She kneed Duke's seat again.

Duke kept his poker face on. "What about the other grand for the first one?"

"You didn't give that to him last night?" Marty asked.

"I forgot to," Marsha apologized in her best cutesy.

"We could give you full price for third one if you stayed until tomorrow," Marty added. "That kind of cash is not that easy to get your hands on. I'm sure you know."

"Let me think this over," Duke said. "I'll make some calls from the airport while we're waiting. I also need to talk to Remy because he's involved in all this."

They toured through residential streets of Beverly Hills, admiring the manicured landscaping and fancifully appointed houses on their way back to the Santa Monica Airport. After they crossed under the 405, Duke showed them the residential side street where he usually parked. They found a spot, lowered the windows, and stealthily passed the stash bottle around while listening to the birds and channeling through the radio. Paul McCartney told them, *"With a little luck we can make this whole damn thing work out."* Then Marty and Marsha waited in the car while Duke went to the airport office to use the pay phone. He dialed the studio in Boulder.

Diane answered. "BlueStar Studios; how may I help you?"

Duke loved sound of her voice. It was soft, inviting, and completely professional. "Good afternoon BlueStar. Talk to me."

"Oh hi, Duke," Diane friendlied up. "We were waiting for you to call. Dennis needs to talk to you about the console, and I need to talk to you about the party. Cynthia told me you gave her the go-ahead, but I just want to make sure before I start making too many plans. You know how she can sometimes get ahead of herself."

A Piper Cub with a noisy engine taxied slowly past the pay-phone like a furious bumblebee that couldn't beat its wings fast enough to fly. Duke put his finger to his other ear and tried to concentrate on the phone call. "We'll talk about the party afterwards. Can you get Dennis on the phone, please?" The Piper Cub revved its engine even harder as it attempted to turn one way, then the other. Duke could see an instructor in the right seat and hoped the

119

novice pilot wouldn't let go of the brakes and send the plane toward him. The battle for control slowly moved out of earshot while he was stuck on hold.

Dennis finally picked up and said, "Hey Duke, sorry that took so long. Walter and I were in the middle of it."

"What're you doing?"

"Wiring in the new desk."

"How's it going?"

"Good. I heard about the party so I figured we should try to get some sounds going. Not sure how far we'll get, but we should be able to listen through the mains by tomorrow night."

"Fantastic. Can I talk to Walter?"

"I think the cord will reach, but he's under the desk with his hands full right now. You want me to relay a message?"

"No, let him work. Is that kid from the high school helping you?"

"No, but the bass player in the Cells band is. He was in Walter's AV class, and now he's working for us. I hope that's okay."

"No problem. Just so long as it all gets done. What are we paying him?"

"Same as the other kid; just a minute." Dennis put the phone to his side and asked Walter what he was saying, then picked up the phone again. "Walter wants to know if you got a chance to listen to the Aphex."

Duke couldn't hear well enough to continue the conversation because of the commotion outside. "No. I'll tell him about it later. I've to go now. Talk to you later." He hung up. Someone nearby was yelling and a jeep with a flashing emergency beacon raced by. Duke looked up and saw a small high-wing airplane that was coming in for a landing. The Piper Cub with the student pilot had stopped in the middle of the runway, and the incoming plane was too low to pull up. Duke could see that the plane trying to land would have to do an extremely dangerous touch-and-go to avoid crashing into the plane on the ground, and everyone on the field stopped what they were doing, expecting to witness an accident. Both planes revved their engines and Duke held his breath. The student's plane didn't move, but already committed to land, the pilot of the incoming plane touched down at the very beginning of the runway, chirped the tires once, pushed the throttle forward all the way, and yanked the stick back on the first bounce. To everyone's surprise, the nimble high-wing flyer roared back into the air, avoiding a collision with room to spare.

Cursing, Remy circled the airport while the instructor moved the Piper Cub out of the way. Duke was waiting for him when he came in for the second time. Remy touched down and taxied, following Duke to the tie-down they had been assigned. Airport regulars took note of the odd-looking tail-dragger as Remy puttered to the spot and spun into position. Trying to like its altered appearance, Duke had already walked around once by the time the prop sputtered to a halt. The entire fuselage, which had previously been shiny red, had been spray-painted a particularly dull shade of rust, and the messy splotches of paint didn't hide the irregularly shaped welds where the body had been modified. Lines of overspray framed the windows, a swarm of dead insects decorated the nose panels, and the smell of burnt adhesives lingered around the tailpipes like a seeping fart.

Remy extricated himself from the cockpit and hopped out. He was aggravated. "Sheeeet. You see that? Some bozo wouldn't get off the field. Thank God this baby's got stick."

"I saw it. Nice flying." Duke patted the fuselage as if it were a skittish animal. "Glad you got it here in one piece."

Remy retrieved his bag and locked the cabin door. "Wait till you see what else it does," he said enthusiastically. "Came over the border at a hundred feet. Could've picked the pine cones from the top of the trees."

"That's the whole idea. How was the rest of the trip?"

"Well, I had to change the plan a little. The girl's brother didn't want to cooperate unless I agreed to give him a ride, so I dropped him off on a coyote road he knew about. Was in and out of there in less than three hundred feet without turning around."

"And no one saw you?"

"The border radar's set for six hundred now, and I kept it under five hundred feet 'til I crossed the Interstate. Didn't see anything else in the sky 'cept birds."

Duke ran his hand over the meandering seams where the metal had been cut and repaired. The sloppy finish work made him nervous, but he was happy to see that the flathead screws holding the sections together had been countersunk. "It seems like those boys really put this together. Hear any rattles while you were flying?"

"Can't hear much over the sound of the engine. They rushed the paint job, but this thing really does handle. Too bad we had to rip them off."

"I know, but Oswaldo and I go back a ways. We'll make up some bullshit and tighten them up later if they don't come after us and start a war. We can say you had to get out of there because you got a tip about the Federales. How'd you leave it? What about the girl? Did she cooperate?"

"Oh yeah, sort of. Her brother really hates the Oswaldo guy. Some kind of family feud." Remy stroked the modified tail rudder and reflected on his two weeks in Mexico. "But that girl; man, she's something special. If I stayed there any longer I may never have come back."

"Tell me you didn't fall in love and screw the whole thing up."

Remy got defensive. "Screw, yes, but I'm here, ain't I?"

"So what happened?"

"The brother gave me the extra set of keys, but like I said, I had to promise to get him out of there. I gave the girl five grand when she brought me the stuff." Remy patted his shoulder bag. "She was okay at first, but then she started crying."

"Uh-oh. What was she crying about?"

"You wanna talk about this out here?"

"I've got some people waiting for me in the car, so just fill me in here. Schedule's changed on this end too."

They finished their conversation while straightening out the kinks in the tie-down ropes. "She got scared. Wanted me to take her too," Remy admitted.

"What was she afraid of?"

"What everyone down there is scared of – snitches."

"She's the one who said she could trust her cousin."

"Yeah, I'm pretty sure her cousin's okay, but Oswaldo knows the Federales too. No one down there can keep a secret."

"Well, it's her problem now, right?"

"I guess." Remy lit a cigarette.

Duke attached nylon ropes from the ground anchors to the tie-down rings on the body of the plane, then cinched them with quick release knots and motioned for Remy to follow him. They could hear Marty and Marsha arguing through the rolled-up windows of the Jaguar as they approached.

Duke knocked on the window. "I hope I'm not interrupting?"

The car was running. Marty powered the driver's window down and said, "Get in."

CHAPTER 13

Jon left Donna's house at one o'clock to meet Marco at the rehearsal studio. Frankie was still at work, so lacking the inspiration of drums they played through their set on guitars at low volume and explored a few new ideas before their attention gravitated to the dormant console, still sitting in the middle of a small room where they had left it the night before. Jon banged his fist on the bolster like a prospective buyer kicks the tires of a car, and Marco peeked at the bewildering rabble of unterminated wires that were taped to the underbelly. They twisted some dials on the control surface, pushed a few faders up and down, and tried to figure out what all the nomenclature meant for several minutes, but neither of them felt confident enough to do anything more than wonder. Marco was eager to get back over to BlueStar where Dennis was expecting him to help solder, and Jon wanted to go back to the hotel to practice for his gig that night, so they split up and agreed to meet at The Sink before the show.

Diane was at the BlueStar desk and buzzed Marco in when she saw him come back. "They're in the control room." She motioned without getting up.

Dennis was holding a heavy piece of equipment when Marco entered the control room. "Just in time," he puffed. "Here, help me hold this."

Marco threw his coat down and put both hands under one side of a densely wired switching matrix that was attached to wires coming out of the wall.

Walter, who was lying on his back with his head inside the wall cavity, gave them instructions. "Watch the feet, please." Walter bent his knees to give his assistants more room to stand. "Just a few more minutes and I'll have the last of these connected."

Dennis and Marco defied gravity in silence while Walter finished his tasks.

"Okay, ready," Walter reported. "Let's screw it in." The men on the outside positioned the unit against the rails of a vertical equipment rack that was flush-mounted in the wall. Walter helped them hold it in place from underneath as they aligned the screw holes. Marco took the extra weight as Dennis let go with one hand to get the first screw started. Once the first screw was in place, the job of aligning the other holes became more manageable. Walter checked the inside connections one last time before inching out on his back like he was in a boot camp drill. *"The things we do for love,"* he remembered the lyrics as he straightened out his fifty-something creaks and cramps. "10cc" was his wife's favorite group, and that was her favorite song. He had originally taken the studio job to keep his wife interested because his awkward personality and highly irregular work habits made it necessary for him to do something she thought was cool. "Let's fire it up and see if it works," he said gamely.

"No can do," Dennis told him. "We're a long way off from that; I don't even have the console fully terminated yet."

Walter was disappointed. "I thought you needed this done ASAP?"

"We did, but I figured it would take you at least a week to finish. I guess you weren't kidding when you said you work fast."

Walter had stayed in his workshop soldering the whole night before. He was surprised when the first light of dawn crept over the Great Plains and reminded him that the rest of the world ran on a twenty-four-hour cycle. The studio noise-reduction switching matrix wasn't one of his most technologically challenging jobs

– it was just labor intensive. Hundreds of tiny blobs of silver solder had to be dabbed onto minuscule gold-tipped pins so that hair-thin wires could be attached. It was beyond tedious, but Walter did it right the first time because he knew he would be the one who would have to fix it if there were any mistakes. "Well, if there's nothing more to do here, I'll leave," he said abruptly.

Dennis understood Walter's quirks. "Okay, see you later. Thanks."

"Bye, Professor Hardaway," Marco said as Walter headed for the door.

Walter stopped and squinted at Marco through thick glasses. Tall and thin with frizzy hair, he looked every bit the nutty professor Marco remembered. "Oh, I'm sorry, I don't remember you," Walter admitted. "I've had so many students over the years."

"That's okay, Professor. I'm Marco. You used to call me Marco Marconi."

"Of course!" Walter recognized the name and extended his hand. "Nice to see you again. You're working here now?"

Marco checked with Dennis before answering. "Yes, just started. That's an awesome-looking thing you made. What does it do?"

Walter looked at his watch. "I have to go now, but Dennis will explain. Good luck, Marconi."

Dennis and Marco stayed in the studio, soldering and testing connections with a dual-trace scope until Cynthia came to check on them. "You guys want dinner?" she asked.

Dennis was surprised to see her. "Diane went home? What time is it?"

"Six thirty. Hi, Marco. I guess you're working here now?"

Marco grinned. "I guess I am. Maybe we'll have some tea later?" he insinuated.

Cynthia thought he looked cute in jeans and a denim shirt. "Tea and crumpets," she said in a fake English accent.

"Maybe we could get a pizza first?" Dennis interjected. "Sausage and onion on my side."

"Mushroom and crumpets for me," Marco wisecracked.

"How late are you planning on being here?" Cynthia asked Dennis.

"Why? You have somewhere to go?"

"There's a talent contest at The Sink tonight, and some of my friends are playing. I was hoping I could leave by nine."

"Funny thing," Marco said. "I was planning on going to that show too; Jon Cells is doing an acoustic number for the contest. Who are you going to see?"

"One of the girls who works in the restaurant around the corner. Rosella. She's a Buddhist."

"Buddhist folksinger. That sounds exciting," Dennis said sarcastically. "You two go have a good time and leave me here to work."

Marco backtracked. "I can stay if you really want me to."

"Nah, just kidding," Dennis told him. "I've been at it all day. Maybe I'll join you. I could use a beer and a good laugh."

Cynthia said, "I'll go order the pizza," and left.

CHAPTER 14

The Buddhist restaurant where Donna worked was bordering on chaotic when she got there. Nancy was on the phone giving directions to a lost driver, and Joel was unloading the extra supplies that had already been delivered. A permanent aura of sautéed onions and burnt lentils filled the overheated cooking area. Tara, blowing the messy curls that couldn't be contained by her chef's hat away from her eyes, was pounding dough on a long wooden table next to stacks of empty baking pans. Restricted by his full-length white uniform, Jampo, a gentle giant who used to be called Jesse, was using a long-handled utensil to joust with an oven full of lunch orders. In one alcove of the irregularly shaped kitchen, Tenzin, a Tibetan immigrant who had taken a vow of silence, slowly worked his way through the never-ending pile of dirty dishes next to his sink, mumbling his mantra with every successful cleansing. Near the back on its own sturdy platform, a sixty-quart electric mixer added to the halo of flour dust suspended in the atmosphere with each rotation, and it was impossible to differentiate the rhythmic whirring sounds it made from the Buddhist meditation tape playing in the background.

Donna mouthed, "Namasté," and put her palms together when she entered.

"Thanks for coming in early," Joel greeted her, toting a burlap sack full of carrots. "Can you take over for Tara now? We've got hungry customers practicing patience and only one other server."

"Where should the driver from Longmont exit the Diagonal?" Nancy called out.

"Tell him to make a left on Twenty-Eighth," Joel yelled as he headed back to the van in the alley.

Tara's hat billowed white dust as she removed it. "Namasté," she greeted Donna. "Here's your stupid hat. I don't know how you do this all the time; my arms are killing me."

Donna donned an apron, tied her hair back in a ponytail, put her hat on, and washed her hands. "Got to get your exercise somehow. How many pans are rising?"

Tara dusted herself off. "None. They just got the mixer working again and I was serving tables before that." Thirty pounds overweight, Tara had difficulty tying the Satsang Diner apron behind herself. She positioned her ample bosoms over the top. "Some of those people out there must not have been vegetarians for long because they're still behaving like the animals they used to eat," she said, straightening the curls around her pleasantly plump face and smudging the lip gloss off her teeth with the aid of a small hand mirror. "There, how do I look?"

"Tara!" Nancy interrupted sharply. "Tuck your breasts in please."

Tara obliged but defended herself. "Those yogis I served breakfast to this morning didn't seem to mind. They left me a ten-dollar tip."

Nancy was originally from Manhattan. "Oh please, those goofballs probably just joined the monastery last month and are still living off their parents. For all you know they used all their singles last night on the girls at the Bustop."

Tara shrunk but Jampo came to her rescue. Squeezing her full waist with one arm, he scolded Nancy, "Now you be nice. We all have our own karma to work through."

"Thanks for reminding me, Guru Jampo," Nancy said sarcastically. "I can smell *your* karma burning in the oven."

The other waitress, Crystal, came into the kitchen close to tears. "The man at the table in the corner wants to talk with the manager," she sobbed. "He says I breathed on his food and now he won't eat it."

Nancy ignored the ringing phone and said, "It's okay Crystal, stay in here for a minute. I'll take care of this."

Crystal, every bit as frail as Tara was hale, accepted the sympathy with a sniffle.

"Broccoli dal spicy and baked tempeh for table two," Jampo announced as he removed the hot dishes from the stove and deposited them on the serving counter.

"You take them out, please," Crystal begged Tara. "I have to go outside and meditate before I can go back in there."

"When can I have an oven?" Donna asked Jampo.

Jampo opened the oven door and peeked in. "I can give you the bottom shelf in a few minutes. The lunch specials will stay warm on top. You're doing the rest of the chapattis first I hope?"

"I can have them ready to go in five minutes," Donna said. She placed an empty tray on the table in front of her. "I'll have a batch of khapse for the party order ready after the lunchtime rush."

Joel came in to deliver another crate of produce and asked, "What happened to Crystal?" as he set it down. "She's sitting in the alley with her head in her hands."

Donna answered while kneading, "She said she was going to meditate."

Joel, who grew up in Los Angeles and was married to Nancy, didn't see Crystal when he went back out, but the distinctive smell of burning marijuana led him to find her around the corner smoking a joint. "Crystal! Not at work," he scolded. We've talked about this before." He and Nancy owned the Satsang Diner and used the profits to support the Naropa Institute. "It's not good for your practice either," he voiced paternal concern.

Crystal was embarrassed to be caught but too giddy to stifle a smile. "Oh come on Joel, you want some?" she offered. "I know you and Nancy still smoke."

"We do not!"

Crystal smiled more broadly. "Not what I heard."

The pungent pot smell, combined with Crystal's mischief, was a contagion that reached the undisciplined part of Joel's brain. His pre-Buddhist years as a fun-loving stud were involuntarily stimulated. "What gives you *that* idea?" His nostrils flared as he wavered.

"Come on, Daddy. I won't tell Mom," Crystal teased.

First looking to make sure he wasn't seen, Joel grabbed the joint and treated himself to a satisfying drag. "Just one hit, and then we really have to get back to work," he managed to say without exhaling. "And don't say anything about this!"

Crystal took the roach back and suffocated it her wooden stash box. "I won't tell if you won't." She rose up on her toes and planted a kiss on Joel's cheek.

Joel had to control his infatuation. "Don't look so happy all of the sudden," he warned. "You were just crying, remember? Everyone will be suspicious."

"I love you," Crystal said airily as they went back inside.

Jampo saw Crystal come back and knew she was stoned. "Glad to see *you're* feeling better," he noted.

Donna smelled the evidence as Crystal passed her. "Save some for me?" she asked.

"Namasté," Crystal answered before going into the dining room.

She ran into Nancy on her way in. Nancy told her, "Tara is taking care of your problem table now. Please go see that table of four. They're ready to order."

Then Nancy went out the front door to check the appearance of the restaurant from the street. One of several storefronts in the eighteen hundred block of Pearl Street, the restaurant identified itself with an ornate sign that was visible for several blocks. In keeping with Tibetan tradition, the gouged wood letters that spelled "Satsang Diner" were painted red and edged in gold. Nancy used the back of her sleeve to wipe some the hand marks off the custom glass door with the same logo and stood back to admire her enterprise. Satisfied that her father would be proud of her, she looked at the posters that she had allowed local clubs and organizations to tape inside the front glass windows. They advertised Buddhist meditation retreats, live music shows, a Native American Pow Wow, new herbal remedies, the Red Zinger cycling event, a sorority fundraiser, and Buddhist candidates for the local election. Everything was representative of Boulder community life except one poster that obviously didn't match the spirit of her enterprise. She immediately went inside to remove it and, and held the offending flyer in her forefingers as if it were contaminated as she went to the kitchen. "I found this in the window," she announced dramatically. "Anyone know how it got there?" The kitchen staff looked quizzically at the provocative picture. Against an all-black background, the Halloween movie poster showed a fisted hand holding a bloody knife. The image's ghosted repetitions implied that it was in the process of stabbing something.

"That's gross!" Donna gasped.

"Ew!" Crystal complained. "That's scary."

Jampo muttered, "Not nice."

Joel came in and saw Nancy folding it so it would fit in the garbage. "Wait! What are you doing with that?"

"Someone put this horrible thought in our window."

Joel took the poster from her. "That someone was me," he said, straightening out the creases.

"It's awful and disgusting," Nancy said indignantly. "Why would you do that? Have you forgotten your vows or something?"

Joel defended himself. "That's an advertisement for a movie. They're having the opening party for it at the Boulderado tomorrow night and they ordered ten trays of baked goods, so we already have karma with them." He didn't mention how cute the promo girl who asked him to put it there was. "I promised we'd leave it up for another two days, and we can throw it out after that," he rationalized as he went to re-tape it.

Nancy sensed there was more to the story, and since her family had supplied the money for the restaurant she felt like she had the final say about what was and wasn't allowed. "Jampo?" she said after Joel was gone. "You'll do the right thing?"

"Of course," Jampo agreed to her unspoken request. "Right after Guru Joel leaves tonight."

"Thank you, namasté. Speaking of tonight, Donna, I hope you can work all the way through?" Wiry and wired, Nancy's slim stature and intense style made her questions sound like orders.

"Tara told me there was lots of baking to do, so I thought I'd use the oven in between lunch and dinner. Is that what you mean?" Donna clarified.

"No, not exactly." Nancy consulted the work schedule. "We're going to be a little understaffed tonight so I was hoping you could also help in the kitchen."

Donna stopped kneading and stared through the mask of pastry dust that had adhered to her face. "But I have plans tonight, and if I work all day and then through dinner … ."

Nancy was unmoved. "You're still young. I could go for three days without sleep when I was young and living in New York."

"On what drugs?" Donna challenged her.

Nancy bristled at the mention of her rough-edged past. "It doesn't matter what drugs – coffee, diet pills, a little pot – what matters is that now I'm completely free from artificial stimuli," Nancy preached. "Joel and I take our vows seriously, and the food we serve here provides all the nutrition we need. Do your practice and you'll have all the energy you need to cover for Rosella."

Donna had heard the bullshit before and knew it was pointless to argue. "Why can't Rosella come in this time? Car broke down again? Boyfriend's dog has a cold?"

"Be nice, Doh-na. Angry words are bad for your practice. Rosella's group is performing tonight so I gave her the night off." Nancy saw her youth in Rosella's wild streak. "I put it on the schedule last week."

Donna wasn't ready to give up. She didn't get along with Rosella, and the idea that she might miss Jon's performance because Rosella had one annoyed her further. "Well, I can only work until eight," she acquiesced. "I'll prepare the specials before I go, and Jampo can take them out of the oven when they're done."

"Thanks, Doh-na," Nancy consented. "Eight-oh-one and you're out of here." The kitchen regained its composure after Nancy retreated to her office. Tara and Crystal deposited dirty plates by Tenzin's sink and picked up the ready-to-be-served meals as they rotated in and out of the dining area. Jampo hummed along to the meditation tape while tending the oven and stove. Donna broke off sections of dough, stuffed them with filling, rolled them into shapes, and arranged them on a greased pan.

Joel, still pleasantly buzzed, came into the office while Nancy was on the phone. She was facing the window, talking to a supplier, when Joel put his arms around her waist and nuzzled her from behind. "Stop it!" she mouthed silently, then brushed his hands away. Joel's libido hadn't settled down from Crystal's peck on the cheek, and he reached for Nancy's breasts. She slapped them away before he touched her and hissed, "Not now!" with a hand over the receiver.

The other phone rang, and Joel answered it. "She's on the other line," he told the caller.

Excited about her upcoming performance, Rosella jabbered while Joel listened patiently.

"I'll tell her," he promised before hanging up.

"Who was that?" Nancy asked when she had finished with the other call.

"Rosella. She wants us to come to her show tonight."

Nancy was already one of Rosella's biggest supporters. "Of course. What time is it?"

"Around ten o'clock."

"Ten o'clock! I'll be tired by then."

Even though they were both barely forty, Joel had heard that excuse a lot. "She said she needs lots of people in the audience to clap so she can win."

"I don't think I'll have the energy."

"You need to loosen up a bit," Joel complained, coming closer. "A couple of beers at The Sink might be a good idea. I don't know about you, but I'm not ready for celibacy."

Nancy answered him with her nose buried in paperwork. "We'll see."

CHAPTER 15

After she'd hung up, Rosella sat cross-legged on a chair in her parents' basement as she worked her way down the list of people to invite to the show. Still rebellious at twenty-four, she cared more about having a good time than cultivating an honorable place in society. She told her parents that she was taking courses at the Buddhist University, and that working at the Satsang Diner was part of her student curriculum, but what she really wanted was to live like the rest of Boulder's nouveau hippe.

Rosella's musical group, the Cowboy Liberation Army, had started out as joke in the alley behind a meat-processing plant in Denver where she worked with her mother. She had developed a crush on Roddy, a strapping young man from an immigrant family who worked in the slaughterhouse with the animals, and the original idea of playing music with him was just an excuse for them to spend time in bed. His hardworking mother didn't approve of Rosella, but Rosella's access to middle-class American society, along with her enthusiastic breasts, made it impossible for him to resist. Hipolito, a wiry young skinner who worked alongside Roddy, was the third member of their performing trio. His energetic guitar playing was what spurred the Liberation Army Cowboys into a gallop, and Rosella accompanied the acoustic guitars with suggestive antics, lyrics, and maracas. They drank beer, smoked pot, and didn't try to do anything more than have a good time until Roddy got an idea for writing a meaningful song. The idea – the one that inspired their name – came to Roddy when someone left the holding pen gate unlatched. He and a few of the other workers were pulled off the line to help round up a small herd of cows that had wandered up to Shoeshone Street and were found grazing in the weeds under Interstate 70. The workers felt sorry for the ruminating beasts, who weren't keen to abandon the fresh sprouts of concrete-defying native buffalo grass they had discovered, and no one was particularly motivated to steer the cows back toward their grim destiny. The cattle bayed and snorted in protest as the workers pulled on their tails and hit their backsides with small sticks, and one particularly stubborn heifer actually became so aggressive that Roddy was forced to let her trot off in the wrong direction rather than risk confrontation with an animal ten times his weight. That's how the whole liberation thing started. Hipolito, who was attempting to wrangle another cow nearby, saw what happened to his friend and thought it was so funny that he smacked the beast nearest to him with his hand and urged it to follow the other runaway. Another cow followed voluntarily, and the three escapees found refuge behind the giant columns that held up the overpass. That day, after the five o'clock bell that announced the shift change had sounded, Roddy and the rest of the line crew huddled in the alley around the corner to smoke and gossip.

"I wonder if we got them all?" one of the workers said slyly, sucking the life from an unfiltered cigarette.

"I hope at least one of them got away," another commented as he filled the tiny pipe he had pulled from his pocket.

Hipolito peered into the sharp shadows between the warehouse buildings. "I wouldn't be surprised."

"Why not?" Roddy asked innocently.

"They're so fast." Hipolito smirked when he said it.

"And tricky," someone else joked.

Hipolito took his turn on the pipe being passed around and held his breath. His eyes bulged as the potent smoke tickled his throat, but he held his mouth shut and refused to laugh. Then, after hissing a long plume through thin lips, he finally cracked a smile. Even though he was a long way from his family farm in Azueta, the spirited racehorses he had grown up riding still galloped through his imagination. "I made sure some of them got away," he admitted proudly.

"What did you do?"

"You will get us all fired!"

Hipolito's gold-toothed grin advertised his guilt. "It's not my fault. You were all there too. I couldn't help it if one or two of them wandered to the other side of the road where we couldn't find them."

"Aye corumba! We thought you had rounded them up."

"How many got away?"

"One, two, three; I don't know. It was so hot and the sun was shining in my eyes and – "

Roddy burst out laughing. "Diablo!" Originally from Mexico City, Roddy had city sense, but Hipolito's rustic upbringing exposed him to a logic they don't teach in schools. "I hope they don't find out for a few days," he reasoned. "We can blame it on the night shift."

CHAPTER 16

There were only two restaurants in Steamboat Springs where anyone took company, so Agent Walker wasn't surprised when they
ran into Farah and an out-of-town visitor having lunch. She was
friendly and made the polite introductions, but her guest, a chis-
eled blond man dressed in an expensive knit sweater and nylon
ski pants, made it clear he was not on a date by acknowledging
the agents' salutations with stiff posture and an arrogant smirk.
Preoccupied with their own business, the agents buried their noses
in the menus and unsuccessfully tried to ignore the conversation
at Farah's table.

Speaking louder than polite volume in a thick Norwegian accent, the man's voice rose over the hubbub of a busy tavern full of
beer drinkers waiting for the weather to change so they could get
on the slopes. "Where do you get such *delicious beef*?" the visitor
asked, wiping the juice from a rare burger off the corner of his
mouth.

"Everything they serve here is local," Farah told him proudly.

"Well it's certainly fresh." He took another bite and looked
around the restaurant to make sure people were noticing him.
"Must have been killed recently. You think this might have been
hung upside down for a few days to ripen?" he insinuated. "Tastes
awfully good."

The agents at the next table cringed, and the murmur in the
bar decreased noticeably.

Farah deflected. "I don't know who supplies the meat here, but I can ask the owner if you like."

"That won't be necessary," her guest informed. "I'm not complaining. It's delicious, really." He jammed the final piece in his mouth and washed it down with a swig from his mug.

Farah finished her plate and acknowledged her agent friends' concern with a shrug.

"So," Farah's guest continued, "where can twenty or thirty people stay around here? It doesn't look like there are too many hotel rooms available. Is this the only restaurant near the basin?"

"Steamboat's growing fast. Holiday Inn will have sixty new rooms by next season, and there're all kinds of construction going on at Trappeur's Crossing. I'm sure you'll be able to find accommodations for everyone if you book far enough in advance." Farah worked for the company that managed the lifts and maintained the trails, and it was her job to present the area in the best possible light. "There're two or three good restaurants in town, but most of the bars serve food so no one goes hungry around here."

Her prospect leaned back in his chair listening, looking, nodding. "Well, I must say, one thing they were right about; Colorado does resemble the Alps. Fresh air, good slopes, and great beer. What kind is this?" He help up his glass and studied the pale orange color.

"Coors special Halloween Blend. I don't know what they use for color, but it's the water that makes it taste so good."

Her guest belched in agreement. "There's no doubt about the brew and burgers, it's just, how do I say it?"

"You're worried about the rumors?" Farah guessed.

"Of course not! I don't believe in such nonsense. It's just that my company gets questions from people. No one wants to go on a ski vacation and get abducted by aliens and wind up dead in a tree."

The agents at the other table stopped chewing as Farah's grit rose to the occasion. "Well, you can tell your customers that the aliens around here seem to prefer cattle, so they have nothing to worry about unless they walk on four legs and moo a lot."

Her guest was shocked. "You mean it?" He didn't know whether to think she believed in aliens or was just the rudest woman he had ever met – or both.

Agent Falin burst out laughing and Officer McKnight couldn't help grinning from contagion.

"Are they laughing at me?" Farah's guest asked her.

Farah turned around and made an angry face that none of the agents took seriously.

"No one is laughing at you, sir," Agent Walker said, trying to heal Farah's guest's ego. "You'll pardon us for listening in on your conversation, but we've known Farah for a long time. She means well, and everyone loves her, but let's just say we don't all agree with everything she says."

"I see," the visitor said, wondering which parts of her stories were true and which parts were salesmanship. Embarrassed, Farah got up to go to the washroom. Her direct manners, long dark hair, and strictly functional clothes were very unlike the Nordic beauties and European sophisticates he was accustomed to. He smiled blandly at the agents, and when she returned, he said, "Well, this has been most interesting. I must thank you for the excellent food and drink, but I think I've seen enough of your lovely hamlet."

"But you haven't been to the hot springs or taken an aerial tour," Farah protested. "It's stopped snowing now so we could get up in the air this afternoon. You haven't seen Colorado until you've flown over it in a small plane."

"Excellent idea. We can fly over the slopes, and perhaps the pilot can let me off in Aspen. I have other places to see before we decide where to set up an office. How long is the plane ride from here to Aspen?"

"The flight takes less than an hour, but finding the pilot may take longer."

"Really? I thought you had this all worked out."

"We did. But we planned on doing the aerial tour either at the end of the day or tomorrow. Everything around here depends on the weather."

"I see." The visitor checked his ostentatious chronograph and assessed his surroundings. The midday drinking had begun in earnest, and a crust of regulars adhered to the doglegged end of the bar. The departing lunch crowd fantasized about slicing through the fresh powder as they exited in boots and parkas. Farah's visitor sat silently as the lunchers left, cursing the broken ankle that had ended his competitive career. A minimum-wage busboy who spoke no English cleared plates from the table with a polite smile that wasn't returned.

Farah made eye contact with Agent Walker and mouthed, "Help me."

Agent Walker checked with Officer McKnight before accepting the challenge. "Perhaps we can help," Agent Walker volunteered aloud. "We're flying over to Aspen this afternoon. Would you like to ride with us, sir?"

Farah's guest jumped at the chance. "Well, if it's not too much trouble?"

Agent Walker replied, "No trouble at all. We've got four seats so Farah can come along for the ride if she wants to."

Farah joined in. "We can fly over of the slopes on the way out?"

Agent Walker knew the terrain. "Howelsen ski area is right near the airport."

Farah asked, "When do you plan on leaving?"

Agent Walker excused himself and consulted with Officer McKnight before replying. "We're all finished here, and the field is probably plowed by now. Why don't you meet us out there in thirty minutes?"

Farah grinned relief. "Thank you so much, William. We're even."

"This all seems to be working out well," her guest said with typical Nordic understatement. "I really did want to see what my countrymen found so wonderful here, and I'm sure Mr. Temple will want to know that Ms. Farah showed the resort in its best possible light."

Farah led her guest out and explained, "The field is right at the edge of town, so I'll have some time to drive you around a bit before we meet them."

After they left, Agent Falin, who hadn't said much during lunch, needed a briefing. "What was that all about?"

Officer McKnight answered him. "Steamboat's a small town and we all look out for one another. Farah's been here for years, and Jim Temple is investing a small fortune to make this an international destination. Helping them out is like helping ourselves."

"How are we going to fit them and all the luggage in the plane?" Agent Falin asked. "Don't we need to fly light up here?"

Agent Walker had the answer. "We're not taking our luggage. Officer McKnight is staying here for the first leg. He'll meet us when we get back and drop Farah off."

"Aspen's that close? We'll have enough time for a round trip and still be able to scout our locations?"

"Aspen's less than a hundred miles from here, and we can do some scouting on the way back. Officer McKnight's got work to do here and probably won't miss another bumpy ride. We'll stay in touch and see how the weather holds up."

The agents paid the bill and piled into Officer McKnight's Travelall for the trip to the airfield. The airport plow was just finishing clearing the runway, and through a series of hand signals scooped the snowbank away from in front of their Skyhawk. Agent Falin didn't know whether to laugh or curse as he brushed the snow off the windows of the plane with his bare hands. "Well, we certainly never had to do this in LA." He cupped his freezing palms and blew on them.

Agent Walker unlocked the airplane door and made arrangements with Officer McKnight before climbing in. Once both men were seated and the engine started, Officer McKnight waved good-bye and left. They taxied onto an approach ramp and left the motor running, and by the time Farah drove up and parked, the heater coil was warm enough to start clearing the windshield fog. Farah and her guest braved the icy blast of driving powder that the prop sent down the fuselage, struggled against the wind to open the cabin door, and clambered into the tight quarters. Once everyone was belted-in, Agent Falin revved the Cessna's engine and released the brakes, allowing it to rumble down the snow-packed runway and lift into the crosscurrents of an overcast gray afternoon. Beneath them, strands of plowed road stood out against the otherwise uneven white terrain. Rolling hills and drooping pines laden with fresh snow defined the wilderness that extended to the edge of town. Geometric rooflines spread out from the center of the city in a jagged fireworks pattern that extended the boundaries of civilization. Working on hand-signaled instructions, they banked left for a flyover of the resort and a closer look at the slopes of the ski basin.

It was too noisy for normal conversation, but still trying to connect her visitor to Steamboat, Farah said, "Howelsen," as they passed over the narrow black diamond trail. Her visitor nodded, proud of his countrymen but bitter with the knowledge his own personal-best slalom time had already expired. The Steamboat flyover took less than ten minutes, and the rest of the short trip to Aspen was a bumpy ride through the undulating valleys of the western slope. It wasn't until they had dropped their passenger off at Sardy Field that Farah felt free enough to be herself.

"Whew! Thanks," Farah blurted. "That guy was such a stiff. You saved me!" She unzipped her down parka, bunched it into a pillow, and laid her head down on the empty seat beside her. "I'm exhausted. Mind if I lay down awhile?"

"Go right ahead," Agent Walker said from the right seat as they taxied onto the end runway and came to a stop.

A voice from the control tower cackled through the speaker. "Xray Zebra clear to leave."

Agent Falin answered. "Roger, Xray Zebra 243 taking off now."

Agent Falin pushed the throttle forward, and they lost touch with the ground well before the end of the jet-length runway. Farah, relieved to be airborne and on the way home, said, "Wake me up if you see any aliens," and closed her eyes.

They flew in silence, following the vectored exit of the airfield until leveling off at nine thousand feet. Agent Walker unfolded an elevation map and consulted the instruments, trying to establish exactly where they were in relation to the twisting melted lines. He traced his fingers along the ink markings that Officer McKnight had made and looked out the window for confirmation. "Take up a heading of two-seven-zero," he instructed. Agent Falin gently cocked the wheel to the left, and the plane aligned with the center of a long, wide valley with a river on one side. Agent Walker took out his high-powered binoculars and scanned the slopes.

"What do you see out there?" Agent Falin asked, navigating through a restless sky.

"Not much," Agent Walker replied. "Can we get a little lower?"

Agent Falin checked his altimeter and the terrain ahead. "We can drop down a thousand feet for a few minutes, but I'll have to pull up before the next pass."

"Okay, let's go in for a closer look. I've got a few dots on my map of this valley. We can circle back if we see something interesting."

Farah had been listening to them talk. "What are you guys looking for?" she asked without getting up.

"Go back to sleep. I promise to wake you up if we see any UFOs," Agent Walker said dismissively. "Let's see if we can get a good look at where the stream exits that canyon," he told the pilot, pointing.

The uneven expanse of rock stubble that covered the tree-less valley floor was bisected by a narrow, snow-covered road that ended at the edge of a canyon and disappeared under trees. Agent Walker studied the terminus with his binoculars but couldn't detect any human activity.

"What is this place?" Agent Falin asked him.

"Remember that picture we showed you?"

"You mean the one with the cow hanging upside down?"

"Yeah. This is where it was supposedly taken. Not too hard to imagine someone hauling the thing here in the bed of a pickup truck and hoisting it up with a winch. Now all we have to do is figure out who lives around here. Just pull up and let's keep going."

"Looks like we're going to be up against some weather ahead," Agent Falin warned. "I wouldn't want to guess how high that peak is."

Agent Walker put down his binoculars and saw the dark gray clouds rolling down the slopes of the mountains ahead. He consulted the map. "Okay, let's take up a heading of one-eight-five and head over to Craig. It's fairly level all the way, and there's a small airport where we can land if we have to."

Agent Falin banked left. "How far is it? We must be close."

"Keep it at eight thousand feet and start looking for the field. It should be on our right in a few minutes. I'll make some calls when we land and get a better idea of flying conditions. Craig's only about an hour from Steamboat, so McKnight can pick us up if we can't fly back there." Agent Walker went back to his binoculars.

Farah couldn't lie still. "We're not going back?" She sat up again. "I'm supposed to meet with Mr. Temple this afternoon."

"We're trying to get there," Agent Walker assured her, "but we've got other things to do than run a taxi service for the idle rich."

Staring into the clouds, Farah saw tiny flecks of light twinkling against the shades of gray outside her window. She rubbed her eyes, trying to make the vision disappear, but it didn't. The

Cessna hit an air pocket that forced the seatbelt around her waist to irritate her motion sickness. She tried to calm the cluster of ground beef inside her stomach and stifled the thought of vomiting on the Flying Norseman she had taken to lunch.

"Wait! What's that?" Agent Walker suddenly said, pointing without putting his binoculars down. "Get me closer. Hurry."

Agent Falin pushed the steering arm in, ruddered right, and went into a steep descent.

Agent Walker was excited. "See it? Something's moving over there."

Agent Falin saw a figure trudging through fresh snow at the edge of the tree line. It was dragging something bulky, and dark streaks in the trail behind it were visible even without binoculars.

"Well, I'll be!" Agent Walker, who had the most detailed view, exclaimed. "Looks like we've got our perpetrator." Agent Falin was too busy flying to get a better look, but Farah thought she saw a cow being dragged into the woods. "Pull up and let's find that little strip in Craig." Agent Walker ordered. "This location can't be far."

"What was that?" the pilot asked.

"Looked like part of a cow to me," Farah volunteered as the Cessna veered back on course.

Agent Walker put down his binoculars and made a mark on the map. Then he turned around and yelled to Farah over the drone of the engine, "See, what did I tell you. That alien of yours was just a big old grizzly bear making himself a steak dinner."

The sudden changes in elevation had caused Farah's meal to crawl halfway up her esophagus, so she kept her mouth shut to keep it from coming out.

"I think I see a field up ahead," Agent Falin said pointing at two o'clock. "Just one runway, right? Do they have a control tower or anything?"

Agent Walker saw it too. "No, this is only used by locals. Strictly VFR. Go around once to make sure there's nothing in the way, then put us down. I'd like to get a hold of some snowmobiles before it gets too dark. I've got a camera with me."

"But what about our mission?" Agent Falin asked as they turned on final. "This is nowhere near the crash site."

Agent Walker caught the pilot's attention and put his finger across his lips. "I'll tell you later," he mouthed and pointed to the map.

Their plane touched down on the narrow strip of runway and rolled to a stop in front of manmade snowbank. A ribbon of plowed road connected the runway to an area where they pivoted and killed the engine. The man in the four-wheel-drive pickup truck that was busy clearing the airport wiped an accommodating swath between his visitors and the small office building, then waved hello before continuing his plow. Farah and the agents went into the simple structure that housed the airport operations, but no one was there except a big friendly dog so they snooped around looking for the bathroom and its owner. Ten minutes later, the driver of the plow truck, who was also the airport manager, came in.

"Welcome to Craig," he said with a hearty handshake. His Bernese companion rose up on two legs to greet him. "I'm Tom Carter. I guess you already met Buster. What brings you out this way?" His smile emanated from a scruffy beard and country manners.

"Well, it seemed like a good day for ice fishing." Agent Walker said, grinning back while they shook hands. "I'm Agent William Walker, friend of Greg McKnight."

Tom was comforted by familiarity. "Well, how is old Officer McKnight? Haven't seen him for a while, but I heard he visited my brother a few days ago." Tom sized up Agent Walker's companions and stopped to consider the possibilities. "You're not here for the same reason?"

"Guess it's true what they say," Agent Walker admitted. "Nothing happens in the high country that somebody doesn't know about. This is Agent Todd Falin and a mutual friend of ours, Farah."

"Well, go figure, nothing happens in little old Craig for months, and now we're the center of attention. So what is it now: The cattle mutilations? The plane crash? Or them crazy Indians?"

Agent Walker hadn't heard anything about Indians but kept it to himself. "You know we can't talk about state business Tom. How is your brother doing? Maybe we should pay him a visit."

"His new house isn't far from here, and I don't expect any more traffic today. I could give you and your friends a ride out there if you want. Us Carters are always happy to cooperate with the law."

"That's a real generous offer, Tom, but we weren't planning on seeing your brother this trip. Is that his field just east of here, the way we came in?"

Tom planted his feet and crossed his burly arms. "That's Carter country alright."

Agent Walker saw that some disclosure would be necessary. "Well, I certainly respect that. It's just that we saw something out there that we wanted to see up close. It may be important. You have any snowmobiles we could borrow for a few hours? The government will reimburse you for the rental."

"Of course we've got sleds. With all this snow, we'd be awful stuck without them." Tom took a head count. "Only I don't think I've got four running right now."

"Well, how many do you have?"

"Two I'm sure of. I've got an extra suit that will fit you, but I'd feel better about it if I went along. It may look flat, but one good gully could eat my machine and you with it."

Agent Walker couldn't argue the point. "I've been riding since I was kid, so I know you're right. Are you volunteering to take me out there? It's probably a few miles from here."

"Wherever it is, I'm your best bet. No one knows that pasture better than the cattle and me. I do the fence mending, run the roundup, birth, brand, and butcher." Tom cracked his knuckles. "My brother Josh depends on me, and well, I reckon he'd want me to go with you."

"I reckon he would," Agent Walker agreed.

"No need to explain," Agent Falin said. "Farah and I will stay here and keep Buster company." He noticed the receiver/transmitter crackling on a side table. "What frequency do you use around here?" he asked, inspecting the vintage device. "I'll say hi to anybody who drops in. Just try to make it back before it gets too dark to take off again. I didn't see any runway lights when we landed."

"You can overnight at my brother's guest house if it gets too late," Tom offered. "Let's get those buggies gassed up and get a move on. I figure we've got just enough time to make it back before sunset."

Agent Walker followed Tom out to the garage, where they zipped themselves into one-piece nylon jumpsuits, laced up the shin-high rubberized boots, and topped off the snowmobile tanks. Outside, stray flakes were swirling in the constant wind of the high meadows. Both men put on gloves, goggles, and helmets before motoring down the snow-covered road that led to the pasture's gate. Tom went first and followed the fence line for several minutes. They stopped to get their bearings at one of the small corrals situated in the rolling fields along the Yampa River.

"How much further you reckon?" Tom asked Agent Walker. "And what exactly are we looking for?"

Agent Walker stood on the rails of the corral and looked out over the pasture. "I'm not sure where, but what we're looking for is blood."

"Blood?" Tom was alarmed. "Good thing I brought my gun." He patted his saddlebag. "Whose blood – or what's?"

Agent Walker checked to make sure his own gun was in the holster under his arm. "I think it was one of your brother's cows. I wanted to come out to be sure. We saw a good long streak of red in the snow when we flew over."

Tom had never lived anywhere else. "That's not so unusual around here. We lose a few head every winter to hungry bears and mountain lions. Sometimes one of the herd breaks a leg and freezes to death, and some just die young. We used to lose more when the wolves were around. Ranching in the Yampa Valley is no picnic."

"I'm sure it's not, but I'm pretty sure I saw a big bear dragging one of your cows into the woods. I wanted to see it firsthand and take some pictures. Part of what we're doing here is trying to get some facts to combat the rumors. Someone's got to put a stop to all this silliness about aliens."

Tom reverted to his adventurous demeanor. "Well why didn't you say so? I bet I know exactly where that happened."

"You do?"

"'Course. There's only one canyon on this side where we ever see bears. You said you saw something moving today? Most of the bears should be asleep by now. Maybe one of them needed a bedtime snack. The sound of the engines will probably scare them off, but maybe we'll be able to find some fresh tracks." He pulled a short-barrel shotgun from his bag and laid it across his lap. "Let's go see." Tom restarted his snowmobile and led the way up to the top of a small rise. "That what you're looking for?" He pointed to a red streak of snow that connected the field to the edge of the woods."

Agent Walker took off his goggles, got out his camera, and took a few shots. "Let's go down on foot. I want to get a good look at the tracks."

Tom followed him, clutching his gun, keeping an eye out for danger as Agent Walker started taking pictures of the blood-streaked trail. "Must have been a pretty big bear to have dragged something so far," he said, snapping away.

Tom looked at the scene and was confused. "I don't see any bear tracks."

Agent Walker started walking the compacted path. "Maybe the tracks got covered by the carcass. Where did it make the kill?" he wondered aloud.

They followed the red color down a small depression and stopped abruptly in front of a still-smoldering fire pit. The severed head and front haunches of a full-grown cow lay bleeding in the red-caked snow. Human footprints had flattened the area around the fire, and a rope of gutted entrails was tangled on the perimeter. Offal splotches of brown and yellow snow soiled the butchering site, and the sickening smell of death hung in the moist cold air.

"Well, I'll be; rustlers!" Tom said, aiming his gun and looking around suspiciously. "Haven't had anything like that happen since I can't remember when. They can't have gone too far." He crouched defensively and began following the trail as fast as the snow would allow. Agent Walker lagged behind long enough to take some pictures of the grisly scene, then followed. The path became harder to follow as they traipsed over fallen trees, around rock outcroppings, and alongside a narrow ravine. It stopped at the base of an enormous blue spruce, but there were no signs of the carcass and no footprints leading away from the tree. Agent Walker peered up into the thick branches while Tom pointed his gun at shadows in the darkening forest.

"See anything up there?" Tom asked, panting from the excitement of the chase.

Agent Walker put his hands on the lowest branch of the tree and tried to imagine someone climbing up. "Not from down here." He bent his knees and picked his feet up, putting all his weight on the sturdy branch as he swung in the air. "They must still be up there," he whispered.

Tom was energized. Waving his shotgun like a skeet shooter, he pointed it upward ready to fire. "Want me to bring them down?" he asked for permission.

"Not just yet. I don't want to start a shooting match when they've got the upper position."

"What should we do?"

Agent Walker drew his pistol and gestured. "Let's move away from the tree and see if they come down themselves," he said cautiously. "They probably heard us coming so we might have to wait them out."

Tom was reluctant to lower his weapon, but he zipped his jumpsuit and nodded. "Whatever you say. I've stayed out all night in these woods more than a few times, but are you going to be okay?"

"I'll be fine; part Indian on my mother's side."

The men retreated to the shelter of the ravine and squatted under the trunk of a fallen giant. The pristine sounds of the forest whistled and creaked in the wind. Distant crows announced the end of the day, and nothing moved except lifeless aspen leaves, clinging to the past like spirit rattles.

Tom said, "I'd have brought some matches if I knew we were going camping."

After a while Agent Walker returned to his agenda. "I don't want to stay here too long," he announced. "I'll look at the pictures after they're developed. Right now I have people waiting for me and other business to do. You and your brother can figure out who did this without our help. Let's head back to the vehicles."

Tom liked what he was hearing. "I'm with you," he agreed. "Let those bastards freeze their nuts off all night. We'll be out here first thing in the morning to round them up."

They emerged from the hiding place and relocated the trail back out of the woods, but they hadn't gone a hundred feet when something moved in the underbrush ahead. They both heard it and went into stealth mode with hand signals. Leaving the main path, they crept toward an impenetrable thicket of mountain mahogany, sharp rocks, and fallen branches. Furry scavengers fled at the sound of their approach with chirps and squeals. Tom smelled the unmistakable odor of death, and before he could get his gun pointed, Agent Walker was kneeling next to the headless carcass of a cow.

"I don't know how we missed this," Agent Walker said as he carefully peeled back the bearskin hide that was covering the body.

Tom, who had seen his share of butchered animals, was much more interested in the bearskin. "What the hell is this?" he asked, handling the edge of the hide. He could tell that it had been tanned a long time ago because the claws were broken and the hair was worn thin in spots. The still-attached bear's head was hollow, toothless, and missing eyes. "Well, I'll be," was all he could say.

Agent Walker turned his attention to the hide. He was confounded. "What do you suppose this is doing here? It looks like someone's rug. Why would rustlers do something like this?"

Tom tried to come up with an answer. "Maybe they just left it here and are going to come back to pick it up later."

Agent Walker took some pictures, but couldn't reconcile the vision he saw with the reality in front of him. "I guess we'll leave this situation to the Carter family. You know how to handle this, and you know who to call if you need help from local law enforcement. I need to get back, so let's go."

The men found their snowmobiles and buzzed back in the fading light with a curious story and undeveloped pictures. Farah and Agent Falin, who had spent most of the afternoon on a well-worn sofa in front of a flickering television, listened to Tom and Agent Walker relate the details of their findings. There were more questions than answers, and the only thing that wasn't confusing was their collective hunger. It was too dark to fly, so Tom called his brother and promised to tell him everything when they got there for dinner. Agent Walker put in a call to Officer McKnight, who agreed to drive out to Craig to pick them up later that night.

CHAPTER 17

The ride back to Marty and Marsha's house was long and uncomfortable. Duke and Remy said as little as possible while the feuding couple sniped at each other in the front seat. Marty jerked his bulky Jaguar sedan around the twisty roads as if it were a sports car, and Marsha rolled her window down and stuck her arm out, slicing the wind with her hand like a rudder. The pleasant aromas of flowering jasmine and wild sage, tainted with the smell of heated blacktop and exhaust fumes, gusted into the passengers faces and challenged their hair. Marsha turned the radio up to the edge of distortion and sang "If I Can't Have You" along with Yvonne Elliman, and everyone was relieved when they finally pulled into the Freedman's driveway.

"Who's here?" Marsha asked as they maneuvered past an unfamiliar black Mercedes parked in front.

Two other visitors' cars were taking up the empty spots in the turnaround and Marty was annoyed. "That's Duane's Spyder, but I've never seen that Mercedes before." He said as he pressed the garage opener. Everyone but Marty got out.

The front door was unlocked and Marsha called out, "Hello," when she entered. African-inspired music featuring an incessant drum and bass pulsed through the house-wide stereo system. A sentinel Buddha statue presided over unintelligible chanting that murmured through a layer of pot smoke in the living room. Anesthetized, a brindle cat sunned herself under an arching dracaena.

A tall, thin man with glasses holding a beer came up the stairs and greeted them. "Welcome home," he said. "Stacy said you'd be here soon." He raised his bottle. "I'm Patrick. Thanks for the hospitality."

"Nice to meet you, Patrick." Marsha shook hands. "And where is the fabulous Ms. Stacy?"

"Down by the pool with the others," Patrick said. "I just came up for a beer." He took a swig. "Cool place you've got here."

Patrick followed Marsha downstairs.

Duke and Remy drifted over to the window with the commanding view. They heard Marty come in and a minute later saw him out by the pool talking with Marsha and their houseguests. While they were looking, a short man with thick glasses and greasy hair emerged from the bathroom and sat in an armchair behind them. Duke didn't turn around until he heard the clink of a drink on the glass side table.

The man greeted Duke and Remy in a gravelly voice. "Nice weather we're having. How you doin'?" he said without meaning it. He was wearing a partially buttoned silk shirt, a jeweled pendant twinkled in the forest of black hairs on his chest.

Duke's radar blipped. "Just fine," he answered tersely.

Remy, dressed in his usual army fatigues, touched the derringer in his pocket, and nodded hello.

The man took a sip of his drink and pretended to be friendly. "Some view!" he said, crossing his legs to show off the expensive loafers lurking under gabardine pants that shimmered like snakeskin.

Duke kept a polite distance. "Yeah, Marty's got a front-row seat."

The man chuckled and his olive skin wrinkled into a grin. "That's my company," he said in a throaty rasp.

Duke didn't understand what he meant any more than where his thick accent was from. He wasn't in the mood for chitchat and didn't like doing business with strangers around. He looked out the window, hoping his hosts would notice him and come back upstairs. Remy bumped him, looked at his watch, and jerked his head in the direction of the door.

The man in the chair was much more perceptive than either of them knew. "Which one of you is Duke?" the man inquired abruptly. Duke's red hair and mistrustful glare answered for him.

Unperturbed, the man extracted a small cigar from his pocket and tapped it on the table a few times. "So tell me, Mr. Dunn, how are things in Colorado?"

Duke bristled at the realization that he was at a disadvantage. "Excuse me," he said defensively. "I'm not sure we've met?"

The man flicked his lighter open and agreed. "No, I suppose we haven't. I'm Benzi, Benzi Mogul. You might have heard of me." Benzi lit his short cigar.

The foreign accent made Remy suspicious. He applied pressure to the valuable satchel under his arm and wrapped his fingers around the handle of the revolver in his pocket.

"Yeah, I've heard of you," was all Duke would admit to.

Marty came upstairs and interceded. "Oh hi, Benzi. I see you've already met my friend Duke."

"Yes, I have." Benzi smoked and smiled smugly. Unaffected by everyone else's tension he added, "Nice day we're having," while tapping his ashes.

"Duke, can I see you in private?" Marty motioned him to the other room.

Benzi's subtle aggression didn't fool Remy, who submerged like the crocodiles he used to hunt. He kept one eye on Benzi and one hand on his pistol while Marty and Duke were gone.

Marsha joined them in the spare bedroom where they were talking.

"So what did they decide?" Marty asked Marsha.

"They want a whole one for themselves."

"They have the cash?"

"Yes, but they want to taste it first."

Marty was annoyed. "We gave them a sample yesterday. They don't trust us?"

"It's not them. It's Benzi."

"Figures." Marty turned to Duke to explain.

It wasn't necessary. "I get it," Duke assured him. "Go do your thing and let me know soon. Remy and I have to get out of here. We've got a long flight ahead of us."

"Thanks, amigo," Marty said. "You want a cold drink or something?" he added as they all went back to the living room.

Patrick, wiry and alert, was sitting across from Benzi when they returned. Stacy, innocent with attitude, knelt next to them. Marsha hosted the gathering. "Remy, Duke, Patrick, Benzi, Stacy," she introduced them with palm gestures. "Anyone thirsty?" she asked. "Ice tea, beer, soda, wine?"

Duke couldn't take his eyes off Stacy. "Perrier for me, please," he said with a phony British inflection. "Awfully hot in here with the sun coming in." He wiped his perspiration with a handkerchief.

Remy recognized Duke's flirtation-inspired inflection and drawled, "I'll have me a beer if you all got one," to compensate for his partner's charade.

Stacy petted the house cat who had come to greet her. "No thanks. I'm good – really good!" Her winsome smile glowed a thousand watts, and the men were momentarily stunned by her unassuming light.

Ceding the moment to youth, Marsha said, "I'll be right back."

Patrick held up his beer and said, "Alrighty then, can we please get down to business?"

Marty turned to Duke. "Want to show us what you've got?"

An experienced criminal, Duke knew the room had too many witnesses. "No, Remy and I will wait for you down by the pool. We can only stay for a few minutes, and then we've got to get going."

Marty was miffed but recovered immediately. "Whatever you say, amigo."

Marsha handed Duke and Remy their drinks and followed them downstairs. As soon as they were out of earshot, she asked Duke, "You have the stuff, don't you?"

Remy patted his shoulder bag and nodded.

"So can I see it?" Marsha asked impatiently.

"It's okay, Remy," Duke told him. "Show her one."

Marsha took the see-through baggie and held it up to her face. Then, with Duke's permission, she brought it upstairs and handed it to Marty, who laid it on the table in front of the sofa. There was no mistaking the iridescent glimmer of the crystalline contents, and Marty adjusted the blinds to shield the delicate powder from the direct rays. Everyone's nose twitched in anticipation as they watched Marty extract a hard fragment with his penknife. He put it directly on the glass tabletop and used the edge of a marble ashtray to gently crush the crusty formation back into loose granules.

Patrick readied his silver tooter as Marty chopped long, thin lines with a black American Express card. The dosage prepared, Patrick gallantly handed the tooter to Stacy and said, "Ladies first."

Stacy, dressed in a ruffled cotton skirt and halter top, bunched her light-brown curls in a ponytail with one hand and ingested the airy powder. Swallowing and leaning back, she stroked the nestling cat and beamed.

Patrick picked up the silver straw next and descended on his lines, erasing them with two extended sniffs. Benzi declined the invitation to go next, as did Marsha, but Marty tidied up the remains by wiping the leftovers with his finger and licking it. No one spoke as the African roots music thundered softly in the background of their collective high, and wordless chants gave form to their individual dreams. Unable to sit still for too long, Stacy squirmed in the spotlight, and her languishing pose demanded a comment.

After a long swig of beer Patrick finally broke the silence with a satisfied, "Damn!"

Marsha loved the sexual tension but stayed focused on business. "So what do you think?" she asked rhetorically.

Benzi asked Patrick. "Is this the same stuff?"

Patrick smiled affirmatively. "Oh yeah, this is the shit! Let's get as much as we can; we've got a week more of rehearsal and a big tour coming up."

Marty excused himself to attend to the bloody mucous dripping from his nose, so Benzi asked Marsha a question he already knew the answer to. "How much is this stuff?"

"Thirty a kilo," she said confidently.

Benzi took a moment to calculate. "Is that a fair price?" He narrowed his gaze and concentrated on Marsha's answer.

She surprised him with her sass. "No, not really. This batch is so special we could easily charge double that." Then she checked her watch and added, "Just let me know if you want to do something because our friends have to leave soon."

Nothing turned Benzi on more than a foxy bitch with an attitude, so he imagined Marsha on her knees with his dick in her mouth and took another puff of his cigar.

Patrick knew how his boss operated and where this might lead. "Marsha's probably right," he butted in. "Thirty a kilo is high for the street, but I do think we're talking penthouse quality here. We can cut this stuff in half for the musicians and they'll never know," Patrick convinced himself and took the last swig of his beer.

"But I'm a musician and I'll know," Stacy said impishly.

"What you know is up to your manager," Patrick told her.

"You're going to keep your mouth shut," Marsha said gently, "unless he's someone I approve of!"

Benzi was aroused by the innuendos. He twisted his vision of Marsha a 180 degrees and thrust. "Okay, Mrs. Freedman, you got yourself a deal." Then he grasped her hand to shake on it but didn't let go. "Let me know how you're doing here," he said hoarsely, staring into her green eyes. "I only hear good things about Ms. Stacy, and I've got a place for *you* any time you want to come with me."

Marsha recoiled at the invitation, and Marty, who had come back in the room just in time to hear Benzi's pitch, marked his territory. "Hands off my wife you old pervert," he said firmly. "We don't need your help."

Benzi was comfortable being despised. "That's not what I hear," he taunted.

"Yeah, what do you hear?" Marty challenged him. "And from who?"

"I never reveal my sources," Benzi schooled him, "but rumor has it that your little lady here is not afraid of doin' her own thing."

Marty ground his back teeth and seethed. "This is my house, so you can either apologize or leave." He raised his arms and readied for a karate-style confrontation. Tongue-tied and glaring, he wanted to say something clever about bringing a knife to a backstabbing party but couldn't figure out how.

"Marty!" Marsha interjected. "These are our guests. I'm sure Mr. Mogul was just trying to be supportive."

"FrontRow is a great company," Patrick added, pitching peace. "We love Stacy. Maybe we *should* join forces. We like Duane's band a lot, so you're welcome too Marty."

Marty's tooth grinding loosened a filling, and the disturbed nerve sent a shot of pain into his head. He winced, and Marsha held his hand to calm him down.

Satisfied with the damage he had caused rivals, Benzi arched his back and dug into his pants pocket. "Business is business," he grumbled and withdrew a wad of folded bills. The money was held together with a thick rubber band and separated into clusters by smaller rubber bands. He counted out loud in what was obviously not his native tongue. "Thirty, you say? Five, ten, fifteen." He laid the currency on the table next to the drugs and put the rest of the bundle back in his pocket. "Count it yourself; it's all there."

"So we're just getting one?" Patrick confirmed.

"I don't want to keep too much around," Benzi explained. "Musicians have a hard time controlling themselves. Bad things happen if they're too happy."

Business concluded, Marty changed the music on the stereo to guitar-driven country-rock of the group he was producing. A torrent of twanging reshaped the moment as Duane bent the strings to his irreverent will.

Stacy was the first to celebrate the change in mood. "I love this," she said, swaying seductively in the furious flurry of fifths and thirds."

"This is Duane's group?" Patrick asked.

Marty swelled with pride. "Sure is. This is a mix from last night. You like it?"

Patrick, intentionally overacting, swung his arms and bent his knees to the one-three kicks. "Yeehaw! Dosey doe. You might just have another hit on your hands." Turning to Benzi he added, "See, I told you; the Freedmans know talent."

Benzi thought the music sounded like the frantic folk songs of his old-country homeland, and there were some quirks of American pop culture he just couldn't understand. "I don't get it," he admitted, "but that's why I have you." He stood and straightened his clothes. "Ready to go?"

Patrick followed his boss's cue. "Always a pleasure to see you," he said, kissing Stacey's hand respectfully. Then he repackaged the booty and stuffed it into his man purse. "Guess we'll see you folks later," he said cheerfully, still vibing with the music as he and Benzi left.

As soon as the door had closed, Marsha said, "I'll go settle up with Duke."

"Good idea," Marty agreed. "Are you going to give them a ride to the airport or am I?"

"I can do it; we both don't need to go." She thought it through and added, "Stacy can come along for the ride if she wants."

"Can we go somewhere after?" Stacy asked. "I might want to stop at my place and get some clothes for tonight."

"Sure," Marsha agreed. "Maybe I'll bring something to wear and change at your apartment. You live much closer to the Strip, so we could have dinner there and head over to the club."

Marty liked the idea too. "Sounds like a plan. I'll head over to the studio with Duane. Maybe we'll see you down there, maybe not. Depends on how the overdubs go."

Marsha peeled ten grand off the stack of bills on her way downstairs. Remy was outside by the pool and Duke was inside on the phone. He didn't see her coming, so she sneaked up, hugged him from behind, and put her hands in his front pants' pockets. Duke felt her hot breath on the back of his neck and lost his words as she squeezed his cock from inside his pocket. "The money's in your other pocket," Marsha whispered, rummaging playfully through his jeans before taking her hands back out.

Duke fumbled through "good-bye" and ended his phone call. He felt the bulges in his pants as he turned around and said, "Thank you."

Flirting made Marsha feel young. She brushed her chest against his arm and pecked him on the cheek. "You ready to go?" she whispered. "I'm driving you to the airport." Duke tried to hug her, but she backed away. "Not now, not here."

Remy came inside. "All good?"

Duke patted his pocket full of cash. "Marsha's taking us to the airport now."

"Good," Remy said. "The sun 'round here's almost as bad as Mexico. Can't wait to get out of Hell-A."

Duke and Remy followed Marsha up the stairs and said their good-byes. To Remy's delight, Stacy came out to the car and slid into the back seat next to him. Driving, Marsha backed up until the rear bumper hit a landscaping rock with a thud. "Marty's going to kill me!" she said, and got out to inspect the damage.

Duke got out too. He brushed his hand over the tiny mark in the bumper and said, "It's nothing. No one will notice. Want me to drive?" His comforting hand found the small of her back.

Marsha melted. "That's probably a good idea." She got into the passenger's seat and Duke took the wheel. "You know how to get there?"

Duke was already halfway out of the driveway. "I got here yesterday," he reminded her.

"Good, because I'm a little dizzy; lots of excitement today. I might have to close my eyes for a while if you don't mind." She reclined the sumptuous leather seat and curled her legs up.

"Go right ahead," Duke encouraged, piloting the Jaguar through the twisty roads. He was eager to get up in the air and on his way home, but Marsha put her head on the center armrest and touched the inside of his leg with her extended hand. Conflicted, he had to keep a firm grip on the wheel to avoid an accident. In the back seat, Stacy hummed along to whatever was on the radio in her head, her loose hair streaming in the breeze through an open window. Remy inhaled her reproductive pheromones like a coonhound fresh on the scent, and everyone was disappointed when they arrived at their destination twenty minutes later. Duke parked next to the entrance gate and felt farewell with wishful hands. Then Marsha and Stacy took over the front seats and headed for town.

Back on their own schedule, Duke and Remy walked briskly to their plane. Once there, they released the tie-down knots, climbed aboard, and started the engine. The airport wasn't busy, so Remy taxied to the end of the runway, lined them up, and pushed the throttle full. The tricked-out plane had such good lift that they were already a hundred feet off the ground by the time they passed over the airport fence.

Duke was impressed; he hadn't ridden in his own plane for months. "Never could do that before," he commented while familiarizing himself with the new instrument cluster. The tropical sprawl and scraggly hills of Los Angeles receded beneath them. He calculated fuel levels and checked his watch. "We'll refuel in Las Vegas. They have lights on the field and I'll fly the next leg from there."

CHAPTER 18

Jon's performance at the talent show was a masterly display of intricate fingerpicking. The song he chose, a well-rehearsed rendition of "Buckdancer's Choice," had always been a crowd pleaser, and he was sure he won the competition before he finished with a flourish. There was only one more act, and all the others, in his opinion, had been completely lame, so he raised his red Gibson twelve-string triumphantly to the audience's cheers and frowned a smile as he departed. Joining Donna and Marco at the table, he accepted their congratulations with mock modesty. "Thank you, thank you very much," he goofed on Elvis' famous line.

Donna planted a wet kiss on his cheek and gushed, "You were great!"

"Best I ever heard you play it," Marco complimented.

Cynthia, who had been sitting at another table, came over to congratulate him. "Hi," she said to Jon. "I didn't know you could play like that!" She sat down next to Marco and put her hand on his thigh. "I really want to see you guys perform together."

A waitress brought another pitcher of beer to the table and smiled approvingly before departing. Donna waved at Joel, Nancy, and the rest of her Satsang Diner workmates seated nearby. The MC for the night made an announcement, "Now let's give a warm welcome to our final contestants, "'The Cowboy Liberation Army.'"

The packed crowd, many of whom were friends of the band, gave a rousing welcome as the costumed crew of three musicians took the stage. Rosella, dressed like a buxom cowgirl in pigtails, engaged the audience with mooing sounds and a bullwhip, while Roddy and Hipolito, wearing cowboy boots and ten-gallon hats, checked their tuning.

"We'd like to dedicate this song to all our vegetarian friends in the crowd," Rosella announced, snapping her whip. The audience clapped and bayed approval. "It's called 'Let the Buffalos Roam.'" Roddy and Hipolito played the parody of "Home on the Range" with an acoustic guitar and a mariachi-style acoustic bass while Rosella sang.

> *Let the buffalos roam cause that's what they do.*
> *Have they ever done anything bad to you?*
> *Let the buffalos roam because they are free.*
> *They don't look like dinner to me.*
> *Home, home on the range*
> *Where the weather is all that will change*
> *Where the grass is like silk*
> *And no one drinks of milk*
> *From cows that are acting strange.*

The inebriated crowd sang along to the chorus as Rosella repeated it, teasing them with cleavage and poses. Donna, who didn't usually like Rosella, was won over by her irreverent antics. Cynthia and Marco lifted their glasses and joined in, but Jon was not amused. Where was the musicianship? This was supposed to be a talent contest, not a vaudeville performance. How could he compete with those tits? It wasn't fair!

Rosella ended with a cowgirl yelp, and the MC retook the stage as the other musicians departed. "I don't think there's any question about who the crowd favorite is tonight." He gestured to Rosella, still onstage. Another chorus of cheers confirmed his decision. "But let's not forget our second place finisher, Jon Cells." He motioned for Jon to join them onstage.

Jon was too upset to comply. Staying in his seat, he wiggled his fingers around his beer mug in acknowledgement and muttered, "Let's get out of here," to his friends.

Marco was puzzled. "Aren't you going to collect your prize money, man?"

"Whatever," Jon scoffed. "I make more than that on a half a pound."

Cynthia's eyes lit up at the mention of marijuana. "You have anything good to smoke?"

"Nothing but the best," Jon boasted. "Wanna try some?"

"Now?" She reached under her blouse and touched her dream-catcher, looking for guidance.

Marco put his arm around her. "Come on, I'll give you a ride home and you can make me some bedtime tea."

A popular student watering hole, The Sink was located within walking distance from the sprawling campus of the University of Colorado. Leaving as couples, Marco and Cynthia followed Jon and Donna through the neighborhood cluster of student housing to Donna's rented cottage. Evening birds chirped in the autumn branches of the residential block as they sat on the front porch smoking a joint. Late-night studiers trudged home on the dark-ened streets where neighborhood cats hid under parked cars. The bright Colorado sky sparkled between the treetops, and a mild breeze reddened the end of the joint.

"Good stuff," Marco said, passing the burning blunt to Cynthia. "Where'd you get it?" he asked Jon.

"Just came in from Oaxaca," Jon answered before inhaling. "I've got a whole pound fronted, so if you know anyone who's looking."

Donna came back from the kitchen holding a painted tin serv-ing tray that rattled with four steamy cups of herb tea and a plate of fresh banana bread.

Jon picked up one of the slices. "Mmm-mmm, my favorite," he said, waving the warm smell under his nose.

Donna beamed. "Just made it this afternoon."

"You really are a good cook," Marco said, selecting a slice for himself.

"Da best-is in the west-is," Jon complimented her in stoner-speak. "And what do we have here, my sweet?" he asked, touching the misting mug to his mouth..

"Mountain Meadows mix."

"Mountain Meadows? The same stuff we smoke?"

"Smoke it, eat it, brew it. The Good Earth provides."

"I drink it cold in the summer," Cynthia added.

"Nothing better than tea and 'nanna bread to satisfy the munchies."

"True dat."

Donna sat across from the musicians in one of her homemade serapes the size of a dress. She didn't wear any makeup, and her hair was wrapped in a half bun that didn't account for all the strands. There was nothing sexual about her appearance, but when she crossed her legs and showed her lace up boots, Jon was reminded of twisted pleasures she concealed.

Cynthia joined the subtle female competition by standing to stretch. She extended her arms outward, then bending at the waist, touched the floor on either side of her flat sandals with her fingertips. Her limberness did not go unnoticed by Marco, and as she straightened up, the swinging dreamcatcher revealed her skin between the buttonholes.

The evening high buzzed in their ears like mating insects. They nibbled on bread, sipped their tea, and talked about how unfair the competition was. Frustrated, Jon adjusted his jeans and belched. Marco rocked in a creaky porch chair, hoping the evening's romantic promise would be fulfilled. Cynthia brushed her loose red stands away from her face and smiled at the darkness. Donna stood, put her empty cup back on the serving tray and collected the others. "What time is it anyway?" she announced the moment.

Marco took the hint. "Time to go, I guess." He grabbed Cynthia's hand and pulled her up.

"Where are we going?" Cynthia asked cooperatively.

"I'm parked around the corner. I can give you a ride home," Marco offered.

Cynthia squeezed his hand. "I don't need a ride. My house is a few blocks away on Arapahoe." She slipped her sandals back on. "But I'd like it if you walked me home."

Marco's ears sizzled as he stepped off the porch still holding Cynthia's hand. "See you tomorrow at the studio," he called out. "What time?"

"Time is of the essence," Jon responded in non sequitur.

Marco and Cynthia kept walking. "Essence of thyme."

"Yours or mine?"

"Pigs or swine?"

They were too far away to continue without yelling.

"Earth divine?" Donna suggested before taking the empty cups into the kitchen and stacking them in the sink.

Jon followed her in and put his hands on her hips. "Valentine?" he whispered into her neck.

Donna leaned over and pushed against his crotch. The effect was immediate, and she had to brush Jon's groping hands off her chest. "I'll go run a tub," she hissed, pinching his midsection to extricate herself.

Jon pulled an armless wooden chair from the dining table and fetched the house guitar from the sofa. Welcoming the dark mahogany Gibson steel-string into his arms, he lightly plucked the first few chords of "Mystical Mountain" before stopping to bring the high E back into pitch. Pedaling on a first-position G major until he was satisfied with the tuning, the song elevated in volume and intensity before descending to the relative minor that marked the B section. Inspired by his own musical outburst, he hammered the high string trills that supported the melody and sang quietly.

Mystical Mountain is my new home,
Its fields and streams are where I do roam,
Close to the sky, I'm never alone,
And I'm feeling right at home.

And you know I rise, you know I rise,
You know I rise, you know I rise,
You know I rise for you.

The fingers on his right hand picked nimbly between the tightly spaced strings, touching each one just gently enough to scratch it into sonic vibration. Machine-like fingers of his left hand, rutted with concave calluses in the shape of the strings, pressed and lifted the taut wires on the fret board with assembly line precision. Fused with his muse, the flurry of notes became a swirling storm as he upped the tempo to challenge the limits of his dexterity, and the lyrical worship of Colorado's natural beauty matched the musical escalation. His feet accompanied the reverie with rhythmic stomps, and fully absorbed in his own performance, singing with his eyes closed, he never heard Chodya enter the house.

Chodya, a friend of Donna's from college who used to be called Trudy, stood in front of him, communing with his inspiration and waiting for an opportunity to say hello. Finally, during a relatively quiet musical passage she spoke. "Good evening, maestro. That is such a beautiful song," she complimented in a throaty low voice. Startled, Jon tried to adjust to her presence and the bright lights. Chodya's recently shaved head made her dark eyes more mysterious than they naturally were, and her appearance had undergone a complete transformation since she became a Buddhist. "Is Doh-na home?"

"She's taking a bath or something," Jon mumbled, his hands feeling for familiar chords.

Chodya tightened the end of a broad orange sash that was wrapped around her body like a sari and tucked it into a fold along her waistline. Wearing one of Donna's patchwork shawls over her shoulders and a beaded pendant in the shape of the sun hanging against her chest, she looked like a visitor from another universe. "May I see her?" she asked with a smile that was meant to ease Jon's obvious discomfort.

Jon was glad she didn't want to talk to him. He motioned in the direction of the bathroom. Chodya bowed slightly and withdrew, following the sound of running water. Jon tried to reprise his song, but his guitar refused to play any major chords with Chodya in the house. He changed songs and tried to sing the chorus of "Jesse Boy" to escape from her spell.

Jesse boy what have you done?
To a girl of seventeen,
Who had only to be seen
To be desired.

Unable to recapture his muse, he gave up trying. Still high, he absently pinged harmonics and tried to hear what they were doing in the other room. He heard the bath water stop, and trickling whispers leaked into the hallway. Drawn to the mystery, he stood outside the bathroom door and knocked gently.

"Who's there?" Donna called out in singsong.

Donna's friendly voice restored his confidence. "It's the big bad wolf coming to get you. I'll huff and I'll puff and I'll – "

The door opened slowly. A layer of scented smoke hung in the humid atmosphere. Chodya sat next to the tub with a lit pipe in her hand. "Come on in, big bad wolfie," she said smoothly. "You can huff and puff with us." She handed Jon a small meerschaum toker. "Your little lamb is waiting for you to eat her all up," she added as he inhaled.

Donna raised a naked leg from the claw-foot tub and waved with her toes. Candles were the only illumination. "Come on in and join me, wolfie," Donna beckoned.

Jon didn't want to undress in Chodya's presence and was alarmed at the invitation.

"Don't be shy; Chodya's seen it all," Donna coaxed. The two women giggled mischievously. "She's going to help us have some fun."

Jon was caught off guard with the idea. He wanted nothing more than to nestle into Donna's fertile imagination, but Chodya's presence gave him a strange feeling. Without agreeing, he sucked some extra stimulation from the pipe.

Chodya emptied a small bag of salts in to the steaming water and the aroma of lavender and sage filled the room. She slid her chair closer to the tub and instructed Jon to breathe deeply, pulling him closer to the steam by his arm. Jon felt flush. Looking down, he could see Donna's dark pubic hairs flickering in the depths of the water. The potent humidity and sexual excitement made him sweat, so he knelt next to the tub, breathing heavily as if he might pass out. Chodya stood behind him, and after some tension-relieving shoulder rubbing, helped him remove his shirt. She worked his neck muscles with strong thumbs that squeezed moans from his throat while Donna lounged expectantly in the misty bath. Feeling better, Jon reached into the water. Donna grasped him close enough for a long kiss. Held in her embrace, he was in no position to defend himself when Chodya undid his belt and slid his jeans down to his ankles.

"Wanna get wet?" Donna teased as she pulled him halfway in.

Jon caught his balance on the side of the tub and stepped out of his pants. Self-conscious about his erection, he quickly submerged and lay on his side. There wasn't enough room for two people, and the water sloshed onto the floor as they tried to find a comfortable position. Chodya took her sandals off so they wouldn't get wet and rolled up the loose-fitting cotton pants she wore under her wrap. Standing over the bathing couple, she took control. "Be still," she commanded. "A restless spirit finds no peace."

"Restless? I'm not restless," Jon argued. "I'm uncomfortable." He shifted his position until Donna found a way to wrap her legs around him so that his boner was pressed against her flesh.

"Better?" she asked coyly. "Now what were you saying, Chodya?"

"Now that you're settled, we're going to do a little experiment."

"Experiment?" Jon asked suspiciously. Donna pinched him into silence.

"It's not really an experiment," Chodya went on, "because we know what's going to happen."

"We do?" Jon's buzz itched his throat, and he thought he might be coming on to a migraine.

Chodya blew a palmful of flammable dust over the candles, and the immolation left a pungent odor. "Let's let some of the water out so we can make it hot again," she said, pulling on the drain chain. The tub emptied slowly as the bathing couple touched each other sensuously. When it was halfway empty, Donna replaced the stopper, and Chodya twisted the hot water faucet back on to a steady trickle. The scalding-hot water poured in, and the bathers paddled it around themselves, shivering from the air and burning from the water until the tub was full again. Chodya added more salts and scented oil to the water, then seated herself cross-legged in a padded wicker chair next to the bathers. The candles flickered as she began her incantation. "Ohmm *het!*" she accented the second word. "Hohmm *phat!* Ma-no-hmm *ni!* Hohmm *dak!*"

Donna and Jon stopped moving as Chodya repeated her spell several times, each time drawing out the length of the ohm sound a little longer and accenting the second word sharply. A deep silence grew in the small room until only the occasional drip of water and singe of burning wax were heard. Chodya clasped her hands together in her lap with her thumbs touching and breathed the cosmic forces through her body. Unconsciously, the bathing couple's breathing cycle aligned to hers.

Soon, Jon felt a sting of energy beneath his scrotum as his serpent power awoke. He twisted to accommodate his growing excitement. As Chodya had told her to do, Donna imagined a tide of blue sky descending through the top of her head each time she inhaled, washing it away from below with the yellow fire of the sun as she pushed the air back out. They meditated, breathing as one, and after a while, Chodya became motionless and stopped breathing altogether. A few moments later, she got up quietly and left without saying a word.

As soon as the door latched shut, Jon struggled to control the surge of bindu filling his manhood. Donna felt his appendage grow bigger than it ever had been, and she squeezed her hand around its vigor. Alone at last, they touched each other erogenously and kissed. Their naked bodies slid against each other in the oily waters, but the tub was too small and slippery to position themselves for insertion, so they left the water in favor of the wood floor. Urges racked their bodies, and too unsteady to stand, Donna knelt on a bathmat beside the tub. Jon held her shoulders as he mounted her from behind and slid all the way in on the first thrust. After the first few frantic minutes, Donna twisted onto her back, and they slowed to their usual pace, undulating rhythmically until climax.

They stayed conjoined for a few tender moments, relishing their sexual compatibility – and then Chodya's magic took over. Spent and mostly flaccid, Jon's appendage began to resuscitate as if it had a mind of its own. Powered by a force hidden somewhere within Donna's muliebria, they felt a sharp surge of hypersexual energy that was not limited to any particular part of their bodies. Neither of them moved as the transmuted bindu rose up between them and snaked its way through their energy centers. An intense internal heat collected in their heads, and when the pressure in their skulls had built to the edge of pain, the ojas erupted through their crown chakras like a chute of overheated mercury explodes through the top of a thermometer tube.

I looked into your eyes
And I saw the edge of pain,
And if I had my choice
I'd do it all over again.
In a tube,
I was only testing.

Paralyzed in coital clench, with their psychic forces drained, they lay motionless, unable to speak. The candles eventually burned out and dropping temperatures chilled them to their senses. Thirty minutes later, weighted by the fatigue of sensory overload, they staggered to the bedroom and sought refuge under the covers.

Chapter 19

Josh Carter's new house was still under construction. A stack of snow-covered lumber marked the edge of the open area where his brother Tom parked the four-door F-250. "Careful when you get out," Tom warned his guests. "It's still kind of messy around here." His companion Buster hopped out and bounded ahead of them.

The sole front porch light was only strong enough to guide them toward the house, leaving visitors ample opportunity to trip over the random cutoffs and frozen ruts in the unfinished driveway. Agent Walker followed Tom's path to the front door, and Agent Falin, who had been riding in the back of the extended cab with Farah, let her use his shoulder for support as she hopped down from the elevated passenger compartment.

"Thanks," Farah said as she landed safely. The oversized tires of Tom's truck came up to her waist. "They ought to put steps on the back of these things," she complained, picking her way through the shadowed obstacle course. Agent Falin, who was attempting to lead without infringing on her independence, smiled to himself. The few hours they had spent together had given him time to deepen his appreciation of Farah's peculiar appeal. Agent Walker was waiting for them at the front door landing, not surprised to see his undersized friend hold an arm as she negotiated the gully between the driveway and bottom step.

Tom was already inside when his younger brother welcomed them. "Welcome, Agent Walker. Nice to see you again." They shook firmly. "It's been too long."

"Hi Josh, thanks for the rescue. I think you might know Farah," he said, making the introduction.

Josh, a handsome, third-generation Coloradan with pure Christian roots, put on his manners. "I've heard your name but don't think we've ever met," he said, looking down as he gently shook Farah's hand. "Nice to finally meet you."

Farah was annoyed at the patronizing deference to her size and sex. "Nice to meet you too, Mr. Carter," she said, pumping his arm much more vigorously than expected. "Lose any cattle recently?"

Josh was surprised at her aggression and looked to Agent Walker for guidance.

Agent Walker redirected. "We can talk about that later, if you don't mind. Right now, I want Josh to meet our new man, Agent Falin." The strangers shook. "This is only his second day in Colorado so go easy on him."

"Welcome to Craig," Josh said, leading his guests into the two-story great room of his custom log home. A massive stone fireplace with a floor-to-ceiling chimney made from rounded river rocks dominated the spacious area. It was framed by two large trapezoidal windows that connected the interior to an expansive skyline. In its own special corner, a three-foot-long, tripod-mounted telescope was pointed toward the heavens. Thick Douglas Fir logs, two stories high, carried the weight of a semicircular ceiling made from rough-hewn branches and wide planks of pine. The whole room was paved with end-cut spruce, and the rest of the house, made from smaller logs and boards, started opposite the fireplace. "Everything we used to build this place was grown, cut, and milled on site," Josh explained as he guided his company to the leather seating arrangement in front of a burning hearth. His guests, like everyone else when they first entered his wood-sculptured masterpiece, marveled at the peaceful symmetry and flow of natural colors. "The whitish-gray wood is all beetle-kill," Josh pointed out. "Everything else is just as God made it. Other than the flooring, all we did was give it a coat of clear." He gestured proudly. "Let's warm up a bit before we eat. Lauren's just putting the boys to bed." He moved some plastic Halloween toys off of a chair, and after everyone had found a spot, he asked Agent Walker, "So how are things down in Denver?"

"Pretty good, I guess. Broncos are five and three."

Tom was a big football fan. "You see the game Sunday? Colts had Upchurch and Moses wrapped up all day. Morton couldn't throw anything downfield. How're you supposed to win if you don't score any touchdowns?" Tom complained.

"Sometimes we need the mile-high advantage to win," his brother commiserated. "Too bad they're not all home games."

"Yeah, we didn't score anything in San Diego last week. At least we kicked two field goals in Baltimore. Who's got the Jets tickets for next Sunday, you or Dad?"

"Dad's taking one of the boys – whichever one wins the best behavior contest. I was supposed to go, but with all this," he looked at Farah and hesitated "stuff going on, I figured I should stay put."

Farah had settled into a small rocker next to the fireplace. The life-like head on a very new bearskin rug was facing her. "So how many calves did this girl get?"

"None," Josh told her. "That one got hit by a drunk Indian on the highway last year. Poor thing was pregnant too."

"That was some accident," Tom commented. "That pickup must've been doing eighty when it hit. Highway 40 was closed for half a day. Killed the bear, ruined the truck, and wouldn't you know – that damn Indian walked away. Cops say he was so loaded he didn't know who he was."

Agent Walker's ancestry made him sensitive to the topic. "Seems like you've been having quite a bit of trouble with the locals lately. Any idea what's got into them?" he asked.

"No idea whatsoever," Josh admitted. "We've been letting them hunt on our property since the first peace treaty, and we've been trying to work out a water deal with them for years. Some Lakota Sioux from Montana have been down here looking for land to buy – I think they must have some rich hippy backers – and since the old Ute chief died a few years back we simply don't know who's in charge. A couple of Indians work for us during the high season, and they seem okay when they're sober."

"Okay? We'd be up a creek without them," Tom corrected his brother. "Those braves are my best helpers. They can ride all day, eat almost nothing, sleep under the stars, and keep going for weeks."

Agent Falin, who had been studying the wall-mounted trophy heads, commented, "Sounds like the Vietcong. We never could figure out how they survived."

"The local people always have the advantage," Agent Walker observed. "They know the land and everything in it."

"Well maybe we should ask them if they've seen our missing pilot," Agent Falin suggested. "We used local trackers all the time over there. They could spot things that none of us even noticed."

"So you were over in 'Nam," Josh noted. "What division?"

"I was in Intel. We were based in Cambodia."

"Agent Falin was working for Customs in LA, but he's here to help us now. I'm sure you know we lost a good man last week."

"So we heard," Josh confirmed. "Greg McKnight came out to talk with us about it."

"I already told him everything I knew," Tom added. "I kind of had a strange feeling when you guys landed 'cause your Cessna was a dead ringer for the one that went down. Thought maybe I was seeing a ghost or something."

"How well did you know Agent Dobson?" Agent Walker querried.

"Not well, he only came in a few times when Steamboat was socked-in."

Josh's wife, Lauren, came in to greet her houseguests. Overweight and plainly dressed, she was tired from a long day of managing young Irish twins and a house still under construction. She stood with her arms folded, nodding impatiently as Josh made the introductions. The Carter homesite was a half-mile away from the nearest neighbor, and living on the frontier, even with electricity and hot water, was not an easy life. She ran rough red hands through unbrushed hair and wiped them on her apron. "Welcome. Dinner will be ready in a few minutes," she said before hurrying back to chores in the kitchen.

Farah saw her struggling to keep up appearances and went to help. Agent Walker was relieved that Farah was out of earshot and continued their investigative conversation. "So, did Agent Dobson ever tell you anything about what he was looking for?" he asked Tom.

"'Course not. You government types never let on what you're up to. All he ever did was ask questions like 'What did I see and who's using the field?' I told McKnight all that already. When's he coming?"

"Probably not for a while. He had some things to do before picking us up. You say he asked you a bunch of questions. Did he seem interested in anything you told him? Anything that might explain what we saw a while ago?"

Living by himself and working alone most of the time, Tom embraced his role as a vital communication link. "Truth is," he said with some enthusiasm, "I *have* heard some strange things recently." After he had everyone's attention, he went on to say, "It's only happened a few times, and I can't say what it was for sure, but at first I thought it was a plane heading toward Steamboat or Hayden – and it might have been – I still don't know. But I didn't see any running lights, and the damn thing, whatever it was, was flying real low. It was making this weird droning sound." He leaned in and tried to imitate the sound by growling. "Oohhrree oohhrree."

Josh laughed at him. "That sure doesn't sound like an airplane to me. More like a sick cow."

Agent Walker hadn't forgotten what he'd seen earlier. "Maybe it was."

Josh agreed. "That's what I told him. I think we must have some kind of bug going through the herd. One of them gets sick and starts moaning, then they all start. The bears or cougars hear them, and next thing you know, they've got one by the neck. If Tom or I don't scare them off with a shotgun in time, they haul it up a tree to eat. All this alien talk is so stupid. That's why we got this telescope." He pointed. "Me and the boys have to keep a lookout so we can see the spaceships coming," he mocked the idea.

Tom defended superstition. "Well you haven't heard about what these guys saw today."

"What did you see?" Josh asked Agent Walker. "A mothership full of little green people?"

"No, we saw something that we thought was a bear dragging one of your herd into the woods. That's why we landed."

"Like I said," Josh concluded.

"Not exactly. I guess Tom didn't get a chance to tell you. He and I took the snowmobiles out to check it out and, well, your brother thinks it was rustlers."

"Rustlers? Out here in God's country? I don't think so. What's this all about, Tom?"

Tom looked perplexed. "Truth is, I don't know. I thought it might've been rustlers 'cause who else would've tried to cover up a dead heifer with an old bearskin?" Tom ground his teeth and pondered. "And I still can't figure out how come the tracks led to that big tree and then stopped. It's almost like whoever grabbed that old girl just disappeared."

Farah came in to summon everyone to dinner, and the men suspended the conversation. "Never heard of rustlers who wanted the livestock dead," Josh muttered as they moved to the dining area. "We'll talk this out after dinner." Before seating himself at the head of a rustic wood table with a picnic bench on one side and shaker chairs on the other, Josh raised his arms and said, "Thank you Lord, for all you do. Bless this meal and all who eat it."

"Amen," Lauren testified. "Let's eat before it gets cold."

Glasses of water were already poured, and everyone took a seat. Sauce-covered ribs from a full-sized cow were stacked on an aluminum serving platter in the middle of the table. Each person self-served one or two of the meaty pieces, then set to separating the seared flesh from the bone with sharp knives and teeth. Sauce dripped down chins, sticky fingers had a hard time holding on to the slippery bones, and no one's red gingham napkin was underused. Steaming cut-and-peeled white potatoes doused in butter were passed around in a wooden bowl carved from the gnarled base of a tree, and eating choked out conversation. Indestructible white enamel dinner plates clinked with the abuse of stainless steel cutlery, and the substantial meal was still settling in their stomachs when Lauren got up to answer the door.

Officer McKnight trailed her back to the table. "Looks like I'm late for supper," he said.

The diners attempted to be mannered while extricating the sinews of flesh stuck between their teeth with forks and fingernails.

"There's plenty left," Josh welcomed. "Lauren will make you a plate if you're hungry."

"Very kind of you, but I had dinner in town already." Officer McKnight sat down opposite Josh and addressed Agent Walker. "Some things have come up; I think you'll want to get back to Steamboat soon," he said soberly.

Agent Walker detected the serious tone. "Okay, I think we're all finished here. Do we have time to sit by the fire and talk? Can it wait?"

Officer McKnight realized that he had interrupted an otherwise pleasant dinner. "Sure, we can stay a little while."

Agent Falin was enjoying the rustic hospitality and thought Officer McKnight was suffering from a case of self-importance.

"So that means we'll get to sample that incredible apple pie I see on the counter?"

The answer surprised him. "Well, you might actually have to spend the night here," Officer McKnight informed him bluntly. "Here or somewhere else close by. A full busload of skiers from Texas rolled into town this afternoon and took over all the hotel rooms. We never have this many early birds. I don't know what they told them in Texas, but everyone in town's scrambling to find places for them to sleep. I lent the police department my truck so they could get to some of the cabins that hadn't been plowed out yet, and I had to come here in my wife's two-seater Volvo."

"Finally some good news for the economy," Josh observed.

"What kind of Volvo only has two seats?" Tom asked.

"A P-1800. It's a little sports car. My wife uses her Jeep most of the time, but she's busy helping the out-of-towners too. We only take the Volvo out in the nice weather unless it's an emergency."

"Emergency?"

"Maybe emergency's the wrong word. I guess I just got caught up in the hassle of trying to accommodate the visitors. Half of them seem more interested in where they're going to have their Halloween party than hitting the slopes."

Agent Walker had other concerns. "What about the plane?"

Officer McKnight had already thought that through. "I figured Agent Falin could fly it back in the morning. I moved all your stuff over to my house because the hotel had to rent your room. You can stay with us tonight. The weather report for tomorrow looks good so we should be back up in the air before noon. Big high-pressure system rolling in."

Agent Walker hadn't finished finding out all he could from the Carters. "Okay, sounds like a plan, but let's just sit for a little while and work out the details."

"Like where am I supposed to sleep?" Farah interjected. "My boss is probably going crazy with all those tourists. I have to get back there tonight."

"I already talked to your boss," Officer McKnight told her. "Jim's got his hands full, but I explained the situation and he expects you back in the morning sometime."

"Well thanks, I guess. Nothing like having other people make decisions for me."

"You can stay with us, honey," Lauren said, extending the invitation. "There's a pullout bed in the boys' room. The other gentleman can sleep on the sofa by the fire if he wants. Right, Josh?"

"He can stay with me," Tom volunteered. "Buster and I don't mind the company."

Buster, who was loitering near the table waiting for a handout, nudged his master at the mention of his name.

"Wherever Agent Falin is most comfortable."

Agent Falin remembered the telescope in the corner and thought it might be fun to use. "I'll stay right here if nobody minds. I haven't used a good telescope since training."

"Okay," Agent Walker concluded. "You and Farah get a ride out to the field first thing in the morning and call me before you take off. Officer McKnight and I will meet you when you land at Steamboat. Farah can get a ride back into town from the airport, and we can get back up in the air to follow our flight plan. Agreed?"

There was no dissension. Farah helped Lauren clear the table and slice up dessert. The men huddled around the fireplace, comparing information and theories in between bites of fresh apple pie and homemade ice cream. Officer McKnight was reticent to share the details of his investigation, and one small Jameson nightcap was not enough to loosen his tongue. He steered the conversation into dead-ends, accelerated departure plans as best he could without alarming anyone. Tom reprised his attempt to imitate the eerie humming sounds he had heard, but Buster's sympathetic growl was much more convincing – and amusing. After he escorted Officer McKnight, Tom, and Agent Walker out, Josh showed Agent Falin and Farah a map of the Colorado sky, pointing out the best places to aim the telescope. "Don't be alarmed if you hear some strange noises," he told Agent Falin and Farah. "My wife says my snoring can get pretty scary."

"Boys' room is the first door down the hallway. Bathroom's next to it," Lauren said and put some blankets on the sofa. Then the Carters retired.

Alone, Agent Falin asked Farah, "So what did you make of all that nonsense?"

"What nonsense?"

"You know, the weird growling sound."

"Oh, that's nothing. You hear all kinds of strange things in the mountains." Farah eyed the bottle of Jameson. "You think our hosts would mind if we borrowed a nightcap or two?"

Agent Falin smiled. "Well, he did say to make ourselves comfortable." He overturned two shot glasses.

Farah approved. "I knew you were okay the minute I picked you up at the airport. The cops that usually come from Denver are all stiffs."

Agent Falin filled the shots. "Well, business is business," he defended the profession.

Farah took her glass and downed it in one gulp. "And pleasure is pleasure. We're off the clock now," she said, smacking it on the table. "Hit me."

Agent Falin drained his own glass and refilled both of theirs. Farah's plan to get him drunk enough to tell her all he knew started by recounting the eventful day's highlights, meandered into making fun of her foreign visitor, and wound up talking about aliens. Out of his environment and far above sea level, Agent Falin had trouble keeping up with Farah's alcohol tolerance and spirited theories. Heated pockets of sap crackled and popped at surprising intervals, punctuating her assertions with uncanny timing. Her wide-eyed wonderment made her look younger and more attractive than she naturally was, and unable to follow her Jameson logic, Agent Falin tried to twist her agenda into an invitation to bed.

The fresh lumber inside the great room creaked and moaned as its burdens settled, and the constant wind of the high plains whistled through the irregularities of log construction. Tipsy, they eventually made it over to the telescope. Farah pointed it at the moon and focused. Agent Falin welcomed the intimacy of sharing the viewfinder, and they were both studying the feminine principle when an airborne silhouette crossed in front of the gibbous crescent.

"Did you see that?" Farah, who had most of the viewfinder, said.

Agent Falin had seen it without the telescope. "I think so. It looked like a small plane, but I didn't see any running lights."

"It was awfully close to the treetops, whatever it was." Farah rotated the device to scan the horizon.

Agent Falin slid the door to the outside open and searched the night sky for clues. The chill wind refreshed his sense of the hunt, but he couldn't see anything unusual. Farah stood beside him as the drone of a distant engine faded into the distance.

"What was that?" she whispered. "Flying around with the lights off?" Extraterrestrials populated her imagination.

"I'm guessing a pilot in trouble," Agent Falin postulated. "Unless they're smugglers." He thought about what he'd said and added, "We might have lucked into something."

"What's so lucky about smugglers?"

Agent Falin realized he had said too much and tried to change direction. He put his arm around Farah's and squeezed her playfully. "*Snugglers*, I said *snugglers*."

"No you didn't," Farah protested and squirmed free. "I heard you; you said *smugglers*. Is that what you guys really came here for?"

"Let's go back inside. It's so cold out here I'm starting to feel sober."

They went back to the warmth of the fire, but Farah wasn't ready to get off her train of thought. "Smugglers," she repeated with a mischievous grin. "Why didn't you say so? Want me to introduce you to them?"

Agent Falin thought he was hearing things. "You know … some smugglers?"

Farah relished the upper hand. As a diminutive woman, there was nothing more satisfying than giving a big man a hard time. "Maybe," she teased. "Is that what you're after? I won't tell Agent Walker if you tell me."

Agent Falin sorted through his grab bag of interests and chose the professional one. "Okay, you win. Yes, one of our missions has to do with smugglers. And yes, I'd like to find out what you know about them."

Farah was disappointed. "You're too easy." She removed her boots and tucked her legs underneath herself. "That information will definitely cost you another drink."

Agent Falin tipped the bottle into her cup, but only a trickle came out. "Sorry, I guess we overdrank our welcome."

"No we haven't," Farah corrected him. "There's a whole other bottle in the cabinet by the kitchen," she assured. "I saw it when I was helping with dinner. These Jesus people never run out of spirits."

Agent Falin followed her directions and found the next Jameson. He couldn't remember the last time a woman was telling him what to do, and it was strangely enticing. The evening wind had suddenly subsided, and the house was so quiet that the pendulum clock, echoing off the hard wood surfaces, sounded loud. He turned off the kitchen lights before padding back to the fire with the full whiskey bottle. Farah turned off the table lamp so that the room was only lit with the twinkle of stars and glowing embers.

"You were saying," Agent Falin prodded as he handed her a refilled drink.

Farah hoped he could see the cleavage in her loosened plaid shirt. "What were we talking about?" she said coyly. "Snugglers? Aliens? Dead cows? Crazy Indians? I forget."

Agent Falin knocked back a swig and engaged. "Smugglers. You were going to tell me who they were."

"No I wasn't. I only asked if you wanted me to introduce them to you."

"Same thing."

"No, it isn't. I don't really know who they are."

"So how can you introduce them to me?"

"I know someone who knows some friends of theirs."

Agent Falin was disappointed. His years of working intel had preconditioned him to know how unreliable friends-of-friends could be. "That doesn't sound too promising."

"I never promised you anything."

Agent Falin rubbed his eyes and said nothing. The long day, thin air, frustrating conversation, and potent nightcap were starting to manifest as sleep. He unfurled one of the blankets and lay down on the couch. "I'm beat. Maybe we can talk this out tomorrow." He covered himself and said, "I hope you don't mind," with his eyes closed.

Farah took the other blanket and curled up on the chair. Sipping her drink, she thought she saw faces in the flickering flames before giving in to exhaustion.

CHAPTER 20

Highway 40 was plowed and salted, so once Officer McKnight and Agent Walker made it out of the driveway, the meandering road next to the river that led back to Steamboat Springs was only treacherous because the spray from trucks barreling in the other direction at sixty miles per hour in the westbound lane caked up the windshield faster than last year's wiper blades and clogged spritzers could clear, and the muddied headlights of the small car they were driving were incapable of illuminating anything more than twenty feet in front of them in the pitch-black countryside. Fortunately, Officer McKnight was a skilled driver. "This little Volvo isn't so good in the snow; rear-wheel drive," he said, downshifting into third as they approached an inclined curve. "But we've got Pirelli's, so it's steady around the turns."

Agent Walker asked the obvious question, "So what made you buy *this*? There aren't many Volvos around here."

Officer McKnight was used to the question and enjoyed answering it. "She's Swedish." He patted the dashboard. "And the Swedes love Colorado; reminds them of home. One of Howelsen's relatives owned a condo in Aspen and shipped this over to use in the summer. I bought it when he sold the place a few years ago."

Agent Walker was anxious to know what Officer McKnight had found out but didn't want to distract him from driving, so the conversation didn't get serious until Highway 40 changed into Lincoln Avenue and they saw the downtown lights of the city. "So what did you hear?" he asked as they slowed down to pass a plow-truck adding height to the banks of snow lining the boulevard.

"The rescue team found a body," Officer McKnight told him, carefully maneuvering around the obstacle course created by a double-parked Grayliner bus.

The accident had happened a week ago, so Agent Walker was expecting the news. "Was it Agent Dobson's?"

Officer McKnight bowed his head, downshifted, and headed up a side street in the direction of his house. "We're not positive."

Agent Walker winced at the confirmation. "Why couldn't they ID it? Too messed up?"

"Too high up in the tree. They might have to bring in a chainsaw to cut him down."

They passed a house Agent Walker's family had rented one summer when he was an undisciplined teenager, and the dark winter weather brought back memories. "Is that all you found out?"

"That's the main thing." Officer McKnight said, slipping and zigzagging through the icy streets until he made it into his driveway at the end of Ninth. He left the motor running and pulled the handbrake.

Agent Walker sensed that there was something else to talk about. "I thought you said you had something to show me?"

"I just said that to get you out of there," Officer McKnight admitted. "The Carter family is nice and all that, but they're a little too wrapped up in their own interests and they have friends everywhere. I figured it was best to keep the state business separate."

Agent Walker hadn't spent much time in Steamboat since his appointment to the Bureau and had lost track of local politics. "Okay, so is there any other news?"

Officer McKnight could tell from the other car in the driveway that his wife was home. He didn't want her to hear what he was going to say so he and Agent Walker stayed in the car and talked. "It looks like Agent Dobson must have been ripped out of the cockpit by a branch when he hit the woods. Most of the wreckage was pretty far away from where we found him. It got too dark to see the breakup pattern. I guess we'll be able to check that out from the air tomorrow. Hopefully, that'll explain how he got there."

Agent Walker clenched his teeth at the thought of his dead colleague's remains. "What do you mean?" he said watching wind-borne flakes perish on the windshield. "He wasn't in the wreckage?"

"No, and there were tracks in the snow around the base of the tree."

"What kind of tracks? Bear? Mountain lion?"

"All kinds, including human ones."

Tracks around the base of a tree hit a nerve, and Agent Walker tried to imagine what might have happened. Why were so many dead things winding up in trees? It wasn't natural. First the cattle mutilation pictures, then whatever got Josh Carter's cow, and now this. "Maybe he survived the crash and climbed up there to get away from something. Did anyone follow the tracks? See where they went?"

Officer McKnight expected the question. "No, it got too dark. They'll retrace tomorrow. We're hoping that explains a few things because the tracks – the human ones – were barefoot."

"Barefoot? In this weather?" The thought of Agent Dobson's suffering clenched Agent Walker's jaw.

Officer McKnight waited a respectful moment. "There's another problem," he added gravely.

"Oh?"

"All the tracks were fresh. It snowed there last night so somebody was there earlier today."

"What?" Agent Walker was stumped. The only people he knew who ever walked barefoot in the snow were Native Americans. "Any reports of Indians in the area?"

Officer McKnight had thought of that too. "No, but we don't keep tabs on them. The crash site is pretty far from the nearest reservation, but they've been hunting in these mountains longer than we've been here. I guess it's possible one of them heard about the crash or stumbled on it."

"Did you speak with anyone at the regional office?"

"Of course. I called it in as soon as I got the preliminary report. The bureau chief had already gone, but I told his secretary. My team is going to take some pictures and continue to search, but they might not be back here for a couple of days. We should be able to file a full report by midweek."

"You think your guys are safe? They'll be able to get the job done and make it back without any help?"

"Bobby and I grew up together. He knows these mountains almost as well as the Indians and I trust him completely."

"Well that makes me feel better. Who's he got with him?"

"His dog."

Agent Walker was surprised. "His dog? That's it? No one else?"

Officer McKnight was unfazed. "That dog is better than any other man we could send. He smells better, hears better, runs faster, and fights harder. No one in their right mind would go hunting without a dog like that."

"But he's not on a hunting trip," Agent Walker argued, "and bureau policy – "

Officer McKnight's grip on Agent Walker's arm cut off his sentence. "Listen William, we both know about policies and procedures, but this is why they wrote 'field judgment' into the manual. I would have gone with Bobby myself if I could have, but he knows a few friendlies in the area and he'll be alright."

Agent Walker unzipped his jacket all the way. "I don't know about you, but this heat is making me tired. Let's go inside. It's been a long day and I want to be lying down before I fall asleep."

Officer McKnight's wife had laid some blankets on the couch, and Agent Walker took off his shoes before bedding down. He tried to blot out images of a mangled body stuck in the trees, but the spirit of the steak drowning in his stomach haunted his dreams about teepees in the snow.

CHAPTER 21

Even experienced pilots are fascinated with seeing the terrain from an aerial perspective, but after it got too dark to make out the features on the ground, the flight over the desert to Las Vegas was boring enough that Duke finally had time to think. The trip to LA had been more successful than he could have hoped: he and Remy had ripped off Oswaldo for three keys of coke that he had already turned into a wad of cash, and even though his hacked transponder never worked right, his tricked-out plane was flying even better than he thought it would. Marsha had treated him to forbidden sex with a married woman, and the memory of that salacious encounter made his saliva run. And as if the emotional satisfaction wasn't enough, the news that his Boulder banker had approved an unwarranted loan in order to earn a kickback opened up the BlueStar skies. With money in his pocket to pay off debts, two more bricks to sell, a new console in the studio, and Marsha's perfume lingering on his collar, Duke's problems drifted down to the darkened earth like sediment settles on the bottom of the ocean. Inhaling the rarified atmosphere, he and Remy cruised through the trackless wilderness a thousand feet over the desert. How far could he ride this lucky streak?

The idea for a Halloween party at the studio wasn't his, but turning it into a grand reopening was. Promoting his visions was as close as Duke ever got to a natural high. His explanations would start out vague and general, but then, he'd lure his audience in with details about things they were only dimly aware of; that was the trick. He had to know more than whoever was listening, so he developed an expertise in subjects that were mysterious to the average listener. Both aviation and sound recording were perfect fits. His charm worked best with just a few minds to impress at the same time; that way he could measure their interest with each pause and make adjustments – a little repetition here, a little graphic description there. Duke's whole presentation, delivered with a sophisticated southern drawl, made everything he was saying seem all the more genuine, and his obvious enthusiasm was made all the more believable by his appearance. Six foot two and ruggedly handsome with a rock-and-roll edge, his thick red mane was usually trimmed to business length, and he looked like Colorado royalty in expensive jeans, Italian loafers, and a custom leather jacket. Looking at and listening to him, it was hard for straight people to see the megalomaniacal insanity lurking beneath the surface of his slick logic. He was so confident that it really didn't matter what anyone thought of him; that was his other secret. That was how he could talk to anybody about anything. And his conversational skills weren't limited to talking; he was also an excellent listener. But he didn't listen to just anybody. Like any smart person, he listened to people who knew more than him about subjects he found fascinating – like aviation.

Duke had big ideas – really big ideas. It didn't matter if people knew he started out as a bass player in a southern rock band; he used that to his advantage. He didn't care if everyone in Boulder thought of him as a guy who used to sell wooden spoons and ice cream makers to retrograde mountain hippies; he was proud of that too. It all made sense to him, even the way he funded his ambitions with daring drug deals. Everyone worth knowing smoked or snorted or hung out with people who did; he was just a middleman making enough money to build his empire into world-class status. Everything he did had to be cutting edge. He had to have the newest and nicest and hippest stuff. It was his right, and he was born to rule because he knew so much more about life and the way things ought to be than regular people. And he was so much more sophisticated than those stuffy white Klanners who were his father's friends. Their time had passed. It was a new day, and he was one of only a handful of people on the planet who realized the importance of this moment in the history of mankind. Apart from the size of his dreams, the most amazing thing about his revelations were that they lasted so long after the effects of LSD had worn off. He couldn't even remember the last time he dropped, and it didn't matter. He never woke up the next day with his eyes buggy wondering what happened. It was like he never came down. That's why he had stopped tripping; he didn't need to anymore.

"I think that's Vegas up ahead," Remy interrupted.

Duke scanned the cluster of lights on the horizon. "The airport is at the edge of town. Just follow the highway and it'll be on the right."

Lights from the constant traffic on Interstate 15 between Los Angeles and Las Vegas made navigation over the desert at night easy. The road through the Mojave was one of the few stretches of highway where cops didn't bother trying to catch all the speeders in a hurry to lose their paychecks or get back to their day jobs. Rich posers in Ferraris and Porches pushed their machines beyond the limits of safety, and middle-aged suburbanites used the emptiness to check the accuracy of their speedometers. That's what the desert did; it made people want to fill it up with something – even if that something was just motion.

Remy picked out the lights of two particularly aggressive speeders and tried to overtake them. "I'm doing a 120 knots and we're barely catching them."

"Let's get right on top of them," Duke suggested. "I want to see what they're driving. Could be a Lambo or Lotus."

Remy pushed the stick in and descended to a few hundred feet. They were about a half-mile behind when the trail car lit up with the angry glow of police lights. The strobing colors splashed on their bug-splattered airplane windshield, temporarily blinding the pilot.

Duke realized they might be spotted and yelled, "Up, up! Let's get out of here," over the engine noise.

Remy jerked the stick toward him and ruddered into a left bank climb. Spotting the lights of another plane coming toward them at two o'clock, he aimed for the open space at a higher altitude. The other plane, having just taken off, was also climbing, and if it weren't for Remy's combat experience, they might not have been able to avoid a midair collision. By the time he had finished cursing the other pilot, the runway lights of McCarran Airport were clearly visible.

Turning around, Duke could see the patrol car's headlights glaring at the back of a low-slung racer, and he was glad he had graduated from youthful joyrides to more prosperous mischief. The strobe on the airport beacon bounced off their windshield as they neared the field.

"Should I call the tower?" Remy asked.

Duke pressed the light on his watch. "It's after seven, so I think we're on our own."

"I'll go around once to make sure."

They buzzed the field at five hundred feet to monitor the activity. A high-wing passenger prop was poised for takeoff at the end of the runway, and two other planes were inching into position behind it. The floodlights in front of the main hangar were on, a truck was towing something behind it, and several people were walking in and out of the control tower building.

Duke checked his watch again. "Looks a little too busy down there. How much fuel do we have?"

"Still got a quarter tank, but we're going to need to refuel before we head into the mountains. Where else can we go?"

Duke studied the map. "Reno's close enough, but they might not be open." He stared out the window at McCarran, calculating the risk of putting down in the midst of so many nosy people.

When they made a wide circle over a large patch of undeveloped land, he came up with a plan. "Let's put down there." He pointed into the darkness.

Remy tipped the wings so he could see. "There?"

"See that road? There's plenty of room to get down. That road leads right to the airport."

Remy could make out a faint sliver separating two uninhabited regions. "You want to land here and drive to the airport? Talk about suspicious!"

"We're not going to the airport."

"Then where are we going?"

"To that gas station." There was a dimly lit, small neon sign on the road. "We can run on ninety-two, right?"

Remy did a low altitude flyover of the narrow two-lane road before lining up a landing. There was just enough light to set down on the pavement, and they only had to taxi a few minutes to get to the gas station. The one car that passed them going in the opposite direction simply swerved to get out of the way of the wing, and the crusty old-timer who filled them up knew better than to ask any questions when they paid in cash. Both of them got out to pee behind the building, then devoured some stale cookies they coaxed out of the station's vending machine. Topped off, Duke took the left seat and taxied back to the feeder road and were airborne twenty minutes after touchdown.

"You were right," Duke said, feeling the tightness of the yoke. "Oswaldo's guys really put this together." He pulled the flaps down and made sure the throttle was pushed full. Full of gas and confidence, they soared into the night sky and left Las Vegas shimmering behind.

Cast your stones into a raging sea,
And they land back on your feet.
Cast your shadows onto the ground,
And you darken all you see.

For the next hour, they flew low enough to follow Interstate 15 through the Utah flatlands up to the intersection with Route 70. Then they turned right and headed east toward Green River. Flying through the mountains at night with no running lights was the trickiest part of the trip. Patting his contraband for inspiration, Duke stayed as close to Interstate 70 as he could. The Western Slope grew hillier and more hazardous as they flew, and when there was no moving traffic he had to guess where the road was. The waning moon, playing hide-and-seek between fast-moving clouds, didn't do much to help. Gusty headwinds swirling in the high country bowls buffeted their progress, and both men had to summon all their courage to withstand the gut-checks of impending doom each time the plane bounced off the bottom of an air pocket. Eventually, they picked up the Colorado River reflections and crossed over Grand Junction, barely making it through the first gauntlet of Rocky Mountain peaks. Then, using the simplest of navigational tools – a compass, watch, and speedometer – they turned north and descended to the elevated plateau around Craig near midnight. Spotting headlights along the meandering Yampa River, they stayed low and followed Route 40 into Steamboat Springs before they were sure of where they were again.

Remy was relieved. "Nice flying, cowboy." City lights illuminated the snow-laden branches of Douglas Fir and Ponderosa Pine. "I thought for sure we was gonna be Christmas ornaments."

Duke checked his watch as they flew over Bob Adams field. A plow truck was working the runway, and there were too many lights on in town to make him comfortable. "I think we better put down in Granby. Don't want to push our luck." He turned southeast along Route 40. "Check the map. I think it's about seventy-five miles if we follow the road."

Remy used his flashlight and traced the route. "We should be good if we stay right over it. Nothing too high on either side except right before we get there." He used his finger to calculate the distance. "'Bout five miles out, I'd say." They were passing over a white-blanketed wilderness when he had another thought. "So where're we gonna stay? You know some people there? Looks pretty cold and we're not smuggling Mexican blankets."

Duke felt good to be through a difficult part of the journey and over familiar territory. "What's the matter, swamp boy, left your alligator snow boots home?"

"Aw shit, cut the crap, Rusty. Your red neck ain't goin' to keep you warm around here."

Duke was amused. No one had called him Rusty since he was ten. "Well, I guess you're not going to complain if we sleep indoors."

"Indoors? Where? Not some – " Remy stopped himself midsentence when he remembered. "You're not planning on calling those weirdo hippy friends, are you? What do they call themselves? The STP family?"

"No man, they don't stay here in the winter, but I know where they camp. The other side of the lake is right near the airport. I heard they built some illegal cabins on state land."

"You got to be kidding me, man. How'n the hell we going to land in the middle of the night, walk through the snow, and find some frozen shack in the woods? I'd rather sleep in the plane."

Duke paused for effect. "Okay, well, how about I call a lady I know and she picks us up and take us to her nice warm house?"

Remy wasn't buying it. "Yeah, sure. You take the front, and I get the back."

"Janice might like that."

"You fibbing me?"

"No, man. I've popped in on her before." Duke patted his stash pocket. "She knows I never show up empty-handed."

"Sheeet, you dog!"

Other than the windsock, Granby Airport looked like an undeveloped side street on the outside of town. The midnight moon illuminated enough of the runway that they were able to touch down and stop without bumping into anything. They were putting on their coats and bundling up for the trek to refuge when the headlights of a car stopped in front of them. Duke squinted through the glare, and panicked when he saw a rack of police lights on top.

"Shit! Play it cool," he gasped.

"I've got my gun." Remy showed him. "Got an extra one for you." He rummaged through his carrying bag.

"Let's hope we don't have to use them."

A lone officer got out of the car and knocked on the window of the plane. "You boys okay? I heard you coming in and thought you might be in trouble." He shined a flashlight into the cabin and saw Duke's face.

Duke squeezed the piece Remy had handed him and held it in his lap. "Evening, Officer," he mouthed through the window and waved with his free hand. "We're okay."

The cop trained his light on the poorly concealed welds that Oswaldo's men had slopped paint over. He ducked under the modified wing and inspected the foot-high call letters all aircraft are required to display. It was too cold to take out his pad to write down the number-letter sequence, but easy to remember as a mnemonic. AM12BE, he repeated silently. Movement inside the cabin caused the plane to shift on its struts and the officer had to make some quick decisions. It wasn't hard to figure out why a customized airplane might want to land on a small, unlit runway in the middle of a cold night; smuggling activity in his territory was an open secret. His real concern were who was involved.

The door opened, and Duke popped his head out. "Good evening, Officer," he re-greeted. "Great to be back in Granby." Duke wriggled out of the cabin and stood facing him with his hand in his pocket.

The officer calmly held his own hand close to his gun as they engaged in conversation. "Where you all headed?" he asked cautiously.

"Nowhere," Duke answered, sizing up his opponent. "We were supposed to get here sooner, but you know how the weather is."

The officer's mind was alive with possibilities. "I suppose."

Remy moved closer to the open door but stayed in the plane with his gun ready.

The officer acknowledged him. "Your friend planning on sleeping in there? I'd appreciate it if he came out and introduced himself." Tensions rose at the mention of instructions. "And by the way, what's your name? I've never seen you in these parts before?"

Duke played it cool. "Name's Duke, Duke Dunn. We don't get out here too often. How long you been on the force?"

"I'll ask the questions if you don't mind."

Remy hopped down and faced the officer silently. The officer lit his face with his flashlight, but Remy didn't blink.

"Where do you plan on going now? Everyone around here's in for the night except for a few regulars at the tavern," the officer said.

"Janice Redding one of them?" Duke asked. "She's expecting us."

The officer knew the name. "Well, I don't know who's still drinking, but we can go see." He sized up his collars. "Why don't you come with me and we can check if that friend of yours is there? The tavern's not far from here."

"I know," Duke told him. "Granby's a small town. We were thinking we'd have to walk there, but seeing how you're offering, a ride sounds like a much better way to go."

Remy knew how Duke operated and didn't need to be convinced. He made sure the door was firmly shut, shouldered the stash bag, and slid into the back seat of the patrol car. Duke turned on the charm. "Sure is nice of you to give us ride, Officer."

The officer was relieved to have them trapped in the back seat of patrol car. He spoke to them through the perforated panel of bulletproof plastic that separated the seats. "Must have been pretty hairy flying in here at this hour. Didn't see any lights on your plane."

Duke knew they were temporarily trapped, but played along. "We managed."

"Where'd you fly in from?"

"Salt Lake; we were at a Mormon Convention."

Officer Walker registered the sarcasm and guided his Plymouth cruiser toward the center of town. "Yeah? You boys with the Latter Day?"

"No, just visiting relatives."

Remy was never comfortable being restricted. He paid careful attention to where they were going so he could get back to plane without a guide. Most of the town was iced over and dark so it wasn't hard to notice when they passed the one establishment that appeared to be open.

Duke saw it too. "Is that where we're going?" he asked cautiously.

"That's Granby's Dam," the officer said as they glided past the tavern, "but I don't think Janice is drinking there tonight."

"So, where're we heading?"

"Mr. Dunn. May I call you Duke?"

"Er, sure."

"Not much goes on 'round these parts that we law officers don't know about. Catch my drift?"

"Not really, Officer?"

"Oh, that's right, I never introduced myself. I'm Officer Wedge Walker. Now suppose you tell me what you fellows are really up to?"

Duke put his hand on Remy's to prevent him from being trigger-happy. "Like I said, we're just coming to see our old friend, Janice. She's expecting us."

Officer Walker turned down a side street and stopped in front of large frontier house on a corner lot. "Well, I guess her bulbs must've burned out 'cause she forgot to leave the light on for you."

Duke knew the trick and didn't bite. "She doesn't live here anymore. She said to ask for her at the dude ranch."

"She's over at Bar Lazy J? I hadn't heard that. Let's go see." Officer Walker backed up and turned around.

Duke backed up too. "She didn't say she'd be there. I always just go to the bar and call. You know Janice gets around."

"I'll say she does!" Officer Walker and everyone else in town knew that Janice was a lush and there was no telling whose bed she might have wound up in.

"Okay, then let's go to the station. You can call from there."

It was after midnight, and even though Duke didn't like being driven around in a cop car, it was better than traipsing through the snow. "Thank you, Officer, or may I call you Wedge?"

"That depends."

"On what?"

"On whether you're going to level with me."

"About what?"

"About why you'd be flying all the way up here to squeeze a few drops of juice from one of the most overripe fruits this side of the divide."

Duke knew "check" when he heard it. "So how's old Janice doing? You seem to know her well."

"Not much to know; she's been around here for years. Goes from one guy to the next. Last I heard she'd taken up with another lady."

Duke played his hand. "Well, I guess you don't know her as well as I do."

Officer Walker turned around. "Really? What am I missing?"

"Her spiritual side; Janice is a Buddhist."

"Buddhist! Now that's funny. You sure are full of surprises. Now how about you make up a story about that home-built, drug-running plane of yours on the way to the station?"

Duke restrained his partner with a hand signal and said. "Okay, Officer, you got us. We'll tell you everything once we get to the station."

"Darn right you will." Officer Walker wanted to get them locked up before calling the state troopers. He was the only one on duty and didn't want to be outnumbered, so he left them parked in the back seat and called his deputy to help move them.

Duke watched him go inside.

"I knew we shouldn't have gotten into this car," Remy said. "Now what're we going do? Come out shooting?"

"Easy does it; this ain't over yet."

Officer Walker came back to the car and observed protocol. "It'll be a little while before my deputy gets here. You boys need some water or anything?"

"A little water sounds good," Duke said. "And I wouldn't mind taking a piss. We were up in the air a long while and – "

Office Walker was experienced enough to know about how a trip to the men's room might end. "Okay, and I suppose your friend has to go too?"

Remy nodded.

"One at a time then – and let me see your hands before I open the door – both of you!"

Duke and Remy left their guns hidden in the seat and raised their hands.

Officer Walker drew his revolver. "You first," he told Duke, "and please don't try anything funny. We just finished scrubbing the blood off the floor from the last guy who got cute."

"Whatever you say, Officer." Duke went to the men's room, and when he came out he asked, "Can I get my phone call now?"

Officer Walker pointed his pistol to the desk with a phone on it.

"May I?" Duke asked for permission to reach inside his jacket pocket and withdrew the small book of contact numbers he always carried. Finding the entry he was looking for, he dialed and waited.

CHAPTER 22

After winning the talent contest, Rosella and her band had gone to Joel and Nancy's house in Sunshine Canyon to celebrate their victory. Roddy parked Rosella's parents' Pontiac under the ponderosa pines that marked the edge of the turnaround, and they entered the house through the garage door. Rosella, who had been there before, led the way. After dropping their instruments off in the basement den, they went upstairs into the modern mountain home Nancy had bought and decorated with her parents' money. She greeted them with a glass of wine in her hand, and Rosella joined her in a goblet of Chardonnay. Crystal, who had come to the show and shagged a ride with her bosses, said hello from the kitchen. Joel handed Coronas to her, Roddy, and Hipolito.

Comfortable in her role as Nancy's protégé, Rosella took an ownership interest in pointing out the highlights of the large open space. The tiled floor echoed like a museum, and Roddy and Hipolito, who rarely nestled in the bosom of the white middle-class, salivated in the posh atmosphere. The textured plaster, vaulted ceilings, and angular walls were only partially separated into kitchen, living, and eating areas by half walls covered in dark, rounded river stones and topped with granite. Nancy showed off a large oil painting of colorful wedges that shared the vertical space with a giant beaded macramé. Joel pointed out the pounded copper sink and imported tile in the downstairs bathroom, and Crystal was fascinated by the randomly placed objects d'art made from painted pottery and twisted metal. Built-in, stainless steel appliances were integrated into the custom wood cabinets of the food preparation area, and a giant Sub-Zero refrigerator big enough for a small village purred in the kitchen's recessed alcove. Rosella plopped herself on one of the sumptuous leather sofas huddled in front of an elevated masonry hearth, and the others joined her in the tribal circle seating arrangement. Kiln-cast ceramic sconces with perforated sides sprinkled the room in subtle patterns of light, and twinkles of celestial illumination trickled through the skylights. "You guys were great tonight!" Nancy complimented the band. "So much better than the last time I heard you."

"Thanks!" Rosella beamed. "We've been practicing a lot."

"Where'd you learn to use a bull whip?" Joel asked.

"Hippy taught me."

Joel was unnerved by Hipolito, whom he had never met before. "Where'd *you* learn?" he asked, not really wanting to know.

Roddy answered for him. "Hippy grew up on a farm."

Hipolito's toothy grin revealed the yellow teeth and crude silver fillings of his origins. Crystal, who had been raised in a white Presbyterian neighborhood in the suburbs of Chicago, caught a whiff of the slaughterhouse clinging to Hipolito's clothes and made a trip to the ladies room to change the smell in her nose.

Nancy asked, "Who did your costumes?"

Rosella took credit. "I did. We always dress up for Halloween." She was still wearing the heavy eyeliner, mascara, and the laced bustier she had performed in.

Joel tried to keep his gaze away from her bust and asked, "Who does the writing? Who makes up the words?"

"We all do," Roddy answered. "Rosella usually comes up with the idea and then we see what fits in with the music. Should I get the guitars and show you?"

"That's a great idea. A private concert!"

Nancy excused herself and clacked up the exposed concrete stairs in stylish leather boots. Watching her, Roddy and Hipolito couldn't understand why people with enough money for carpeting had elected to leave the steps uncovered. Looking forward to some late-night fun, Joel finished off his beer and raided the pantry for another bottle of wine. He solicited Crystal's opinion on her choice of vintage and filled Roddy's and Hipolito's order for two more Coronas. It wasn't their usual gathering of invited guests, but Joel and Nancy rarely partied anymore and knew that sharing the wealth was good for employee retention. Rosella joined Joel and Crystal in another glass, and they nibbled on pretzels and talked about work while waiting for Nancy's return. Roddy and Hipolito, who didn't know anything about Buddhism or vegetarian diets, were satisfied to just listen and drink free beer.

Nancy came back downstairs in her house robe and made herself a cup of green tea. "I have to get up early tomorrow," she explained her appearance. "Lots of party orders." She sipped her tea, let Joel make conversation with their guests, and eventually said, "Stay as long as you like; just save some energy for tomorrow," and padded back upstairs to her bedroom.

Joel knew that a concert in the living room would keep her up, so he directed the gathering downstairs to the den. Roddy and Hipolito were happy to be reunited with their instruments and started tuning while Joel, Rosella, and Crystal found spots in the sectional sofa. Rosella led the trio through a few rowdy standards, and the admixture of Friday night fun and Buddhist precepts fused together with the aid of alcohol and acoustic guitars. The volume increased as the night wore on, and Nancy fell asleep listening to the downstairs ruckus of a cleverly reworded parody of Guan Tanamara.

Wanton tomato,
I'm just a wanton tomato.

You need a wanton toe-may-toe,
To make your salsa hot.
One-ton tomato,
You need a one-ton tomato,
I've got a one-ton toe-may-toe,
To fill my salsa pot.

Everyone sang along, and after some hearty laughs, Roddy and Hipolito put down their instruments. Still wired from the excitement, Joel's evangelical streak emerged. He got into a long conversation with Roddy about the spiritual benefits of being a Buddhist, demonstrated how to sit in the lotus asana, and showed the proper way to breathe. Imitating his example, Roddy was surprised at how quickly it cleared the beer fog from his brain. Rosella joined them, seizing the opportunity to strike another busty pose, but Crystal just lay back in the cushions, sipped her wine, and watched through half-closed eyelids. Hipolito took the opportunity to go outside to smoke a cigarette.

While they we sitting in meditative repose, Joel assumed the role of spiritual guide. "Spine straight," he commanded. "Deep breath in. Hold. Exhale."

Roddy and Rosella followed his instructions.

"Now imagine that your spine is a straw whose end is inside a glass of blue liquid. Every time you breathe in, the fluid in the glass is sucked up to the top of your head. When you exhale, the fluid runs back out again."

Rosella knew how to do it already and secretly let some of the energy collect in her second chakra before transmuting it. Roddy had trouble at first, but got the hang of it with a few more tries.

"Now let's try something different," Joel continued. "This time, when you breathe in, imagine the straw is filling with yellow sunshine from the top. When you exhale, it gets released back to the sky the same way it came in."

Following Joel, they repeated the pranayama exercise several times, then lapsed into concentrated silence. Crystal closed her eyes and drifted off with them. The mountain air was still, the house was creaky but quiet, and the distant hiss of 3:00 a.m. buzzed in their ears. Hipolito came back and thought they were all sleeping, and before he could catch it, the screen door slammed shut and startled them awake.

"I never felt like that before," Roddy said as he stretched his legs out. "That was good. You have to try this sometime, Hippy."

Hipolito was still buzzed from beer and tobacco. "Sure thing, man. Try what?"

"Joel just taught us a special way to sit and breathe." He demonstrated.

"I think my uncle knows how to do that; only he snores when he's on siesta."

Rosella laughed and corrected him. "We weren't sleeping; we were meditating."

Hipolito picked up his guitar again. "Okay, whatever. Wanna play some more?"

Roddy got up and retrieved his instrument. "Sure thing, man. I feel liberated. Come on Rosy, get your cowgirl back on."

Joel vaguely remembered the name of the band had something to do with cows. "What's the name of your group again? What do you call yourselves?"

"We're the Cowboy Liberation Army!" Roddy strummed for emphasis.

"How did you come up with that name?"

Roddy loved the question. "Well, you know where we work?"

Joel looked confused. "Rosella works for us at the restaurant."

"Part time," Roddy corrected him. "The rest of the time she works at the slaughterhouse with me and Hippy," he said without seeing anything wrong.

Rosella cringed. "I told Nancy I had another job," she said defensively.

"Yes, I know," Joel said, trying to hide his shock. "Everyone needs to make a living."

"My mother works there too," Rosella explained. "I go to the office a few days a week to help her."

Roddy picked up the story. "That's how we met. My mother works for the Lombardis – they own the business. That's how I got the job on the line."

"The line?" Joel asked. He didn't know anything about slaughterhouses and couldn't believe he was even asking about them. Even though he had only been a vegetarian for a few years, the thought of killing animals made him feel wrong.

Roddy knew that what they did might be shocking to an outsider, so he tried to make it more relatable. "I just bring the cows in from the pen," he explained. "I love them." Then he told Joel the story about how some of the cows escaped and how he and Hipolito helped them. "We thought about what it would be like if everyone got together to set the animals free. That's how we became The Cowboy Liberation Army."

Rosella picked up the thread. "All our songs are about freedom; freedom and liberation. Isn't that what Buddhists believe in?"

"They do," Joel agreed, "but Buddhists are against killing animals." He looked at Hipolito skeptically. "What does *he* do there?"

Rosella answered, "Hippy works on the line, but I don't know if you want to hear what his job is."

Never chatty, Hipolito simply said, "I'm a skinner. They're mostly dead by the time they get to me."

"Mostly?"

Rosella gave permission. "Go ahead, Hippy. Joel can handle the truth."

"Well, sometimes the knockout box – they don't want to waste electricity so it doesn't work so good. I try to do my job fast so they don't feel it."

Fully awake, Crystal gasped at the graphic truth. "That's horrible!"

Painful images of bovine suffering filled their collective imagination. Joel's righteous indignation was overstimulated, and no one felt like playing music anymore.

Rosella emptied the last dribbles of wine into her glass. "Looks like we may need another bottle."

Crystal swallowed whatever she had left in one gulp. Making eye contact and a hand signal, she asked Joel for permission to break out a joint.

Her pleading eyes reminded Joel of a suffering animal, and he responded by saying, "I'll go get another bottle of wine." He didn't want to cross the green line with employees, but he was so upset by the slaughterhouse conversation he welcomed the idea, tacitly giving his approval by saying, "Make yourselves comfortable," before leaving.

Much to the band's delight, Crystal lit up as soon as he left. She passed the joint around, and by the time Joel returned with an open bottle, the room was filled with smoke. Joel got a contact high from the marijuana relief therapy, and the conversation drifted into plotting revenge on the bloodthirsty, misguided, and commercialized bastards that were driving Western society to the brink of self-destruction. They petered out by 4:00 a.m., but before they called it a night, Crystal, subtly vying with Rosella for feminine attention, sent Joel to bed horny.

After Joel left, the guests turned off the lights and rustled quietly into the dim light of early morning. Roddy and Rosella's unguarded intimacy, unlit by the darkness and unmuffled by the leather cushions of the adjacent couch, encouraged Hipolito to try to get Crystal to join their chorus of breathy grunts and creaking springs. Crystal was repulsed and resisted Hipolito's advances with stiff shoulders and mosquito swipes. Frustrated, Hipolito drained another beer and then his erection before passing out. Crystal barely slept, and was wide awake when Nancy, still married to her work schedule, came down and saw the guests sprawled out on the basement sofas in a mess of blankets and pillows at 7:00 a.m. The lingering smells, empty bottles, and used ashtray were all the clues she needed to deconstruct the evening, and by the time she drove down the canyon and opened the restaurant, Crystal had sneaked upstairs to see if Joel was awake.

SATURDAY, OCTOBER 28, 1978

CHAPTER 23

The snow in the higher elevations had been restricted to news-casts, and by the time sunrise was less than an hour old, the traces of frost that remained on the ground in Boulder were hiding in morning shadows. Donna's cat was perched on the kitchen counter watching the birds at the feeder while she and Jon waited out the early morning thaw under a down comforter. Sexually satisfied, they kept their hands to themselves and allowed their minds to wander out of bed before their bodies. Donna had a full day of baking ahead of her and wasn't looking forward to being covered in sweat and flour. Her mind went numb trying to calculate how long it would take to make the forty trays of fresh pastry that were supposed to be delivered by six o'clock. Jon was on a musician's schedule and didn't have anywhere to be until the afternoon. He knew Donna would be working, so he planned on having some coffee, toking up, and playing guitar at her house before going back to his room at the hotel. The rest of the college neighborhood was on the same, hung-over, post-Friday-night schedule, and the occasional car rumbling through the quiet streets on its way to a weekend seminar or service job was in no hurry to get there.

Marco, who was still lying in Cynthia's bed a few blocks away, was anxious to get to the studio to continue his apprenticeship. He wasn't sure how to leave, but Cynthia, who was much more experienced with one-nighters, facilitated his exit gracefully.

"You can use the bathroom first," she said, putting on an unflattering full-length flannel robe. "Want some tea or coffee?"

Marco was relieved there was no romance in her heart and said, "Coffee would be great," without budging. Dennis was expecting him first thing, and the thought of stripping wires, soldering connectors, and twisting the dials of the dual-trace oscilloscope excited him. He was lost in thought, trying to remember the principles of a linear frequency scale when Cynthia brought him a hot mug. He said, "Thanks," but looked bewildered.

She thought his confused look meant that he wanted to start a conversation about their relationship, so she said, "I can put some more honey in that if you want." Marco wasn't the best lay she had had that month, but at least he was harmless. Her phone rang, and she added, "I'll go get dressed now," hoping the idea would accelerate his departure.

After she hung up, Marco asked, "What time are you going to work today?"

"I'm going in early because we have to get ready for the party tonight."

"What party? Where?"

"At the studio; I told you. Duke gave us a budget to throw a Halloween party tonight. There're going to be some cool people there."

"But there's going to be a big bash at the Boulderado tonight. I think everyone's going *there*."

Cynthia came back already dressed. "We know. That's kind of what gave us the idea. Everyone in town will be at the hotel, and then the special people – the ones we like – will come to the studio afterwards." She pulled the bedcovers off and scolded him, "Time to get up, lazy boy. Dennis and Walter are probably at the studio already. This is only your second day so better show up early. Plus, I don't want them to blame me if you're late."

Naked, Marco squirmed with embarrassment as the blankets disappeared. He hopped out of bed and pulled his pants on as quickly as possible. When he was all dressed, they both paused at the idea of hugging. "Want me to give you a ride?" he offered, lacing his sneakers.

"No thanks, I've got some things to do around here before I go." Cynthia moved toward the living room so he would follow her. "You go ahead and I'll see you later." She held the front door open.

Marco's good-bye kiss landed on her cheek, and he made it down the hill to the studio in a few minutes. Diane buzzed him in, and he went directly to the control room where Dennis and Walter were already working.

"Good afternoon," Dennis greeted him lying on his back under the console. "Have some fun last night?"

"Hi, sorry I'm late. Yeah, we had a good time," Marco admitted. "I thought you were going to come."

"I got out of here too late. How was the show?"

"Jon played his twelve-string acoustic and got second place."

Dennis shifted positions. "So I heard. Do me a favor, hand me those pliers."

Marco crouched down to hand them to him. "How'd you know?"

"Cynthia and Diane already talked this morning."

"Well, I guess there're no secrets around here." Marco shrugged and took off his jacket. "So where do you want me to start?"

Walter handed him a nest of thin twenty-four-gauge wires that were once a twelve-foot-long snake. "Here you go, Marconi. Straighten these out. Every kink is a problem waiting to happen."

Marco bent the delicate wires to his will, while Walter and Dennis were occupied with more serious tasks.

CHAPTER 24

Nancy was the first one to get to work, and the core kitchen crew was complete when Jampo, who always gave Tara a ride, arrived. Jampo lit the oven to give it time to warm up, then hefted the heavy bags of whole-wheat flour, rice, and cornmeal from the storage room to the mixer. Tara put on her favorite meditation tape and began the tedious job of peeling and slicing the fresh apples for the turnovers Donna would be baking. As assistant chef, she had to pre-grease pans and stack them so Donna would have room to knead, roll, fill, and fold. Nancy, who, despite owning a restaurant, didn't like to get her hands dirty or cook, went to the office to organize paperwork and look over the bank statement. In keeping with Buddhist principles, conversation was kept to a minimum.

Tenzin the dishwasher usually didn't come in until breakfast was being served, because that barely left him enough time for his early morning rituals. His trip down the mountain to Boulder took over an hour, so he had to get up by 5:00 a.m. in order to meditate before doing his monastic chores. Having renounced his worldly possessions, he rode the high-mileage Volkswagen van that shuttled residents of the monastery into town every morning for work, shopping, and personal business. Some of the riders stayed at the Dorje Dzong Buddhist Temple where the bus ended its commute, while others, like Tenzin, walked a few blocks to their daytime destinations and returned in time for the evening trip back up the mountain. Originally from Tibet, Tenzin had been living at the Punkah Monastery since it was established ten years earlier. Everyone at the restaurant liked him, though his vow of silence made him hard to get to know.

Chodya, who was in her second year of nunhood, was also a resident of the Punkah Monastery. Along with Tenzin, she frequently rode the Dharma Bus into Boulder to her part-time job at the Dorje Dzong Temple, located a few blocks from the Boulderado Hotel. Born on a farm in upstate New York and used to manual labor, Chodya helped maintain the temple grounds, and when she wasn't wielding a rake or shovel, served as liaison between the Tibetan-speaking monks and English-speaking visitors. Like most Western converts, the deprivations and disciplined behavior of Buddhist culture didn't come naturally to her, and she was still in the process of deciding which vows she could live with. She and Tenzin shared the silent commiseration of menial task workers, but because he never spoke, Chodya had no idea how far advanced Tenzin actually was.

When Tenzin showed up at the Satsang Diner, a stack of dirty mixing bowls and dough-covered utensils was already piled up next to the washbasin. He greeted his kitchen-mates with a slight bow and namasté hands, then hung his thin jacket on a hook and filled the soaker sink with hot water. His mumbled mantra, the only conscious sound he ever made with his mouth, blended seamlessly with the background meditation tape and rinse water.

Tara, the only early morning waitress, served morning chai, herb tea, flat breads, and fruit cakes to the scatter of regular customers, and it wasn't until nine o'clock that the usual sampling of Friday night revelers showed up for Saturday morning repentance breakfast. The Satsang didn't serve bacon or sausage, and many of its regular customers didn't eat eggs or dairy, so very few of the non-Buddhists who came in were drawn by the menu. Stir-fried vegetables over quinoa, masala dosa, lentil naan, and spicy string hoppers were destination foods for acquired-tastes only, so when

Tara approached the table of bleary-eyed frat rats, she was not too surprised at their confusion.

"What do you mean you don't have regular coffee? This is a breakfast place, isn't it?"

"Yes, it is," Tara answered politely. "We serve breakfast, lunch, and dinner. Would you like to try some hot roasted chicory? It tastes very similar to coffee."

"You don't have coffee?" one of the diners asked incredulously. "I told you guys we should have gone to the Aristocrat."

"I'll try some of that chickadee stuff," another diner said. "How bad could it be?"

"One hot chicory," Tara noted on her pad.

"I'm hungry," another said. "What do you have to eat here that's good? I want something to make me feel *spiritual*." His buddies tittered at the idea.

"Spirituality is in all of us," Tara answered calmly. "Most people like the string hoppers. They're kind of like spaghetti."

"Spaghetti for breakfast? Yech! Will that make me holy?"

"They come with a nice coconut sauce," Tara explained. "They're really good – and filling."

One of the young men remembered that his uncle told him to trust the recommendations of plump waitresses. "Okay, sold," he said. "String hoppers for me. How many do you get? I'm starving."

"There're four per plate, but you can always order more."

"What do you have that cures a hangover?" one of the other wiseasses asked.

Tara was used to the question. "Banana and orange juice lassi is very popular, but most people just drink water to clean themselves out."

"Water all around then."

"Three filtered waters," Tara repeated.

"Can't I just get regular Boulder tap water?"

"We filter our water with arsenic minerals and activated charcoal. It's the only way to remove the impurities."

They shuddered at the mention of arsenic. "Okay, I guess. What else is good here?"

Tara pointed to menu board. "We've got all sorts of egg dishes with vegetarian bacon or sausage, and I really like the pancakes."

"Now we're talking! Pancakes and eggs for me."

One of the frat boys had a second thought and asked, "Are they regular pancakes or – "

Tara smiled and folded her arms under her substantial bust. "Now where do you think you are?" she sassed. "All our food is organic, and the pancakes are too."

"So you can put some fresh blueberries in mine?"

"Of course. Do you want the whole grain or rice meal pancakes?"

Neither sounded good. "Well, maybe I'll just have the eggs. They're from chickens, right?"

A regular at the next table who had been listening to the conversation couldn't resist interjecting. "Oh Tara, can I have another order of turtle eggs? This time with mustard seed relish."

Tara smiled at the joke and played along. "We're out of the snapper eggs, but the mallards' taste very similar."

The frat boys were rattled. "Don't you have anything normal around here? Maybe some tea and toast?"

"What kind of tea would you like? Chamomile? Licorice? Maybe some Darjeeling?"

"Lipton?"

"No, sorry," Tara apologized.

"What kind of toast is there?"

Tara realized this was going poorly and tried to be extra friendly. "We don't have plain old white bread, but the toasted naan with ghee is really good. That's what most people order."

The nearby regular customer delighted in upsetting outsiders. "You guys should try the salted ghee; it's made from yak milk. They import it all the way from Tibet."

One of the college students pushed his chair back abruptly and stood. "That's it! I'm outta here. I'll be over at the Aristocrat. They've got an all-you-can-eat scrambled egg breakfast with greasy home fries. You guys can stay here if you want."

The other two followed suit. "Scratch the whole order please. I guess we came to the wrong place."

"There are no coincidences," someone said as they walked out the front door.

Donna came in through the back just before ten. Preternaturally relaxed from last night's tantric orgasm, she carefully hung her coat and put her apron on.

It wasn't the first time she had come in late after a hard night, and Jampo noticed. "Good afternoon, sunshine," he joked. "I see your flower has already risen," he punned.

Donna smiled as she stood in front of the work table stacked with empty baking pans, mixing bowls, and utensils.

"Tenzin made sure they were all nice and clean for you," Jampo said sympathetically. "I put the rest of the ingredients on the bottom shelf."

Donna bent down to look and count, and Tara was in front of her when she stood back up.

"What happened to you?" Tara asked. "You look strange."

"Namasté," was all Donna could say.

"That boyfriend of yours, the musician, what's his name?"

"Jon."

"No, his other name. Something creepy like a disease."

"You mean Cells? You think that's creepy?"

"Ew!" Tara hesitated while conjuring up images. "He's such an animal. Look at you!"

"Jealous?" Donna guessed correctly.

Nancy came in from the office with the order pad. "Well, I'm glad you finally made it in," she told Donna. "I was beginning to worry. We've got all these orders to fill. I hope you don't have plans tonight because we might be here late."

Jampo tried to soften the confrontation. "The ovens are already hot, and we're not that busy. I can keep an eye on the baking while Donna preps."

"That's very nice of you, Jampo," Nancy said, looking down at her list, "but everyone's going to have to pitch in to fill all these orders."

Tara had planned on going to the Halloween party at the hotel. "So when do we expect Joel and Crystal and Rosella to come in?" she asked.

Nancy's intuition cringed. "Uh, they'll be along soon. You three keep working, and I'll make sure no one's car broke down or anything." She went back to her office and phoned home.

Crystal answered in a sleepy voice on the fourth ring. "Hello?"

Nancy didn't recognize the voice. "Who's this?"

"Uh, Crystal. Who's this?"

"Crystal! Why are you answering my phone? This is Nancy! Where's Joel?"

Crystal rolled over in Nancy's bed and saw that it was after ten o'clock. "Joel's in the kitchen," she lied smoothly. "Rosella and the others are still asleep."

Joel, who had heard the phone ring, came in from the bathroom in his robe. He mouthed, "Who is it?"

Crystal's eyes bugged out, and she covered the receiver while mouthing, "Nancy!"

Joel took the phone from her. "Good morning, dear. How's it going?"

"Where are you?"

"Downstairs. I'll have everyone there in a half hour. Restaurant busy?"

Nancy heard her bedside alarm clock go off. "Don't lie to me. What are you doing upstairs?"

Joel turned off the alarm. "I moved the alarm downstairs so everyone could hear it. I'll put it back tonight. Are you okay, sweetheart?"

Nancy always got suspicious when Joel called her sweetheart. "No, I'm not okay. We've got all these orders to fill and half our staff is asleep at our house. After you're done flirting with Crystal, please get your asses down here. We'll talk about this later." She slammed the phone down, caught sight of herself in the mirror, and for a moment, missed her pre-Buddhist life of privileged partying.

CHAPTER 25

Saturday morning broke clear and bright in the thin air of Steamboat Springs. Officer McKnight's wife's exit from the house had awakened Agent Walker, but he didn't get off the couch and fold the blankets until thirty minutes later. There was a pot of hot coffee and some defrosted donuts on the table, and he was sipping himself awake in the kitchen when Officer McKnight joined him at eight-thirty.

"Sorry I slept in," Officer McKnight apologized. "Long day yesterday."

Agent Walker squinted at the snowy blanket, amplified to blinding by the early morning rays. "Might be a longer one today," he said, closing his eyes. The sputtering hiss of the coffee pot made him think of the sweat lodge his paternal grandfather had taken him to when he was a child. Dreamstate phantoms still haunted him with images of bloodstained snow and broken tree limbs. He wasn't sure how the plane crash and cattle mutilations were connected, but his intuition insisted they were.

Officer McKnight, a wholesome Scot who wasn't gifted with Native American vision, respected Agent Walker's process. His own musings were limited to reassembling the crash site clues so they would conform to standard Agency protocol: Cause of accident – unknown, cause of death or injury – trauma from impact, status of personnel – one presumed dead. He turned on the radio to hear the weather report.

"Gonna be a beauty for all you lucky skiers today!" the announcer stated. "We usually have to wait a month to see conditions like this, but we've got plenty of sun, temperatures warming into the fifties, and ten new inches of the freshest powder Colorado has to offer. Welcome to the first good snow of the season! You'll find whatever you need to attack the slopes at the Howelsen Basin rental shop, and plenty of good times waiting back in town."

"Is that an advertisement or the regular broadcast?" Agent Walker asked.

Officer McKnight knew what he was talking about. "Money talks, my friend, and guess who owns the local radio station? Jim Temple."

"You're kidding. How did that happen?"

"You know Jim. Nothing's changed except – " Officer McKnight stopped himself.

"Except what?"

"Except we're not sure where he's getting the money from."

"Well, I know he doesn't come from money; he had to borrow a car to go out on a date when we were in college, and I had to spot him twenty more than once back in the day."

"Exactly. That's why we checked his financial records as best we could. He paid off the personal loan at a local bank three years ago, and the outfit in Denver that financed the ski basin property said he'd paid them off too. He bought the radio station last year."

"Well, I'll be. Old Jim Temple finally made good on his promise."

"Promise?"

"He told me over drinks one night a long time ago that he'd own this town. Looks like he does now!"

Officer McKnight, who lived in Steamboat full time, didn't like the sound of that. "Well, he does own a hefty chunk, I'll give you that, but we don't *all* work for him – yet."

"Yet? Don't tell me he's going to run for mayor."

"Didn't you see the posters in the lobby of the hotel?"

Agent Walker started to see the problem that Officer McKnight and other officials had been wrestling with for the past few years. "So who's behind him? And what do they want?"

"Beats me." They ran out of speculative ideas by 9:00 a.m. and left for the office. Driving, Officer McKnight asked, "When do you think we'll see Farah and your new guy?"

Agent Walker checked his watch. "They're probably awake by now. I guess it all depends on how fast the Carters can get them to the field." He put the sun visor down to shield his eyes from the intense white glow. "Nice high pressure; they shouldn't have any problems once they get up in the air." He lowered his window to connect to his environment, but was greeted with the smell of gasoline fumes from snow-removal equipment. Steamboat's love-hate relationship with snow was a winter-long affair. It was good for the ski business, but hard on the people who made a living from it. Metal plows scraped the pavement with shrill rasps, sputtering snowblowers tore through the tranquility, and Agent Walker closed his window to block out the high-pitched whining of cars trying to spin themselves to freedom.

The walkway in front of the municipal building had already been cleared, so Officer McKnight parked the Volvo on the street and led Agent Walker through the lobby and down one flight of stairs to his office. He was a little surprised to see Margaret Strothers at her desk already. "Good morning Margaret," he greeted. "I didn't think you'd be plowed out so soon."

"Good morning, Officer McKnight. The guys in town did our road to make sure our boarders could get to the slopes early. Lord knows we need them to buy lift tickets and rent equipment."

"I see. How many did you put up last night?"

"Six of them, but two were kids. The kids slept on the living room sofas. We put the two couples in the downstairs den on the foldaways. It wasn't bad. They were real nice. We stayed up with them and played some cards before going to bed. George couldn't believe how much they paid us."

"You remember Agent Walker," Officer McKnight said, making the reintroduction.

"Of course. How do you do, sir?" Margaret got up, shook his hand, and opened the door to Officer McKnight's office. "Not too often we get important visitors around here."

"Any news?" Officer McKnight asked.

"The machine picked up a few messages about UFOs from the usual nuts, but nothing from Denver or National. Josh Carter called right before you came in. He said his overnight guests were on their way home, whatever that means."

"So nothing from search and rescue?"

"Not yet." She looked at the wall clock. "Bobby usually calls in by noon." Margaret's phone rang. Before answering, she asked, "Is that all? You folks have coffee yet?"

Officer McKnight waved her off and closed the door behind him.

Agent Walker stood next to an awning window that opened to the level of the sidewalk. The basement office was safe and warm in the cold weather, but the snow drifts blocked everything but the light. He thought about the view from his own office and realized he wasn't going to be comfortable until he was above ground – high above ground in clear skies.

Officer McKnight sat at his desk and arranged some papers. "I was working on a flow chart last night." He spread out one of the maps that he had left there. "This is as far as I got before I drove out to Craig."

Agent Walker stood over his shoulder and watched.

"I checked with Aspen and Telluride, then merged their data with ours. We've got a pretty good idea of where Agent Dobson was all day Saturday. He stopped for gas at Sardy about two hours before we lost him, so we know he didn't run out of fuel. The illegal field near Kremmling was socked in, so if he were tracking someone, it would have taken some fancy flying to follow them in there."

"Agent Dobson was a damn good pilot."

"True, that's what makes this all the more strange. Something must have happened."

Agent Walker studied the data. "What about the strips we don't know about? He had been complaining about how good the smugglers were getting at disguising them as construction sites."

"It's a real problem; the more people we have moving into the mountains, the more building we have. We really don't have enough manpower to keep track of all the permits and visit all the sites regularly. These are the areas where we've had the most uninspected activity." He pointed out.

Even though the satellite photos were clear, it was impossible to know the composition or purpose of the irregularly shaped dashes of color. "So it's fair to say that we have no idea where he was headed when those trees got in the way?" Agent Walker asked.

"Not exactly. We have a pretty decent network of ground intelligence now. Bobby visited some of the good people up there, and they gave him a few leads. That's how he found the wreckage." Officer McKnight changed overviews. "Here's a recent satellite photo of Estes Park, and this might be a landing site near Trail Ridge Road. Our informers haven't reported any comings or goings out of Granby for two months, so we're thinking the smugglers might have started to use another field. This is their season, so they must be landing somewhere."

Agent Walker digested the information and scanned the written report. He didn't want to see Agent Dobson's remains, but the mystery of the tracks around the base of the tree aroused his instincts. "When do you think we'll see the photos?"

"Bobby's not due back until tomorrow. There's a friendly in the area with a good short wave but no way to see the pics until we get them developed."

Agent Walker wasn't satisfied with the answer. There were too many loose ends, and he felt a personal obligation to determine the fate of his colleague. "You say there might be an illegal field there?"

"Near here." Officer McKnight pointed at the map. "About fifteen miles from where Agent Dobson went down."

"How long is it?"

"Short; probably only a couple of hundred feet. Why?"

"Think we could put the Cessna down there?"

Officer McKnight was surprised at the idea. "I don't really know; never thought about it. It's probably pretty rough, and I'd rather not break a strut there. I'm sure it's covered with snow so that makes it doubly dangerous."

Agent Walker saw his point. "You think we could drive there somehow?"

"It'd be a hard drive, even in my Travelall. We'd have to go far out of the way to get there by road. Why not stick to the original plan and just do a flyover?" Officer McKnight tried to soothe the consternation on Agent Walker's face. "Bobby's really good; he knows how to do his job. He'll get you all the pics and information you need for the report. I'm sorry about Agent Dobson too, but there's nothing we can do for him now. I'm glad we didn't have to wait till summer to find the body, so let's not risk too much on the recovery."

They heard Margaret answer her phone. "Call for Agent Walker on line one," she said through the intercom.

"Send it in," Officer McKnight answered and handed Agent Walker the phone.

"Hello, Agent Walker speaking."

"Gooood morning, boss. How's things at headquarters?"

"Good morning, Agent Falin. We're working. Where are you now?"

"Ms. Farah and I are at the bustling Craig airport. Beautiful day out today. I could get used to this."

"When are you planning on taking off?"

229

"Soon; that's why I'm calling. We can be outta here in like ten minutes, provided I can get clearance from the tower." Agent Falin pretended to cover the phone. "Hey, Tom? Mind if I take off now?" He waited a beat for comedic effect. "Okay, thanks. Guess I'm cleared for takeoff, sir!"

Agent Walker wasn't in the mood for levity. He checked his watch and said, "Good, here's what I want you to do: Have them top you off at Craig, and we'll meet you at the field. Just follow the river east and approach from the north. Shouldn't take you more than thirty minutes."

"Over the river and through the woods," Agent Falin repeated in singsong. Farah, who was developing an appreciation for Agent Falin's irreverence, smiled, but his carefree attitude annoyed Agent Walker.

"Agent Falin," Agent Walker addressed him formally. "Please confirm your understanding of the plan."

"Yes, sir! Take off now, fly to Steamboat, land. What about my passenger?"

Agent Walker had forgotten about that wrinkle. "Yes, we'll have to get Farah a ride into town. Thanks for reminding me."

"Roger and out!"

"See you soon." Agent Walker hung up and addressed Officer McKnight. "Can you call one of Jim's people and have them pick Farah up? I'm sure they need her at the basin."

"Will do."

Agent Walker went back to the maps and mysteries while Officer McKnight made a phone call. They left contact instructions with Margaret, headed out to the airport, and were sitting in their car when Agent Falin touched down and taxied toward them. He left the prop running while Farah exited.

"Good day, gentlemen," Farah greeted them cheerfully, her hair pulled back in a fresh ponytail, her down jacket unzipped.

"Lovely weather we're having!" she said, stretching her arms and twisting her torso to realign her spine.

"Good morning, Farah. Jim's sending someone out to pick you up."

"So I heard. Great day for skiing and all that, but I'd rather be up in the sky looking for aliens." She put her thumbs through the belt loops on her jeans and showed off the handmade silver buckle in the shape of a UFO. "Sure you don't need my help? I know how to speak their language."

"Well, that's a mighty fine offer," Agent Walker said patiently, "but we're not looking for little green men today."

"Never know when you might bump into one though."

"That's true," Agent Walker humored her, "but it's a risk we take every day."

Agent Falin revved the engine, temporarily drowning out the conversation while he wheeled the Cessna back toward the runway. The rumble of big snow tires on the airport service road announced the arrival of the Howelsen Basin transport van.

Seeing the van approach, Farah said, "Well, I guess this means a girl's got work to do."

"We'll see you up there," Officer McKnight consoled her. "Give us a wave from the top of the chairlift."

Farah was halfway in the van when she suggested an afterplan. "What time are you gents getting back tonight? There's a big Halloween party down in Boulder. My sister said it was going to be awesome. Maybe you guys want to give me a lift over there later? It's not that far. Take a load off?"

Agent Walker was already boarding the Cessna and didn't hear what she said but Officer McKnight appeased her. "Let's see how the day goes."

"Party hardy!" Farah repeated the call of the wild from inside the van.

Officer McKnight, who was the most familiar with the local terrain, rode in the right seat, and Agent Walker spread out his maps, notebook, and binoculars across the back. They cleared Howelsen Mountain and stayed low as Agent Falin steered them over the Trappeur's Crossing construction site in a northeasterly direction. Within minutes, the patchwork of developed parcels, defined by truncated roads and clearcut, gave way to precipitous peaks and craggy conifer forests. They followed a compass vector toward the area of the crash, deviating from their heading for safe passage over and around terrestrial obstructions.

"It'll be on our right at two o'clock in a few minutes," Officer McKnight announced. "Why don't we drift left and circle around so we can make a few passes."

Agent Falin piloted them to the east of their goal and banked the wing so they could see the ground clearly. Officer McKnight readied his camera, looking for signs of disturbance in the treetops. Agent Walker adjusted his field glasses and trained them on the horizon. The bright sun, saturated with white reflections, made it difficult to see anything clearly, and it wasn't until they made a full quarter turn and were looking south that they were able to confirm their exact location relative to the ground. Flying just a few hundred feet above the barren peaks, Agent Falin fought the gusting winds and downdrafts with the yoke and rudder. His spotters were challenged to keep their focus on the land that jiggled through their lenses.

"There!" Officer McKnight said. "See the broken branches?"

"I'm looking," Agent Walker said slowly, "You mean over there?"

They came around to the western side of the target, and a sketchy pattern of sheered limbs seemed to line up.

Agent Falin, who had been on his share of reconnaissance missions, saw it too. "You saying those few broken branches were made by a plane like ours? How do you know it wasn't just wind sheer or the weight of snow on weak limbs?"

"Hard to know for certain until we see the actual wreckage."

Everyone on board kept their eyes on the area, and when they were almost finished with the circle, they received the confirmation they were looking for.

"There!" Officer McKnight pointed. "You see that? That must've come from the wreckage. Maybe the windshield or part of the fuselage. Only something manmade reflects like that."

"Unless it was ice," Agent Falin said skeptically. "Let's have another go-round and take a second look."

"Good idea," Agent Walker agreed. "Did Bobby leave us anything to hone in on? A beacon? A flag? A fire? Something?"

"He usually does; maybe we just haven't seen it yet."

Agent Walker trained his binoculars on the ground. "Where do you think Bobby is now?"

"I don't see him." Officer McKnight said as he played with the focal point of his zoom lens and clicked a few pictures.

Agent Falin spotted movement beneath the trees some distance from where they were. "I think you guys are looking in the wrong place," he said, leveling off and heading north.

The aerial searchers trained their equipment on the side of a steep ravine where a few dark figures could be seen trudging through the high snow. Officer McKnight got eyes on them first. "Congratulations, city slicker," he said. "You've seen your first Rocky Mountain elk. Now can we please go back to where we were?"

"Not so fast," Agent Walker weighed in. "There may be more than a few elk down there."

Agent Falin swooped perilously low and buzzed the canyon. A small herd on unsure footing scattered in desperate leaps at the approaching noise, falling into drifts and rolling down the mountainside in a tangle of flailing legs. Officer McKnight thought it was funny, but as they turned around and watched the wind from the plane kick up a blizzard, Agent Walker saw something else.

"Go back! Go back!" he said excitedly. "Go back; I saw something back there."

Agent Falin put the Cessna on a steep climb and looped around the valley for another pass, this time in the opposite direction. The elk had regrouped at a lower elevation and were moving as fast as they could. A lone figure was following the path they had made through the deep snow.

Officer McKnight was pretty sure it was a human. "That doesn't look like Bobby."

"I don't see any rifle, so it's probably not a hunter," Agent Walker noted as they approached. "Maybe it's an Indian?"

The noise of the plane caused the figure on the ground to hunch down on all fours as they raced by overhead.

"Or maybe a bear?"

Agent Walker immediately thought of what he had seen the day before in Craig and sensed the connection. "We've got to land. Now!" he commanded.

Officer McKnight was surprised at his level of conviction. "We do? Why?"

"I can't explain right now," Agent Walker said, his glasses still trained on the mysterious figure barely visible through the trees. "It's just a gut hunch."

Agent Falin respected intuition. "Where do you want to land?" he asked. "Is there an airport around here – I mean, an actual one?"

"No safe place to land, that's for sure," Officer McKnight answered. "What did you see down there? My camera zoom isn't nearly as good as your binoculars."

"I'm not sure what I saw, but that's not the point. It's what I saw yesterday, combined with what I just saw that makes me think we have to find out more."

Agent Falin understood. "You saying that the weird thing we saw over in Craig is somehow connected to this?"

"That's exactly what I'm saying. Maybe whatever's chasing those elk is the same thing that got Josh Carter's cow."

"And this relates to our mission how?"

"I'm not sure, but I'd like to find out."

Officer McKnight was starting to understand. "Maybe whoever is down there knows why Agent Dobson went down."

"And maybe they know how he wound up in a tree."

"And maybe we can ask him – or it – where the nearest airport is too," Agent Falin said as they soared into the unknown. "Where to now, guys?"

"Let's try the site by Trail Ridge you think may be a landing strip," Agent Walker suggested. "I don't know if we can find the place in the snow, but maybe we can put down."

"How far is that, and in what direction? I'm sure they won't have a windsock."

Officer McKnight checked his map. "It's about fifteen miles from here. Take up a heading of three-four-zero."

"What good will that do?" Agent Falin said as he lined up the compass. "How do you plan on getting back here? I don't see any roads, and whoever or whatever is down there isn't going to wait for us."

Agent Walker was too invested to let go. "Maybe they have snowmobiles we could use. There must be some trails."

Officer McKnight had never seen Agent Walker lose his judgment and tried to cover for him. "With all due respect sir, it might not be such a good idea to land. If there is an illegal field – assuming we can find it and land safely – the people there might not be so friendly. In fact I wouldn't be surprised if they fired on us, and I certainly wouldn't count on them to lend us their snowmobiles." Agent Walker was silent so Officer McKnight continued. "Why not let Bobby do his job? He's up here somewhere, and he'll be able to find out what we need to know. I say let's go back to the crash site, take some pictures, then head back to Steamboat. We don't have the clothes or equipment to go hiking and camping today."

Agent Walker relented. "Okay, we'll let Bobby do the ground-work, but I still want to fly over the Trail Ridge site. Even if we don't land – and I agree it's probably not a good idea – I'd like to see the layout in case we have to go back there for any reason. It's just a hunch, but I'm guessing Agent Dobson knew about that field and was following up on something when he got in trouble."

Agent Falin, feeling the effects of the altitude, agreed. "That sounds like a good idea to me. There's a drink with my name on it back at that tavern we went to yesterday." Surfing the western winds of the jet stream as they rose in elevation, they followed the compass heading toward Milner Pass, and tracking Trail Ridge Road as it passed from Grand to Larimer County, they made it over the pass and down to an open expanse of broken meadows. The terrain was all part of the Roosevelt National Forest, and the icy slit of runway next to Stanley's cluster of buildings was easy to spot because it was next to the only manmade structures in the area. Agent Walker saw someone standing next to the house look-ing up, and another figure behind one of the out buildings. Smoke was rising from the main house, and Officer McKnight took some pictures before a sudden wind turned them around. They didn't want to be seen, so rather than fight the elements and risk detec-tion, they headed back to Steamboat.

CHAPTER 26

Remy and Duke waited for the light of dawn before attempting the most treacherous part of their trip; making it over the Continental Divide at Milner Pass. Their all-night snort with Janice Redding, who had rescued them from Wedge Walker's jail with a saucy combination of bullshit and blackmail, left them wired and alert to the task. She drove them to their airplane in her beat up Saab and waited in her car to make sure the engine started. Remy climbed into the freezing cockpit, got the motor to turn over after a few tries, and blew on his hands for heat. He checked the gages while it was warming up, and Duke knocked the thin layers of icy condensation off the flaps and rear stabilizer with his bare fist. Janice put in a cassette of a band she had heard in Boulder and sang along.

> *Uh oh,*
> *Washing your fingers off with snow-oh.*
> *Taking your time cause you don't know,*
> *Which one of us has to go-oh.*

After several minutes, the plane's RPMs settled into a steady tone and the heater coil started working. It was too cold for long good-byes, so Duke climbed on board and blew Janet a kiss through the foggy window. The prop kicked up loose powder as they inched forward, and Janice drove off with her thank-you payment, anxious to grind out the tension with her roommate.

Remy, who had taken the left seat so Duke could navigate, taxied to the edge of the open field and wheeled around to face the wind. A thin layer of snow had covered the dirt runway, so he aimed to the right of the wind sock, summoned his Cajun guides, and pushed the throttle full, hoping to be airborne before reaching the chain-link fence that separated the airport from the street. To his relief, Oswaldo's recreation roared into the sky like a mountain lion attack, shattering the early morning calm with sound waves that frightened the native prey. Wedge Walker, finishing his overnight shift with cold coffee and a paperback crime thriller, knew what the noise was and didn't even look out the window to see them escape.

They followed Route 34 north along the western side of the Divide where the scarcity of towns and rugged terrain protected their anonymity. Flying through the heart of Rocky Mountain National Park, the ground grew closer over the procession of peaks, and they had to rely on the altimeter to keep them under twelve thousand feet. The rock-face juts and conifer-stand jabs that splotched and split the rocky barrens were palpably breathtaking in the rarified atmosphere. Suffering from oxygen depletion, Duke conjured faces in the rays of an orange dawn that lit up the nimbus swirls, and both men winced from the shards of pain knifing through their heads as their capillaries expanded in the low pressure. The extremely buoyant, high-wing design, which was much better suited for farming than mountaineering, bobbed and eddied with every surge of air current, and even though their destination was less than an hour away, the nausea caused by motion sickness and spasms of fear from the sound of a sputtering engine starved for air, seemed to last a lifetime.

Tracking Trail Ridge Road, the highest paved road in the continental United States, they skimmed a few hundred feet over the treeless tundra of Milner Pass and rode the currents down to Stanley's two-hundred-acre spread. Located in the mountains above Estes Park, Stanley's property was mostly steep slopes and deep ravines, but one relatively level area accommodated a house, barn, dirt runway, and outbuildings. With the field in sight, Remy went downwind, turned base, and dove into the prevailing headwinds that complicated their landing. They briefly touched down on the ice-covered runway before a sudden gust lifted them off again, and without enough room to avoid the huge snow bank at the end of the runway, Remy pushed the throttle forward and went around for a second try. Circling back, Duke saw a snowmobile moving between the buildings. A large dog loped behind the snowmobile, and the rider looked up and waved. Remy aimed for the runway again, but the yoke developed a mind of its own, and he struggled to control it. Fighting what he assumed was ice, he finally managed to get the plane to stay on the ground on the next pass. The greeting committee was waiting when they came to a stop.

Duke put on his leather jacket and scarf before opening the door. "Howdy!" he greeted the snowmobiler from inside the plane with a big smile and wave.

The snowmobiler, dressed in a bulbous, one-piece jumpsuit with a fur-lined hood, held his mittened hand up like a police officer making a stop signal and seemed to smile back. The dog sat impatiently at his side.

Duke couldn't see the man's eyes through the dark ski goggles that covered most of his face, and realized that the noise from the engine and howling wind made him hard to hear. "Morning!" he tried again louder.

The snowmobiler grinned, and the shaggy Tibetan mastiff, happy to have visitors, barked hello.

"Where should we park?" Duke asked with his palms.

The snowmobiler pointed in the direction of one of the buildings and led the way there on his snowmobile. They followed him to a Quonset-roofed garage and waited while he hoisted the door open with a pulley chain. Remy would have taxied inside, but there was another plane in the way, so they waited with the engine running and heat on. The man on the snowmobile unchocked the wheels of the other plane and pushed the tail into a corner to make room for the visitors, then he came outside and waved his arms in an X pattern that pilots know means to turn the engine off. Remy, who was suspicious of dogs he didn't know, reached into the back seat for his overnight bag and made sure his revolver was easily accessible. Duke bundled up, jumped down first, and the hundred-and-twenty-pound dog welcomed him with a greeting that almost knocked him over. The travelers were relieved to be on the ground, but the relentless wind burned their nostrils with icy gasoline fumes, and almost two miles above sea level, they felt the sway of high-altitude malaise.

"Push it in?" Duke asked, leaning on the strut of their plane to keep his balance.

Their stocky host nodded, took up a position by the tail, and made arm signals.

"The dude don't talk?" Remy noted as they twisted and rolled their plane carefully into the cramped hangar.

"Maybe he doesn't speak English."

Once their plane was chocked, the man ushered them out of the hangar and closed the doors. It was only a few hundred feet to the main house, and although the dog seemed to enjoy the climate, following on foot without full winter attire was a losing battle with the elements. Airborne flakes stung the areas of exposed skin that their garments didn't cover, the insides of their ears throbbed from the cold, and their vision was blurred by involuntarily secreted tears. Their guide led them to the entry door, where they were relieved to feel the warmth of civilization.

The snowmobiler went back to his outside rounds, and a dark-haired woman greeted Duke while he was hanging his coat on a rustic, wall-mounted peg. She stood in the doorway of a tiled mudroom with her arms folded inside a wide-stitched wool sweater. "I'm Nima. You must be Duke?"

Duke stomped the caked snow from his shoes. "Yes, and this is my partner, Remy. Is Stanley here?"

"No, but he told me to expect you," she said pleasantly. "He went down to Boulder yesterday."

Duke thought he detected an accent but couldn't tell where she was from. "When's he coming back?" he asked, entering the main part of the house.

Nima's long skirt hid her feet, and she seemed to hover in front of him. "In a few days. You can stay here, or we can give you a ride down when you're ready."

"Great, maybe we can go this afternoon? I have some pressing business in town."

"No problem. Did you want to eat or rest before going? Breakfast is still warm."

Remy was ready to get comfortable. "Coffee sounds good to me."

"Okay, I'll see what we have." Nima led them through the vaulted living room of a modern rustic house with irregular spaces.

Duke, who hadn't changed clothes since Los Angeles, stopped to defrost near an elevated stone fireplace, and Remy joined him, extending his hands to absorb the heat.

Nima saw that her guests weren't dressed for the weather. "Oh, I'm sorry. You can both wait here and warm up if you like. I'll bring you something hot to drink."

"Thanks, light and sweet for me," Duke ordered.

Remy said, "Just black."

Nima glided to the kitchen in sheepskin slippers over a rough stone floor. Still jerked up from the lack of sleep and harrowing flight, the men stood by the fire and tried to settle down to domestic speed. Stanley's wooden chalet was finished in tongue-and-groove pine paneling, and the morning sun sliced the walls with sharp wedges of light that complicated the post-and-beam design. Decorated with Native American rugs, it was furnished with sturdy hand-hewn chairs and a distressed leather sofa set. Wrought-iron lighting fixtures, switch plates, and outlet covers, crafted with themes of the old west, matched the mountain motif of the entire compound. There was a bearskin rug at the bottom of a spiral metal staircase that ascended from the main room to the second floor sleeping areas, and the panoramic picture windows were made of double-paned plate glass in order to withstand the assault of winter weather. The log walls that faced the weather still had their bark, but the insides had been stripped, oiled, and chinked. The low-slung roof, angled to reduce the effect of fierce winds, was covered with a layer of thick-cut cedar shake. Duke had been to Stanley's property once in the summer a few years ago when the house was being built, but hadn't seen it completed. Remy was completely out of his element, light-headed from the altitude and lack of sleep, and anxious to get back to their commercial agenda. He saw the wordless man on the snowmobile through a window and mumbled "weird dude" to himself. The mastiff, frolicking with an unseen friend, bounded behind Kundun.

Nima came back and set a serving tray on the polished log table in front of the hearth. There was only one pot, two cups, and an earthenware jar with a spoon in it.

"No milk?" Duke asked as she poured their drinks.

"No, sorry. We don't do much dairy around here," she apologized.

"Sugar?"

"Bad for you. We try to avoid that too." Nima smiled serenely. "Take a taste. You may like it plain, but here's some honey if you need a little sweetener."

Remy took a sip of the hot black liquid in his cup and nearly gagged. "What is this stuff?"

"Chicory. That's what we all drink around here."

Duke studied his hostess, but her loose and casual clothes concealed her figure, and her straight black hair and bangs framed a face that lacked any defining characteristics except a subtle smile. He knew Stanley had tried to change his lifestyle since his health problems, and wondered what Nima knew of his past. He noticed a small Buddhist prayer wheel on the mantle and took a guess. "Namasté," Duke said, sipping his drink politely.

Nima smiled more broadly. "You're a Buddhist?"

"Not exactly," Duke answered, winking at Remy over the rim of his cup.

"Stanley said you were spiritual."

Remy's eyes bugged out, but he held the warm mug and went along with the charade.

"Well, I don't practice as much as I should," Duke explained, "but I do believe in the cause."

Nima sighed with satisfaction. "The world needs as many true believers as possible."

Duke dosed his cup with honey and said, "I agree. You said breakfast was still warm?"

"Yes, of course. You must be hungry; rice porridge okay?"

Duke's game had come back to him. "Exactly what I had in mind!"

When Nima went back to the kitchen, Duke clued his partner in. "Stanley comes from old money. We have some common ancestors so we're kind of like family – only his side has all the money. He's been through some rough times, and I haven't been up here since he moved in."

"Some spread," Remy noted, "but who are these people?"

"I'm not sure. Maybe they're the caretakers or something," Duke said, looking around for clues.

"Not what I expected. You think he's doing this lady Nima?"

"I don't know. His ex was an absolute bombshell so it's hard to imagine."

Remy caught sight of the bronze head of a Native American chief staring at him. "This place kind of gives me the creeps. I mean it's nice and all that, but."

They heard a door close, followed by the sound of footsteps on the stairs. An orange-clad monk with a shaved head led an equally bald young woman with dark eyes down to the living room. They were blissed out and surprised to see company.

"Oh, good morning," the monk said in a high-pitched voice with an English accent. "I didn't know we'd be having visitors."

Nima came in to introduce them. "Good morning, Gyalpo. This is Stanley's friend Duke, and his friend, Remy."

"Namasté," Gyalpo welcomed them with a slight bow. "This is my student, Chodya. You have been here before?"

Duke followed protocol. "Namasté. I was here when it was being built, but not since then. They did a great job." His roving eye fell on Chodya, who smiled with a trace of embarrassment.

Nima played hostess. "Yes, the construction was quite an ordeal. We couldn't have done it without the help of the monastery."

"Monastery?"

"Yes, the Punkah Dzong Monastery is only a few miles away. The monks, especially Gyalpo, were very helpful."

Duke was fascinated with the idea that monks did anything but sit and meditate. "The monks are carpenters? They have tools?"

"Oh yes; they are very skilled with hand tools. A crew from Estes Park did the heavy construction, but residents of Punkah Dzong did most of the finish work. Gyalpo supervised because his English is very good."

"The Tibetans are quite comfortable at this altitude," Gyalpo explained patiently. "Cold air clears the mind." He fell silent but saw that a further explanation was needed. "I came to this beautiful country with Lama Yeshe twelve years ago. There were only a few of us then, but other Tibetans have come to escape the problems in our home country. Many Westerners have also flocked to the Teachings."

Nima continued, "Stanley's family sold the property for the monastery many years ago. They needed more space for the new people, so I convinced him to donate some as part of his practice. Stanley and I, we've been together for a few years now," she revealed.

Duke didn't remember if he ever met her before and couldn't imagine it. "Oh, I see."

"Yes, we met in a most peculiar way, but, well, that's another story. How long have you known him?"

"Stanley and I go way back; we're distant cousins."

Nima squared her impressions of Duke with her expectations. "Stanley said so. I'm looking forward to getting to know you," she said without changing her expression. "I'll go get your breakfast."

Gyalpo and Chodya followed Nima to the kitchen. Once they were out of earshot, Remy tried to make sense of what was happening. "What is going on around here? I thought Stanley was a businessman."

Duke made sure they couldn't be overheard. "He is; don't let appearances fool you."

Remy shook his head. "Sure don't feel like any smuggling operation I ever been part of."

"That's what's good about it," Duke whispered. "It works."

"You saying these people are part of it?" Remy asked incredulously.

"I'm not sure who knows what, but Stanley always has his shit together. Look at this place!"

Remy didn't like the idea that he'd left his gun in the pocket of his coat. "I don't know," he drawled. "S'long's we ain't abominable snowman bait." He peered out the window to see if he could spot the snowmobiler and thought he saw someone else near the garage.

"Relax, man. I know what I'm doing. The whole Buddhist thing is a cover – well, maybe not the whole thing, but most of it. They built a big temple in Boulder and Stanley gave them some money – that's all. Then the Buddhists started a spiritual university, and now people from all over are taking classes and teaching there. It's been great for local businesses, and everyone in town's affected, one way or another."

Remy couldn't grok it. "A Buddhist university? What do they teach there?"

"Yoga, meditation, spirituality. Religious stuff."

"Whadya mean? It's some kind of school for priests?"

"No, man; it's for regular people. You don't have to make any promises to God to go there. Hell, they don't even really believe in God, not like we do."

Remy needed some clarification. "So they can drink and smoke and screw whoever they want to?" he asked skeptically. "Seems to me they're either church folk or they ain't."

"It's not like Christianity, man. Didn't you learn anything over in 'Nam?"

Remy got his back up. "I learned how to shoot straight and who the bad guys are. Y'all ferget where y'all come from?"

"I left all that Jesus stuff back in Mississippi," Duke said dismissively. "You can think whatever you want to. There's a big ole world beyond the Delta. Everyone's got their own God, and whatever they think he looks like is fine by me."

Remy pondered the universe beyond his comprehension. Even though he had traveled abroad and met lots of different people, he had never considered himself anything more than a good ole boy from Mississippi. "Well, I may do some bad stuff, and I know I'm a sinner, but at least I know the rules."

"Religion is just religion. People just make up their own rules. Buddhists are a lot like Baptists – except for the sex part."

Remy still didn't get it. "They got sex rules?"

"Yeah, they've got rules, but they play the game differently."

Nima interrupted them with two bowls of hot cereal. "I thought you might not like the plain taste so put a little yak butter in for seasoning."

"You've got yaks?"

"No, but they keep a few at the monastery. Gyalpo brings their milk and curd sometimes; it's a real treat."

Remy eyed his bowl suspiciously. "What else you got in here?"

"Just plain old brown rice, Himalayan salt, and treacle. Try it; it's really tasty," Nima pitched. "Stanley and I have it almost every morning. Keeps you regular too."

Duke heard a cue. "By the way, where is the washroom?"

"Down the hall on your left."

Duke found the bathroom and locked the door behind him. After emptying his bladder, he tapped a mound of coke on the custom tile sink and recharged his nose. On his way back, he palmed the stash bottle to Remy who went and did the same. Their appetite dulled, they nibbled at their porridge and returned to their agenda. "So when do you think we can get a ride into town?" Duke asked.

"I'll talk with Kundun when he comes in," Nima said, looking out the window for him.

"I'd like to go as soon as possible. I've got a big Halloween party at the studio tonight."

"At the studio?" Nima said with some surprise in her voice. "Your studio? Stanley said there was a party at the hotel."

Duke recalibrated to cover what he assumed was Stanley's deception. "There're probably going to be Halloween parties all over. I heard the one at the hotel is going to be extra special because some people from Hollywood are sponsoring it."

The mention of parties triggered Nima's pre-Buddhist desires. "Stanley wanted me to come to town with him, but I said I'd stay here in case you showed up. Kundun doesn't understand much English and Gyalpo is only here some of the time. Maybe I should go?" Nima asked herself out loud.

"Halloween party?" Gyalpo asked from the kitchen. "Where? Is everyone invited?" He and Chodya came in and joined the conversation.

Duke sensed that he was in control of the information and took advantage. "I don't know about the party at the hotel, but you can all come to *our* party at the studio." He made sure Chodya understood.

The invitation broke Gyalpo's serious bent. "I love Halloween!" he admitted, then stopped to hide his joy. "We Tibetans … Halloween is so much like some of the old rituals." He and Chodya exchanged a knowing glance. She tucked her arms into the sleeves of her robe, rose up on her toes, and rotated her head in a neck-cracking circle. Gyalpo felt like he had said too much and made an excuse to leave. "The floor is cold; I forgot my slippers," he said, leading Chodya back upstairs.

"Why don't you both come?" Duke reinvited them.

"Maybe we will."

"Is the Dharma bus doing a second run today?" Nima asked Gyalpo.

Gyalpo called down from the second floor landing. "It's Saturday, so it might make an evening trip."

Nima addressed her guests. "Well, if you want to go this afternoon, I guess I'll have to take you myself," she concluded. "I wasn't planning on it, but Stanley told me your visit was a priority. Do you want to shower or anything?"

"No thanks," Duke answered for both of them. "We'll just rest here until it's time to go."

Gyalpo had heard the plan. "Mind if we hitch a ride too?" he called from the balcony.

Nima looked up. "Sure, whatever you want; we can all fit into the Land Rover. I'll have Kundun drive us."

When she found him, Kundun was outside with his canine companion, standing very still, listening intently to messages on the wind, trying to determine if the low frequency drone he heard was an airplane engine or psychic communication from Tibet. Nima got his attention by knocking on the window, and he met her in the mudroom. She spoke in gesticulated-assisted English. "Car start. Drive to town."

CHAPTER 27

With Donna already at work and his life force temporarily drained from tantric sex, Jon didn't get out of bed until late Saturday morning. He knew Marco would be working at the studio all day so there wouldn't be a full band rehearsal, and playing with just Frankie, who used the practice space for percussive therapy on the weekends, was a form of punishment he didn't feel up to. The disappointment over losing last night's talent show to the vaudevillian Cowboy Liberation Army dampened his desire to perfect another display of musicianship, and in the absence of any other pressing business, the only urgency he felt was supplied by his bladder.

Donna's cat followed him to the bathroom, demanding a stroke when he exited.

"Gooood morning, Mot." Jon obliged.

Mot, whose name was Tom backward, arched his back and followed Jon to the kitchen. The intense, mile-high sunlight had warmed Donna's cloistered back yard to near-spring conditions, so Jon went outside in his underwear and bare feet, enjoying the simple pleasures of fresh air and leisure time as Mot dutifully marked his home turf. A rumbly stomach sent Jon back inside while Mot cracked nuggets of kibble in his dish on the back step. Jon turned on the tea water and snooped through the fridge. He found some of yesterday's zucchini bread in a baggie, but the moment he put a morsel in his mouth, the teapot started whistling and the phone rang at the same time. Flustered by the sudden activity, he turned off the gas and filled his mug quickly, splattering some of the boiling water onto his foot. Hopping in pain toward the insistent ring with a mouth full of masticated mush, Jon wondered why he experienced disruptive synchronicity so frequently. "Good morning," he answered, trying to sound nonchalant.

"Good afternoon," the woman caller corrected him. "Is Donna there?"

Jon checked the clock and saw that the caller was right. "Uh, she's not here right now," he mumbled with a sticky tongue.

The caller hesitated. "This is her mother; is this Jon?"

Jon was shocked. He hadn't spoken with Donna's mother for a long time, and their last conversation was not pleasant. He regretted answering and swallowed. "Yes, Mrs. Garfinkle," he said politely. "How've you been?"

"We've been fine. How are *you?*" she asked forcefully. The Garfinkles' were not shy about sharing their disappointment with their daughter's decisions. Donna had failed to graduate with a degree, opting to follow Jon, who had also dropped out of college, to Colorado, and neither of them had any plans to return to the sanity of the east coast.

Jon knew that Donna's parents disproved of their relationship. He responded with the defiant bullshit of a problem child. "I've been great! We love it here." He knew that the Garfinkles had been providing financial support for years and wanted to sound convincing.

"Yes, we know that Donna is very happy in Boulder. Are you working now?"

Jon offered a less-than-convincing "Of course."

"Really? What are you doing?" Mrs. Garfinkle asked with a trace of hope.

"Music, mostly."

She was re-disappointed. "Uh huh."

He could tell she wasn't pleased so he added what he thought she wanted to hear. "Doing some construction and other stuff too; got to pay the bills."

Mrs. Garfinkle, who had gone back to teaching after her children left home, wasn't fooled by the misinformation. "Music, construction, and?" She assumed the third occupation was drug dealing but wanted to hear how Jon would lie about it.

Jon knew what her suspicions were and felt cornered. Why were straight people so uptight about a little pot? Why was a little toke so much worse than a stiff drink? He defended his lifestyle choices with a creative outburst. *"Business,"* he said emphatically, blurting out the one word he knew would impress her. The rest of the words just tumbled out of his mouth before he knew what he was saying. "I've gotten into the equipment business," he said expansively. "Music making equipment. We just bought a big new console for the rehearsal studio and we're going to start charging people to practice and record there." Jon liked the sound of his bullshit so much that he kept going. "Yeah, my partner Marco is working at the biggest recording studio in the state, and we're going to get all the customers they don't have time for. I think we're going to make a lot of money. How's Mr. Garfinkle doing? Feeling better after the surgery?"

Jon's spirited storytelling was almost believable. "Good for you, Jon," Mrs. Garfinkle allowed. "I hope it all works out." She took comfort in knowing that even if Jon couldn't do anything she considered credible, at least he seemed to care for her daughter. "Mr. Garfinkle is home now, resting. Please tell Donna I called. Do you know where she is?"

"She had to go into work early today; lots of baking to do." Jon took a sip of tea.

The thought of her daughter slaving over a hot oven didn't match the socialite expectations her mother still clung to. "She's at the Buddhist restaurant today?" Mrs. Garfinkle asked rhetorically. "What does she make for them?" She couldn't imagine.

"Her pastries are really popular now. You'd be really proud!"

Mrs. Garfinkle tried to stay positive. "I am proud," she lied. "Proud of you both. Please remember to tell her I called."

"Will do, okay bye." Refreshed from his imaginary PR victory, Jon finished his bread and tea in front of the kitchen window while watching Mot chase a squirrel up the crabapple tree in the back. When he was done, he fetched his guitar from the living room chair and tried some chords out. Then, recognizing his lack of inspiration, he went back to the bedroom to light a fresh joint. Within minutes, the part of his brain that last night's sex had emptied was refilled by the soundtrack of chirping birds and the high frequency buzz of blood circulating through his eardrums. He sat on the edge of the bed in his underwear, fascinated with the harmonic scratches of flesh on wound steel as he explored open G tuning for he wasn't sure how long. Afterward, he got dressed and strolled back to the hotel via the Ninth Street corridor. The Chamber of Commerce afternoon weather was having its usual positive effect on Boulder residents, who raced down the hilly stretches of road in sporty cars and ten-speed bicycles until they hit the traffic lights on Canyon Boulevard, and by the time Jon got there, the Boulderado was a beehive of activity. Mr. Lawry didn't seem to notice, but preparations for the Halloween party were in full swing. A thirty-foot ladder, leaning on the railing of the second floor balcony, was positioned in the middle of the spacious marble-floored lobby. A glossy movie poster on a freestanding sandwich board forced visitors with brochures and questions to navigate around it, and two slick-jeaned hipsters with clipboards were orchestrating the Hollywood-style promotional buzz. A man near the top of the ladder was using a staple gun to affix sparkly orange and black streamers to the outside of the wood railing around the balcony while his helper stood on the second-floor landing, dispensing lengths of the decorations from giant rolls. A stained glass roof separated the lobby atrium from the sky and trapped the sounds inside, so each shot of the staple gun echoed through the hotel like sniper activity. Jon moved away from the ladder in case something fell, and was caught off-guard by a surprisingly assertive pinch on his ass. Simone, in his usual beret and open vest uniform, said hello with his eyes and jerked his head in the direction of his quirky shop inside the hotel. Accustomed to Simone's antics, Jon followed him, curious to see if the unexpected contact contained any hidden meaning. It did.

Once they got inside, Simone whispered, "Major snowstorm coming in from the west," in riddle-speak.

Jon never listened to weather reports and was too stoned to care, so he waited for the next clue with a pregnant grin. He knew that most of what Simone said was completely ridiculous, and Simone's reputation as the minister of misinformation made conversations with him like a game of Find the Truth.

Simone added another clue. "Janice Reading has a telephone."

"Good for her. Who is she?"

"She who has seen the glory."

"Glory hallelujah."

Direct communication was against his religion, so Simone distorted a Marvin Gaye song. "*Merci merci me, rien est la meme,*" he half-sang. Then he dug into his pocket and pressed a small glass vial into Jon's hand.

Jon assumed it was coke, but when he sneaked a peek, he saw it was empty. "*Pourquoi?*" he tried speaking in Simone's native tongue.

Simone answered in a thick western accent. "No *pour*, just *quoi*. Fill 'er up, pardner."

Jon and Simone had dealt weed to each other, but Jon had only dabbled in coke. He patted his pockets and turned his palms up in the universal sign language that he wasn't holding.

Simone was annoyed that he was so dense. "*Mon dieu! Mon ami! Que tu est bête!*"

Jon didn't know what he was saying and gave up.

Simone, who seemed to know everyone's business, shooed Jon back to the lobby like someone dismisses a foolish child and closed the door behind him.

Still fidgeting with the empty vial in his pocket, Jon wandered over to the Fleur de Lis Restaurant and saw Mavis and Sasha still serving the lunch crowd. It was much busier than usual for two o'clock in the afternoon, and he couldn't help but notice the contingent of suburban women who had finished lunch and were entering the hotel lobby. Dressed in expensive pants, tailored tops, and polished shoes, they were obviously out-of-towners, and as they moved into the lobby, the sound of the staple gun startled them. After determining it was safe to proceed, they stopped to read the movie poster placard.

"They made a movie about Halloween?"

"I think it's just a scary movie with that name."

"No little goblins and ghosts and pumpkins and candy?"

The women pondered the meaning of the menacing knife images.

"Why are there butcher knives? It reminds me of Lombardi's meat store."

"It doesn't look like a nice movie to me. Certainly not what I'd want my kids to see."

"I don't think it's playing here. The billboard says it's just going to be a Halloween party."

"Well, that's better. What time does it start?"

"It says around eight; I wonder if we're invited."

"Open to all guests of the hotel," one of the women read.

"I guess we picked the right place, ladies!"

"Fun! I haven't been to a good party without my husband since the kids were born."

"Me neither."

"What are we going to do about costumes? It says it's a Halloween party and I don't want to look out of place."

"Just wear something black and open your top button; that always works." The women tittered in agreement.

"The party doesn't start until tonight. What are we going to do for the next few hours?"

"I want to take a drive up Flagstaff Mountain; anyone want to come?"

"How far is it?"

"Only about half an hour each way. There's a cool amphitheater on top and a really great view of the Plains."

"No thanks, I get vertigo going around all those hairpin turns."

"And I have a hair appointment at four."

"Okay, let's all just meet back here at six and figure out where we're going for dinner."

"We could eat here; the sign says there's going to be free food and live music."

"What time does the band go on?"

"Nine o'clock."

"Who is it?"

"Gangbusters; they play in Denver all the time. They're supposed to be really good."

"Who cares about the band? Maybe there'll be some hot guys from LA. Glad I brought my heels!" The ladies giggled as they cliqued through the lobby. One of them bumped into the ladder, almost knocking the man on top off, but she never looked up to see him glare, and none of the women felt anything portentous about the evil-faced psycho on the movie poster. They wandered into Simone's shop, drawn by the pearl-strung torso with a racy bra, but were shocked into leaving by the display of handmade dildos and other sex toys.

Jon was about to go back to his room when he caught sight of a raggedly dressed man speaking to Mr. Lawry. Mr. Lawry, who only left his seat by the front door to go to the bathroom – when someone remembered to take him – and whose ability to verbally communicate was firmly rooted in the frontier dramas of the early twentieth century, seemed uncharacteristically engaged. He nodded as the man, who's wizened features were occluded by greasy strands of hair that had once been part of twin braids, spoke to him in the undecipherable low tones of a language Jon didn't recognize.

Mr. Lawry's eyes widened as the man touched his head and stroked his arm, but the sound of the staple gun crashing to floor of the lobby behind him made Jon look away. When he turned back, Mr. Lawry was slumped in his chair – asleep or dead, Jon didn't know which – and the mysterious man was nowhere to be seen.

Ken Ken, the Buddhist practitioner who had once been an accountant in New York and now managed the financial affairs of Naropa Institute, noticed Mr. Lawry slumped in his chair as he entered the hotel. He put his finger under Mr. Lawry's nose, determined that he was barely breathing, and quickly proceeded to the front desk. "I think you'd better call a doctor," he told the hotel manager. "Mr. Lawry doesn't have far to go."

"Where's he going?" Jack acknowledged, continuing to look through the registration book. "He lives here."

Ken Ken tried to be careful talking about spiritual matters with the uninitiated. "I mean he's ready to go to the beyond."

Jack looked up and saw Mr. Lawry slumped in his usual chair. "I'll make sure he's got a ride."

Ken Ken checked his watch and practiced patience. "Thank you," he said with prayered hands. "Namasté."

Ken Ken went to his meeting on the mezzanine, the man on the ladder came down to retrieve his tool, and Jon summoned the elevator. Busboys clanked dishes in the nearby kitchen. A pall of cigarette smoke and musty odors seeped through the lobby as Gerry Rafferty cast the somber spell of "Baker Street" through the house speaker system. The eerie calm slowed everyone's agenda, but a loud screech startled them out of malaise. Confused, no one was sure if what they heard was a scream coming from inside the restaurant or part of the sax solo.

Jon let the elevator close without getting in and went to join the mounting commotion at the entrance to the Fleur de Lis. Inside, Mavis was trying to calm the woman diner who had shrieked at the sight of a freshly severed finger stuck in her crème brûlée. Mavis had quickly removed the dessert from the table, but the busboy she handed the heated dish to burned his hand, tripped, and dropped it on the floor. The ceramic bowl shattered, sending a splatter of scalding-hot creamy eggs onto the legs of adjacent diners, setting off a second round of moans and curses. Sasha tried to calm her table with soothing words and napkins, but when she squatted down to wipe the floor and saw the bloody finger, she gasped, hit her head on the table, and landed ass first on top of the mess. The ceramic shards cut her hands when she tried to get up, and she looked like an accident victim when she wiped her hair away from her face with bloodied palms. The women diners were horrified at the sight of their pretty bleeding waitress, but one of the men had the good sense to reach down and wrap the severed appendage in a cloth napkin. The rest of the diners were either too close to continue eating or too far away to know what was going on, and by the time the police arrived there were a quite a few statements to record.

It was the most exciting thing to happen at the Boulderado since the drug overdose in William Burroughs' room last year, and everyone had a perverse fascination with being part of the proceedings. Jon edged his way into the crowd and voluntarily joined the line of customers and staff waiting to be interviewed by a detective. The police, already seven cars strong, set up a perimeter around the hotel and fanned out to investigate. One group focused on the kitchen where they presumed the digit had been amputated – either accidentally or intentionally. They were unable to identify any victims, but they took photos of the workers, recorded their names, collected all the butcher knives they could locate, and handed them to the forensic specialist for DNA testing. The forensic specialist examined the human evidence in a private booth at the restaurant while her colleagues were dealing with the public. She wrapped the bundle of knives in a towel and cleaned the brûlée off the severed digit with dabs of water. Her cursory inspection determined that it was probably the left pinky of an old man, so she gave this information to the other officers on the scene, then took the finger and cutlery back to the station for further testing.

Armed with the biological clues, the officers took a heightened interest in anyone over the age of fifty, paying special attention to the hands of everyone who was interviewed. Still without either victim or perpetrator, a trio of officers confiscated the hotel register and used it to identify occupants as they went door-to-door through three floors of twenty-six rooms each. Many of the occupants were long-term residents who rented by the month and had turned their not-so-temporary quarters into decorated apartments. At three o'clock in the afternoon, there were mostly unanswered knocks. Someone was dispatched to find the judge authorized to issue search warrants on a Saturday, and news of the impending investigation spread quickly. Hotel residents scrambled to hide, disguise, or remove evidence of their questionable behaviors before their rooms were examined for criminal clues. After he gave his statement at the restaurant, Jon went back to his room on the fourth floor, wiped off the glossy magazine cover he used to roll joints, and put the rest of his stash in his pocket. The flurry of activity had sobered him up, so he headed for the roof of the five-story edifice to get out of the way and smoke a cigarette. Those that knew about the roof access had set up a few chairs near the edge overlooking the street, and Jon wasn't completely surprised to see Simone's girlfriend Miko sharing a joint with her friend as if nothing unusual had happened.

"Hey, Johnny," Miko greeted him. "Up for a toke?"

Jon always wondered what it would be like to bed Simone's kinky squeeze, but he was even more attracted to her exotic-looking friend whom he'd never seen before. "For sure," he said, entering their aura.

What was in the air?
A chemical reaction.

I was made aware
Of a physical attraction.
I would follow you right down
The only road I know.

They stood near the edge of the roof, passing the joint and watching the police activity below.

"What's going on down there?" Miko asked.

"How long have you been up here?" Jon asked, holding his smoke-filled breath.

"I don't know. About an hour, I guess."

Jon exhaled. "Then you sort of missed it."

"Missed what," Miko's friend asked innocently. Her huge dark eyes, perfect complexion, and shoulder-length black hair were startlingly beautiful.

"*Missing all the action.*" Jon brushed his own hair off his face and unsuccessfully tried to conceal his infatuation. "Cops all over the place; didn't you hear the sirens?"

"We heard them," Miko said, unconcerned. "The cops are always up to something. They think they're so important. They can't wait for something bad to happen so they can blow their whistles and boss everyone around."

"I like to think of police with their pants off," her friend Sarquette added cattily.

Miko and Sarquette were dressed in blue-jean casual with no makeup or fashion accessories – they didn't need any – so when Sarquette exhaled a breathy column of unabsorbed smoke, the hiss it made slithered into Jon's ear like the scales of a reptile on dry grass. The audible serpent traveled down his spine, activated his second chakra, and sent a wave of elevated blood pressure surging into his lower head.

Miko noticed his complexion change. "You okay?" she asked, handing him the roach for a final hit.

259

"I'm good, and so is this!" Jon took the roach clip and sucked the life out of the burning remains, hoping to regain his composure.

Miko, who had a deep understanding of chi, helped him transition. "Oh, I guess I should introduce you two," she said slyly. "Sarquette, this is Jon. Jon, this is Sarquette."

Sarquette was very skilled at manipulating male attention. "Pleased to meet you, Jon." She offered her soft, lotioned hand and squeezed Jon's energy into herself. "You're a friend of Simone's?"

Jon blinked in an alien landscape. "Yeah, everyone knows Simone."

Sarquette studied Jon's priapic presence and looked to Miko for direction.

Miko understood her unasked question. "Jon lives here at the hotel. He visits us in the shop sometimes."

"Well, maybe you'd like to come hang out with *us* sometime," Sarquette said suggestively. "I just got into town and don't know too many people."

Jon would have sexed her on the spot if he could but said, "Er, that sounds like a good idea. Maybe we'll all hang out sometime."

Seeing the potential, Miko was about to arrange a tryst when the door to the roof opened and Gyalpo appeared with Chodya in tow.

Gyalpo seemed very agitated, and his sudden appearance disrupted the rooftop cathexis. "Miko! What are you doing up here?" he said brusquely. Then he smelled the pot. "The police are probably trying to get into your room," he added. "They've blocked the store and are asking Simone questions; I'm sure they'll be looking for *you* soon."

"Have they arrested Simone? Is he okay?" Miko asked.

"I don't know. I only saw them talking to him."

Sarquette retracted her receptors and said, "I think we'd better go; I left my purse in the room."

Jon remembered the vial Simone had given him. Where was it? He patted his pockets. Did it have any residue? He got paranoid. What would the police find if they searched Simone's room? Was

Simone going to turn everyone in if he got busted? Was there a murderer on the loose or just someone who liked to cut people's fingers off? Jon hated the sight of blood, and the thought of the severed finger helped anxiety subsume lust.

Gyalpo steered the awkwardness. "Everyone back downstairs now please; Chodya and I need to use the rooftop for a meditation."

Miko and Sarquette thought it was a good idea, but Jon bristled at the tone of the bossy monk. "Who are *you*?" he asked defiantly.

"I'm Gyalpo," the monk answered sternly.

"Gyalpo's my teacher," Chodya told Jon. "Jon's my friend," she told Gyalpo.

"I think she's told me about you. You're Doh-na's friend?" Gyalpo asked Jon.

Jon was amazed that the monk knew him, and embarrassed that his girlfriend was mentioned in front of Sarquette. He covered his tracks with old dirt. "Yes, Donna and I go back a long way, all the way to Baltimore."

"Well, you might think about going there for a visit soon if you don't get out of here fast," Gyalpo snapped back. "There's much more going on around here than you know about," he added portentously.

Jon was completely confused. Gyalpo, with his shaved head and monkish attire, looked like all the other harmlessly preoccupied Buddhists who were seen around town, but he didn't appear to be at satvic peace with himself. In fact, if it weren't for the robes and beads, Jon couldn't have told the difference between Gyalpo's attitude and any other dude he might meet doing a high-stakes drug deal. Seeing Chodya brought on a whole other cloud of concerns. What was she doing with the bossy monk who knew Miko and Simone? Would Chodya tell Donna that she saw him on the roof getting high with two sexy girls?

Miko and Sarquette slinked through the downstairs portal and disappeared.

Chodya spoke after they had gone. "I don't think Jon has anything to worry about; his aura is clear," she testified.

Gyalpo took a hard look. "I guess you're right, but I don't think he should stay here; we need privacy."

Jon was completely lost. He didn't know what his aura looked like and couldn't imagine what they were planning to do. Chodya's friendly smile always made him nervous, and he didn't see the point of arguing with the forceful monk. "I don't know what you two are up to, but the roof's all yours. Say an ohm for me," he said as he retreated below.

Buzzed and ready to chill, Jon was hoping the chaos in the hotel had subsided. It hadn't: barking search dogs roamed the hallways, uniformed officers were posted by the elevator, room doors clacked and slammed shut, serious voices squawked through walkie-talkies, and the hotel's endless supply of soothing rock comforted no one. Jon slipped into his room, made doubly sure there was no incriminating evidence lying around, and took the stairs down to the lobby, joining the collective who had assembled there. Frightened vacationers, restive tenants, idled workers, earnest officers, and curious passers-by asked each other questions in an insistent drone that the stained glass canopy amplified to angry-hive volume. No one was really sure if they were out of danger, above suspicion, free to leave, or just victims of circumstance, so the noisy crowd buzzed with speculative fervor until someone reported the sight of actual blood. A circle quickly formed around the drops of evidence that were dripping onto the floor from Mr. Lawry's left hand, and after determining that his pinky finger was indeed missing, an on-scene detective spoke to the onlookers.

"Please stand back, folks. We don't want to disturb the crime scene."

"Who would do something like this?"

"He looks like such a harmless old man."

"Is he sleeping or dead?"

The detective felt for a pulse and reported, "He's alive," as he held Mr. Lawry's sleeve over the wound.

A small dark puddle had formed under Mr. Lawry's chair, and the onlookers spread around the area in a semicircle. Suspicions traveled through them like an airborne disease. The people nearest the octogenarian covered their mouths to hide horrified gapes, trying to prevent the scent of crime from entering their system with shirt sleeves and Kleenex, and those who were too far away to taste discovery crowded closer.

Jack, who had been reassessing party plans with the movie promoters, cut through the crowd and asked, "What's going on over here?"

"They discovered where the finger came from," a bystander informed him.

Jack saw who it was. "Mr. Lawry! Who would do such a thing?"

"No one knows."

"It doesn't look like he's dead."

The discovery of the victim, which ruled out any possibility of an accident, increased the urgency to find the perpetrator. They couldn't shut down the hotel and detain everyone because it wasn't a murder, so the authorities took photographs, talked to anybody who looked like they might know something, and made plans to analyze their findings back at the station. A few of the curious stayed and watched the EMT bandage Mr. Lawry's hand, but the rest of the crowd dispersed.

Jon joined Sasha and Mavis, who were sipping herbal tea in the empty restaurant. Mavis was particularly animated. "Very strange," she spoke mostly to herself. "I feel the presence of ghosts."

Sasha had borrowed some of Mavis's books but wasn't a convert yet. "Ghosts don't usually cut people's fingers off," she said with a trace of fear.

Mavis communed with a far-off unknown. "Some very unusual things can happen around Samhain," she reported dreamily. "The veil between the worlds is extra thin."

A hotel worker wheeled Mr. Lawry back to his room and a janitor started scrubbing the floor. Jack and the promoters paced around the mezzanine inspecting the party preparations. "How does this affect our plans?" one of them asked. "Can we have this mess cleaned up in time for the party?"

The other said, "Maybe we can say this had something to do with the movie? Nothing scares people more than finding out their fears are justified."

"What do you have in mind?"

"I don't know … got it! We can say we found a bloody knife in the bathroom. We'll help the police solve the crime!"

"Brilliant! What do you think, Jack?"

The idea was beyond Jack's imagination.

Alone on the roof, Gyalpo pressed Chodya against a wall and summoned his creative energies as the police cruisers came and went.

CHAPTER 28

The afternoon sun cast long shadows as the Customs Bureau plane taxied to a halt at the Steamboat airfield. Agent Falin, who was dizzy from flying them around in circles over unfamiliar and treacherous terrain, was relieved to be back on the ground where the horizon wasn't moving and oxygen was more plentiful. "Never thought I'd miss the tropics," he said as the engine sputtered to a halt.

They folded their maps, collected their thoughts, and zipped up against the chill. After they locked the Cessna and wiped the condensation off their sunglasses, Officer McKnight phoned his office from the pay phone on the side of the only building.

Margaret answered, "I was hoping you'd get back before I left; things have been a little crazy around here."

"Really? What?"

"Well, for one thing, the chairlift broke right after you left and it won't be fixed until tomorrow – they hope! So now the town's full of angry skiers who are trying to drown their frustrations wherever alcohol is served."

"Sounds like trouble; I bet Jim Temple isn't too happy."

"Oh, you got that right! You should hear what the jocks on the radio are saying. I think they may have crossed the line this time."

"Really? What did they say?"

"They're saying that the reason the chairlift broke has something to do with aliens."

"Huh?"

"Yes, you heard me right. They said, only half-kidding you know, that the aliens want everyone to stop skiing so they will get drunk and celebrate Halloween. That way, the aliens can come to the Halloween parties and, I don't know, fit in I guess."

"I'm not following this. Why would they say that?"

"I think Jim's just trying to get people thinking about something else. Maybe spend money at The Tavern or buy stuff from the Strawberry Springs store. It's so crazy no one can stop talking about aliens in Halloween costumes."

Officer McKnight paused for a breath of sanity. "Okay then, what else is going on?"

"Oh, I almost forgot. Bobby called in. Pretty weird stuff too. Something happened to his dog."

Officer McKnight wanted to hear more but Agents Walker and Falin were ready to go. "Listen, I need someone to pick us up at the airport right now. Can you send a cruiser over?"

"All the police are pretty busy right now. How about I come get you myself?"

"Good idea. See you soon."

The government men watched an orange-tinted sunset and stomped their feet on the frozen ground until Margaret rumbled down the service road to fetch them in her Dodge Club Cab. Befitting their ranks, Officer McKnight and Agent Falin wedged themselves into the jump seat and Agent Walker got in front.

Margaret was uncharacteristically chatty. "Is it okay if I just drop you off at the office?" she said as they passed onto the paved part of the road. "We have overnight guests are at the house, and George is still working. Their kids want to go sledding before it gets too dark, the mothers want to go shopping before the stores close, and the dads have already started drinking. I've got to get back there."

Officer McKnight tried to calm her down. "It's okay, Margaret, go home. Do whatever you have to do. It's close to five o'clock anyway."

"Thank you, sir. I really appreciate it. They don't have a car, and I know what it's like to be stuck in the house with kids. I promised to make them something to eat for dinner, so I need to stop by the grocery store too."

"Just take care of yourself, we'll be fine. Did you leave me any notes? When is Bobby coming back? Any update?"

Margaret stopped the truck in front of the municipal building. "Oh, right; I'm sorry, I haven't told you what he said." She left the motor running and rolled down the window as the men got out. "He said he found an elk that had been attacked. It was all cut and bleeding like it had just happened."

"Where did he find it? Did he say?"

"It was really close to the crash site so he's going back to look for clues." Margaret fidgeted with the shifter and apologized. "I wrote down the coordinates on a piece of paper when he told me. It's on your desk."

Officer McKnight reviewed his mental list of elk killer suspects: A hungry mountain lion was his first thought, but Yellowstone grizzlies could have wandered down from Wyoming, and a wolf pack that had successfully been reintroduced in the upper Routt were possible perpetrators too. There were also recluses in the area, outlaws in hiding, and poachers who might be hunting out of season. "When's Bobby going to call again?"

"He said he might spend the night at someone's cabin he knows, but he might come back to Steamboat tomorrow because of the dog."

"What happened to the dog?"

"He said the dog smelled something and ran off. Bobby heard it yelp, and when it came back, it was limping."

"Maybe it stepped on something sharp, or maybe whatever got the elk got the dog too. "

"I don't know; I just don't know," Margaret admitted while she was rolling up the window. "Can I go now, please?"

Officer McKnight gave her a wave, and she sped off to pressing business.

Agents Walker and Falin had been standing to the side and hadn't heard the conversation. They followed Officer McKnight into his basement office and he told them everything he had just heard. They located the coordinates Margaret had written down on a geologic survey map, but without more information the prospect of solving any part of the mystery was fading with the setting sun.

"How far is the dead elk from where the wreckage is?"

"Real close, I think. Maybe only a mile or two."

"Where did we see those other elk that were being followed?"

"Just down the mountain a little. I know what you're thinking. Whatever we saw chasing the elk caught one. Sounds like a bear to me."

Agent Walker had another idea. "You think someone in the area might be using a bearskin for camouflage?"

"Who would they be hiding from? The elk?"

"Or the warden."

Agent Falin was more interested in chasing people than animals. "What the hell do dead animals have to do with our mission? That's got nothing to do with smuggling or a plane crash."

"Well, I guess we've got two separate mysteries then," Officer McKnight concluded. "We won't hear from Bobby until tomorrow so – " A ringing phone interrupted, and he picked it up. "Oh hi, Farah," he said with some disappointment. "Yes, we're all here. We got back a little while ago." Officer McKnight listened while Farah talked, then relayed her question to his companions. "Farah wants to know if we can meet her for drinks. She says she knows something but won't tell me over the phone." Officer McKnight covered the receiver and added, "Probably something about aliens," with a wink.

"Well, we're not going to find out anything new just sitting here talking to each other," Agent Falin observed.

"We don't have any hard evidence to write a report with, so I guess there's no reason we can't go to dinner."

Agent Falin liked the idea. "I knew what they said about you Colorado boys wasn't true. Let's call it a day."

After Officer McKnight told Farah they'd meet her at The Tavern, he asked Agent Falin, "Just out of curiosity, what did they say about us in LA?"

"Mighty, tighty, whitey," Agent Falin teased.

Officer McKnight objected. "That's not nice – or true."

"So you're going to prove them wrong tonight?"

"I'm married, but I've still got an open mind."

"Good 'cause when you've got an open mind there's always a way out," Agent Falin quipped.

Officer McKnight wasn't sure what he meant, but he and Agent Falin continued their friendly banter on their way to The Tavern as Agent Walker aligned the collected clues with intuition. Farah saw them come into The Tavern and waved them over to the table she and a friend had taken over. Her friend gave the detectives the seats they had saved and joined the mix of friendly locals and frustrated skiers who were drinking their way to familiarity.

"Thanks for saving us a spot," Officer McKnight said as the men sat down.

"Thanks for coming," Farah welcomed them. "I'm a little freaked out so it's good to have company."

Agent Walker scanned the room warily. "What's the matter? Somebody threaten you because the lift broke?"

"No, no; nothing like that. Most of these people can't ski anyway. They just like to dress up and feel like they're on vacation. I think they're happy to have an excuse to start drinking early."

"Sounds like they've got the right idea to me," Agent Falin commented. "What was that local beer we had yesterday?"

Farah held up her mug of unnaturally orange brew. "Coors Halloween Blend, cheers!" She took a celebratory swig as a waitress appeared.

"Works for me; all around?" Agent Falin asked his partners.

The waitress acknowledged their order and went to fill it. The men opened their jackets and got comfortable with their surroundings. Farah sipped her drink, waved at one of her friends, and loosened another button on her flannel shirt.

"So what's got you freaked out?" Agent Walker asked. "I've never known you to be a scaredy-cat."

Farah, who had established a tomboy reputation in her youth, corrected him. "I'm not scared, not like you think."

"No little green men after you this time?" Agent Walker condescended.

"Don't be so smug, William. You want me to tell your friends what *you* were scared of when you were young?"

Agent Falin remembered what he liked about Farah. "I love secrets. Do tell."

Agent Walker didn't want her to. "Come on Farah, you know I didn't mean it like that. Officer McKnight said you had something to tell us. That's why we're here. Did you hear something that made you upset?"

"Yeah, kinda," she admitted. "A guy I know – someone who lives in the middle of nowhere – called me and left a message." She had everyone's attention but stopped talking while their beers were delivered.

"What did he say?"

"Not much except that it was important to call him back as soon as I could."

"Did you?"

"Of course. He's one of the people I know who's seen things."

Agent Walker hid his skepticism. "What did he see?"

"It's not just what he saw. It's what your guy Bobby saw that's got us freaked out."

Officer McKnight was surprised that Bobby would share the details of the investigation with strangers. "What did Bobby tell him?"

"Well, I don't want to get anybody in trouble. My friend the Professor and Bobby are sort of friends."

"So Bobby went there to call us?" Officer McKnight guessed.

"Right. I don't know how he does it, but the Professor can tap into the phone lines with his short wave radio. He's called me from there before. When they couldn't get a hold of you, they got to talking and realized that they both knew me and that I might know where you were."

Agent Walker was surprised at the breakdown in protocol. "Did you talk to Bobby yourself?"

"No, he had already gone by the time I called back. But he told the Professor to tell me to tell you that they think the missing pilot may still be alive."

The news was riveting. "Alive? After all this time?" The law enforcement agents' critical faculties returned to active duty. "How could that be? That's not what he said to Margaret."

"Your office person was already gone by the time he called her back. That's why the Professor called me; Bobby wanted you to know as soon as possible."

"Why do they think he's still alive? Did someone see him?"

"That's where it gets complicated."

"Complicated? Is he injured? Should we get a helicopter up there right away?"

"I don't think so, not from what the Professor said."

"C'mon, Farah, level with us," Agent Walker commanded. "What the hell is going on?"

"I'm not sure," Farah said convincingly. "The Professor told Bobby that he saw someone who looked like a pilot a few days ago. He got freaked out because the guy looked dead, but he was walking around."

"Well, he obviously wasn't dead then!" Agent Walker said with exasperation. "Your friend has been smoking too much weed. I don't know why we're even listening to this crap."

"I knew you'd think that, and so did he. That's why Bobby told him to mention that the guy wasn't wearing any shoes – and he ran away as soon as he saw them."

"He ran away?" Officer McKnight repeated. "Very strange – but not very dead. Why does Bobby think it might be Agent Dobson?"

"According to the Professor, he had one of those Air Force jumpsuits on. It was all torn but the Professor saw the patches and zipper. I know you think me and my friends are kind of kooky sometimes, but the Professor's neighbor saw the same guy too. They thought it might be the missing pilot because they couldn't figure out who else it could have been."

Agent Walker recapped. "So your friend saw someone in the woods he didn't know and got freaked out because of what he was wearing? Listen, Farah, we're policemen; you know that. We appreciate you and your friend trying to help us, but making up stories about dead men walking and telling us it's one of our own, well, it doesn't come across as reliable information. "

Farah was frustrated that she wasn't being taken seriously. "The Professor is a scientist. He used to work for NORAD; your father probably knows him. He's been living up there for years, and he's not a stoner."

"That part's probably true," Officer McKnight agreed. "Bobby wouldn't be hanging out with any hippie types."

Agent Falin thought the whole conversation was very curious. "You're telling me you've got scientists and professors living in the mountains like hermits? Maybe there's a good reason – theyre too nutty to get jobs!"

"That might be true," Officer McKnight agreed, "but some people who could live anywhere choose the solitude of the mountains. It may not make sense to you – coming from LA – but there're some very intelligent people who value tranquility."

"I know how to get a little instant tranquility. Watch." Agent Falin took a long draft of his beer and belched.

Agent Walker interrupted. "Is there anything else your friend said? Any actual evidence?"

"The Professor said he's been hearing strange things lately," Farah reported shyly, hoping to avoid more derision.

Agent Falin didn't cooperate. "Oh, come on! Hearing things too?"

Farah rose to the challenge. "Kind of like a motor running." Her eyes widened. "Maybe there's an alien space ship in the area."

"What did he say it sounded like?"

"Oohhrree, oohhrree."

Agent Falin's mug hit the table with a punctuating clack. "Now that sounds like a ghost story I heard in 'Nam."

Farah pointed to the mug. "That reminds me; I almost forgot! The Professor also said he's heard banging too." Her voice lowered to mystery pitch. "Like maybe they were repairing the spaceship."

"Whoa! Slow down, girl," Officer McKnight interjected. "This whole thing is way too out there for me. What's the Professor's number? I want to talk to him myself. I want to know what Bobby saw."

Farah handed Officer McKnight a scrap of paper with the number on it. "I figured you'd want to. Please don't be mean. My friend's name is Edward Hardaway, but we just call him the Professor."

"Okay, thanks. I'm going to call him right now." Officer McKnight left to use the pay phone.

Agent Walker automatically dismissed the alien part of Farah's story and focused on the similarities to the reliable information they had. "Barefoot?" he repeated. "Are you sure?"

"That's all I know," Farah admitted. "Bobby said he would try to call you tomorrow. There's something the matter with his dog so he might come back early."

"So we've heard. Is Bobby going back to the professor's house?"

"I don't know where he's going tonight, but I have a question for you." Farah paused to consult her beer. "Level with me, do you think aliens have anything to do with this? Lots of us have seen things we can't explain, and we want to know what's going on around here. Why won't the government tell us the truth? They think we're too stupid to understand?"

Agent Walker gave the textbook reply. "You know I don't believe in aliens Farah. I'm sure there's a reasonable explanation for all this."

Agent Falin disagreed with his boss. "Well, I'm not so sure aliens don't exist. One thing I learned over in 'Nam is there's always one thing more to learn before you get to the truth." He winked at Farah and said, "This place sure has it's share of mysteries."

"I agree! What about what we saw last night?"

"What did you and Agent Falin see last night?" Agent Walker asked tentatively.

Farah's lips were two beers loose. "We were looking through that huge telescope in the Carter's living room. You know, looking at the moon and stuff, when all of the sudden, a shadow came flying across it."

Agent Falin took up the story. "It looked like a small aircraft. We only saw it for a second, and then it disappeared over the horizon."

"Yes, but we heard it too. You said it might be smugglers."

"I didn't see any running lights," Agent Falin explained, "so that was just a guess."

"Why didn't you say something before?" Agent Walker asked. "Those might have been the guys we're looking for."

Agent Falin realized his mistake and covered his amorous tracks. "I didn't remember until just now. It didn't seem like a big deal; I figured maybe that sort of thing was normal around here."

Farah remembered what had distracted Agent Falin the night before and smiled at his fib. "Normal's only normally normal," she quipped. "The rest of the time it's anybody's guess."

Agent Walker ignored the personal intrigue and stayed professional. "Well, my guess is that what you saw and heard might have something to do with what we came here for."

Farah was delighted that she'd got Agent Walker to disclose more about his mission. "So you *are* looking for smugglers! I thought so. You should have told me; I know how to get a hold of them. You want an introduction or do you want to figure out who they are yourselves?"

Agent Walker was astonished. "Farah, you never cease to amaze me. Does your father know who you've been associating with? I doubt he'd approve."

"My father's so old-country the only smugglers he knows about still ride camels and mules."

"When was the last time you saw him? Has he been here recently?"

"Of course he's visited me; I've been living up here for three years. I tried to teach him how to ski last year, but it was hopeless."

"So who *are* the smugglers, miss busybody?"

Farah realized she had the informational advantage. "Oh, I don't know," she said coyly. "My boss usually deals with all the high rollers himself."

"Jim Temple knows about the smuggling in the area?"

"You'll have to ask him."

"I'm asking you," Agent Walker said, all business.

Officer McKnight came back and interrupted, "I just got off the phone with Bobby. It's more serious than I thought."

"You spoke to him? What did he say?"

Officer McKnight tipped his mug and swallowed. "There's definitely someone out there; Bobby saw him too."

"Really? Is it Agent Dobson? Could it be?"

"He only saw a glimpse, so he's not really sure. It's like the Professor said, the guy had some kind of jumpsuit on; the kind most pilots wear."

"Really?"

"Bobby said he went back to check on the elk after he called Margaret. The elk had been skinned and dressed since the first time he saw it. He saw someone way up in a nearby tree and yelled to him, but the guy just sat in the branches without speaking or moving. Bobby could see the flight suit with his field glasses, but the branches hid most of the guy. He's guessing that the guy killed the elk for food and was keeping an eye on his dinner."

"Well, Agent Dobson was trained for wilderness survival, so it might have been him, but how do we know someone didn't find his body and steal his uniform to stay warm?"

"Or maybe the crash landing sent him into shock, and he's not thinking clearly?"

No one had any answers, and Agent Falin was starting to feel the altitude again. "I'm not thinking so clearly myself; another round?"

Dinner was being served, and the alcohol buzz in the restaurant rose to a level that made quiet conversation impossible. The detectives' instincts were overmatched by hunger and fatigue, and everyone at the bar was starting to look like a suspect. A female friend of Farah's came by, whispered in her ear, and both of them laughed at the private comment. Agent Falin caught the humorous contagion, but Officer McKnight continued to monitor the room for known criminals.

Agent Walker tried to stay on point. "How far away from Bobby was the guy in the tree? He couldn't tell if it was Agent Dobson?" he asked Officer McKnight.

"He was pretty high up, and it was almost dark. Bobby couldn't make out the face. The only other thing he said – the part I can't figure out – is how the guy climbed up there."

"What do you mean?"

"The tree didn't have any lower branches, so he must have had to shimmy up there."

"Maybe one of Farah's aliens just jumped way up there," Agent Falin said with hops-inspired irreverence. "I hear they're really athletic."

Farah liked the idea of having another believer at the table and expanded on the theory with her own sloshy logic. "Now you really have me wondering. What did the skin look like? All smooth? Was it kind of greenish? Could they see the nose? Aliens hardly have any noses, just nostrils."

The waitress came to take their order. Farah and Agent Falin continued to bond over alien perpetrator theories, a firefighter friend of Officer McKnight's came over to make small talk, and all the noisy distractions prevented Agent Walker from hearing himself think.

After Officer McKnight's friend and the waitress left, Agent Falin focused on Farah. "You say you have a sister in Boulder?"

"Yes, how did you know?"

"You said so earlier today."

"Oh, now I remember. I told you my sister Sasha said I should come to the Halloween party at the Boulderado Hotel tonight."

Agent Falin liked the direction their conversation was headed. "You like to party?"

"Of course, don't you?"

"Only when I'm off duty."

"When's that?"

"Never."

"Too bad; I was going to invite you guys to come with me."

Agent Walker only heard the last sentence. "Invite us where?"

"Boulder."

"When? Why?"

A mischievous idea flew into Farah's head and escaped out of her mouth. "You said you wanted to know who the smugglers were. Well, I think some of them may be at the Halloween party in Boulder tonight."

The conversation paused for the distribution of steaming burgers, and the seduction of food was palpable. Agent Falin used both hands to maneuver his oversized patty close enough for a hearty chomp, and the other men surrendered to the tempting taste. Farah's sole concern was getting her mouth around the beef while demonstrating feminine charm. The discussion resumed on sated stomachs, but only their corporal appetites were satisfied.

"So are you going down to Boulder tonight?" Agent Walker asked Farah.

"That depends on whether I can get a ride."

"Your truck won't make it?"

"My Blazer will get me there, but I might hitch a ride with friends. I don't want to drive through the mountains at night by myself. I was hoping one of you guys would give me a lift."

"I'm sorry to disappoint you," Agent Walker said. "We're here on business so that can't happen unless you're going to lead us to suspects."

Farah pressed her case. "I probably know more about who's who around here than you do. We might find someone interesting down in Boulder."

Agent Walker considered the distinction. "Should I ask you if you plan on doing anything illegal there?"

Farah enjoyed being treated as an equal. "You can ask."

Officer McKnight wasn't interested in Farah's gamesmanship. "Well, I've definitely had enough for one day, and I want to get home before my wife falls asleep. Tomorrow's going to be a busy day, so tonight will have to proceed without me."

"That may not be possible," Agent Walker said. "I was hoping to follow up on the Jim Temple lead tonight."

"How can we do that?"

"Don't you know where he lives?"

"Of course I know, but what do you plan on doing? We can't just go over there on a Saturday night and interrogate him."

"Maybe he's not going to be home tonight. Farah, do you know if Jim plans on throwing a Halloween party tonight?"

Farah was delighted to be in the loop. "As a matter of fact, I do. There's going to be a private gathering at the main lodge. Only

Jim's close friends and important people are invited, so he'll definitely be there."

Officer McKnight put the clues together quickly. "I see. Well, maybe we need to be included in that group. Never know who we might bump into or what we may learn."

"Can you call Jim and get us invited?" Agent Walker asked Farah. "Tell him you ran into old friends. What time does the get-together start?"

Farah saw the Coors Mountain clock over the bar and checked it against her watch. "They usually don't get started early, so I'd say ten o'clock would be about the right time to show up."

Agent Walker saw the time too. "That's in four hours. Do you think there'll be a problem getting us an invitation?"

"I'm not sure Jim would be very happy having policemen at his private party – some of his guests may not be following all the rules of the state of Colorado – but if I tell him it's just some old friends."

Agent Walker understood. "Can you make the call? I'd owe you one."

"Another one?" Farah reminded him. Seizing advantage, she added, "Okay, but here's what I want."

"You name it. Shoot."

"I want a ride to Boulder tonight, and I want Agent Falin to take me."

"Farah! You know Agent Falin is here on business. I can't just send him to Boulder to take you to a party."

"But there may be some business at the party. I can point out who's who. You *are* looking for someone, aren't you?"

Agent Walker consulted Officer McKnight. "What do you think?"

"Well, I don't think all three of us need to go to Jim's party, so maybe it's not such a bad idea. Where would Agent Falin go if Jim didn't want strangers there?"

"I'll go wherever you want," Agent Falin volunteered, liking the direction of the planning. "It may be a good idea to follow up on the other leads. You and McKnight seem like you've got Steamboat covered."

"How would you get there? It's too dark to fly," Agent Walker asked.

"We can drive my Blazer," Farah volunteered. "It's got four-wheel drive, and I know the way. We could be there by nine o'clock if we leave soon."

Agent Walker gave tentative approval. "Okay, why don't you call Jim and see if McKnight and I can get invited to his little get-together. We'll make a decision once we hear." He waited until Farah was gone before opening up to his colleagues. "This is definitely not textbook," he pointed out.

"Successful investigations never follow all the rules," Agent Falin recited his usual excuse.

"Do you think Farah actually knows something?" Officer McKnight asked.

Agent Walker had known her longest. "I wouldn't put it her past her."

"Well, we can't do anything about what Bobby saw *tonight*, so we might as well try to accomplish something else."

"I'm game," Agent Falin chimed in, a little too enthusiastically.

Agent Walker tried to get comfortable with the plan.

Farah came back with a smile on her face. "All set. You and McKnight are invited."

"Did you tell Jim it was us?"

"No, he was in such a good mood he didn't even ask. The only thing he said was to make sure you had good costumes."

"Costumes?"

"Everyone is dressing up – they're expecting a lot of aliens – so you have to fit in. Jim said it'd be fun to figure out who everyone really is."

Agent Walker was confident he could make a headdress from something. "This could get interesting."

Officer McKnight rolled his eyes and repeated "costumes" as if it were a swear word.

"Do we have to have costumes to go to the party in Boulder?" Agent Falin asked.

"Nah, costumes are for squares. Boulder is too hip for that."

Agent Falin liked the plan. "Well, I guess we better get on the road soon—provided it's okay with my boss?"

Agent Walker acquiesced. "Please remember why you're there and call me in the morning. I'll be staying at McKnight's."

Agent Falin put his jacket on and said, "Yes, sir!"

Farah waved her friend over. "Ruby's going to hitch a ride with us." The women were excited. "Let's go!"

CHAPTER 29

Kundun dropped Stanley and Nima off at the Boulderado before delivering his other passengers to BlueStar Studios. Duke had only been gone a few days, but the studio was not the same as when he left. Cynthia buzzed him in the front door and he stood, mouth agape, somewhat horrified at the alterations. The sophisticated atmosphere had been tastelessly violated by Halloween decorations, randomly taped and pinned to the midnight blue walls of the lobby. Lengths of tinseled streamers were draped over the expensive furniture, and crepe paper pumpkins, witches, and ghosts dangled from threads attached to the ceiling. Even the space-age studio clock, an iconic, ultramodern creation that had inspired the BlueStar logo, had been defaced by oversized plastic candy corns attached to the ends of its polished titanium indicator arms.

"You like it?" Cynthia asked expectantly. "Diane and I have been going nonstop since you gave us the go-ahead."

Duke bit his bottom lip and inhaled patience. "I didn't think you were going to be doing so much … decorating."

Cynthia was disappointed but still excited. "Dennis wouldn't let us do the control room, but there's more in the studio. I hope you like it 'cause we tried really hard to make it festive and cool. Diane and the new guy are in there setting up tables."

Remy, who had no appetite for silliness, swatted a dangling mummy and followed Duke down the hall. "Who all's recording here?" he asked sarcastically. "The Grateful Dead?"

Duke's second thoughts about allowing Cynthia to talk him into having a party multiplied as soon as he opened the control room door. The old console was gone, and the new one was in its place, but when he finally spotted them, Dennis and Walter were on the floor in a mess of wires, testing the connections to the custom noise-reduction system. None of the big tape machines were where they normally lived, the furniture was pushed into a cluster against the back wall, the grill covers for the main speakers were propped up against the control room window, and tiny bits of multicolored cut wire were splattered amongst the hodgepodge of tools on the floor like confetti.

"Welcome home, boss," Dennis greeted them from the floor. "Great idea, having a party here tonight," he said in a tired voice that didn't hide his displeasure.

Duke moved around the console for a better look. "I thought you were further along. Cynthia said the new console was in and – "

"Cynthia said," Dennis mocked and held up the head of an unterminated snake. "A lot she knows. Why don't you ask her where I should plug this in?"

Duke saw Diane and Marco arranging chairs in the studio area and chose to ignore Dennis' bad mood. He and Remy were still buzzed and the idea of a party still felt like a good idea. "So how fast can you two button this up?"

Dennis was incensed. "How fast? Are you kidding me? This will take weeks!"

Duke asserted himself. He needed and trusted Dennis, but he was the one with his ass on the line, and he was the one with the vision. "I don't care if everything works; I just want to be able to play something through the speakers," he clarified. "What do you think Walter? Doable?"

Walter sat up and wiped his glasses with his shirt. He didn't want to get in the middle of a studio power struggle. "We can just bypass the noise reduction for now. As far as everything else is concerned, you'll have to ask Dennis."

Duke reached into his bag of tricks for a palliative. "So, Dennis, I know you must be a little burnt, but I think I can help you out with that," he offered.

Dennis knew what he meant but said, "Whadya mean, jelly bean?" just to confirm.

Walter understood too. "I didn't hear that, and if you guys are going to be taking drugs, please go in the other room."

Duke scaled Walter's facade. "Oh, Walter, don't be such a prude. We know you smoke. Samantha's got some funky friends."

Walter tried to uphold his civic reputation. "You can't believe everything my wife says. I've got government clearance and – "

Duke didn't let him off the hook. "And what? Like everyone in the government is straight? My friend Remy here was in the army for a long time. Tell him how righteous and holy everyone in the armed services is, Remy."

Remy grinned like a crocodile. "Sheeet, man, I think he knows what you're saying. Why don't we just show the man some respect and do your business in back. I'm running low on fuel."

The prospect of energy drugs got Dennis up off the floor. "Man, I ain't getting any younger," he said, stretching his substantial frame. "I could use a little boost to get me over the hump. This place is a complete mess; I can't believe you want to have a party tonight!"

Walter stayed in the control room working, but Duke led Dennis and Remy to the rear lounge and closed the door. "We've been on the road since yesterday morning," Duke said, justifying the length of the lines he was laying out on the sofa table. "What day of the week is this?"

"It's only Saturday man," Remy reminded him, "but I ain't slept more than a few hours since Wednesday night." Remy cleared both lanes, swallowed, and revisited memories of Oswaldo's niece.

Dennis lined up and took off next. "Mmm-hmm," he said, savoring the numbing tingle in the back of his throat. "Now we're talking. What is this stuff?"

Duke knew how to use the power of drug persuasion. "Finest flake for my best buddies," he promised as he partook.

Feeling better, Dennis asked, "So what's the deal with this stupid party? You know we can't be ready to show the studio off the day after we change consoles."

Duke didn't see it that way. "Of course we can," he said, repeating the mantra of positive thinking he had read about in a magazine at the Santa Monica hotel. He knew the studio was much more than a place to record sound. "We don't have to worry about having a recording session; no one's bringing any instruments. We'll have the party in the studio, and anyone who wants to see the new desk can come in the control room for a peek. It looks amazing, and I'm sure everyone will be impressed. This is the most expensive console between Nashville and LA, and it's going to put us into the big leagues!" Satisfied with his own explanation, Duke sank into the comfortable cushions and held court. "Dennis, my man, this is a place where people realize their dreams. That's what the studio's all about. It would be great to be able to listen to something, but nothing has to actually work."

Remy had heard Duke's slick logic a thousand times and considered it his responsibility to keep his old friend grounded in reality. "I'm a few lines short of my dreams," Remy commented, rubbing his nose. "What time is this party anyway?"

Duke understood and laid out another round. "Tonight. This should help you make it through."

"Dream a little dream for me," Dennis said before he took his second turn.

Diane, who didn't bother knocking, showed up right as Duke was hunched over the table. She was one of the few studio women who never lost her wholesome manners in public. "Let me know when your brain and mouth get reconnected because there's stuff to talk about," she said plainly. Apart from testing her limits after a few beers, Diane didn't take drugs and tried to act like the adult she considered herself to be. Even though Duke was her boss, she believed she had a license to sass because she was dating a famous country music producer who was one of the studio's best clients.

Always ready for a confrontation, Duke stood up, turned around with a goofy grin, and smothered her with an aggressive two-armed hug that ended with a breathy nuzzle on her neck. "It's sooo nice to see you good-goddie," he said, using a nickname that was a portmanteau of her surname and reputation. "My brain and body never felt more connected," He stroked Diane's perfectly coiffed hair solicitously. "so let's talk."

Diane shuddered from Duke's physical contact. His affection was like an overly friendly dog's, and besides the fact that she wasn't naturally attracted to him, he smelled from too many days on the road without a shower and his crude manners reminded her of her lecherous brother. She re-gathered and cut through Duke's coke maze with her pent up agenda. "Well, the first thing we have to decide is who's invited. I've been making a list of all the people I think you'll want to invite, and I went through the booking calendar and made a list of everyone who's recorded here in the last few years, and then, there're all the people in town we do business with, and friends, and friends of friends, and I don't know, it seems like there're way too many people for the small space we've got; how are they all going to fit?"

Duke just listened and fantasized about stopping her mouth with his tongue.

Diane continued. "Who should we tell they can't come? We don't want people to hate us so how can we turn some people away and let other ones in? It's too late to send out formal invitations so what are we going to do? Have a bouncer at the door checking people's names off a list?"

Duke processed her rant and asked, "Well, who have you told so far?"

Diane had to think. "Uh, I didn't really keep track. We've been so busy, and I didn't know what you'd want to do, and I didn't want to invite certain people without asking you so I don't know who I told." Diane was startled by her own answer. Then she had a realization and added, "Cynthia's been working on this too, and I have no idea who she's told either."

Flustered women were a turn-on to him, and Duke viewed the problem from a chemically assisted altitude. "Then that settles it," he said smoothly. "There's no time to plan this out, so we'll just have to roll with whoever shows up."

The logic escaped Diane's comprehension. "But there's not enough room. If too many people come, it'll be too crowded; everyone will be bumping into each other and no one will have a good time," she argued. "And how much food and alcohol should we get? How can we make this work?" She had a hard time understanding the motivations of her permissive peers.

"We don't have to make it work," Duke claimed. "Let the force be with you," he explained with a gesture Diane avoided.

Conflating *Star Wars* logic with druggie reasoning was popular, but Diane didn't believe in it. "Nice idea, but that doesn't answer any of my questions."

"I know you think it doesn't, but it does," Duke assured her. "We're just going to let anyone who wants to come, come. We'll have someone at the door to make sure there're no narcs or random strangers, but that's all. If it gets too crowded, some people will leave. If we run out of food, so what? We aren't running a restaurant. Most of the people who will show up are friends in one way or another. It could be fun if everyone's packed in here; some people like rubbing up against strangers. I know you don't do drugs, but everyone else does, and that's what makes it a party." Duke thought he had talked her into submission, so he tried to finish her off by saying, "Have a drink or two, let yourself go; you might have a better time than you think." Then he cornered her, put his arm around her waist, and put his lips to her ear. "And I won't tell James if you need to scratch that itch."

Diane pushed herself free of Duke's disgusting idea. "Okay Duke, whatever you say. It's *your* studio. Who are you going to get to watch the door?"

"I was thinking you and Cynthia could take turns. You two know everyone who belongs here, and I'll be around if you need some help."

Dennis saw that Diane was upset and intervened. "I can take a door shift too. It'll be good to get some fresh air once it gets too stuffy in here."

"How many folks you think there're gonna be?" Remy asked, already sweating from an elevated heart rate. "I don't much like too many people too close. Makes me think sumpin's gonna git me."

The pressure of close quarters pushed the energy out of the lounge, and they all headed back up the hall to where there was more personal space: Dennis went into the control room, Diane continued to the front, Duke went into the studio area, and Remy went to the rest room.

Marco, who had never met Duke, was in the studio by himself arranging microphone stands and gobos so they would be out of the way. A long table with a plastic, goblin-themed tablecloth had been pushed against the control room glass, folding orchestra chairs were lined up along one wall of the large, parquet-floored room, and orange and black balloons with shiny ribbon tails bobbed off the dark textured ceiling as the ventilation system cycled on and off.

"Who are *you*?" Duke confronted Marco.

"I'm Marco. Who are *you*?"

A half-foot taller, ten years older, and thirty pounds heavier, Duke appeared intimidating. "I'm Duke. I own this place. What are you doing here?"

Marco was nervous to meet his new boss. "I'm just helping set up, sir. Is that okay?"

It fed Duke's ego to be called "sir," and he scanned his surroundings like a general reviews the troops. "Looks good in here," he said approvingly. "Carry on." Then he went back in the control room to salivate over his latest purchase.

Owning a studio was a dream come true, and Duke had sacrificed nearly everything to make it happen. He loved equipment, the more complicated the better, and in his mind, there could never be enough buttons, dials, and tiny blinking lights. He ran his hand along the sleek, anodized metal of the new console, and it excited him. Even if he didn't know how all the controls worked, they made him feel smart. He already knew what it was like to play nice instruments through expensive amplifiers, so building a world-class recording studio to capture those sounds had been a natural progression.

Dennis, in a decidedly better mood, was already putting the control room back together. "Whadya think?" he asked, snapping the fabric-covered grill cloths back onto the front of the flush-mounted speakers.

Duke rolled one of the leather engineer's chairs into place and sat down. He casually twisted a few knobs and ran some faders up and down their travel. "Feels good," he confirmed, savoring the mechanical engineering and workmanship. "I like the yellow paint better than I thought I would." Although Duke derived great pleasure from soaring through the sky like an omnipotent bird of prey, sitting behind a massive control panel directing the fate of others was a more intimate form of control.

"MCI really got their shit together," Dennis pointed out as he wheeled a chair next to Duke along the bolster. "I love the way they laid out the subgroups in their own section to the right of the master controls. We've got full metering and dynamics for the monitor mix!"

Duke wasn't as much of an engineer as Dennis, but he appreciated the complexity of the modules. "It'll take me a while to get familiar with all this, but I'm very impressed." He turned his attention to the tape recorders. "What do you think of the machines?

Still think the Germans and Swiss are the only ones who can build reliable equipment?"

"I'll always be a Studer man," Dennis admitted, "and there's nothing like a Nagra, but this JH 24 looks like it'll do the job. We'll have to see how she sounds when we work her out."

Duke had leveraged all his assets to finance the purchase of the new equipment, and he had much more than a passive interest in how it was going to perform. "Well this stuff sure *better* work; I've got everything riding on it."

Walter, who had been sitting on the floor, joined the conversation. "Oh, this is all going to work; I guarantee it!" he reassured Duke.

Duke was surprised that Walter would make such a bold statement. "Really? How do you know?"

Walter stood on the other side of the console, facing Dennis and Duke. He knew they were both high, so he chose his words carefully. "Listen, guys, I know you might think this is the most complicated piece of equipment in the universe, but it's not. All it does is allow noise to go from one place to another. Someone talks into a microphone, and you can hear them through the speaker. If you don't want to listen to them right as they're talking, you can store the sound of their voice on tape and hear it later." He spread his arms along the length of the console like the wings of an airplane. "This whole thing just lets you listen to lots of sounds at the same time, and all these buttons do is let you hear some louder or softer or with more treble or bass."

"Well duh!" Dennis said, reacting the simplistic explanation. "Thank you, Mr. Peabody, but I think we all know what happens in a recording studio."

Walter knew where their knowledge ended and took them there. "I'm sure you do, and I didn't mean to offend your intelligence; it's just that this technology is actually quite primitive."

Duke didn't like Walter's low opinion of his monumental purchase. "What do you mean, primitive? There are hundreds, maybe thousands, of chips in this baby!"

"I know, and I'm not saying that this isn't one of the most advanced pieces of technology consumers can buy, but as a pilot, you know that the military and government don't let the public get their hands on anything until they consider it commonplace."

Calling anything of Duke's "common" was like telling a teenager "no." "This equipment is manufactured to mil-spec," Duke reminded him. "That's why it costs so much. What makes you think that the government's so far ahead?"

Walter didn't want to ruin his relationship with the studio – partly because his wife thought it made him cool and partly for the income – but he also didn't want to violate any of the security clearances he needed to do his government contract work. "You know I can't tell you too much, but let's just say that someday soon, all this analog technology will be replaced by digital."

Dennis knew what Walter was talking about. "I've read that too. Moore's law is revolutionizing everything. The new synthesizers are using chips to generate sound and the control functions are being performed by stacked ICs."

Walter took up the narrative. "And that's just the beginning. Navigation, communication, and scientific calculation device makers are already using chips to make lighter, faster, and cheaper products. Those are big markets with lots of customers. Professional audio is a very small field, so it doesn't make sense to design and manufacture products that, even if they sold one to every possible buyer, wouldn't cover the cost of research and development. Most of the parts to this console were made to do other jobs. MCI just repurposed the components. How many of these consoles do you think they will ever sell? How many studios are there that could afford one?"

Duke didn't like what he was hearing but couldn't argue with the facts. He redirected the conversation by asking Walter, "So what else have *you* been working on? Do you think we can get our hands on some of this newer technology and use it here? It would be awesome if we could be the first studio to have something no one else had."

Walter thought of something that was unclassified and had an audio application. "I built something recently that might be interesting. My brother lives in the mountains near Steamboat Springs. He wanted to see if he could hear anything from outer space, so I made him a kind of digital microphone."

Dennis's ears perked up. "What's that? How does it work?"

"It's not really that complicated. It's just a big dish receiver attached to some amplifiers, chips, and an output board."

"Has he heard anything yet?"

"Of course. Radio astronomy hobbyists pick up all kinds of signals."

Remy, who had returned from the lavatory and come into the control room while Walter was talking, commented, "I've seen those things. The Comm guys in our division made one to listen in on the enemy."

"Interesting," Duke said, "but that doesn't sound like anything we can use here."

Dennis was fascinated. "I'm not so sure about that," he said, breadboarding his imagination into a device.

All the tech talk had sapped their coke buzz, so when Cynthia and Diane came into view through the control room window the men were drawn to the distraction. It was hard to know if Cynthia had already changed into her evening costume because she always dressed like a far-out hippy, but the three-foot angel wings attached to her back were definitely not part of her normal attire. In an obvious good mood, Cynthia spread her arms as if she were going to take off and trotted around the room fast enough to make her wings flap. Marco, who was still trying to be useful, abandoned his professional demeanor and invited her approach with open arms. Cynthia circled him, and they attacked each other like mating birds. Diane, standing with her arms folded across her chest, thought it was funny, then saw the blinking light wired to the outside buzzer and went to see who was at the front door. It was only four o'clock, and they had told everyone that the party didn't start until nine, so she assumed it was someone delivering the food they had ordered. She was wrong.

Stanley, a regular visitor, was waiting outside with Nima, who had only been to the studio once before. "Namasté," Stanley greeted Diane through the design in the etched glass door.

"Oh hi, Stanley," she said, opening the door. "The party doesn't start until nine, but you can come in if you like; Duke's here."

"I know," Stanley said, entering. "That's why I'm here."

Diane was only partially surprised at how quickly news spread in the small Boulder community. "They're in the control room, I think."

Stanley's appearance had evolved along with his spiritual growth. He still sported shoulder-length hair, but had started cinching it into a tight ponytail rather than letting it hang loose. Always conscious about fitting in, his Colorado outfits were defined by designer jeans, tailored shirts, and expensive cowboy boots. "Is he busy?" Stanley asked politely. Well-built, handsome, and with the aristocratic bearing he had inherited from the original Earl of Dunraven, Stanley's tortoiseshell glasses made him look more harmless than he was. "Do you think he'll mind if we join him?"

"Of course not," Diane answered the rhetorical question and stepped aside to let them pass.

Nima blew gently on a hanging ghost as she flowed into the depths of the studio behind her liege.

Stanley opened the door to the control room, saw too many people to feel comfortable. He said, "Oh, I'm sorry, Duke. I'll be in the back when you're free."

A few minutes later, Duke found them in the rear lounge sipping tea and watching television. Following etiquette, he sat down and joined them.

"So, bumpy flight?" Stanley asked.

"Not too bad," Duke reported, playing along with Stanley's unhurried style. "How are things by you? I hadn't seen your house all finished; it looks great."

"Nima told me you liked it. It's a bit far from town, but privacy and a view always come at a price. We've got a few guest rooms if you want to spend the night there before you take off again. I'll make sure we have some Western food next time."

"I never said I didn't like your food," Duke protested mildly.

Stanley's inveterate manners made it nearly impossible to argue with him. "Well, all the same, we'll take good care of you if you decide to spend some time with us. Nima hasn't forgotten how to prepare fish, and the monks from the monastery have taught us some wonderful vegetarian recipes you really ought to try."

A televised promo for the new Boulder-based sitcom *Mork and Mindy* steered the conversation away from food.

"Do they really film that here?" Nima asked. "It looks just like Pine Street."

Duke welcomed the opportunity to display his superior knowledge of the media business. "That *is* Pine Street, you're right. Have you seen an entire show?"

"Yes, we have," Nima said cheerfully. "Stanley and I go to our room at the Boulderado sometimes just so we can catch it. Na noo na noo," she added, playfully imitating the show's signature phrase.

"Well, they tape most of it in a Hollywood studio – television shows don't use film – but they send crews here once in a while to get location footage," Duke described the process.

Nima seemed confused. "So do you think anything on the show really happens in Boulder?" Her foreign background hadn't fully prepared her for modern Western culture. "What about Mork? Do you think he's really from another planet?"

Duke was shocked at the question, but an indulgent look from Stanley guided his answer. "Well, I'm not sure. I don't think I've ever met any aliens, but that doesn't mean there aren't any."

Nima seemed satisfied with the answer, but Stanley elaborated. "You remember what the monks say, "reality is in the mind of the beholder."

Nima considered the wisdom and asked, "Do you think that's what happened at the hotel today?"

"No, what happened at the hotel was real," Stanley told her. "They found the finger and where it came from."

"But they don't know who did it," Nima pointed out. "Maybe it was a ghost or an alien or … I don't know." Nima's logic often ended in mystery.

Stanley reeled her in. "I know you must be upset, but no sense letting your imagination run away with your fears."

Duke wasn't sure what they were talking about, and didn't want to bring up any business in Nima's presence, so he asked, "What happened at the hotel?"

Nima, much more talkative than she was when he first met her, volunteered an explanation. "We don't really know, but we were in our room when the police knocked on our door. They were looking for somebody so we let them in. Stanley knew the officer, so it was all okay, but when we went down to the lobby, we heard that someone in the restaurant found a cut-off finger in their dessert."

Duke interjected, "You're kidding?"

"No, she's not," Stanley assured him. "Someone attacked the poor old man who always sits by the front door. It turned into quite a scene. The hotel was still crawling with cops when we left. That's one reason we decided to come over early."

"That sounds awful!"

"Mind if I use the ladies' room?" Nima asked.

"Out the door and to your left." Duke pointed. Once she was gone, he added, "She's a little … ."

Stanley took it all in stride. "I know she's a little different," he admitted, "but I've learned a lot being with her."

"Really? Are you two a couple?"

"Well, sort of, in the Buddhist sense."

"What sense is that?" Duke asked, not knowing whether to expect any salacious details.

"You wouldn't understand," was all Stanley volunteered, "but one thing I can tell you is that she's nothing like my first wife."

Duke, who always had a crush on the extroverted blond that Stanley had foolishly married when he was young, couldn't resist asking, "So are you celibate now, or do Buddhists have sex as much as I've heard?"

"I don't know what you've heard, but some Buddhists practice celibacy, and some screw their brains out."

"So which is it for you?" Duke asked chummily. "You were always such a player. It's hard to imagine you not interested in getting any."

"Getting any what?" Nima asked as she reentered. Her hair had been brushed into a lustrous mane, and the subtle effects of the makeup she had applied made her face glow.

Stanley was familiar with her sign language. "Getting any younger, dear. I was just telling Duke what a good Tibetan wife you are."

"You two are married?"

Nima blushed. "A Tibetan wife is not the same as a Western wife."

Duke's confusion increased when he realized Nima was looking at him suggestively.

Stanley put his arm around her and stroked her back. "I hope we haven't arrived at your party too soon. You must be busy with preparations. Is it okay if we stay here for a while until the activity at the hotel subsides?"

"I guess so," Duke answered tentatively, his usual confidence melting under the pressure of unknown forces. As extended family, he had a complex relationship with Stanley, whose land and largesse solidified his position as a Colorado power broker.

"No need to fuss over us," Stanley assured him. "You won't mind if we sit and drink our tea?"

Nima had settled on the sofa in front of the television. "It's so cozy in here I could take a nap."

Duke didn't know what to make of Stanley's mysteriously benign companion, and wasn't sure what business could be discussed with her present. "Stay as long as you like," was all he could say. He had planned on transacting with Stanley at the hotel, but he wasn't in a hurry now that he had enough cash to cover his immediate needs. "I'll be up front. Let me know if you need anything special." He opened the hint window.

Stanley understood the inference. "As a matter of fact, your black tea was a little weak. Perhaps you have something a little stronger? It's been quite a day already."

"No problem. I'll be right back," Duke said, closing the door behind him.

"Do you need me to go get you something?" Nima touched Stanley's leg sympathetically. "The Satsang Diner has really strong mate. I could go get you some if you two need to talk old times."

Duke intended to retrieve his leather satchel and fetch them a chunk, but was diverted from his mission once he popped his head in the control room. By the time he remembered, Stanley and Nima had gone back to the hotel.

CHAPTER 30

There were several reasons Joel didn't want to go into work. He knew it was his responsibility, and they were always busy on Saturday night, but the Satsang Diner was more of his wife's business than his, and his overnight dalliance with Crystal had left him strangely satisfied – in a way that several years of marriage and meditation had been unable to do. The prospect of lying to Nancy, who was already overbearing and suspicious, was the main deterrent, but the fact that Nancy's favorite employee, Rosella, was lounging in the living room with her bandmates and knew that Crystal had slept upstairs was another problem. After spending a few extra moments in front of the bathroom mirror admiring his well-toned physique and organizing his excuses, Joel put on a pair of loose-fitting jeans he usually saved for special occasions, slipped on the soft leather loafers he had bought in San Francisco, and was buttoning his Lawrence Covell shirt when he returned to the bedroom. Slightly embarrassed and still giddy from the stimulation, Crystal was sitting up in bed with the covers up to her chin, uncertain how to proceed. They both knew that they would have to hide their romance, so according to agreement, Crystal floated down the stairs behind Joel in one of Nancy's house robes, determined to pretend that nothing had happened.

Rosella, whose bawdy performance the night before had earned The Cowboy Liberation Army prize money, was a proven expert at manipulating male attention and didn't even bother acknowledging their charade. "Well, good afternoon, you two," she greeted them cattily. "Nancy's robe looks a little big on you, Crystal."

Crystal's blush was only one shade darker than her post-orgasm glow, but she didn't say anything.

Joel defended himself. "I know what you're thinking Rosella, but nothing happened," he said convincingly. "Crystal had an anxiety attack, and I gave her one of Nancy's sedatives. Were you three comfortable downstairs?"

Rosella smirked but answered, "We slept fine after we finally got to sleep. I hope we didn't keep you up."

Joel used a subliminal suggestion technique he had learned in college to reinforce their ruse. "Crystal was knocked out, and I didn't hear a thing." He took Crystal's hand and led her into the kitchen like a medical attendant. "Have some of this tea; a strong brew of mate will help take the woozy away."

Hipolito, who was near the refrigerator looking for something to eat, moved out of the way so Joel could fill the kettle, and highly sensitive to animal emissions, smelled Crystal's sex as she brushed by. His manhood reacted before his brain, and as the only one in the house whose early morning intimacy was a solo affair, Hipolito felt out of place. His usual partner Roddy was still submerged in Rosella's passionate depths, and the high concept, richly appointed interior of a wealthy American couple's house made him feel like he didn't belong. Hipolito went downstairs to the den with his wake-up coffee, thinking that playing his guitar would make him feel better, but wound up walking outside instead.

The slight dusting of snow had completely melted, and the ground was damp. The mountain air was clear and crisp, and the overhead sun steamed a layer of fog over the pine canopy over the canyon. Happy to be closer to nature, and noticing the similarities between Colorado's climate and his native Azueta, Hipolito's attention was drawn to a plume of smoke emanating from the woods nearby. He had no reason to go back inside other than to relieve his bladder, so he left his coffee cup on the driveway retaining wall and followed an animal trail into the forest. After stopping to piss against a tree, he walked in the direction of the smoke. The path led down a steep gully, and he quickly lost track of exactly where he was in relation to where he came from. The trickle of water at the bottom of the wedge between the rocky hills had encouraged a growth of thick vegetation, and the ground was a messy tangle of withered vines, downed branches, and careened rocks. Walking carefully by brushing the obstacles away with his hands, Hipolito was surprised to see the dried remains of poisonous lupine seed pods, which he had been taught to keep his farm animals away from, and was alarmed to see a stand of highly toxic monkshood still standing in a protected southern exposure. As he knelt to rinse the residue on his hands in a small pool of water that had collected, the distinct smell of meat cooking over an open flame wafted in his direction. Curious, he crept closer to the source of the smoky odor with the stealth he had learned as a child, until he got close enough to hear the guttural mumblings of the chef.

Despite his best efforts to keep quiet, Chief Niwot heard Hipolito approach and called out an invitation. "Come, stranger; there is meat enough for all," he announced.

Hipolito emerged warily from the thicket. He saw an old Indian seated cross-legged next to a small fire, holding the hindquarters of a large animal over the flame by its leg. The rest of the butchered carcass lay on the other side of the pit, and were it not for the fact that Hipolito was familiar with the butchering process, he would have been disgusted to see the liver and other entrails drying on top of the rocks that formed the fire pit.

Chief Niwot spoke in an unusually familiar dialect. "You have come a long way. You must be hungry."

Hipolito didn't know who he was, but wasn't scared. "Yes, thank you," he said, practicing cautious manners. Meeting strange-looking recluses in the mountains wasn't that unusual where he came from, and Hipolito could tell that the seated man was very old, very dirty, and probably not very dangerous.

Chief Niwot removed a chunk of charred flesh from the heat, wordlessly proffering it with a scarred and blistered hand.

Following atavistic custom, Hipolito took the offering and nibbled politely, trying to please his host. But the ancient Indian didn't make eye contact or move. Hipolito wasn't sure he was breathing and looked more carefully. Strands of greasy hair that had once been part of braids hung like a ragged veil across his face. The Indian's lips were parched and swollen, and the few patches of skin Hipolito could see on his neck were thick folds of yellowed wither. Neither spoke as the fire crisped an aromatic plume into the sky. Hipolito looked up to see a hawk gliding down the mountain thermals, and when he looked down again, he was shocked to be alone. There was no trace of the Indian, the carcass, or the fire, and a rotting stump of a huge cottonwood was his only companion in the small clearing. Hipolito wiped the hair and sweat from his face. Disoriented, he scoured the nearby bushes, looking for a trace of the apparition. His lips were sticky with sap from the pinecone in his hand, and Roddy's voice, echoing his name off the canyon walls, called him to his senses.

"Coming!" Hipolito answered as he set off in the direction of the audible beacon.

"Over here!" Roddy yelled at intervals until he heard his friend's progress through the brittle woods.

Joel, Crystal, and Rosella were outside with Roddy by the time Hipolito returned to the driveway.

"*Que pasa*? What happened to you, amigo?" Roddy greeted him with slack-five concern.

Joel, who was holding the cup that Hipolito had left behind said, "You've been gone more than an hour. Where were you? We were worried about you."

Crystal noticed the dirt on his face and said, "You don't look so good. Did something happen to you? Are you feeling okay?"

Hipolito was surprised at all the attention. He rubbed the bark and brambles out of his hair and said, "I'm okay," in a bewildered voice. "Was I really gone that long?"

"Yes," Rosella informed him impatiently. "Nancy called from the restaurant three times. She's been waiting for us, but we couldn't just leave you here. What happened to you?"

Hipolito looked confused and didn't offer an explanation.

"Maybe he had an accident?" Crystal suggested.

Rosella disagreed. "You don't know him like we do. Hippy has a way of getting into trouble. Right, Roddy?" Roddy knew what she was talking about but defended his friend. "Nancy's a nicer boss than Hans. All Hippy did was get lost."

"Just like those cows got lost?" Rosella reminded him.

"I don't know what you two are talking about," Joel interrupted, "but we better get going now. It's time to set up for dinner, and we've got to be there to help. Rosella, you can ride with Crystal and me if your friends want to go home."

Rosella didn't like the idea of riding in the backseat – especially when she knew Crystal would be riding in front. "That's okay, Joel. We'll follow you."

Joel asserted himself. "Okay, but don't get lost on the way."

Roddy had already packed the instruments into the trunk of the two-door Grand Prix, and they had no trouble keeping up with Joel and Crystal down the twisty two-lane blacktop that hugged one side of Sunshine Canyon. Rosella sat in the bucket-style passenger seat, skillfully touching up her toenail polish as the centrifugal forces pitched the nose-heavy gas burner from side to side.

Hipolito, sitting sideways in the back seat, tried to explain what he saw. "He seemed like he knew me," he repeated several times, mostly to himself, "and I understood everything he said."

"But what happened to him?" Roddy asked through the rear-view. "Are you saying he just vanished like some kind of *fantasma*? Maybe it was your ancestor? It's very close to Day of the Dead."

"No, he was definitely no one I knew. I can still see him in my mind. He was some kind of Indian but didn't look Maya or Yaqui."

Rosella, whose friends had shown her passages from *The Teachings of Don Juan*, made a connection. "Maybe he was a sorcerer?" she said with the excitement of discovery. "Did he give you anything to eat?"

The question shocked Hipolito. "Yes! How did you know?"

"There's a book everyone's been reading. It's about a Mexican Indian who eats peyote and sees things."

Roddy weighed in. "I don't think Hippy wandered off and ate peyote by accident."

"Did you put anything strange in your mouth?" Rosella asked, remembering the pithy taste she still had in the back of her throat. "Maybe some kind of poison that made you see things?"

Hipolito touched his fingers to his lips and tasted them. The motion of the car made him a little dizzy, and the lupine residue burned his tongue. "I don't know what happened," he admitted.

CHAPTER 31

After he dropped his passengers off, Kundun had parked and went to the Satsang Diner to await further instructions. The restaurant was closed between lunch and dinner, but Tara brought some chai and made him feel welcome. Donna's baking had taken on assembly-line efficiency with the rest of the kitchen staff helping. Jampo shuffled the trays in and out of the oven, Tara packed the finished pastries into boxes, and Tenzin kept the bowls and pans and utensils ready for their next usage. Nancy confined herself to her office, where she alternated between processing paperwork and hanging up on Joel at the end of bickering phone calls. Joel's excuse for not coming in was that Rosella's bandmates had slept late, and he didn't want to leave them at the house by themselves. He promised that he and Crystal would show up and help with the dinner serving, but Nancy knew there was more to the story.

When they got to the restaurant, Joel and Crystal pulled into the dedicated parking spot behind the building. Following, Roddy stopped on the corner to let Rosella out. "Come by the restaurant later," she said with a peck on his cheek.

"What time?" Roddy asked through the window. "Do I have enough time to take Hippy back to Denver?"

Rosella was halfway across the street when she yelled, "No. Just hang around town. Pick me up after eight. We're going to a Halloween party tonight."

They didn't have anywhere special to go, and Roddy had never been to Boulder without Rosella, so he decided to go to the

Boulderado and get a drink at the Mezzanine bar where Rosella had once taken him. The two Latino boys were underdressed for the trendy spot, but everyone was too concerned with getting into the mood to notice. The ongoing crime scene and police investigation was a curious distraction, so they ordered a pitcher of beer and peered over the railing of the second floor balcony at the drama below.

Joel was already arguing with Nancy in the office when Rosella walked into the Satsang kitchen. Crystal had disappeared into the alleyway for some fresh inspiration, and Donna was silently snide, so after saying hello to Tara and Jampo, Rosella put on an apron and went to see if there were any customers in the restaurant. There were only a few, most of whom were either reading or waiting for time to pass, and no one needed anything. Rosella knew that Nancy was the only one at the restaurant who liked her, so rather than go back in the kitchen to help cook or bake or clean, she sat at an empty table and finished applying red touch up paint to her nail extensions.

In between washing cycles, Tenzin wandered out of the kitchen with a cup of tea and joined Kundun at a table. Owing to Tenzin's vows, they didn't speak in the same way that Westerners understand dialogue, but their communication was complete. Kundun spoke in Tibetan, and Tenzin responded with guttural groans, tongue clicks, and eye contact. The shared experience of refuge in a foreign land added to the effectiveness of the wordless knowing that was an integral part of their training. A rough translation of their conversation follows.

"How's the tea?" Tenzin asked.

"Weak but warm."

"What are you doing here?"

"Waiting."

"For?"

"Drive back to the monastery."

"The Dharma Bus made a special trip?"

"No, I drove the Stanley car. They had guests. Gyalpo and Chodya came too."

Tenzin had a rivalry with Gyalpo that stretched beyond this lifetime and into the family trees that forested their home country. They had all emigrated together, but because of his excellent language and assimilation skills, Lama Yeshe left Gyalpo in charge of the monastery during his absence.

The news that Gyalpo was in town with Chodya made Tenzin uncomfortable. "Where are they?" he gesticulated.

"I let them off at Djorge Dzong, but I think they're going to the hotel for the Halloween party."

"They're up to no good," Tenzin thought aloud.

Kundun, who was also part of the first wave of Tibetan refugees to settle in Colorado, agreed. He and Tenzin knew that Gyalpo had veered from the Path, and they planned on informing the head monk upon his return. They knew that Halloween was the perfect time for Chöd rituals and shared their disapproval of the practice with deep breaths.

Tara came in with tea and refilled their cups. She was always very polite to Tenzin, who seemed satisfied washing dishes, because she knew that if he didn't do it, she would be the one with her hands in the sink.

Tenzin accepted his refill with a silent stare.

"Lama Yeshe is due back soon," Kundun reminded him.

"We will speak to him about Gyalpo," Tenzin said. "Perhaps *he* will be able to control the tulpas." Both monks blamed Gyalpo for the bad karma that had allowed the tulpas to escape.

Kundun stirred his thoughts through his tea. With so few people in the restaurant, his attention settled on Rosella. He had seen her there before, but she was always moving too fast for him to get a good look. As the youngest founding member of Punkah Dzong, he was the same age as many of the American hippies, and in his eyes, she appeared to be the embodiment of the decadent

Western youth culture. What was it about the freedom of America that caused their young people to act so outrageously? Rosella's blood-red nails and provocative cleavage reminded him of the she-demons he was shown in painted murals before he took his vows. Temptation tested the limits of his resolve, and he used pranic energy to battle his earthly desires.

Older and more advanced in his practice, Tenzin sensed Kundun's meditative struggle. Troubled with weighty matters, their combined concerns were strong enough to reach the consciousness of their teacher, Lama Yeshe. Appearing to them both at the same time, Lama Yeshe summoned them home. As their bodies sat in the restaurant, the monks' temporal surroundings melted back into Maya, and their consciousness were transported to the incense-thick monastery in Tibet where they had received their training. Long bellows from resident monks cleansing their spirits with deep overtone chants, and the random pattern of their damarus, reverberating off the wooden walls like horses trotting through paved air, obscured their sense of their own bodies. Lama Yeshe, seated on a zafu in an alcove with thick drapery walls, stopped his meditation and opened his eyes as his disciples appeared before him. They spoke without speaking.

"I have heard your suffering," Lama Yeshe gestured empathetically. "The new world has many challenges."

"Yes, Teacher," Kundun agreed. "Our practice is difficult. There are so few of us and much work to do at the monastery."

"I understand, but your training is strong, and you will succeed. Has the tulpa you created been helping?"

"Yes, Your Holiness, it was." Kundun was too scared to elaborate.

Tenzin spoke for them both. "The tulpa is no longer useful," he revealed.

Lama Yeshe was supportive. "They do not last forever," he sympathized. "You must destroy that one and make another."

"We cannot."

"Why?"

"The tulpa has escaped."

"Escaped?" Lama Yeshe leaned slightly forward. He had been away for almost a year and had been involved in too many of his peoples' struggles to follow all the tribulations of his own monastery. "How? Where did it go?"

Tenzin laid the blame on Gyalpo. "We do not know. Gyalpo was in charge of him. When the first one disappeared, Gyalpo made another."

"Yes," Kundun confirmed. "Gyalpo made the second one much stronger so it could help with construction. He was very helpful at first."

"At first? Has something happened to the second tulpa as well?"

"Yes," Tenzin took up the narrative. "Gyalpo thought the first tulpa would die by itself, but it came back and poisoned the mind of the second one. Now they are both lost."

"Yes," Kundun said, "and I cannot take care of everything by myself. The novices need so much instruction."

Lama Yeshe was much more concerned with the missing spirit beings than a messy monastery. "How can this be?"

Kundun remembered Rosella's temptations and snitched. "It is Gyalpo's fault. He has violated the remainders."

Lama Yeshe was disturbed by the allegation. "Which ones?"

"He has been unchaste – with a Western nun."

Gyalpo was not the first of Lama Yeshe's disciples to stray from the Path. He tried to imagine what might have happened. "Has the monastery forgotten to polish the Three Jewels?"

"Punkah Dzong has changed since you left, Your Holiness. The local influence is very powerful. We need you to come back."

Lama Yeshe closed his eyes. "There is much needing in Tibet as well." When he opened his eyes again, the monks could see tears. "I thought Punkah Dzong would be safe from local enemies in the new world. Here, we battle the Chinese occupiers who have destroyed many temples. Our young cannot enter the monastery and learn about our culture. Our land is being taken, and our people are suffering. Many have gone to India to seek work and have become strangers to our traditions. The Dalai Lama, and all of us who have escaped, are doing everything we can, but we cannot be everywhere at once."

Kundun felt bad for complaining. "I am sorry, Teacher. I must deepen my compassion."

Tenzin wanted to ask about the family he left behind but said, "You have given us much, Teacher. We will do our part to preserve our ways."

"Good. Both of you sit with Gyalpo and the others; find a way. The tulpas only have the power they can borrow. Punkah Dzong is strong enough without them now. Many are counting on you. Throw out the demons who have interfered and make room for your practice. I will bring many more pilgrims with me when I return." Then Lama Yeshe addressed the dissension between Tenzin and Gyalpo. "Tenzin, you are my successor. Gyalpo has confused his mastery of Western skills with pratimoksha training. You will need his help to destroy the tulpas, and after that, he will be summoned here."

"Thank you, Master. As you wish. Namasté."

Their darshan over and their senses bristling with awareness, Tenzin and Kundun found themselves back at a table in the Satsang Diner. Nothing their teacher had said was comforting or optimistic, but the monks accepted their hardship as one more obstacle on the path to enlightenment. No one had noticed their conscious departure, and only a few moments of earthly reality had passed, so the men stirred their tea in silence and practiced patience. Each of them had been taught how to create and destroy their own tulpa – the successful completion of that ritual was a necessary part of their initiation – but they were in uncharted territory now because the tulpas that Gyalpo had helped create to serve the monastery had developed their own agenda. The monks didn't know where they were, so they looked for signs of mischief everywhere, starting with their present location.

In their brief absence, Rosella had gone to wait on two men who had never been to the restaurant. Her flirty repartee was inappropriate but certainly human, so the monks looked elsewhere. Nearby, Crystal was unable to suppress a satisfied grin while taking a dinner order from a local writer who knew both reasons she was in a good mood. The monks decided that she was not under malefic influence, and everyone else appeared benign, so Kundun stayed at the table with his back to the window that still had the Halloween poster in it and Tenzin went back to the kitchen.

Tara was helping Jampo prepare and deliver the meals, Donna was busy rolling and filling the remainder of the baking orders scheduled for delivery, and Nancy was still arguing with Joel behind closed doors. Everyone within earshot went about their tasks, pretending to not hear them.

A loud bang was followed by Nancy's shrieking invective, "Don't lie to me!"

"Keep your voice down," Joel told her sternly.

Nancy's indignant tirade continued anyway. "Don't tell me what to do. It's my restaurant, and I'll talk as loud as I want to!"

"It's our restaurant," Joel corrected. "And we have an obligation to our sangha to keep it peaceful," he added, trying to keep calm.

Nancy was too annoyed to be polite. "My father put up the money, so this place is mine," she insisted. "And screw the sangha, what have they ever done for us?"

Joel was shocked to hear how shallow her commitment to her adopted faith was. "What have they ever done? I know you're angry, but you're talking like you still live on the Upper East Side. The sangha is our community now. The sangha is the reason we live here and the reason this restaurant exists. Without the sangha, there can be no Satsang."

Nancy turned her rage down to a slow boil. "Don't preach to me, Joel. You're not even close to enlightened!"

"And you are? What about selflessness?"

Nancy paused to consider his point, then boiled over at the thought of his infidelity. "At least I know how to keep my pants on, Mister."

Joel cringed as his secret spilled into the next room. Then he fired back. "I'll say. Maybe you ought to try taking those frozen pants off and feel something human once in a while."

"I'll bet you'd like that. Too bad I'm not interested in feeling what *you've* got!"

Joel was a little stunned to hear the truth. "Well, I guess we've figured out what our problem is. I'll go and do the deliveries while you figure out who or what you *do* want." He moved toward the door.

Nancy didn't surrender to his sympathy defense. "That's it, turn it around like you always do. Fuck someone else in our bed and blame me."

Joel restated his lie. "Crystal was sick, and I gave her one of your sedatives. She couldn't sleep on the sofa next to Rosella's smelly friend, so I let her stay on the sofa in our room."

"And you expect me to believe that? I've seen the way you look at her – so frail and vulnerable," Nancy mocked. "I hope she called you Daddy because you're old enough to be her father!"

"That's it. You've completely lost it!" Joel said indignantly. "I hope you have some of your pills with you because you may need all of them." Furious, he slammed the door on his way out and tried to compose himself in the presence of his employees.

The kitchen staff didn't know whether to say something or pretend they hadn't heard every word. Donna broke the silence by asking, "Can you check on my turnovers, Jampo. I think they're ready to come out, and I've got the next batch ready to go in."

Jampo opened the oven door, poked at the pastries, and followed the path of least resistance. "One more minute, Do-nah. They're almost crispy on top."

Joel welcomed the distraction and joined the conversation by asking, "How many boxes are ready for delivery?"

Tara pointed to the stack of squat cardboard containers with the Satsang Diner stickers on top. "I don't know how many are there, but those are the ones ready to go."

Nancy usually handled the to-go orders, so Joel asked Tara for help. "All these are full? What's in them? Are they labeled anywhere? How do we know which goes to who?"

"I'm not sure anymore," Tara told him. "There were so many that it was too hard to keep them separate; I just packed them the way they came out of the oven."

Joel lifted a lid and peeked inside. "Do they all look the same? How do we know what's what?"

"The khapse and yola are kind of twisted and don't have anything inside," Donna explained without stopping her preparations. "The turnovers are kind of fat. I put apples in about half of them, and the rest have some combination of apricots, raisins, pineapple, and yogurt. There are a few different kinds of cookies, but I told Tara to just put some of each in every box. I hope that's okay."

Joel was peeking under the lids when Crystal came into the kitchen. She was too high to notice the tension and nuzzled against him, sniffing at the delicious odors trapped inside.

Tara, who hated confrontation, thought Nancy might see them, so she said, "Nancy has the order book," in such a way as to warn Joel. "Some of the parties might already be starting so maybe these should be delivered now."

Joel glanced up just in time to see the blinds on the windows to Nancy's office close. He knew he'd have to talk to her sooner or later, so he announced, "I'll be making the deliveries myself," in a resigned tone and went back into the office.

Crystal didn't know they were about to resume their fight. "I can help," she offered with an innocence no one believed.

Tara turned up the tape player in the kitchen so it would be harder to hear the next argument. Jampo tried to mask the ensuing conflict by practicing the basso incantations that were his favorite part of Buddhist practice. Concerned about the unraveling of his sangha, Tenzin used the patterns of rinse water to help him divine whether the renegade tulpa was causing the disharmony. Donna, her arms hurting from the day's kneading and her hands covered in sticky rice flour, blew the hair from her eyes so she could see the clock and estimate what time she would be able to get out of there.

Rosella, oblivious to the drama and energized by attention of the male customers she had been explaining the menu to, came into the kitchen chewing gum and feeling chipper. "Virgins in the dining hall!" she announced to no one in particular. "You should have heard them when I told them we're vegetarian only." She paused to make sure her cleavage was visible. "One of them asked me if I was on the menu and, if so, what kind of vegetable I was. Men; they're so predictable."

"So what did you tell them?" Donna cracked. "A radish?"

"Very funny, pastry girl. You look like you're ready for the oven yourself. What are you going to be for Halloween, a sugar loaf?"

Donna was too tired to escalate the spat, but Tara, whose breasts were bigger than Rosella's, took on the challenge, posing in a way that accentuated her attributes. "I'm going as a nurse."

Crystal, who was almost flat chested, stayed out of the argument. Joel came out of the office, looking upset. "What's the matter?" she asked sympathetically.

"Want to help me make deliveries?" he asked, holding back tears.

Crystal was a little embarrassed by how emotional the invitation was. "Now? What about the dinner rush? Who's going to help serve?"

"Rosella and Tara can handle it," Joel decided. "Nancy will run the register if she ever comes out of her office," he added bitterly. "Come on, let's go. I could use the company," he admitted, then picked up two pastry boxes and handed them to Crystal. "You take these and meet me in back. I'll drive and you can deliver."

Crystal was happy about the assignment but concerned about the logistical implications. "How long do you think this is going to take? I have plans tonight."

Joel was walking toward the back when he answered, "I'm not sure how long we'll be. Better get your things in case we don't make it back tonight."

CHAPTER 32

By six o'clock, the police investigation at the Boulderado had wound down to a few detectives looking over the hotel register and making notes in the small bar situated around the corner from the reception desk. Per their daily ritual, Ken Ken led a trio of novice monks with swinging metal incense burners through the corridors, cleansing the cosmic energies with local sage and sandalwood. Jack, sporting a demon horn headpiece, was unusually energetic, making sure that the Boulderado was prepared to accommodate the big crowd and inevitable overuse of bathrooms. He directed hotel employees to cordon off residential areas so that several hundred high-spirited revelers were mostly confined to the first two floors. Bandaged and sedated, Mr. Lawry had been moved back to his third floor room and out of the way so that preparations for the Halloween party could resume. Acting with exaggerated calm and sincerity, the two Hollywood producers, speedballing with coke and rum chasers, took pains to make sure each aspect of their planned event was in place. They hovered over Sasha, Mavis, and the rest of the Fleur de Lis wait staff, making changes to the flower arrangements and patrolling the party area like vigilante Tinker Bells.

Jon was tired of staying out of the way in his room, and with Marco busy at the studio and Donna still at work, he was without his usual companions. He ventured downstairs to see who else might be around and was relieved that the energy had shifted from a crime scene to a party atmosphere. The hotel staff, many of them Jon's pot customers, wearing the logoed T-shirts, hats, and pins of the movie, circulated through the crowd with fearsome levity as they advertised the hideous message of a bloody knife in midstab. Jon peeked in the restaurant and saw that Sasha and Mavis were too busy setting up the buffet to pay attention to him, and Jack, his sometimes friend, was being bossy and unapproachable. Simone's shop was closed, and he thought about going back to the roof but didn't want to run into Chodya and her hostile monk friend again. The bustling lobby was overrun with straight people from Table Mesa in expensive, store-bought costumes, and college party animals who had already begun to drink and push their way toward the free meal. Feeling claustrophobic, Jon zipped up his vintage bomber jacket with the faux fur collar and slipped out the side door.

The streetlights on the mall had been activated by darkness, and the Halloween decorations, swaying and shimmering in the evening breeze, looked strangely fitting against the backdrop of darkening mountain shadows. All the public buildings around the courthouse plaza were closed, and most of the pedestrians on the promenade were scurrying to the restaurants hosting Halloween-related activities. The temperature had dropped low enough that the homeless hippies and their pets must have found refuge somewhere, because other than Jon, the only people who thought the weather was perfect for just welcoming the night were a trio of impossibly persistent Hare Krishnas and one bedraggled Native American.

Seated in the grass on the opposite side of the walkway from Jon's bench, Chief Niwot periodically raised his arms to the sky. Mumbling while tapping on a small drum hidden in his lap, his ritualistic behavior seemed almost normal for the Pearl Street Mall – an area where existential longings were routinely expressed. Jon, with nothing else to capture his imagination, listened to what the old Indian was saying. He couldn't understand the language, but did find musical inspiration in Niwot's song. The painful, guttural growls, interspersed with the scratching and thumping of calloused hands on stretched animal hide, sounded like something he could imitate by dragging a flatpick across the wound strings of an electric guitar plugged in to an amp with a touch of distortion and short delay. Appreciating the similarities between the Chief's incantation and the rumblings of a Moog synthesizer, he was lost in the old Indian's dirge when the volume and urgency of the singing increased. The last rays of daylight barely lit the cloud cover on the furthest western peaks, and the Indian's bass frequencies seemed to ripple like heat in the chill air. The Hare Krishnas noticed a change in the vibrational atmosphere and became uncharacteristically motionless.

As the evening veils of Samhain parted, Chief Niwot suddenly stopped singing and began speaking. Jon couldn't see who he was talking to until a dimly lit wraith appeared in the darkened ethers and the night seemed to come to a standstill. He saw the outline of a hovering spirit over the Chief, and thinking he must have smoked too much pot, reached for a cigarette, hoping it would help him come down. A sudden gust of air extinguished the lighter on his first try, and Jon, whose deep connection with the physical universe had never allowed for much spiritual realization, relit and took a long drag on his filtered Camel. He was stunned, but completely conscious when the apparition, who he recognized as Gyalpo, materialized out of nothingness and stood next to Niwot.

Agitated, Gyalpo confronted the Chief in an angry voice. The Chief, suddenly attentive, argued with him forcefully. There was very little actual contact as vaporous arms flailed, and neither seemed to have the upper hand as the confrontation intensified. Cursing furiously, Gyalpo swiped at Niwot's head with a long-bladed knife, but the Chief, looking much younger and spry than he did a moment ago, deftly avoided the attack. Distancing himself,

Niwot summoned a deep-bellied roar that overwhelmed Gyalpo's high-pitched diatribe, and commanding the sound-current power with the purposeful beating of his hand drum, thumped his opponent into submission. Gyalpo's image wavered as the Chief asserted his primacy, and Jon understood nothing about their exchange except that it was extremely brief and seemingly hostile. Before he had finished smoking, both Gyalpo and the Chief vanished with the last light of day. The Hare Krishnas celebrated the end of the fight with a round of devotional singing and rhythmic bells, and the mall resumed its real-time functionality without anyone else noticing anything unusual.

Stunned by the experience, Jon tried to relate what he had seen to the passages from Don Juan that Donna had read to him. Sorcerers and spirits appearing and disappearing were instances he had heard about, but the actual experience was different from what he expected. It had happened so fast that he didn't have time to be scared, and the fact that he was just a spectator made him consider the possibility that he had just imagined the whole thing. He got up and walked over to the spot where the Chief had been sitting, expecting to see nothing but the confirmation of a drug-induced hallucination, but a long feather – the kind he had seen drooping from Chief Niwot's head band – conflated his realities. The feather was too long to have come from any of the sparrows or pigeons that frequented the mall, and he didn't see any other feathers like it nearby. Picking up the magic plume and sticking it into his hair seemed like a good idea, and feeling empowered he walked the few blocks back to the hotel with the smirk of discovery and confidence that he was sufficiently costumed to join in the holiday fun.

The Satsang van was parked in front of the Boulderado when Jon got there. He saw Crystal carrying the familiar Satsang Bakery boxes and, knowing they were full of Donna's pastries, offered to help bring them in. Crystal recognized Jon from the talent contest and accepted the help. She followed him into the Fleur de Lis, set the desserts down on one of the serving tables, and went back to the car to get the rest of the order. While she was gone, Jon pried open one of the boxes. He was snatching a snack when Sasha spotted him with a feather in his hair.

"Hey, Chief, hands off!" Sasha scolded. "We're not serving dessert until later."

Jon removed his cookied hand sheepishly and hid the evidence in his mouth. Sasha's busty costume, partially covered by a horror movie apron, made her admonition hard to take seriously, so Jon raised his right hand like a spaghetti Western Indian and said, "White woman look very sexy," after he swallowed.

The people waiting in line for the buffet to open saw Jon eating and took it as a cue that the serving had begun, and once the word spread and the pungent smells of barbecued ribs confirmed the rumor, there was nothing Sasha or anyone else in the restaurant could do to halt the hungry assault on the food as the throng of expectant partygoers answered the call of free dinner by pushing closer to the meal.

Crystal, holding the rest of her delivery above her head so she could pass through the crowd, had mixed feelings about being groped by naughty college boys drunk on beer. She put her hand on Joel's leg when she got back to the car and asked, "Can we go to my apartment so I can change into my party clothes?" Joel welcomed the idea, so they drove to her apartment, smoked a joint, and didn't get out of bed until the next morning.

The press of diners into the restaurant pushed Jon out, and he sliced against the incoming tide with one arm extended in front of him like a rush-hour surfer. Back in the lobby, he grabbed a champagne from a roving server, straightened out his head feather, and careened around the costumed excitement until Simone beckoned him from the mezzanine balcony. Tipsy, he bounded up the spiral staircase and joined Simone's gathering. Miko and Sarquette, sparkling in sequin outfits, sandwiched Simone with sensuous smiles.

Welcoming Jon to their clutch like a master of ceremonies, Simone, his considerable girth confined by a custom-made, gray sharkskin suit that featured a bold orange and black silk handkerchief, raised his right hand, and with a nod to Jon's feather, said, "Good evening, Chief. I'm glad to see they've let you off the reservation."

Jon gamely stayed in character. He bent over so that the feather brushed Simone's face and returned the greeting with a raised hand. "How-*de* kimosa*be*," he rhymed.

Simone loved attitude above all else. He presented his others as eye candy offerings. "*Bon nuit, monsieur. Je pense* you've already met the lovely Ms. Sarquette. She puts the *howl* in Halloween, *n'est pas?*"

Sarquette's provocative pose ignited Jon's serpent fire, and he drained the rest of his drink trying to put it out. Temporarily tongue-tied, he raised his hand again and gulped acknowledgement. "And *how!*"

"*How* do you like it?" Sarquette teased him and touched his arm. "Now that you're away from your reservation?"

"No reservations; *Mon Dieu!*" Simone exclaimed. "Perhaps monsieur doesn't know how he likes it."

Miko joined the seduction by nuzzling against Simone. "Perhaps he needs some instruction," she suggested.

Jon was overmatched by the professional company. Unable to resist temptation, the sights and sounds of the festivities blended into a hazy buzz. He felt like there was a leather strap wrapped around his hardening appendage, and each twitch of Sarquette's expressive lips put pressure on the imaginary binding, causing it to harden more. Seeing Jon's uncontrollable reaction, Miko slithered on Simone's side, celebrating the captivity of Jon's herpetological urges.

Sarquette took the empty flute from his hand, put it on a nearby table, and came close enough to breathe, "I need to see you in our room," onto his neck.

Simone nodded approval and asked Sarquette, "Shall we come too?"

Sarquette ran her hand down the front of Jon's pants and answered, "In a little while; I think we'll need a head start."

Mesmerized, Jon allowed Sarquette to take his hand and lead him to the stairwell. As soon as the pneumatic fire door closed, he grabbed her around the waist, pushed her against the wall, and put his lips to her mouth. Encouraging the vigor of his advances, Sarquette put her arms around his neck and pressed her pubis against his loins. Their tongue-play and touching escalated like a brush fire, and only the sound of someone coming down the stairs slowed them to a less passionate embrace.

The woman on the stairs didn't see who the couple was, and it wasn't until he looked up that Jon recognized Chodya in the dimly lit stairwell. Caught in the act and too excited to make excuses, Jon avoided Chodya's gaze and hugged Sarquette with the animal instincts that controlled him.

But Sarquette could tell there was something was wrong with Chodya and said, "Good evening," smoothly distancing herself from vice. Then, recognizing Chodya from earlier in the day and feeling Jon's hesitation, she added, "Nice to see you again," as she stroked Jon's back with PG affection.

Chodya was drawn to the power of their intimacy, but unknown to Jon or Sarquette, she was too engaged in her own drama to judge them. After turning around fearfully, she came close enough for it to be obvious she wasn't well. Her face was contorted with pain, her headscarf was half off, and the folds of her poorly wrapped sarong were dragging on the floor. Holding on to the handrail for support, she gingerly stepped down to the landing and rested her back against the wall next to Sarquette's. "Help me, please," she whispered. Her presence completely disrupted the couple's foreplay, and they separated as Chodya began to babble nonsensically. "They want to eat me. I am the red meal," she sputtered. "Gyalpo played the kangling. I must be purified."

Sarquette, who knew something about ritual magic, talked to Chodya like a therapist trying to reach a patient in episodic seizure. "Who wants to eat you?" she asked gently.

"The demons." Chodya choked out the words. "I must be purified to save the monastery."

Jon's blood flow reversed direction and activated his brain. "Chodya, it's Jon. Can you hear me?"

She shook as he touched her arm. "Gyalpo is angry. I'm scared."

The mention of Gyalpo's name recalled the hostility in Jon's stomach. "Where is he?" he asked bravely.

Chodya looked up the stairs with the terror of someone who had glimpsed the Darkness.

Jon followed her stare and confirmed, "He's on the roof? What he did he do to you?"

Chodya twisted her mouth but couldn't explain in words.

"Then I'll go find out myself," Jon said valorously.

Sarquette had other ideas. "I don't want you to go up there. It may be dangerous; and besides … ." She squeezed his hand.

Jon didn't know which urge to respond to, but when Chodya melted down the wall, he grabbed her before she crumpled to the ground.

Looking down, Sarquette saw that her head was scratched and bleeding. "She needs to lie down," she told Jon. "Help me take her to the room."

Suddenly sober with a sense of purpose, Jon carried the half-conscious victim up the stairs to Simone's fourth floor lair. In his arms, Chodya looked up and saw Jon's feather. "The Chief is angry," she mumbled as he laid her on the bed. Sarquette peeled Chodya's headscarf the rest of the way off her head and gasped at the geometrically correct pentangle carved into her cleanly shaven scalp. Using skills for treating abuse she had learned in dominatrix training, Sarquette put a damp towel on the wounds to stop the bleeding. Then she unwrapped Chodya's outer layer of clothes and tried to assess the extent of the damage. Lying down, Chodya relaxed and drifted further into a ritualistic stupor. The scented privacy of Simone's tapestried quarters eased her breathing into a deep rhythmic cycle. "Cut my body, free my soul," she sang the Tibetan prayer weakly, humming in between repetitions.

As the urgency to seek medical help subsided, Sarquette put her hand inside Chodya's wrap and soothingly rubbed her skin. She touched Jon's arm with her other hand, and her careful, sensuous stroking rekindled his serpent fire. Battling powerful surges of pity, lust, and duty, Jon chose war over peace. "Where are you going?" Sarquette asked as Jon abruptly headed for the door.

"I'll be right back," he told her, clenching his teeth as he started toward the roof. The musty carpeting in the wide hallway muffled the sounds of life leaking through the thick wooden doors of the old hotel. Murmurs of the party a few floors below gurgled up the stone and metal stairwell as he climbed to reach the rooftop portal. Outside, the cool wind refreshed him, and a hundred feet above the street on with no man-made illumination other than what glowed through the yellowish atrium skylight, he moved cautiously, looking for his adversary around the giant air-conditioning units and numerous pipe vents that protruded through the flat expanse. Jon was naturally strong and unafraid, but he had no training as a fighter in this or any other dimension, and his instinctive combat skills were limited to outbursts of a short-fused temper. Scanning the perimeter, he couldn't see anything other than a commanding view of the city and the dark rooftops of other buildings, and the emptiness made him second-guess his sudden rush to defend Chodya, whom he barely liked. Unable to locate an adversary, it crossed his mind that he had no business being there. He went to the safety railing that skirted the front facade like the top railing of an ocean liner and looked down on the ebb and flow of Halloweeners. The fires that Sarquette had stoked burned away his vestiges of revenge, and the idea of resuming where they had left off pumped through his veins. He decided to retreat to the warmth of inside, but as he reached for the door to the stairway, an ornamental dagger with no visible hand attached, suddenly sliced the air right over his head. He recoiled defensively, and the floating phurba disappeared as quickly as it had manifested. Stories of the Boulderado's famous hauntings accelerated his descent to the perceived safety of indoors.

Simone saw him coming briskly down the hallway.

Jon greeted the familiar face enthusiastically. "*Bonjour, monsieur.*"

Simone was surprised to see him. "Good evening, Chief. What happened to your headdress?"

Jon put his hand to his head and plucked the stubble of feather from it. He held it in front of him, staring in disbelief at its truncated height. A fear, born of confirmation that the rooftop encounter hadn't been an illusion, crept across his face.

Simone noticed the horror in his eyes. "Come, come, Jonny boy," he patronized. Sarquette awaits in the garden of delight." He steered Jon back to his room.

Chodya was alert, telling Miko and Sarquette what had happened when they got there. Jon noticed Chodya's accent showing signs of her pre-Buddhist persona –. "I didn't want to do it, but he made me," Chodya explained through tears. "He's so strong, and I thought it was all part of my training."

"What did he do to you?" Miko asked gently.

"I, I'm not sure. I was kind of in a trance." Chodya wrinkled her face as if to squeeze out the truth. "My … ; it hurts down there." She motioned to the area between her legs. "I tried to get away, but he had this horrible knife."

"Maybe we should call the police," Miko suggested. "I think there are still some detectives downstairs."

Simone didn't like the idea. "You can take her to see them, but I don't want them coming in the room again."

"I don't want to take her," Miko responded. "They know I'm with you."

"She might need to go to the hospital," Sarquette said. "I felt something wet underneath her clothes."

"Maybe *you* should take her," Miko suggested.

Sarquette was reticent. "I'd like to help, but I just don't think I'm up to it."

Chodya, in obvious pain, moaned like an injured calf. Urgency gripped the gathering and indecision searched for commitment. Finally Miko told Jon, "Sarquette is just visiting and doesn't know the area. This woman is a friend of yours, sort of, so why don't *you* take her to get some help?"

Chodya's dark eyes pleaded before he could answer. "You would do that for me, Jon?" she asked meekly.

Jon eyed Sarquette longingly, but chose chivalry. "I can take you – if you really want me to."

Simone accepted the invitation for everyone. "Hail to the Chief!" He opened the wet bar and extracted a bottle of gin. "Drinks on the house."

Sarquette squeezed thank you into Jon's hand, and his scattered energy coalesced around the clarity of the mission. Chodya's mood brightened at the prospect of deliverance, and he helped her to her feet while Sarquette and Miko made sure her wrap wouldn't come off by itself. Chodya held Jon's arm as he slowly escorted her to the elevator, but once inside, she had second thoughts.

"I don't want to go to the police right now," she told Jon. "There's something I didn't tell your friends."

Jon's mistrust competed with his compassion. "What is it? Are you sure you want to tell *me*?" he asked nervously, wondering what he had gotten himself into.

"I know their secrets," Chodya confided. "I just don't know what to do about it."

"Whose secrets?"

"Gyalpo's. The monastery's."

Jon scanned the air for sharp objects as the elevator doors closed. "The Buddhists have secrets?" he asked.

Chodya pressed the stop button and asked, "Can you please take me somewhere else? I don't feel safe here."

Jon was starting to regret accepting his mission. "Where do you want to go *now*?"

"I don't know, somewhere quiet. I don't feel so good."

When they reached the ground floor, the elevator doors opened to a party in full swing. As if on cue, the mass of people in the hotel had swollen to the point where Jon had to pry Chodya out to let other passengers in. As they edged around the main gathering toward the side door, he recognized several people he knew but didn't want to talk to. Roddy and Hipolito spotted him from above, and a few of his customers, looking to replenish their stash, unsuccessfully tried to get to him before he got away. He was almost outside when Frankie caught him from behind with a bear hug.

"Hey, man! Where you been? I've been looking for you all over," Frankie shouted over the noise.

Jon pointed. "Upstairs in my room."

"Really? I knocked there a while ago. Why didn't you answer?"

"I thought it might be the cops again." He made a smoking gesture.

Frankie saw Jon's arm around Chodya and smiled conspiratorially. "Yeah, smoking. I won't tell Donna if you don't."

Jon was annoyed at the accusation but knew it was useless to tell Frankie the truth. "Thanks, man. It's not what you think but who cares? Why were you looking for me?"

"They want you to come down to the studio. Marco told me to find you."

"Why? What's going on down there?"

"They want us to play! They're having a party and need some musicians to liven it up. Marco said there's already a drum set there."

Jon liked the idea. "What about my guitar and amp? I was supposed to meet Donna here at nine."

"I'm going to the practice space to get Marco's bass rig, and I figured I could get your guitar at the same time. You don't have to come to the studio, but Marco's already there, and I'm going too."

Jon wasn't about to let his band perform without him, so he prioritized. "Good. Pick up my axe, and I'll meet you there in a while." Then he spoke to Chodya, who seemed to have stabilized. "I can drop you off somewhere on my way to pick up Donna."

Donna was one of the first people Chodya met when she came to Boulder, and the thought of seeing one of her best friends appealed to her. "Can't I just come with you? I really don't want to be alone."

Frankie rolled his eyes at what seemed like sexual intrigue. "Whatever man, I'll see you there."

"Later." Jon fived him and led Chodya outside to the parking lot where he kept his car. Once they were inside with the motor running he asked, "So what happened to you? That creepy monk rough you up?"

Chodya ran her hand along her scalp to feel for scabs. "It's hard to explain. I mean, he's my teacher, and I'm not supposed to question what he does because everything he does means something that I'm not spiritual enough to understand."

Jon put his Peugeot into reverse and said, "Sounds like mumbo-jumbo to me."

"I know you don't believe in these things Jon. Donna and I have talked about it. But this stuff really works. Didn't you feel something extra special the other night when you and Donna made love after I left?"

Jon was embarrassed that Donna had told her what happened but realized that Chodya was the one who helped plan it. "Well, I guess you already know." Jon put the car in first and accelerated. "I'm not sure what you did but … ."

Chodya felt a sympathetic twitch that made her private parts throb. "I love Donna. It'll be good to see her."

CHAPTER 33

Agent Falin's pilot training was good practice for driving the steep and narrow roads that twisted through the mountains between Steamboat Springs and Boulder. He spent most of the three-hour journey listening to Farah and her friend Ruby jabbering about people only they knew, but the car's disorganized collection of cassettes provided a welcome relief from the gossip. Driving with one hand while shuffling through the tapes, he tried to find something familiar amongst Farah's archives of local bands. He sampled the Freddi-Henchi tape, The Tim Duffy Orchestra and Poco's release, but related most strongly to Tommy Bolin's music. Blasting Zephyr's male attitude through the Blazer's custom speakers, he tried to drown out the female chatter. The band's dominating drumming, nuanced rock solos, and airy, imaginative vocals were a reflection of the grandiose scenery and ubiquitous cocaine culture that had recently claimed Tommy's life, and the spirit of the newly anointed demigod blew through the twisty canyons like the wind that had inspired the name of his band. When they emerged from the foothills and started their glide onto the darkened Great Plains, Agent Falin changed tapes. "Vacant Lot," a song by one of Farah's favorite artists, Jon Cells, was the soundtrack for the undulating descent of Route 93 that ended in Boulder.

I'll meet you.
Next Saturday.

Saturday.
You were all dressed up in blue,
And nothing you won't do.
Downtown your cover's up,
Pictures of your lovers are
Up at the corner store
Staring out forever more.

The twilight twinkles of South Boulder were laid out in predictable patterns. Home to the employees of locally headquartered, scientifically inclined institutions; including the National Commission of Atmospheric Research; the Rocky Flats nuclear weapons facility; the IBM spinoff, Storage Technology; and Colorado University; the Table Mesa development was so culturally isolated from downtown Boulder that it might as well have been in a separate state. Agent Falin related to the inherent structure of alphabetically organized street names, homogeneously designed homes, and perfectly paved thoroughfares, but Farah and Ruby couldn't wait to get through what they considered the wasteland of suburbia. They reached downtown a little after nine o'clock, intent on going directly to the Boulderado.

The parking lot next to the Indo Ceylon eatery on the north side of the hotel was full, so Farah directed them to a spot on nearby Pine Street where the large historic homes had been converted into townhouses and duplexes. There they parallel parked and joined the flow of pedestrians on their way to the party at the Boulderado, trickling through the quiet chill of the residential neighborhood like Boulder Creek itself. As they neared the hotel, the street noise of exuberant frat boys, squealing Saturday night tires, and decisive car door slams increased, and Agent Falin, who had been memorizing the landmarks and looking out for possible threats, tried to not be too distracted by the intoxicating brew of uninhibited college coeds dressed for Halloween in revealing costumes. When they entered the lobby, Ruby disappeared into the cocktail of inexperienced drinkers and unleashed hormones, but Farah kept her promise and stayed with Agent Falin as his guide, escort, and interpreter. They didn't see Jon helping Chodya out to his car, and didn't know enough about what had happened that afternoon to do anything more than smile, say hello, and sample the canapés, shrimp, and champagne from roving servers.

Farah led them to her sister's restaurant, but Sasha and Mavis, were still busy accommodating the surge of diners at the free buffet. Sasha didn't know Farah was coming and assumed that Agent Falin was her sister's uncharacteristically straight-looking date. Farah knew what her sister thought and, always competitive for male attention, slid her arm through Agent Falin's to perpetuate the misconception and earn girly points. Sasha's eyes widened at her sister's handsome catch, and Agent Falin couldn't help notice that ample bosoms were a family trait. They agreed to meet up with Sasha later and wedged out of the restaurant and into the excitement of the main lobby. The first screeches of Gangbusters, plugging in and tuning up on a riser at the far end of the common area, sent of jolt of electricity through the air that amplified everyone's already elevated anticipation. Agent Falin, waiting for Farah to emerge from the ladies room, didn't need the signature smell of pot smoke to know there were illegal stimulants talking, and Farah, having run into an old acquaintance in the bathroom, came out in an exceptionally good mood with only the tiniest telltale sniffle. Emboldened by the powdery stimulation, she pressed her chest against Agent Falin's and stood on her toes to tell him a secret. She spoke with her lips touching his ear. "Don't look, but one of them is over there."

Her full body contact clouded Agent Falin's law-enforcement perceptions, but when he looked in the direction she had indicated, he didn't see anyone particularly suspicious. "Where?"

Farah stayed within his auric field. "The guy with the fancy jeans." She squeezed his hand for emphasis. "He's talking to some people near the front desk."

Agent Falin saw one of the Hollywood promoters surrounded by a group of very attentive hotel employees. He was archetypically handsome with a stylishly long haircut and wide-toothed smile. If Farah hadn't fingered him as a bad guy, Agent Falin would have made him as an undercover vice cop. "Him? Are you sure?"

Farah nuzzled closer. "Mmm-hmm," she confirmed. "I just ran into a mutual friend in the bathroom, and I know for sure that he's holding." Blending in as a couple was easier than either of them thought, and Agent Falin rested his hand on the small of her back as they discussed the details. "Want me to introduce you?" Farah asked, casually sipping a fresh flute she had lifted off a passing tray.

"Not just yet; let's watch him for a little while." Agent Falin deposited a canapé in his mouth, threw the toothpick into a nearby garbage, then moved closer to the bandstand. Always alert for aliens, Farah followed him into the thickening crowd, sidling cautiously between masquerading witches, ghosts, and gangsters.

Stanley and Nima, having tired of waiting for Duke to finish his other business, arrived at the hotel during the first song of Gangbuster's set. They were planning on practicing kundalini together before joining the evening festivities and didn't want to stop and talk with anybody. But Jack saw them come in, and because he knew that Stanley was a friend of the hotel's owner, came over to reassure him that the situation was under control. "Glad you made it," Jack said them over the noise. "Raging success!" he hyped. "These Hollywood people really know how to make things happen. Free buffet in the restaurant if you're hungry; courtesy of the movie."

Stanley answered, "Thanks Jack, but I think we'll just go straight to the room. Everything okay here now?"

Jack followed him. "Yes, sir. There are a few detectives in the downstairs bar, but other than that, the coast is clear."

"They found the finger surgeon?"

"Well, no, but they gave us the 'all clear' right after you left. They're guessing he or she must have escaped."

Quiet conversation became impossible, and Nima stayed close to Stanley as he edged toward the elevator. The second song of Gangbuster's aggressive rock set thundered off the domed glass ceiling and electrified the smoke and alcohol haze. The elevator door opened, and after stepping aside to let Roddy, Hipolito, and two drunken coeds out, Stanley and Nima got in and pushed the button for the top floor. They were relieved when the car didn't stop on the mezzanine level, but surprised at what they saw when the door finally opened on their fifth floor hallway. Nima knew something was wrong immediately. "Gyalpo! What happened?" she gasped as she got out of the elevator.

The normally stoic monk was leaning against the wall, bent at the waist with his hands resting on his knees. Only partially cognizant, he looked at her with tortured eyes from another dimension and didn't speak.

"Are you okay?" she asked rhetorically.

"He looks hurt," Stanley observed.

Gyalpo tried to stand but was in too much pain.

Nima, who had developed a pragmatic dependency on Gyalpo, was alarmed. "I think we need to get him to a doctor."

Gyalpo's usually beatific face was contorted, and a sound Nima had never heard growled from his stomach like an injured animal. A sheen of sweat reflected off the top of his shaved head, and they could see that he was barefoot. Instinctively, Nima reached out to touch him, but he jerked away, slid down the wall like a recoiling jack-in-the-box, and began chanting to himself in a low, unsteady monotone. Despite their familiarity with quirky Tibetan behaviors, neither of the uninitiated Westerners knew what to do.

"Maybe we should just leave him alone," Stanley suggested.

Gyalpo sunk deeper into his trance, his torso pulsing with a slow heave of inhalations and incantations.

Nima's codependency covered all the territory from mother to spouse. "I don't think he knows where he is," she said, concerned for his safety.

They were standing near the crumpled monk, pondering their next move, when an unseen shadow passed in front of the hallway sconce, rippling the light. Gyalpo's hand suddenly emerged from his robe brandishing a large ritual knife, and in an apparent battle with an invisible enemy, swiped the air in self-defense. The Westerners, relegated to bystanders of the etheric contest, moved further away from the inexplicable activity. Stabbing at his invisible foe with short jabs. Gyalpo's utterings became higher-pitched and more forceful, and although his head moved from side to side, his arms seemed like they were struggling against a mighty pressure. Hisses and groans accompanied his spasmodic movements, his face contorted into that of a demon possessed, and then he suddenly sprang to his feet and eructated a violent guttural scream.

The unearthly noise sent the Westerners scurrying to the safety of their threshold, and other residents could be heard locking their doors. In the safety of her room, Nima revisited the stories of supernatural enlightenment that had attracted her to the faith. Eventually, when the commotion in the hall became silent, she and Stanley went to check on Gyalpo's condition. He wasn't where they'd left him, and a sprinkle of white feather barbs on the scuffed carpet was the only trace of where he had been. Mystified and unsettled, they hurried down the stairs rather than wait for the elevator, but their exit was hampered by Simone's slow-moving entourage, inching cautiously down the same stairs in front of them. Chemically handicapped, Miko held the handrail so as not to trip in her six-inch platform shoes, and Sarquette demonstrated her skimpy outfit with the courtesan confidence of one-step-at-a-time. Escorting his harlequins in silk butler clothes, Simone knew who Stanley was and played to his status. "Good eeevening, sir," he intoned with his usual artifice. "*Bon nuit!*"

Stanley had no fascination with Simone's foolishness. "Hi there, Simone," he said dryly. "Mind if we pass you on the way down? We've got somewhere to go."

"*Vite, vite, allons!* Happy Halloween!" Simone commented as they looped down the flight in front. "Save some fun for us!"

When they reached the ground floor, Stanley pushed the stairwell door open with a sense of urgency, and Agent Falin noticed him leading Nima through the crowd with a purpose. "Who's that?" he asked Farah.

Farah trained her eyes on the disappearing couple and admitted, "I don't know."

Agent Falin sensed that Stanley and Nima seemed to be fleeing, and told Farah to wait while he followed them to the side door. Watching them hurry down the sidewalk from inside, his policeman instincts were rewarded when he caught sight of them being confronted by someone who came up from the shadows. He couldn't see who it was, but when he opened the door to listen, he heard Nima shriek. When he went to investigate, Stanley was hunched over, holding his side.

"Are you okay?" Agent Falin asked as he approached. "What happened?" He felt for his service weapon and looked around for perpetrators.

"I'm ... I don't know," Stanley said, wincing in pain. He held up his hand and felt moisture. "It happened so fast. I think I've been stabbed."

Agent Falin held Stanley's hand up to the streetlight and saw it was wet. The smell of blood coursed through his law enforcement personality like a vampire in search of prey. "Be still," he commanded and assumed a defensive position. Turning to Nima, he instructed her to stay low. They all froze, but no imminent danger appeared. After a brief moment, Agent Falin said, "Let's get you some help. Come with me."

"Who are *you*?" Stanley asked, recovering his composure. He was unaccustomed to being bossed around and thought Agent Falin might have had something to do with the assault. "I'm okay, really. It's just a little cut," he claimed, lowering the tension.

Agent Falin wasn't ready to reveal his badge so he backed off. He made a mental note of Stanley's face and apologized. "Okay, if you think you're alright. I was just trying to help. Where are you folks going anyway? The party's back there." He pointed to the hotel.

Stanley nodded and acted nonchalant. "We know; we just came from there. There're too many people and the music's too loud," he explained. And then he said too much. "We're going to a private party at our friend's studio a few blocks away."

Agent Falin heard the clues and asked, "You sure you're okay?"

Reverting to the stiff upper lip manners of his native culture, Stanley straightened out his coat and offered a chaperone arm to Nima. "We're fine, thanks. What's Halloween without a few surprises?" he joked as they sauntered away. "Thanks for your concern. Enjoy the evening!"

As Agent Falin watched them recede into the dimness, he realized that he didn't have a flashlight to thoroughly examine the surrounding area for traces of the conflict. Reluctantly, he ambled back toward the hotel with his senses on high alert, hoping someone or something would reveal itself. The smell of beer, piss, and vomit lingered in the bushes along the sidewalk, and the hubbub from the hotel spilled down the side street in echoey car door bangs, fading whistles, and hoarse yells. Patches of refreshingly cold night sky breezed between the buildings, blanketing human constructs with the magic of Boulder's rarified atmosphere. Agent Falin couldn't help being transported by the nocturnal charm, and wasn't particularly surprised to meet someone dressed as an Indian sitting on the steps of the hotel's side door.

The Indian stared at him with eyes that emitted no light. "You will help us?" he asked as Agent Falin approached.

Confused, Agent Falin looked around to see if the Indian was talking to him or someone else. "Of course," he answered as a member of the force. "What's the matter?"

The Indian spoke gravely. "They came for the gold, they took our land, killed our buffalo."

Agent Falin assumed the specter was a tipsy college pledge. "Yeah, that's a bummer," he commiserated, "but what can we do about that?"

The Indian stood up and pulled out a rusty knife. "They must leave or die!" he said, forcefully thrusting his weapon to the sky.

Instinctively, Agent Falin, swiped the air between them and knocked the knife from his grasp. He bent down to retrieve the weapon before the owner could get it, but when he straightened up, his adversary had disappeared. Agent Falin's concerns shifted from self-defense to a head-spinning search for sanity, and when Farah saw him, she could tell something strange had happened.

"There you are!" Farah called from the half-open door over the music. "What's going on? Where'd you go?"

Agent Falin was relieved to see a familiar face but couldn't answer either question easily. "I just needed some air," he said without believing it.

Farah knew he was lying. "Oh right! Come on, we're in this together, sort of. What's going on? You look like you've seen a ghost!"

"I do? How'd you know?"

"Just a guess; it is a Halloween party!"

Agent Falin found several reasons to like Farah's explanation. "Yeah, I guess you're right," he agreed, dusting his injured psyche off. "There was some guy dressed as an Indian who dropped this so I was looking for him." He held up the knife.

"Ahhcht! Put that down!" Farah screeched. "It's all bloody!"

Agent Falin held it up to the light and saw she was right.

"What did you do? Kill someone?" Farah asked, backing away in fear. "Maybe we should call the police?"

Agent Falin tried to calm her down. "I *am* the police!" he said and came closer.

Farah ducked into the hotel and closed the door between them. "Don't hurt me; I didn't do anything!" she said through the glass partition, only partially kidding.

Agent Falin realized that he might appear to be a guy with a bloody knife, intent on getting at a frightened woman hiding behind a door. He needed to set the record straight before anyone else got involved, so he hid the knife in his pants pocket and tried to reason with his frightened friend. "Please don't be scared. It's not what you think. I'm one of the good guys, remember?"

The music in the party was too loud for Farah to hear what he said, but when she saw him put the knife away, she opened the door and extended her hand. Their tactile communication re-sparked the promise of intimacy, and it felt completely natural for her to be led down the steps and into his embrace. After they hugged, Agent Falin led her to the side of the building where he could explain the details without shouting. "I definitely saw something," he spoke into her hair with one eye on the lookout.

"Mmm hum." Farah nuzzled for warmth.

"There was a guy dressed as an Indian sitting on the steps of the hotel. He said something to me about ... I don't know, the buffalos and someone stole his land. I thought he was kidding. You know, like someone in a Halloween costume just having fun."

"Ooh, that does sound scary!" Farah mocked.

"No, really, that's not all. He asked me if I was friend and then he kind of jumped up and started waving the knife."

Farah stiffened at the mention of the knife. "Uh huh."

"He wasn't trying to stab me, but I know karate, so I knocked the knife out of his hand. After that he just disappeared." Agent

Falin felt relieved that Farah had let him share his secret. "Have you ever heard of anything like that?"

Farah pushed back and stood on her own. "Actually I have," she said with surprising confidence.

As soon as she said it, Agent Falin realized where this might be heading. "You're not going to tell me it has something to do with aliens are you?"

"No, but that could be an explanation too. Actually, I think you might have met Chief Niwot. I'm very impressed."

"Chief Niwot? You know his name? Who, or what is he?"

"He was the Chief of the Arapahos and he's pretty famous around here. Lot's of people in Boulder have seen him over the years, but I'm surprised he would talk to an outsider."

"Have *you* ever seen him?"

"No, but my sister and I came here when we were younger and heard stories. I once went to a sweat lodge ceremony where some people said they felt his presence." Farah paused reflectively. "But I never heard of him attacking anybody. Maybe it was somebody else. What did he look like?"

Agent Falin reverted to his training. "Listen, it was dark and it happened fast. I have no idea who or what that was, and if I didn't have the knife in my pocket to prove it I might not even believe it myself." He patted his thigh to make sure the weapon was still there. "What's the story behind this Niwot guy? Who is he and what does he want?"

"I don't know the whole story, but everyone talks about Chief Niwot's curse. They say that he tried to make peace with the white men but they killed him anyway."

"So this happened when – like a hundred years ago?" Agent Falin didn't know the protocol for apprehending a violent ghost and squinted into the evening shadows. "I think we'd better go back inside," he concluded.

Farah was enjoying the pleasure of his company and tried to prolong the moment. "When do you get off work?" she asked with body contact. "My sister has a place we could … crash."

Agent Falin hated to pass up romantic opportunity, but wasn't done being a policeman. "There's something else I haven't told you."

"You're married? Have a girlfriend?"

"No, but I do have a mystery, and maybe a crime to solve." He hugged Farah affectionately. "I will get tired eventually though, so it's good to know I can save the state some money by sleeping at your sister's house."

Farah accepted the plan with a twinge of excitement. "I thought you just wanted me to point out who the smugglers were. What else are you investigating?" she probed, calculating how long it would be before her sister was off work. "There's nothing you can do about the plane crash or missing pilot from here, and we're not going back to Steamboat tonight."

Agent Falin wasn't used to working with a female partner, but Farah was more knowledgeable about local conditions and proving to be more of an asset than he expected. "I'll let Agent Walker know what I come across tomorrow. What I didn't tell you," he confided, "is that I think this Indian guy attacked those people I followed out right before he met me."

"He attacked them? Now this is getting weird."

"Any idea who those people were? I get the feeling they were up to something because the guy was bleeding but didn't want my help."

"The Indian actually cut someone?"

"Yes, I saw the blood myself."

"And you have the knife in your pocket now?"

Agent Falin felt for the blade. "Evidence."

"Now I see why you were holding onto it. I'm sorry I was so freaked out. I thought you were … ."

"I *am* dangerous," Agent Falin completed the thought and squeezed. "Maybe I'll get to prove it later."

Farah felt like she had been deputized. "So where did that couple get off to? They go back inside?"

"The guy said they were going to a party at a studio."

"Hmm, interesting. Maybe my sister knows where this other party is."

Agent Falin opened the door for her. "Let's go back inside and see what else we can find out."

They re-entered the hotel as partners.

CHAPTER 34

By closing time on Saturday night, the Satsang Diner was a weak imitation of a friendly meeting place where spiritual pilgrims could gather to nourish their bodies and souls: Nancy had called Rosella into her office for an inquisition into Joel's behavior the night before, and their conversation turned into a feminist bitch session on the weakness of men; Tara was hurrying the last patrons out of the restaurant so she could go home to change for the Halloween frat party that her chest had earned her an invitation to; Jampo was occupying the bathroom, sponging off sweat, changing underwear, and using lotion to prepare for his secret date with a pre-Buddhist girlfriend in Denver; Tenzin mechanically worked his way through the last clutter of plates and pots while his troubled mind was elsewhere; And Donna, who had just burned her fingers in a rush to get the last tray out of the oven, was beyond frustrated when Jon and Chodya came into the kitchen through the back door.

She greeted them with involuntary curses. "Shit! Damn it! That hurts." She shook her powdered hand in the air, stomped an angry foot, and barely acknowledged her friends.

In the presence of greater suffering, Jon and Chodya remained mute and stayed clear of the kitchen hazards.

Tara bustled in and asked, "What happened?" but knew the answer when she saw Donna licking her fingers. "The butter isn't helping?" she asked, hanging her apron.

"No, I really got myself this time," Donna complained.

Donna's scream brought Jampo out of the bathroom. "Someone die out here?" he asked, looking for victims. Then he saw Donna. "I can't leave you alone with that oven for a minute. How bad is it?"

Donna sucked her right hand and shook her head. Nancy popped her head out of the office, assessed the situation and implored her staff to be careful before closing the door again. The flurry of activity brought Tenzin back to his terrestrial surroundings and he noticed something about Chodya had changed.

"I'm so sorry," Chodya said, comforting Donna without the pretense of her Buddhist persona.

Donna was very surprised to hear her talk like that. "Are you okay?" she asked her old friend.

Chodya came toward her with open arms. "I feel better now that I'm with you."

Donna looked at Jon quizzically while she and Chodya hugged. "I *feel* better too."

The excitement of the moment over, Jampo and Tara resumed their exit plans while Donna, Jon, and Chodya made theirs.

Donna dusted the pastry powder off Chodya's orange wrap. "What happened to you?" she asked, temporarily forgetting her own pain.

Chodya's eyes filled with tears that clogged her throat, and she couldn't get any words out of her mouth.

Jon answered for her. "I think one of the monks did something to her. We don't know what."

"*We?*" Donna asked. "Who are we?"

"Uh, Simone, you know, the guy who has the shop at the hotel."

"What does *he* have to do with this?" Donna probed while consoling her friend.

"Nothing," Jon said, editing the facts. "I carried Chodya back to his room when we found her."

"Where did you find her?"

Jon avoided self-incrimination. "She found me. I was on the stairs at the hotel, and she kind of came stumbling down."

Chodya knew what Jon was trying to hide and covered for him. "It was Gyalpo." She sobbed the name and redirected. "He – I can't talk about it here."

"Then let's go." Donna brushed herself off and dumped the last of the cooled cookies into a box. "I can't wait to get out of here. It's been a looong day."

Tara agreed. "I've got one more table to clear, so I need to stay. You go and wrap that hand. I'll tie this last box and leave it for Joel if he ever comes back."

"Thanks Tara, you're a sweetheart. Namasté." Donna blessed her with a throbbing thumb.

"Namasté, have a nice day," Jon rhymed as he followed Donna and Chodya out.

Nancy's door remained closed, Jampo turned the ovens off before he left, Tara tidied up, and Tenzin stacked the pots on the drying table, upside down like a collapsed pagoda.

"So where to now, ladies?" Jon asked as they walked toward his car.

"I thought we were going to the hotel party tonight," Donna said. "I was going to go home and shower first. I can't wait to change my clothes and put some ice on my hand." She hadn't planned on Chodya being with them and was confused by her uncharacteristically clinging presence. "You can come with us if you want," she invited, but was surprised when Chodya got in the car with them.

Jon fielded Donna's curious glance with a tell-you-later eye roll. "Change of plans," he said, driving quickly. "We just came from the hotel and, well, I'm going over to the party at BlueStar Studios. They want our band to play there to liven things up. I figured you could come too."

"Okay, I guess. I don't care where we go as long as it's somewhere fun," Donna consented.

It only took a few minutes of lurching shifts and steep corners for Jon to hurry up the hill to Donna's house, and by the time they got there Donna knew something was seriously wrong because Chodya hadn't said a word. Donna told Jon to wait in the car and Chodya followed her in. When she turned on the light, Donna noticed the bleeding scabs on Chodya's scalp. "What happened?" she gasped in horror.

Chodya put the damp end of her headscarf back on her wounds and said, "I don't want to be a Buddhist anymore," with tears in her eyes.

Donna was shocked. "You don't? But I thought – "

Chodya felt the pain between her legs and said, "I need to sit down." She melted into an upholstered chair in Donna's living room.

Donna stood over her and examined the pattern of cuts on top of her scalp in the light. "How did this happen? Who did this to you?"

"Gyalpo. He was trying to protect me from them but it hurt. I'm so confused."

Donna went to the kitchen and came back holding some ice on her bad hand and a warm damp towel in the other. "Put this on your head. I'm going to change, and when I get back you can tell me more." She knew Jon was waiting in the car, and was torn between wanting to be supportive of her friend and having a good time, so she showered quickly, changed into one of her multilayered fertility goddess outfits, and suggested that Chodya stay at her house and rest while she went out for the night.

"You look beautiful," Chodya said as Donna came back dressed.

"Thank you. I made this myself." She twirled around to show how the motion of slinky material momentarily revealed bare legs.

"I love that!" Chodya said, perking up a bit. "Do you have an outfit for me?"

"Of course, but I think you'd better stay here and rest."

"I know you're right, but I'm scared to be alone. Can't I please come with you? I promise to not get in the way."

"But you're bleeding. Why don't you stay here? You'll be safe."

Chodya's face drooped with fear. "Please let me come. You don't understand. I'm scared to be alone; they can find me anywhere."

"Who?" Donna asked. Then her concerns got personal. "They know where *I* live?" she asked, alarmed at the idea.

"Yes, no, maybe. They don't really use street addresses."

Donna heard Jon toot his horn and tried to shorten the conversation. "Who are *they*? Who's after you? What are you talking about?"

"It's hard to explain. I know you must think I'm crazy or hallucinating, but look at my head! I helped Gyalpo make a tulpa, and now we have to destroy it before it destroys us." Chodya retched up the truth and felt relieved.

Donna didn't know what she was talking about but saw the anxiety in her face. "Okay, I guess you can come with us. Let's go get you dressed in something that doesn't look like you're about to be sacrificed."

Released from her secret, Chodya regained energy and emerged from Donna's closet with a frilly shawl that covered her injured head. Clomping clumsily in a pair of Donna's square-toed witches' boots, she came back to Jon's waiting car disguised as a normal twenty-eight-year-old hippie from upstate New York in search of Halloween fun.

Jon was anxious to get to the studio, and it was too dark to notice much about his passengers except that they seemed like they were both in better moods than before, so he passed them the reefer he was smoking, put a tape into the cassette player, and sang along with a song his band had made at rehearsal as they coasted back down the hill to the studio on Pearl Street.

Stayin home alone at night,
And watch the satellites.
Through the vapors of your eyes,

Your thoughts are televised.
Though you're somewhere else tonight,
Your love is on my mind.

That song reminded Donna of screwing outdoors, and with the help of the pot, she squirmed into a party mood. Chodya took a toke and hummed along to something other than the autonomous mantra that had sawed through the forest of her Western precepts like a Tibetan chainsaw.

Cynthia was watching the door when they got to the studio and greeted Jon like the rockstar he occasionally thought he was. "You made it!" she said enthusiastically. "Marco and your drummer are already setting up. It's going to be awesome!" She saw Donna and Chodya with him and added, "And you even brought your own groupies! Come on in! Never too many hot chicks at a studio party."

BlueStar was abuzz with costumed excitement and pretentious posing, and Jon, Donna, and Chodya burrowed in like members of the hive. Local celebrities, including Mark Andes from Firefall, David and Candy Givens, and entertainment impresario Barry Fey, drank the attention of the tightly packed, wineglass toting crowd that included music store owner Nick the Greek, the Buddhist jazz percussionist Jerry Granelli, Randy California from Spirit, and other Boulder regulars. Trust fund hippies who only left their mountain hideouts for the most exclusive gatherings, a few international stragglers who happened to be in town for a Naropa event, and a core sample of local shopkeepers, aspiring Colorado musicians, and wannabe cools completed the crowd. Duke was in the control room, refereeing the competition between control room egos who vied for supremacy in front of the cassette player that was providing a jump-cut underscore of rock, country, and acoustic music. No one was completely sober, and none of the blabbering was a conversation that lasted more than a moment or two.

The wholesome pastries from Satsang Diner shared a serving table in the main room with platters of condiment-laden crackers, cubed cheese, and sliced fruit. Under the halo of black and orange balloons with shiny ribbon tails, Donna sampled one of her creations while Jon joined his bandmates, who were set up on the opposite side of the room. Jon and Marco had trouble tuning over the dominating sound system that didn't stay on one song long enough for them to cop a tonic, and Frankie, joyously beating his skins through every passage, only made it more difficult. Frustrated, Jon waved Donna closer, put his finger firmly over her earhole so she wouldn't go deaf, and told her to go into the control room and ask them to stop the tape player so the band could perform. Chodya guzzled some alcoholic relief and followed her. They easily located the imposing redheaded man Jon told them to look for.

Duke had never met Donna and assumed she was another sexy earth-mother goddess who couldn't help being interested in making his acquaintance. He turned the sound in the control room down far enough to make small talk, and Remy, positioned alongside him, was drawn to Donna's newly liberated, lapsed Buddhist companion. Before Donna could say anything, Duke raked his hand through his hair, smiled, and thanked her for coming through a row of coke-clenched teeth. "I'm Duke and this is my place," he announced expansively.

Donna's marijuana high put her at an alternate altitude, and she only managed to say, "Hi, I'm Donna," while limply accepting his handshake.

Donna said something about the music he couldn't hear, so Duke assumed she was looking for something different. He removed the tape from the player and shuffled through a stack of cassettes, trying to pick one out that might heighten romantic possibilities. In the other room, Jon took the silence as a cue that Donna had accomplished her mission and launched into his band's only established local hit.

Uh oh,
Washing my fingers off with snow-oh.
Taking my time, because I don't know,
Which one of us has got to go-oh.
Your left one says that your right one might,
I just can't be alone tonight,
'Cause I'm so low,
Hard to swal-low.

Jon could barely hear his vocal through the makeshift PA system, but several people who knew the song celebrated the coke-themed lyrics by singing along with the chorus and making awkward dance moves that resembled hikers climbing through deep snow.

Duke heard the live music, saw the party's reaction, and claimed credit. "They're great! I just signed them to a record deal," he told Donna with a triumphant grin.

Donna was surprised at the news. "Really?"

"Yep, that's why we wanted them to play tonight. They're going to be the first band to break in the new desk." He patted the big sleek console like a proud father.

Donna was impressed by the size of the equipment. "You know how this whole thing works?"

"Sure do. You live in Boulder?" Duke asked, moving close enough to assess her availability.

Donna saw that Chodya seemed to be enamored with Remy, and she was trying to be polite when she answered, "Mmm-hmm," in her usual sultry tone. "I work at the Satsang Diner." She was watching Jon through the window of the control room when she said, "Did you try some of my cookies?"

Duke got the unintended impression that Donna wanted him to sample her wares and, without warning, plunged his nose between Donna's breasts like a friendly horse greets its rider. "I love cookies!" he explained with a whinny of delight.

Startled, Donna crossed her arms in self-defense, but thinking it playful, Duke pawed at her sleeves and nuzzled her neck. Frustrated, she tried to brush him off and get away, but the control room was too crowded to flee, and Duke turned her protests into a harmless game of paddy cakes.

Seeing what he thought were Duke's successful advances, Remy moved close enough to Donna's mysterious-looking friend to smell the fresh dose of patchouli she had used to mask the camphor-based healing ointment on her head. Still psychically vulnerable to male domination and not used to being alcohol-tipsy, Chodya's remaining defenses melted from Remy's body heat and her knees buckled. Remy put his arm around her waist to keep her from falling and felt stiffness in his pants before either of them knew what was happening. Grateful for the support, Chodya breathed, "Thank you. I'm Chodya," into the side of his head as he drew her near.

Holding the first flask of female comfort he'd had since Mexico, Remy gurgled, "Mmm-hmm," like he had just sampled white lightning, then swallowed the moonshine with a name-bending quip. "Well, hello, soda, you can call me pop."

Happy to be renamed and feeling protected, Chodya responded to the lighthearted wordplay by saying, "Pop pop, fizz fizz."

Donna was surprised at how quickly Chodya had paired, and assumed she must have known Remy from before. She saw that Jon was entertaining other admirers, and felt strangely abandoned by her friends. Duke was still hassling her, and with her hand still hurting, the only thing she could think of to protect herself from his playful assault was to raise her knee into his crotch with a sharp thrust.

Duke was shocked that his advances had been so forcibly rejected, but was too cool to show how much it hurt. He said, "Excuse me," and turned away to hide his pain.

Chodya didn't see what happened and held on to Remy as Donna escaped. Facing the wall, Duke took two quick snorts and attempted to regain his altitude, hoping that no one had seen him kneed in the balls. Sniffling, he fiddled with the new console, pressed the wrong button, and an ear-splitting screech, followed by a loud grinding hum, pierced through the party atmosphere like an unterminated ground.

Dennis rushed over and switched the channel back to neutral before anyone's ears actually bled, but he was unable to completely silence the disturbing noise. Never too high to tame a technical glitch, Dennis ignored the party around him as he chased down the source of a phantom rhythmic pulse. Putting his ever-handy pencil light in his mouth, he peered behind the equipment rack, wiggled the TRS jacks to made sure they were pushed in all the way, pulled on each wire to check for cold solder, followed the snake to the point where it disappeared into the floor, then turned down the master fader before rotating the selector knob through its settings to overcome possible oxidation. Nothing worked, and the annoying buzz, undulating like electric pulses from a distant motor, persisted.

Stanley and Nima showed up at the front door just as other people were leaving. Annoyed at the lack of oxygen and disturbed by the sonic interference inside, one of exiters, Dan Fogelberg, a well-known recording artist who lived on a ranch near Stanley's, warned his neighbor not to go in as he left. Stanley was inclined to ignore the advice, but catching sight of someone inside who was dressed like a Native American, he reconsidered. His side still hurt, and he couldn't be positive that he wouldn't run into someone he didn't want to see. As much as he wanted to finish his transaction with Duke, he knew that there were too many people around for a high stakes drug deal to happen safely. The walk from the hotel through the crisp air had resuscitated Nima's transcendental desires, and she communicated her preference for a more intimate setting by gently pulling Stanley away from the door. "Let's go home. I don't feel safe here," she said, peering down the darkened alley to see whose footsteps were approaching. "I told Kundun to wait for us at the restaurant. Maybe he's still there." The Satsang Diner was around the corner from the studio, so she and Stanley hurried over, hoping to catch a ride back up to the mountains before Kundun left town with their car. The restaurant was closed, but the light was on so Nima knocked.

Thinking Roddy had come back for her, Rosella answered the door. She recognized Stanley and Nima as customers but said, "I'm sorry, we're closed."

"Is Tenzin still here?" Nima asked.

"No, he left with that other monk who drives the bus."

"When did they leave?"

Rosella looked at her watch and told her, "About a half hour ago," then locked the door again.

Disappointed, Nima said, "Thanks." Her spiritual senses were keen enough that she didn't feel safe out in the streets, and they didn't want to go back to the hotel, so she suggested they go to the Dorje Dzong. "Maybe Kundun and Tenzin are at the Temple. I don't think Kundun would go back without us." Stanley didn't have any better suggestions, so they headed back toward the Buddhist Temple in the center of town. It was only a ten-minute walk, and after two encounters with supernatural forces and the general chaos of Halloween night vibrating through the akashic clouds, the meditation hall seemed like a good place to find sanctuary. There were a few lights on inside the monastery, and Stanley was overjoyed to see his Land Rover parked in the lot.

The Dorje Dzong was located in one of the oldest industrial buildings in Boulder, and its original purpose, warehousing dry goods for the burgeoning population of Boulder County, had been modified over the past hundred years to adapt to the needs of changing economies. After completely gutting and removing all traces of the sequence of offices and retail establishments that had lived and died there, the Buddhists had reincarnated the soul of the building into a house of worship. More than half of the cavernous ground floor was converted from the frontier functionality of shielding livestock and survival provisions from the weather to a large meditation hall. It was appointed with the touchstones of Tibetan tradition: bare wood floors for the zafued practitioners; thick, orange-themed tapestries that covered the walls and made partitions; always-lit incense dispensers; and numerous strings of hand-painted prayer flags that hung from the ceiling carrying messages to and from the ethers.

Tenzin and Kundun, who had retreated to a sectioned-off corner of the meditation hall, didn't hear the knock on the front door, so Nima rapped again, this time more forcefully. Then, after waiting a few minutes and getting no response, she and Stanley headed toward the rear entrance near the parking lot, hoping the back door was unlocked. The idea to light the outside of the building at night never occurred to the rugged mountain people who had survived the harrows of the Himalayas for hundreds of years, so they had to move cautiously through the deep shadows, hoping to avoid danger and the unexpected. Seeing a flicker of candlelight on one of the windows, Stanley put his face to the glass and looked inside while Nima kept a wary eye on her surroundings. Neither of them were able to see anything unusual, but they both heard the tonal throb of a small drum. Thinking they might be targeted for another attack, they assumed a defensive position with their backs against the building. As the drumbeat got louder and closer, they saw an oscillation in the shadows near the back door of the building. It wasn't clear, but with the chimeric reflections of city lights and a veil of moonshine to help, they were able to make out Chief Niwot and another very large Indian Brave approach the monastery in rhythmically locked step. The Chief's drumming ceased at the entrance to the back door, and the apparitions paused to assess the supernatural conditions. Nima and Stanley were relieved when the phantoms didn't acknowledge their presence, but were shocked when the Chief and his Brave simply oozed into the building and vanished. Stanley suggested they get into his car and leave the haunted area as quickly as possible, but Nima reminded him that Kundun had the keys to the car. They put their faces to the window again, hoping to catch the attention of their driver.

Deep in meditation and mostly hidden from outside view, Kundun, Tenzin, and Gyalpo were seated together in the innermost sanctum of the temple. Their pranayama had slowed to the point where they were able to include Lama Yeshe's consciousness in their midst. No words were spoken aloud, but the well-trained monks were able to communicate with their inner voices. After exchanging the ritualistic pleasantries that always preceded important conferences, Lama Yeshe steered the proceedings toward its ultimate goal – the survival of Tibetan Buddhist traditions in their new Western home. He began by asking Gyalpo for a chronology of the events that had precipitated the crisis.

Gyalpo had recovered some of his vigor, but his frequency was higher pitched and more warbly than usual. "It started out so well," Gyalpo began, rocking slowly where he sat. "The tulpa took the form of an able-bodied servant just as I had envisioned."

"It was only *your* vision?" Lama Yeshe asked.

"Yes, at first. We – Kundun, Tenzin, and I – all meditated together to give it strength, but we had agreed ahead of time that it would be my tulpa."

"So it was also your responsibility," the Lama clarified.

"Yes, but he was the servant to us all."

"At first he was," Kundun confirmed.

"For how long was he obedient?" the Lama asked.

Tenzin answered, "About three months."

"And how old is he now?"

"He was made in the summer."

"So he has been on his own for a few months? What happened? When did you notice something was wrong?"

"It was little things at first," Kundun said. "The robes were not washed right, or they fell from the drying rope. The floor wasn't swept, or the incense wasn't relit."

Tenzin said, "I noticed him sitting in the garden one day while he should have been working. He wouldn't look at me; that's when I knew something was the matter. I would ask him to do something simple like water the plants, and he would say yes, but he wouldn't do it. That's how it began."

"Did you become angry with him? Did you strike him? Any of you?"

Gyalpo confessed, "Yes, when he purposely spilled the dinner kettle. We had many visitors who had come to see the monastery that day and had prepared a special meal. I asked him to get some plates, but he became very agitated and pushed the stewpot off the table." Just recounting it raised Gyalpo's blood pressure, and his fellow monks had to calm him down so he didn't lose collective consciousness. "I cursed him, and when I ordered him to clean it up, he ran away."

Lama Yeshe said, "I see. Is that the last time you saw him?"

"Oh no," Tenzin said, taking up the narrative. "He stayed with us at first, mostly in his room. But soon, he began to live in the barn with the animals. He still took care of *them*, but he wouldn't do any chores in the main building. After a while – maybe a month – we wouldn't see him every day, and then one day, he came to us during meditation dressed as a Native American – an American Indian!"

Lama Yeshe was concerned. "Independent thinking is a bad sign."

"He said his name was Chief Niwot now," Kundun reported.

Lama Yeshe took in the facts. "Very strange – and very unusual. Tulpas have been known to escape their masters, but I never knew of one who assumed another identity. There must be an explanation. What else can you tell me? You said there were two tulpas."

"That's correct," Gyalpo told him. "We still needed help at the monastery, and I thought the first one would die on its own, so after he ran away, I made another one."

"By yourself?"

Gyalpo hesitated at the point in the story where he knew his actions would be criticized. "No," he admitted. "I had the help of a getsulma."

Lama Yeshe knew some of what was going to be said but made Gyalpo explain it anyway. "A getsulma? A Tibetan nun? I didn't know we had any at Punkah Dzong. Someone came?"

"No," Kundun said, "all the nuns here were born outside the holy land. None have been ordained yet."

Lama Yeshe knew the important distinction between novice and initiate. He needed Gyalpo to tell him everything so he made his questions more about finding facts than faults. "And did you do kundalini with this nun?"

Gyalpo shuddered and couldn't speak, but Tenzin volunteered the information. "Yes, Honorable Teacher. Gyalpo has committed one of the four defeats."

"Is this true, Gyalpo?"

Gyalpo felt Chief Niwot's inimical presence and, without moving a muscle, fled to the safety of his faith. "Yes, Honorable Teacher. I used the kundalini forces to create a second tulpa. It was a great mistake. The second tulpa was much bigger and stronger than the first, and it escaped my control in just a few weeks."

"Where is it now? Do you know?"

"Yes. Both tulpas are here with us now."

Kundun was surprised to hear that danger was so near and opened his earthly eyes. He didn't see the Chief and his Brave, but through the separation in the curtain, he did notice Nima at the window. When he closed his eyes again to rejoin the convocation, Lama Yeshe had withdrawn and Gyalpo's breaths were becoming more frequent as he reentered the earthly plane. Feeling threatened, Tenzin reinforced their magic circle with a sonic barrier, and Kundun contributed to the defenses with audible gusto as the monks domed themselves in light. When the Native American spirits in possession of the tulpas tried to enter the reinforced circle, it set off an otherworldly struggle. A sudden flurry of robes rustled the curtained quadrant where the monks were seated as they defended their territory. Stanley and Nima saw the interdimensional conflict as moving curtains and flashes of light, and heard intense grunts and low-frequency emissions through the windows. Hoping that stillness and silence would render them invisible, they huddled together for protection and waited for the monks' urgent chanting to subside. After several minutes, a change in the glow of candlelight inside the temple seemed to signal an end to the disturbance, but uncertain of the outcome, Nima and Stanley stayed hidden where they were.

Inside, after the spectral combatants had dematerialized, the monks re-inhabited their earthly bodies. Tenzin ministered to Gyalpo's psychic injuries with compassion. "We are one people," he counseled his sometime adversary. "Your transgressions are our burdens."

Gyalpo folded his arms tightly around his midsection and rocked forward in pain. Although the cuts were only superficial, the stab wounds from Niwot's knife oozed real blood that soaked through his monk's habit.

Kundun untied a large prayer flag, tore it into strips of cloth, and wrapped Gyalpo's chest to soak up the bleeding. Then, recognizing that the injuries were not fatal, Kundun emerged from the conclave and took stock of their surroundings. No other parts of the monastery had been disturbed, and the possessed tulpas had vacated the premises. Tenzin stayed with Gyalpo, and Kundun found his Western hosts crouched outside beneath the window. Relieved that they were unharmed, he said, "Keys," and held out the roped jangle.

Embarrassed to have been discovered cowering in fear by someone he considered an underling, Stanley compensated for his emasculation by saying, "Nice of you to come out," as he dusted the leaf litter off. "We've been knocking for quite a while."

"Sorry," Kundun apologized. He didn't know what they might have seen, and didn't want to reveal the existence of supernatural servants to seculars, so he pretended all was well. "Back door open," he added with a knowing twinkle.

The evening's stress had fractured Stanley's patience, and he was in no mood for humor. "So thoughtful of you, Kundun. Might we get a lift home? Or do you have other plans for this evening?"

Nima interpreted Kundun's apparent disregard of the extraordinary circumstances they had witnessed as another Tibetan mystery. She knew Kundun's English wasn't good enough to understand Stanley's sarcasm, so she squeezed the haute out of Stanley's hand and said, "I'm ready to go."

Kundun said, "Namasté," before heading toward the Land Rover.

When they got to the car, Stanley demanded the keys and told Kundun to sit in back. Nima got in the passenger's seat and prepared for a long, socially uncomfortable ride back up to their mountain retreat. Kundun retreated to mantric silence, hoping to calm the restless spirits that troubled their path, but as they reached the parking lot exit, Tenzin and Gyalpo appeared in the headlights.

Tenzin assumed Kundun was driving, so he walked in front of the square British civilian tank and rapped on the fender to indicate his intention to board. Stanley had no choice but to stop, and before he could assert his dominion, Tenzin helped Gyalpo climb into the back seat.

Nima was glad to see them. "Gyalpo! Are you okay?" she asked.

Gyalpo, not fully recovered, answered, "Yes, mostly," as the vehicle started moving again.

"What happened? We saw you in the hotel and – " Nima wasn't sure whether he remembered. "Are you hurt?"

Gyalpo didn't answer, and neither of the other monks volunteered an explanation of what they were forbidden to reveal. Tenzin acknowledged Nima's question with a blameless shrug and aligned his meditation with Kundun's.

Dissatisfied with the lack of answers and spineless response he took as Buddhist wimpiness, Stanley made an intentionally hard turn onto Broadway that jostled the back seat passengers, forcing words out of Gyalpo's mouth.

"I, I saw you try to help me," Gyalpo spoke with difficulty. "Thank you."

"Of course," Nima empathized, her roles as consort, housemother, and spiritual adventurer fused. "We saw a big knife and got scared. It seemed like you were fighting with somebody or something."

"Yes," Gyalpo admitted. He wanted to keep monastery business secret, but Stanley's rearview mirror glare demanded more information. "There was a problem with – I cannot say."

The cut in Stanley's side from the wound he had received only a few hours earlier reminded him that there was real danger to be dealt with, and his impatience with the non-confrontational attitudes of his Buddhist friends grew. "You *have to* explain," he said forcefully, putting his foot into the gas so the vehicle lurched forward. "I was attacked too. Maybe it was the same – whatever it was."

The news that Stanley had been injured brought a new sense of urgency to the monks. Suddenly much more attentive, Gyalpo asked, "What happened to *you*?"

Stanley protected his honor by saying, "We were outside on the sidewalk, and some guy dressed like an Indian stopped us and asked me something. I couldn't understand what he said, and then lunged at me with a knife. He cut my side a little, but I pushed him down and he just sort of ran away."

"You say he looked like an Indian?" Gyalpo asked. "An old Indian?"

"I'm not sure. It was dark."

"I saw him too," Nima confirmed. "I thought he was a just someone dressed up for the party until he came at us. Stanley was very brave." She put her hand on Stanley's leg to reduce his aggression.

"So do any of you know why something like that would happen?" Stanley probed as he headed north toward Lyons.

Nima said, "We saw you in the temple, and it seemed like – I don't know – something was the matter."

The monks were alarmed that the tulpas had become dangerous and realized the severity of the problem. "Yes, we had a difficult meditation," Gyalpo explained. "Problems in our homeland." The monks silently agreed to reconvene with Lama Yeshe once they got back to the monastery. "How is your practice coming?" Gyalpo asked, trying to redirect. "I know Nima is over fifty thousand repetitions."

Stanley was annoyed at the dodge but knew he had to respect the monk's authority over spiritual matters. "I think I'm at about thirty thousand; I don't have as much free time as Nima."

"Yes, of course. You are a busy man," Gyalpo noted obsequiously.

The lights of Boulder receded into the background as they passed the turnoff for Left Hand canyon. They had just entered the cover of dark roads when Nima casually asked the question no one could answer. "By the way, where's Chodya? Is she staying in town tonight?"

CHAPTER 35

In BlueStar's control room, Chodya's efforts to escape from Buddhist strictures increased along with the alcohol levels in her blood. Busy with their own party-time antics, no one noticed Remy taking advantage of her lust for freedom by grinding her against the wall, misinterpreting groans from the pressure on her injured pubis as encouragement. Having recovered from Donna's knee-to-crotch rejection with another surreptitious snort, Duke hunted for new female quarry in the next room through the window. He saw familiar faces, some he barely recognized in their Halloween getups, but his search was interrupted when someone he knew – a presumptuous tout who worked the periphery of the music business – blocked his view to make an important introduction.

Using his faux British accent and a deferential gesture, the tout presented his catch, an internationally famous troubadour. "Duke Dunn, this is Cat Stevens. He's interested in making his next record here," the tout said dramatically.

Duke welcomed the starlight. "Hey, Cat, welcome to BlueStar. What's happening?" he said, slapping the bearded singer's outstretched hand as if they were long lost brothers.

Naturally reserved, Cat Stevens answered, "Nice to meet you," and blinked at the chaos he found himself in.

"I just picked Cat up at the airport," the tout bragged. "He's had a long trip. Maybe he needs a little pick-me-up?" Duke touched his nose and gestured an offer. He didn't know that the singer had recently converted to Islam and already declined the tout's offers of hookers and booze.

"No, thanks, but I could use a glass of water if you have one," Cat Stevens responded politely.

"Sure thing," the tout obliged and went to fetch.

Looking for a way to connect, Duke quoted one of Cat Stevens' songs to make conversation. "*It's a wild world!*" Duke sang, grinning foolishly.

The party atmosphere was not what he expected when he agreed to come check out the studio, but Cat Stevens tried to make the most of it by continuing the quote, "*Hard to get by with just a smile.*" Then he asked, "Can I hear something through the monitors?"

Duke hoped the system was working. "Of course! Did you bring a tape?"

A ripe floozy who recognized the famous singer brushed her chest on Cat Stevens' arm before he could answer. The stimulation interfered with the convert's internal dialog and he answered while fending off the woman's palpable interest. "All my tapes are in my luggage; just play me something you've recorded here."

The idea that any critical listening could be done under the circumstances was ridiculous, but Duke seized the sales opportunity anyway. "No problem. Let me get my tech to set something up. It may take a minute, but I don't think you'll be lonely." He winked and went to look for Dennis, leaving the singer alone with his unwelcome fan.

The wanton woman rubbed the singer on the leg, and his battle with sworn-off impulses climaxed when the tout returned with a bottle of water. "Get me out of here!" he snapped. "I thought we were going to a recording studio, not a brothel!"

Unflappable, the corpulent tout put his burly arm around the woman's waist and pulled her toward him, absorbing her sexuality with his flabby midsection. Moving seamlessly between pillars, she embraced the idea that she would have to service the messenger before the king.

Duke came back, unsure of how he was going to skirt the issue that the speakers might not sound good, but before he could obfuscate, Cat Stevens demanded to be driven back to the hotel. At first Duke thought it might mean that he had decided to indulge in the affections of the fawning fan, but when the singer knifed toward the door alone, it was impossible to misinterpret his righteous indignation. The tout followed him, leaving Duke with the most available girl at the party.

In the main studio, Jon's band worked the crowd into an appreciative pulse with a tight rendition of their uptempo, B-side hit "Terminal Thighs."

I saw you walking down the avenue.
I was so frustrated and so are you.
Come on baby donchu tell me no lies,
'Cause I got a little case of terminal thighs.

Stationed in front of the band, Cynthia waved her arms in the air and writhed in an invisible Hula Hoop as a paean to the hippy gods who had blessed the party with success. Diane, whose stint as door monitor had lasted most of the night, gave up trying to keep people out by ten o'clock. With her arms folded across her chest, she sipped white wine through a taut smile and nodded indifferently at the vaguely familiar faces.

For Walter's wife Samantha, the BlueStar party was an apex event. It took all of her Presbyterian training and new age thinking to stay married to her oddly wonkish husband, and the opportunities to let loose and have a good time were too few to miss. She dressed Walter up as a distinguished vampire with spectacles, cape, and cane, and squeezed herself into leather-strapped harlequin dress. Walter adapted surprisingly well to his costumed persona, holding court in the control room and pointing out technical subtleties with his cane, while she explored the borders of decency in front of the band.

Rumors that lines of coke were being laid out in the back room of the studio traveled in whispers throughout the Boulderado, and word that the BlueStar party might be more exciting than the bash at the hotel spread quickly. When Rosella heard about it, she led Roddy and Hipolito over to the studio and into a world none of them had ever experienced. After they got in, they helped themselves to free beer and hors d'oeuvres, but when Rosella saw Donna at the end of the food table, she steered her entourage toward the live music on the other side of the room.

Simone and his consorts, who had refined their costume-party skills to the point where they were always invited – and sometimes paid to show up – also made it to the studio party. Vibing to the live music, they observed the intoxicated antics of amateurs blithely, mingled with Boulder's elite chic, and projected their seductively aloof cool with wine goblets in hand.

Still at the Boulderado, Sasha found her younger sister leaning over the mezzanine balcony, pointing out possible suspects to Agent Falin.

"There you are!" Sasha greeted her over the band noise.

Farah smiled mischievously from under Agent Falin's arm. "Hey, sis! Awesome party!"

Agent Falin stayed professional. "Great place to work, the Boulderado."

"Yeah, this is great," Sasha replied like a jealous sibling, "but I hear the other party is way more fun."

"Really? What other party?" Farah asked.

"The one at the studio."

"What studio?"

"BlueStar, you know, the place owned by Duke Dunn. Mavis used to date him."

"I've heard about it, but I've never been there."

"We heard Jon Cells is playing there tonight so we want to go."

"Cells is playing? I love them! Can we go?" Farah asked.

Sasha, a few years older than her sister, was happy to have regained the upper hand. "Well, I'm not sure; I know Mavis and I are invited."

"C'mon sis, you know how much I love that band."

"I know. Did you forget that I introduced you to them?"

Farah wanted to remind her about the time her sister went off with the awesome lead singer and left her with the icky bass player but said, "Of course I remember! That's what big sisters are for. Now can you pleeease get us into the party to see them?"

Agent Falin was having a hard time following the clawless catfight, and was concerned that his professional agenda was in danger of being completely shredded. "Uh, this party," he interjected. "Do you think there might be some *people* there I might want to meet?" he asked Farah in code-speak.

Sasha was too busy looking around for friends to notice the odd tone of his question, but Farah understood completely. "Yes, definitely!" She pulled Agent Falin down as if she was going to kiss him and whispered, "Drug dealers always hang around recording studios," with breathy excitement.

Sasha spotted Mavis sitting at the bar and excused herself. A few moments later, they came back together. "We're definitely going to the studio party," she said, "and Mavis thinks it's okay if you guys come too," she added with a smile.

Farah hugged her sister. "Thanks! Everyone needs a big sister like you." She took Agent Falin's hand and followed Sasha and Mavis down the stairs and out the door. Mavis, humming a Celtic melody while she toe-stepped, led them through the mall. Inspired by the idea of hanging out with local celebrities and hooking up for the night, the group imitated her Wiccan reverie, paying scant attention to the other Halloween revelers on their way to or from holiday celebrations. Holding Farah's hand as they walked in rhythm, even Agent Falin got caught up in the high altitude excitement of a magical night in Boulder's rarified atmosphere. Smooching couples, sobering drunks, and marginalized hippies occupied the promenade benches, the mountain breeze refreshed their faces, the holiday tinsel glittered, and everything wonderful seemed possible.

They were halfway to their destination, right in the middle of the mall, when the first rebel yells cascaded down the hill and echoed through the city. Curious, Mavis stopped the entourage to listen to the sonic disturbance. Throaty whoops and the sound of running got louder, and the stampede clicked and clopped on pavement with increasing intensity like an approaching hailstorm. Within a minute, the first runner came into view. Dressed like a Native American and carrying the flag of his fraternity, the standard bearer announced the arrival of Sigma Chi with a full-throated blare. "Sigma *Chi*, you and *I*, Sigma *Chi*, forever!" Behind him, much to the surprise of everyone who could see, came several other pledges, barely dressed in loincloths and headdresses, escorting Ralphie, the Colorado State Buffalos' mascot, through the downtown streets. The high-spirited frat pack repeated their mantra, making as much noise as possible, and were having obnoxiously harmless fun until they were confronted by two imposing Native Americans. The collegians tried to avoid the other Indians by steering around them, but each time they made a turn, the challengers appeared to block their path.

"Sigma *Chi*! You and *I*, Sigma *Chi*," the pledges chanted in place, thinking the obstacles were part of the hazing ritual. "Sigma *Chi*! Let us *by*!" they repeated as they faced Chief Niwot and his Brave.

Niwot held up his hand to arrest their momentum and signal peace, then withdrew a small drum from his robe. The pledges shifted restlessly in their places as he began to rhythmically tap his ancient deerskin-covered gourd. Niwot's Brave, who was much bigger than any of the frat boys, stomped his massive legs slowly in time to the drum and chanted as if he was in pain. Chief Niwot joined him, and as the ritual grew louder and more urgent, everyone on the mall was drawn to the unusual sounding activity. Seizing the opportunity to be distinguished as a leader, one of the pledges started singing along, and other pledges joined in, irreverently adding melodic phrases of popular songs to the solemn dirge. Chortling with mischief, the pledges regained their attitude, and thinking that they had bonded with the other Indians in song, the frat boys believed they had passed the hazing test. Then, believing it was all planned, they allowed Niwot's Brave to walk between them and take the leather reins of their mascot. With all eyes on him, the Brave walked Ralphie onto the lawn in front of the courthouse and spoke to him in a forgotten tongue. Ralphie, a full grown, two-year-old male bison, nibbled the grass as the pledges gathered around, patting his sides, imitating the Brave by talking in Indian gibberish. Sasha's entourage, along with several others who had assembled, were fascinated at being so close to the pastoral tranquility of the enormous animal, and their collective curiosity morphed into an appreciation of the docile beast. Momentarily mesmerized by natural wonder, no one was prepared when Chief Niwot suddenly thumped his drum sharply and barked an emphatic command. Following instruction, his Brave raised a long rusty knife over his head for a brief moment, then, when Niwot gave the next command, wrapped both fists around the bone handle and forcefully plunged it into the buffalo's neck, removing it just as quickly. Still standing, the beast's heart pumped a geyser of blood through the wound and sprayed it into the air, splattering whoever was nearby. Shocked, the horrified gasps of the Caucasians turned into moans of disbelief as Niwot's Brave cupped his hands to collect the fluid and slurped it up with his mouth. The whole bloodletting lasted less than thirty seconds, which was barely enough time for anyone to react, but as soon as the frat pack realized what had happened, they rushed to Ralphie's defense. Their ritual completed, the spectral perpetrators melted back into the ethers before they could be apprehended.

Ralphie, who hadn't moved, breathed through his nose as his blood continued to spew, his vacant eyes staring at the ground, seemingly unaware that he had been attacked. The college boys reclaimed their sense of purpose, and with no adversaries in sight, one of them wrapped the long flag of their fraternity around Ralphie's neck to stop the bleeding. Others gently patted Ralphie's sides and tried to make sense out of what had happened. In their midst, a troubled runaway who had been sprayed with blood, imitated the Brave by licking her dirty fingers and repeating "far out" to herself. The rest of the assembled crowd was repulsed at the sanguine spectacle.

"That was the most disgusting thing I've ever seen!" Sasha said as she checked her clothing for traces of blood.

"I've got it all over me!" Mavis complained, trying to brush it off the Halloween movie sash she was still wearing.

"Just take that stupid thing off," Sasha told her. "That party's over."

"What the hell just happened?" Farah asked, looking up at the sky for clues. "Who were those guys?"

Mavis peered into the night with Wiccan receptors. "The ghosts of Samhain."

Agent Falin put his arm around Farah as they continued in the direction of the studio. "That looked like the Indian who tried to get me," he told her quietly. He felt his pocket to see if the knife was still there. It was. He scanned the mall for suspects. "Where the hell are they?"

Visibly shaken, the Sigma Chi pledges abandoned their abandonment and collected around Ralphie. One of them, a bio major, pulled the dressing aside to inspect the wound and was hit in the face with a squirt of blood. Desperately rubbing the impurity from his eye, he declared a fraternal emergency. "We better take him back. It's right on the vein, and I think he'll need stitches."

"Let's hope that's all he needs," another said. "Because if he dies, we're all going to get kicked out of college."

"Shit! You really think so?" another asked.

"Most definitely! We steal the mascot, run him into town, and he comes back fatally injured. What do you *think's* going happen?"

"Well, it's not like we did it on purpose. It was – "

"Yeah right, we can always say it wasn't our fault. Two old Indians stopped us and one of them stabbed him in the neck and drank his blood. Who's going to believe that?" the leader pointed out. "Where are those guys anyway? Anyone see them?"

"Didn't you see what happened? They just friggin' disappeared right before our eyes!"

"They did? Are you sure they didn't just run away?"

"I'd like to get my hands on them."

"It might take all of us, but I bet we could take that big guy down."

"Maybe we should call the police?"

"And tell them what? That we stole Ralphie and some guys we never saw before tried to kill him?"

"We've got to find those two Indians 'cause if we don't everyone's going to blame us."

"Where the hell are they? Anyone see where they went?"

"I think I've had way too much to drink because I could swear they just sort of melted into, I dunno, nothing!"

"You have had too much alcohol, and so have all of us. I think this pledge is over, and we better get our asses back to the frat house and tell our big brothers what happened," the self-appointed leader declared.

No one argued, so the pledges huddled around the injured animal and escorted him back toward campus. "I hope they believe us," one said.

"I wouldn't."

Having put physical distance between themselves and the incident, Sasha, Mavis, Agent Falin, and Farah arrived at the alleyway door of BlueStar Studios hoping to recapture the night's magic.

Diane, who knew Sasha and Mavis from the restaurant, was happy to see some relatively normal friends. "Hey you two! I was hoping you'd come." They hugged like sisters. "How's the party at the hotel?"

"It was great," Sasha said. "I would have stayed, but I heard Cells was playing here. We're not dating anymore, but I still like his music."

"You dated that guy Cells? I didn't think he was your type."

"Well, not really dated. I mean, we slept together a few times but, you know."

Diane nodded and a few other stragglers cued up behind Sasha's party.

Mavis was more direct. "Come on, let's go inside. We'll be safer with people around, and I could use another drink after what we just saw."

Farah and Agent Falin moved closer to the door. "They're with us," Sasha explained as they all went in.

CHAPTER 36

Stanley and Nima dropped Tenzin, Kundun, and Gyalpo off at the monastery before driving the rest of the way to their mountaintop chalet. Gyalpo, still injured but determined not to show it, was the last one out of the car. The three monks waited for the sound of the Land Rover's engine to fade into wind noise, then pulled the roped latch and went inside. Their entrance startled the lone novice who was acting as evening sentry, but they were too preoccupied to remind him of the difference between meditation and dozing. When they reached the area of the monastery reserved for them, Gyalpo pulled his robe aside so that his brethren could see the extent of the wound to the side of his chest.

"It is not too deep," Kundun reported. Then he produced a small handheld mirror so that Gyalpo could see for himself. Gyalpo touched his skin and winced painfully. Embarrassed, he tried to lower his robe but Kundun didn't allow it. "We must put something on it," Kundun explained. "I will fetch the herbs."

Tenzin and Gyalpo were never comfortable alone together. The insults and misdeeds that formed the basis of their mutual dislike were never discussed, and even though they had been sent to the monastery as young boys, both men considered it family duty to perpetuate ancestral hostilities. Gyalpo's roots still found nourishment in the stubborn pagan traditions of Bon, and he was more interested in power than purity. His aggressive verbal abuse had pushed the introverted Tenzin against the wall of silence, and rather than argue, Tenzin had chosen the power of not speaking with his mouth. A portion of their forgiveness meditation was always dedicated to each other.

"Your injuries are our injuries," Tenzin said with his eyes.

"I have shamed the monastery," Gyalpo admitted. "May Lama Yeshe forgive me."

Tenzin nodded gravely. "Only time will heal this wound."

"There are some wounds time does not heal," Gyalpo commented cryptically.

Kundun returned with a small bowl in his hand. "This should keep infection away," he said as Gyalpo lifted his robe. Kundun applied a beeswax salve infused with golden seal, yarrow, mullein, and tea tree oil.

Gyalpo was despondent. "There are some infections which herbs cannot defend."

Kundun looked puzzled. "Local herbs are the best remedies for local injuries."

Gyalpo's face contorted in pain. "This injury – our problem – is not just local."

Tenzin sensed the depth of his agony. "What are you saying?" Kundun finished his ministrations and stood back.

Gyalpo lowered his habit. "I have not told you everything," he said gravely.

Tenzin was alarmed. "But Lama Yeshe asked you what happened. Did you lie to His Holiness?"

"No, I told him the truth, but the tulpas interrupted before I was finished."

"What else is there to know? Have you forgotten your pratimoksha?"

Gyalpo drew his arms close to his body and assumed a protective posture. "I have not abandoned my vows, but I underestimated the power of my ancestors," he confessed.

Tenzin knew enough about the dark rituals of Bon to be truly frightened. "Then the whole Sangha is at risk!" were the first words he spoke aloud in eight years.

Kundun was shocked to hear the deep resonance of Tenzin's corporal voice. "Tenzin! What has become of your silence?"

The sound of his own voice energized Tenzin. "Gyalpo's trespasses have released me from that condition. I must – we must – save the monastery."

Gyalpo grimaced and held his side. "I have been trying."

Kundun came from a family of herders and didn't understand occult Buddhist practice. He instinctively checked the windows and door, looking for intruders. "Protect us from what?"

A loud noise in the main hall announced the answer, and the monks went to investigate. They saw a meditation screen that had been knocked over, and beyond it, a sight none of them expected. The area in front of the supersized Buddha statue that was reserved for prostrations and sacraments held a gathering of Native American spirits. Fluctuating between dimensions like the flickering flames that illuminated them, the entities mingled slowly in the dim light of the large room with a stone floor.

Tenzin led his trio forward. "Who are you?" he demanded. "What are you doing here?" None of the spirits responded, so he asserted himself. "This is a holy place. You are not welcome here. Go now, back to the shadows!"

One of the spirits, a large man with regal bearing, came forward and spoke telepathically. "Niwot has called a tribal council." Others joined him, and they drifted into a specter of motley opposition.

The mention of Niwot upset Gyalpo. "Where is he now?" Gyalpo asked, looking for his adversary. "Go now! This is not Niwot's place."

The spirits seemed to understand and closed ranks defiantly. Kundun threatened them with the long wooden cudgel that had been hidden in the sanctuary, and Gyalpo felt for the phurba within in his robes.

But Tenzin held them back from confrontation. "Who are you? Where have you come from?" he asked.

Their spokesman, wearing a single head feather, answered, "We are your ancestors."

Tenzin didn't see the connection and thought it was just spirit talk. "Why has Niwot summoned you here?" he probed.

"Our time has come again," the spirit answered. A murmur of approval spread through the other ghosts.

Tenzin continued talking to the magical beings. "The Great Spirit is calling you. You must go home now," he urged.

Their response, "This is our home," spread through the ghosts in silent consensus.

The Tibetans heard but didn't understand what they meant. "*Om mani padme hum,*" Tenzin intoned. "All life is suffering. Your liberation awaits. Go now, back to the ethers."

The ragged assembly, clutching bows, arrows, and clubs, grumbled amongst itself. None of their crude wooden weapons were deployed, and dressed in tattered buckskin, they looked as if they had been dead for a long time. Many of their wavering presences were smaller than modern men, so Kundun lowered his weapon and joined Tenzin's peace incantation. Gyalpo sang with them but remained on alert. "*Om mani padme hum,*" they chanted intensely. Within several minutes, the gathering of ghosts seemed to lose its adhesion. The definitions of a few stragglers on the edge faded into barely perceptible, and the monks increased their audible assertions. Believing they had regained control, they seated themselves at the feet of the Buddha statue, hoping to complete the exorcism.

The monks closed their eyes and channeled the presence of Buddha, augmenting their intonations with instruments: Tenzin picked up a finely tuned bell that was kept on the alter and struck it with a wooden mallet; Kundun grasped the handle of a damaru and began rhythmically twisting its strikers onto the drum heads; and Gyalpo added to the audible force by blowing on a ceremonial bone kangling. Their fervent, sound-current purge lasted fifteen minutes, but when they opened their eyes, expecting to see the sanctuary cleansed of the uninitiated, they were shocked to see that the original gathering had actually grown in size.

Besides the recognizable core of deceased Native Americans, the ghosts, now too numerous to count, included beings whose origins were at once completely foreign and strangely familiar. Dressed in the colorful tatters of conquered tribes, the other ghosts carried ceremonial staffs, shields, and swords. A common purpose seemed to unite the disembodied beings, and the over-matched monks longed for the guiding presence of Lama Yeshe. But before they could summon him, Chief Niwot and his enor-mous Brave suddenly materialized in front to them. The startled monks cowered as Niwot spoke to them with authority, "Are not all beings who seek release from the cycle of death and rebirth welcome here?"

Tenzin replied carefully. "Yes. Our boddhichitta welcomes all true liberation seekers."

Niwot seemed pleased with the answer. He raised an eagle-feathered stick and forcibly struck the small drum he kept close. "Come then," he addressed the assembled spirits. "Gather round the living. Drink of their energy. Know what it is to be in this world again."

Attracted to his magnetic presence, the entities crowded around like iron filings. The critical mass of spirits alarmed Gyalpo, who grasped the handle of his hidden dagger. Chief Niwot saw his fear. "Did you not learn? You cannot fight Wakan Tanka with weapons of man?"

Gyalpo drew his blade. "This is no ordinary weapon. It has been forged by magic. Go now, or face its wrath."

The formidable spirit with a lone feather came to Niwot's defense. "Left Hand will not obey you," he warned, using Niwot's Anglicized name. "He has possessed your spirit being and knows your ways."

"What do you mean?"

"Red Cloud speaks the truth," Niwot answered. "You beings, tulpas you call them, belong to us now."

Gyalpo's worst fears were confirmed. He recognized that Niwot's Brave was about the same size as the second tulpa he had created. Stunned, he tried to make mental contact with his creation, but the Brave stared at him vacantly.

Tenzin wasn't sure how the tulpas and the spirits might be connected, and hadn't ruled out the possibility that the whole confrontation might be a hallucination brought on by sorcery. True to his calling, he took the peaceful approach. "You, who have been made of our sacrifices, are welcome here. Break free from the restless spirits who have taken your freedom and come home."

Chief Niwot, a master of language in his earthly days, corrected him. "We have not taken the freedom of your servants. It is they who sought our unity. The same is true for all the others." He gestured to his makeshift tribe.

Tenzin challenged him "You are mistaken. Only two tulpas, the one you inhabit and that of your Brave, have been birthed by our will."

"No, it is you who are mistaken," Niwot answered. "Many of these spirits live through the energy of made beings."

"How is that possible?"

Niwot explained, "For as long as there have been medicine men, there have been spirit beings. Yours were not the first to yearn for their own lives."

"But why have our tulpas become Native Americans?"

Niwot, energized by the collective attention, channeled the vigor of his youth. "Our common ancestors came across the water in the early times," he explained. "The Arapahoe, the Cheyenne, the Sioux – all the members of the great nation here – are made of the same blood and stars as you. We are all seeds from the same great tree."

The monks' knowledge of continental history was limited, and they were temporarily stumped into silence. The confrontation had passed into a realm beyond Kundun's comprehension, but Tenzin stayed engaged. "Yes, our roots are nourished in the same earth," Tenzin said, "but the other tulpas, who made them?"

"Monks just as you."

Tenzin noticed that some of the ghosts wore clothes from his native Tibet. "But the monks in our homeland are far away."

"Spirit beings have no earthly boundaries."

"Then why have they come *here*?"

"Just as you, they followed the iron bird."

Tenzin was surprised that Niwot knew of the ancient prediction.

Niwot continued, "Our medicine men and your monks share the same secrets. We are joined in eternity. You are our blood, and the energy of your creations, your tulpas, have given life to our resistance."

Gyalpo felt the sting of his wound. "Then why have you fought with me?"

"It was you who fought the inevitable," Niwot claimed. "Now your beings belong to us, the undead."

The idea that the tulpas were forever beyond their control didn't sit well with the monks, but even Gyalpo, whose occult training was the most advanced, didn't know what to do.

"What do you want?" Tenzin asked.

"The return of Paha Sapa, the holy land," Niwot replied, "and all the treaty territories."

"Then why have you come here to Punkah Dzong? We do not have the power to grant your desire."

The assembled spirits came closer. Red Cloud spoke for them. "You will help us," he informed them sternly.

Kundun asked, "How? What can we do?"

Red Cloud reprised his role as leader of the nations. "You will make more spirit beings. We will rise up together and reclaim Paha Sapa."

The monks were horrified at the suggestion, and Niwot saw that a further explanation was necessary. "Red Cloud speaks the truth. Our numbers grow stronger every day, but we need the power of new beings. It is only a matter of time before we return as men."

"Left Hand always grasps for peace," Red Cloud said, "but his peaceful blood still stains Sand Creek. The time of peace has passed."

Tenzin tried to reason with them. "Surely that was a long time ago; much has changed since then. The white men have given us sanctuary here. They are our friends now."

"We thought they were our friends too, but their treaties were worthless," Red Cloud told them sternly. "They ruined our hunting grounds and way of life. We tried to get along with them, but sickness and starvation were our reward. Now only our spirits are left to fight."

Kundun understood and sympathized. "It is the same for us. The yellow man has invaded our homeland and destroyed many temples. The old ways are not possible anymore. That is why we have come to the new world."

Red Cloud welcomed the support. "Then we will both fight to regain what was taken from us."

"And what if it is discovered that we are helping you?" Gyalpo asked. "What will become of the monastery?"

Red Cloud, the most successful strategist in Native American history, offered a plan. "You will help us secure our homeland, and we will protect you while your temple grows in strength.

Your teachers and holy men will come here and plot their revenge against the yellow invaders."

Tenzin realized that Red Cloud didn't understand the Tibetan occupation. "Our people are few, the Chinese are many," he explained. "We have come here, to these mountains, to plant our culture in new soil."

"Then you are welcome to live among us. We are many tribes but one people."

None of the monks shared the vision: Kundun, the monastery's groundskeeper and caretaker, fumbled with the logistics of sharing the property with hostile ghosts, Gyalpo shuddered at the prospect of a conflict between the dead and living, Tenzin searched for a peaceful resolution. Deprived of their privacy, the monks sent an urgent telepathic message to Lama Yeshe and retreated within themselves.

Niwot fielded the attention of his followers and commanded his Brave to strike the ceremonial gong. "I have waited – we have waited – many years to take back our land. The magic of these new tulpas is strong. Let us use their energy to act now!" Drawing on the power of his physical manifestation, the Brave picked up a heavy mallet and struck the gong forcefully. The shockwave shattered the years of peace that had accrued in the sanctuary, and Gyalpo knew that the spirits' increased ability to affect objects on the earthly plane was an ominous sign of their potency. Fearing that the thunderous reverberations of the hand-forged gong would invite more trouble, he grabbed the head of the mallet as the Brave recoiled for a second strike. But the power of the wraith was greater than his, and the mallet slipped through Gyalpo's arms. It landed with a thud on the edge of the gong, and the clumsy hit, along with Gyalpo's act of resistance, caused doubt within the meditation hall. Resolute, Niwot commanded the Brave to strike the gong again, and the deafening crash hurt the ears of the living more than those of the dead. Neither the cowering monks nor the gathered ghosts heard the banging on the front door of the monastery, but fully awake, the novice guarding the entrance opened it.

Stanley and Nima brushed past him on the way to the monks' quarters and, seeing them empty, continued to the main sanctuary. Able to see only the prostrated monks, Stanley announced their presence. "Nima said we must come back to the temple tonight. I don't know why. We just heard the temple gong. Is everything alright?"

Gyalpo felt like reinforcements had arrived but wasn't sure if the Westerners could see the ghosts or help. "Welcome, friends."

Tenzin reverted to silence and let Gyalpo do the talking.

"What's going on?" Nima asked, looking around "I had a dream and we got here as fast as we could."

Thinking that the ghosts had vanished in the presence of the uninitiated, Gyalpo considered which falsehood might be the most believable. He picked up the mallet and touched the gong lightly. The low volume sound waves helped the meditation chamber regain its sonorous authority. "We're having a special meditation tonight. I'm sorry if you thought we summoned you."

Stanley didn't believe him. "Special meditation? Just the three of you?" he asked suspiciously. The vision of what he and Nima had seen at Dorje Dzong was still fresh in his head.

"Well, no," Gyalpo's explanation proceeded cautiously. "We are monks; we see things others don't notice."

"We notice more than you think," Stanley challenged him.

"What do you mean?"

"We saw, I don't know what they're called – ghosts? – enter Dorje Dzong tonight."

The news was startling. "You saw *what*?" Gyalpo asked.

"The old Indian Chief and the big Brave. They went right through the back door!" Nima blurted.

The monks prayed for guidance, but their long-distance psychic call for help went unanswered.

Seizing the moment, Chief Niwot rematerialized. "You and your squaw are welcome here," he told Stanley. "I have seen your house, and our people are honored there."

Stanley found the idea that ghosts had visited his house unnerving, but Nima, more attuned to the spirit world, said, "Yes, a statue of your likeness adorns our hearth, Chief Niwot."

Stanley and the monks were shocked that Nima knew his name.

Chief Niwot was not. He held out his hand to touch her. "It was I who came to you in your dream."

Nima swooned. "Yes, I know."

Chief Niwot gestured and other ghosts began to appear. "The tribes thank you, earth mother."

Stanley and the monks were dumbfounded and reduced to spectators as Niwot led Nima into their midst and bade her strike the gong. Trance-like, she obeyed. Eerie yelps that had been pent up for centuries rode the sound waves as the ghosts rejoiced. Temporarily released from death, the spirits gathered with purpose. Visible thought forms, with mounted riders and murmurs of war and retribution, swirled through the ethers. Ignoring Stanley and the monks, the undeceased raised their fists and rustic weapons.

Chief Niwot held Nima's hand and spoke to them. "We must protect this holy womb, this earth mother who has given us rebirth."

Nima's consciousness had been breached, but Stanley resisted the possession. "Wait!" he shouted over the echoey din. "She belongs to me." He grabbed Nima's arm and tried to pull her away.

Nima looked at him with fiery eyes and resisted. "It is okay, Stanley. I have found my purpose. The Chief will not harm you."

Stanley was incredulous. He felt the cut in his side. "But I was attacked!"

Chief Niwot apologized, "Forgive my Brave. He did not know who you were. Our people have watched over you for many years. Did we not keep the flying men away from your door?"

The news was confusing and stunning at the same time. "You –. What did you do?"

"Your enemy, the man in the iron bird. Our arrows kept him away."

Among the thousand other questions he had, Stanley asked, "Why did you help me?"

"You have been generous to our brothers." He gestured toward the monks. "You have returned this land to them. The man in the flying machine is no more, but his body is our servant now."

Stanley hadn't heard about the plane crash, didn't know about Agent Dobson's fate, and didn't believe in zombies. He felt powerless in the presence of supernatural forces and wanted to escape but was unwilling to leave Nima behind. The monks reluctantly mingled minds with their uninvited guests and saw visions of the historic migration through Beringia that seeded the Native American tribes. Under Red Cloud's guidance, tribal discord ceased, and hostilities were directed toward the white devils that had upset the natural order in the new world. Anger was also directed at the yellow devils who had invaded Tibet, and an ad hoc council of resistance formed around shared agendas. Nima, in her new role as Niwot's oracle, blessed the assembly.

SUNDAY, OCTOBER 29, 1978

CHAPTER 37

Colorado's reputation as a fun and adventurous place was written in code on every invitation to every party in the state. Posters with precipitous peaks, some separated by sunny orbs and some modified to resemble women's breasts, were the most iconic symbols, but skiers on snowy sluices, iconic cowboys on horseback, crusty old nugget finders, trout-happy fishermen, and streaking mountain bikers were also used to entice the hard working, hard playing, hardy folk of the Rocky Mountain State to stop what they were doing, have something to drink and smoke, and tell each other how lucky they were to be alive in the rarified elevation of good clean living.

By early Sunday morning, the Steamboat party at Howelsen basin had stopped checking for invitations at the door. Everyone who remained was running on fumes, and some of those fumes were definitely illegal. An assortment of revelers in elaborate spacemen costumes gave the party the air of mystery and intrigue that Jim Temple had anticipated, and the local talent he had hired to come in small gray and sexy green alien outfits were making the most of the funnest gig they had had in years. Agent Walker, still wearing a makeshift Indian headdress, Mexican serape, and borrowed boots he had fashioned into a costume, was several drinks past quitting time, and with Officer McKnight already home in bed, he felt like he was truly off the clock. No one's costume had survived midnight in perfect condition, but Halloween was still being worn with enough conviction that he wasn't able to recognize anybody at first glance. There was one exception, and because the sultry voice of an old flame had given her away, he was in no hurry to leave. Her sparkly, feathered eye-mask, oversized cowgirl hat, and braided pigtails matched the Wild West theme of her studded jean jacket, leather chaps, and rhinestone boots, and Agent Walker felt free enough to flirt with his costumed persona's traditional enemy.

After reintroducing himself, he and his female friend joined a few other partygoers on the outdoor deck to escape the sloppy second set of live music. Being careful not to slip on the rustic planking that was coated with refrozen snowmelt, they inhaled the chilly, 1:00 a.m. air, looked up at the stars, and laughed about long-forgotten details of their youth while searching for what they still had in common. Their alcoholic smalltalk fogged the air and rekindled passions, and eventually Agent Walker put his longneck Coors on the railing next to the other empties and repositioned his arm around his cowgirl friend. "God, I miss the mountains," he confessed. "You never smell the pines down in Denver."

His companion snuggled closer. "I love the winter up here; lots of fun ways to stay warm. How long are you in town for?"

"I'm here tonight," was all he could say without lying.

"Where are you staying? All the hotels are full."

Agent Walker heard the silent invitation. "I was going to go back to my friend's sofa."

His companion put her hands in her pockets and breathed deeply. But before she could voice her desire, another guest, dressed as a Native American, put his hand on Agent Walker's arm and said, "Come, it is time," as if it were a command.

Agent Walker resisted. "Excuse me?"

"Come," the Native American repeated with complete sincerity. "White settler no good," he said, referring to the cowgirl.

Assuming it was a joke, Agent Walker responded, "No, Cochise, white woman very fine."

The Native American wasn't amused. "Me not Cochise." Then he peered deeply into Agent Walker's eyes. "And you not one of us!"

"And you not one of *us!*" someone else said in drunken glee. He had on a Darth Vader helmet and cape, and poked the Native American with his light saber, mocking him.

Agent Walker welcomed the distraction, as the Native American grabbed Darth Vader's light saber and tried to wrestle it away. The altercation soon turned into a shoving match that cast Agent Walker as a reluctant peacemaker. Summoning the strength of his fantasies, Darth Vader battled with the classic martial arts moves he had been waiting all his adult life to use, and was actually winning the fight until someone dressed as an airplane pilot came to the Native American's defense. The pilot attacked Darth Vader from the back, wrapping the torn sleeves of his jumpsuit around Darth Vader's midsection. Agent Walker noticed how closely the Native American's ally resembled Agent Dobson, but as the fighting intensified, all he wanted to do was leave the drunken fools outside to sort out their own problems, so he and his cowgirl date went back to the main room of the lodge where the party was petering to a halt.

The last couple on the dance floor, dressed in authentic lederhosen, were holding on to one another for support as the vocalist rasped his way through one last ballad. Jim Temple's host table was full of empty chairs and bottles, and spent partygoers near the exit were trying to figure out how to reconfigure indoor-only costumes against the cold. Reviving their amorous ambitions, Agent Walker and his date escaped to the relative safety of her pickup and kissed while the engine warmed. The defrosters had just started working when he caught sight of the combative Native American and his pilot friend running into the woods at the edge of the parking lot. It seemed like an odd end to an odd encounter, and he worried about how Darth Vader might be doing for a moment, but there were too many alien perpetrators and drunken fools for him to take official responsibility and he let more urgent impulses guide his actions. Reconnected to part of his past, the cowboy coffee with steak and eggs breakfast the next morning never tasted better.

CHAPTER 38

The people who had been on the mall when the buffalo was attacked caused quite a commotion when they went back to the party at the Boulderado and spread the news. It wasn't an easy story to believe, and no one who repeated it was particularly sober or concerned. Holding court in the small bar off the lobby, Jack Aikens summed up the general feelings at 2:00 a.m. "Frat boy hazing prank; something like that happens every Halloween. I'm surprised they didn't try to crash the party this year."

Ken Ken, who, along with a few hotel employees, was testing the limits of his alcohol tolerance said, "Maybe they were going to, but the Indians stopped them."

Jack thought about it. "Indians; what's so goddam special about Native Americans? I don't get it."

"They were here first."

"Yeah, and then we came and kicked their asses. We own this place now." Not everyone agreed, but one argued with him.

CHAPTER 39

It took more than one beer for Agent Falin to feel comfortable in the midst of so many lawbreakers packed into the tight spaces of BlueStar Studios, but with Farah's encouragement and an insistent beat, he bent his knees and bounced along to the uptempo Cells song.

Don't change your mind!
It happens all the time,
When you read between the lines,
Time's up!

With your punk rock boots,
And your hula-hoops,
It's no substitute,
For a gun that shoots.

Don't change your mind!
Who said that love is blind?
Did you read between the lines?
Time's up!

With your plastic bag,
And your pants that sag,
And your game of tag,
You've been such a drag,
But time's up!

Cynthia, Samantha, and Donna formed the core dance team that welcomed other Boulderites into and out of their midst, and not wasting an opportunity to show off her moves, Rosella competed for attention with a lascivious lasso. Pot smoke choked the sober, wine stains dribbled down party outfits, and full-throated rants glorified subversion. A slow rain of helium-depleted balloons with ribbon tails that tickled the celebrants were batted around like beach balls as they descended. Paper plates covered with half-eaten food overflowed from the garbage that everyone was having too much fun to empty, and no one claimed ownership of plastic drink glasses whose fluids spilled onto the dessert trays.

Sonically isolated from the chaotic atmosphere in the next room, the mood in the control room was decidedly more intimate. With one eye on the visual entertainment, Duke groped the con-sensual Cat Stevens fan like static electricity looking for ground. Having already located Chodya's anode, Remy left the control room and steered her to the privacy of the equipment closet, intent on completing the circuit. Ever the technician, Dennis sat at the console, discussing the merits of the new board with the few people who had actually come to see it, and Walter, sporting the prescrip-tion monocle Samantha had accessorized him with, channeled his gnostic persona by calmly answering drug-induced, tangential questions from bleary-eyed partygoers. Having successfully tamed the previous interference, Dennis was the first to notice the low frequency hum of unknown origin emanating through the moni-tors. He rotated the master volume pot, trying to turn the noise down, but that didn't help. Then Walter heard it, and in an effort to show the studio in its best light, he casually went to where he assumed the source of the problem was located. Sticking his arm inside the wall through the empty rack space, he jiggled the con-nections by memory. There were a few noisy crackles, then one loud pop, and then everyone in the control room knew there was a problem.

Duke stopped his fondling and came to investigate. "What's going on?" he asked Dennis.

Still seated, Dennis answered, "Not much," calmly fussing with the settings as if everything was under control.

"What's that buzz?" a visiting engineer asked.

"Not sure," Dennis told him. "We just got this in here and haven't had time to fully debug."

The sixty-cycle hum pulsed in volume, and Walter joined the ground search party. "Sounds like we've got an open rail," he speculated.

Duke didn't want to advertise the studio's faults in front of possible clients, so he joked, "Well, that must mean the train's about to arrive."

Walter lived in a fact-based world and corrected him. "No, that means something may be wired incorrectly."

No one liked hearing that, especially Duke. Dennis knew that Walter didn't know how to not be serious and intervened. "I think I know what's wrong," he lied. "That kid we hired probably spilled a blob of solder on something. I'll clean it up tomorrow."

Everyone seemed satisfied with the explanation, but the annoying drone through the monitors got more intense. "Maybe you better shut this thing off before it fries," a visiting engineer suggested.

"Good idea," Dennis agreed.

"I'll do it now," Walter said, then knelt down to access the power supply.

The console wheezed and sighed as the power drained, and once the indicator lights had fully dimmed, everyone was relieved that electronic disaster had been averted – except it hadn't. The unexplained humming persisted, buzzing like a swarm of insects flying around a microphone.

"Guess I'll have to power down the mains," Walter explained. "Be right back."

Walter left the room, and the others waited, listening uncomfortably for the droning disturbance to cease. The music in the next room muffled through the walls, and the partiers' furious dancing seemed like it was happening somewhere else, so when the low frequency disturbance in the control room morphed into a barely perceptible chant, no one was sure what they were hearing.

"Oohhrree oohhrree oohhrree," the chant repeated, punctuated by an intermittent *thump!*

"What the hell is *that*?" a visiting engineer asked.

"Some kind of interference," Dennis said. "Could be coming down the electrical feed."

"Sounds like a radio station playing really bad music."

"Could be the RF from a Halloween radio program."

The interference became more distinct. "Oohhrree oohhrree oohhrree, *thump!* Oohhrree oohhrree oohhrree, *thump!* Oohhrree ... ."

"Where the hell is Walter?" Duke asked, annoyed. Then he remembered hearing the same chant in the lobby of the Santa Monica hotel and got confused. "I thought he was going to shut the speakers off."

Walter had come in behind them. "I couldn't open the equipment closet. It was locked from inside so I think someone was in there."

"Oohhrree oohhrree oohhrree, *thump!*" the dirge repeated, more loudly and audibly.

"This is too weird for me," Duke's paw toy said, withdrawing her affection.

Duke didn't want to lose her. "Stick around," he said, holding on. "The party's just getting started." He wrinkled his nose tellingly.

His prospect got the message. "I'm soooo tired," she intimated. "Is there somewhere around here I can lie down?"

Duke's attention shifted from the disturbance to the invitation. "Sure, I'll show you where the back lounge is; it's quieter in there."

Walter had his arm in the wall again when the lights started to flicker. "Are you doing that or?" Duke asked him on the way out.

"It's not me!" Walter said. "These are only audio connections."

"Maybe we've got a brownout? Could be the whole block."

"Someone go outside and check."

The musicians in the next room stopped playing as the power to their amplifiers cycled on and off, and the party ground to an anxious halt. The intermittent lighting and strange humming created a haunted house effect, and someone yelled, "Happy Halloween!"

The idea that the phenomenon was intentional brought a short-lived sigh of relief, but no one was comfortable when the entire studio went completely black.

CHAPTER 40

Despite the protests of the subjugated monks, the war council at the Punkah Monastery intensified. Selecting the magical hour of daylight savings, when the white men lost track of time and the Samhain veils were the thinnest, Chief Niwot's host and Red Cloud's army of ghosts, now several hundred strong, chanted through the electrified ethers, envisioning the Boulder foothills returned to pristine beauty and devoid of white man's pollution. "Oohhrree oohhrree oohhrree, *thump!*" They imagined gold and silver flowing back into the mines, buffaloes grazing on the unfenced plains, houses replaced by trees and teepees, and paved roads vanished under a blanket of native growth. The low-frequency sound waves rolled silently down the canyons like a millennial flood, clouding the minds of those who were able to sense its foreboding. Nightmares haunted sleepers' dreamstates, nocturnal wildlife burrowed for cover, and an avenging wind swept through the treetops like a dense cleansing fog. Like an invading force, the expanding legion of displaced souls rallied around the prospect of rebirth, and surfed down the sonic tsunami submerging the plains intent on mischief. Sensitive to the kinetic force that grounded itself in open water, the electrical grid sputtered with rolling brownouts and the local citizenry paused without comprehension.

Stumbling drunk and paranoically stoned, most of BlueStar's disoriented party guests groped their ways to the exits in the pitch-black, windowless building. Jon, still holding his guitar in the hopes that power would be restored, told his bandmates to stay put, and Marco agreed, pointing out the potential damage to the instruments if they tried to move. Using their remaining senses, Donna gravitated toward to the sound of Jon's voice, Farah used the excuse of darkness to hold Agent Falin close to her, and Rosella clung to Roddy while the timid fled.

The mood in the control room was more stoic, but after a short time in cramped quarters without air circulation, most of them surrendered to instinct and made for the exit. The incessant mantra, droning through the monitors like throbbing headache, permeated the atmosphere. "Oohhrree oohhrree oohhrree, *thump*! Oohhrree oohhrree oohhrree, *thump*! Oohhrree ... ."

But the pure visions of simple primitives, animated by the magical forces who had given the tulpas life, attracted other disembodied beings, many with no redeeming qualities. Criminal spirits who had met violent ends, jilted lovers with revenge agendas, false gods carrying twisted messages, and miscreants of every stripe tainted the collective vision of the united tribes, and having shed the constraints of terrestrial physics, the skies opened wide enough to include subtle influences from beyond the earth's atmosphere. Red Cloud urged his warriors to harness their energies and obey his command, but with too many voices, the message slowly lost its tonal clarity.

The captive monks, who had retained independent thinking, understood the implications of destabilizing natural order, and once they heard the vibrational fluctuations and the irregular thump of Niwot's clarion drum, they knew it was their cue to act. As Red Cloud and the Chief struggled to control the ever-expanding, unwieldy thought-form and the sonic emanation it produced, Gyalpo, whose misdeeds had opened the doors to chaos, left his body and went to locate the source of the Chief Niwot's power.

Inside the studio, no one could see or hear themselves think as the multitoned assault gained strength and added to everyone's anxiety. The narrow hallway was crammed with the costumed and confused, pushing and shoving impatiently, cursing in aggravation. Untethered from manners, the crowd's drunkenness turned blindly hostile: Arguments broke out in yells and shrieks. Gut punches and elbow jabs were exchanged. The weak were jostled, the fallen stepped on, and the boisterous rudeness crescendoed to a full-scale frenzy at exactly the same time Remy's stimulation brought Chodya to orgasm. Her unearthly scream barely leaked through the equipment closet door, but her release had a far-reaching affect.

Gyalpo heard Chodya's etheric cries and realized her vows had been broken. With occult skill, he directed the destructive tantric forces toward the tulpa Chodya had helped him create, and Chief Niwot's Brave, who had commandeered that entity, immediately began to lose his vigor. Chief Niwot sensed the change but, struggling to control the disorganized army of the disembodied, did not have the power to reverse the trend. Without the help of his powerful second, the Chief was unable to maintain focus, and Red Cloud's followers, whose inhabited spirit beings were old and weak, could not stem the tide either. Imploring his assembly to ignore the karmic forces that had caused their death and concentrate their energies toward rematerializing on the earthly plane, Niwot thumped his drum erratically as the magic hour wore on. But the loyalty of his own tulpa, whose sense of independence was awakened by the other tulpa's spiritualized activity, wavered. Tenzin and Kundun, who had helped create Niwot's entity, urged it to surrender to their authority, but as the veils closed and the threads of rebellion unraveled, the rogue entity chose its own destiny. After it abandoned the Chief, the tulpa vaporized into empty space and ceased to exist. The Brave's tulpa followed it into the darkness, and Niwot's ability to influence the material plane diminished like a fading storm.

Most of Red Cloud's warriors were able to retain control of their spirit entities, and the Indians retreated back to the brooding levels of retribution that had sustained their existence since their demise. The other spirits, mischievous, mal-intentioned, and sparkling with life energy like firework fragments, slipped through the Samhain cracks to experience moments of manifestation as Halloween creatures before melting back into their realms. The streets of Boulder and halls of the Boulderado Hotel shivered with a frisson of fright as the local ghosts celebrated their ephemeral yearly life cycle.

As the ghosts retreated and spiritual fog in the sanctuary cleared, the intruders' insidious mantra was replaced by the monks' purging tones. Lama Yeshe and several other Tibetan holy men joined the incantation. Nima awakened from her possession in a cold sweat, dazed but unharmed. Stanley, whose psychic vision wasn't developed enough to have followed the confusing power struggle, was relieved she was back, and they left for home as quickly as possible. Once they were gone, the monks' meditation shifted to more mundane matters.

Lama Yeshe said, "We heard your thoughts but were unable to reach you. Just as you said, the Native Spirits are very strong. We must make sure this never happens again." The other holy men agreed.

"Yes, Your Holiness. What shall we do?"

Lama Yeshe consulted his peers then spoke. "There will be no more tulpas made here; it is too dangerous. We will send novices from the Dharjeeling temple to help polish The Jewels."

"Thank you, Your Holiness. We will make preparations," Kundun said.

The Lama continued, "Tenzin, now that you have found your voice again, you will manage the affairs of the monastery until a successor is chosen."

Tenzin was surprised. "When are you returning, Your Holiness?"

"I am not," Lama Yeshe told them. "There is much suffering amongst our refugees, and the Dalai Lama needs me in India. You know the ways of this country better than me now, and you have proven yourself to be a capable leader." Then he addressed Gyalpo.

"Gyalpo, your impure Bon roots have troubled the smooth bark of our Bodhi Tree. Still, you are a monk and one of us. You will submit to Tenzin's will and use your occult skills to protect the Sangha."

Gyalpo apologized. "I am sorry, Your Holiness. I will obey."

"Kundun," Lama Yeshe continued, "you will welcome the pilgrims and assign them tasks. All of you will be responsible for their training, but they must return to the homeland to be ordained."

"And what of our novices?" Tenzin asked. "What shall become of them?"

"The sons and daughters of the white men may study our ways. So too may the brown and black and yellow children of the West. But teach them slowly, for they do not know patience."

"And what of the red men? Shall they be welcome too?"

"The Native Americans are our cousins," Lama Yeshe said. "Their plight is much like our plight. You shall help them in every way possible."

Gyalpo objected, "But the restless spirits of their dead can cause great mischief, Your Holiness. Must we obey them too?"

"Of course not Gyalpo. You will protect the Sangha from their bad intentions."

"Then what special treatment shall they be afforded?" Tenzin asked.

"The red people still suffer greatly. You will teach them the Buddhist ways and help them get along with those who now live here. Just as they've welcomed us, some of the whites sympathize with their cause."

"The whites have made special places for them, but the people who live on the reservations think of them as prisons."

"They are prisons, but there are freedoms within. You must help them find ways to use their time wisely. Teach them to meditate; only then may they be liberated from the wheel." Lama Yeshe used his advanced powers to gaze into the future. "The red people share our special blood. Like us, their spirits never die. They will find a way to survive and grow in strength and number."

CHAPTER 41

The mantra ceased, and the power to the studio cycled back on while Chodya was still in coital thrall. As light returned, Frankie broke the oppressive silence with a few nervous kicks of his bass drum, Jon picked up his guitar, tentatively strumming a chord or two, and Marco checked to see if his amp was on. Without speaking, the band coalesced around the minor chords of a slow song they had never played in public before.

> *Aaahhh nowhere!*
> *And nothing stays the same.*
> *You shop a lot of windows*
> *Along the streets of main*
> *Heaven is alright,*
> *It's just a little hard to find*
> *And what's been on your mind*
> *More than likely's been on mine.*
> *Cast your stones into a raging sea,*
> *And they land back at your feet.*
> *Throw your shadow onto the ground,*
> *And it darkens all you meet.*

Fearing another power failure, the people nearest the door, including Sasha and Mavis, kept pushing out into the alleyway and scattered. Diane had already gone home, but the other studio regulars remained: Cynthia, who was somehow energized by the excitement, extended her arms and moved to the music like a helicopter rotating too slowly to get off the ground, Samantha, unable to tuck herself back into her tight costume without partially disrobing, sought the privacy of the bathroom, Donna saw that the food table was a complete mess and attempted to rescue some of her pastries from a pool of wine, while the other inveterates who had decided to stay revisited their stashes and picked through the edible remains, determined to remain to the very end.

The changeover from a fractious fray to a private party was aided by more wine and the scent of fresh pot, and by the time the band was halfway through their next song, a new mood was established. Simone and his consorts swayed to the undulating rhythm like tidal weeds, and the band's dreamy ballad calmed everyone's nerves.

> *Stuck her head into the lion's den*
> *Said, "Hey babe, there you are!"*
> *Searched the world round for you,*
> *Now I'm leaving on a star.*
> *Many times in many ways,*
> *You showed me who you are.*
> *All alone and back again,*
> *You traveled very far.*
> *It's the rise and the fall,*
> *Of nothing at all.*

Agent Falin wasn't professionally comfortable in the thick layer of marijuana smoke in the main room, so he led Farah down the hall toward the back of the studio. Looking for a safer place, he yanked on the locked doors of the bathroom and the equipment closet, and the one door he found unlocked should have been. Inside the back lounge, Duke was seated on the sofa with his pants off. The topless lush kneeling in front of him had her mouth around his cock, and even though her stringy hair blocked most of her face, it was easy to see the band of white powder near the base of his shaft where her oral lunges hadn't yet reached.

Farah giggled nervously, but Agent Falin was stunned to have caught them in the act.

Neither of the sexualants had any intention of stopping, so Duke simply said, "In or out, just close the door, please."

Complying, Farah pulled Agent Falin into the small room and closed the door behind them. He wanted to leave, but she squeezed his hand hard enough to let him know that she was aroused and wanted to stay. The racy contagion of stifled moans made it difficult for Agent Falin to resist, and in mid-lust, Duke proffered a coke vial. Agent Falin's hands were occupied, but Farah took it, unscrewed the top, and thrust the tiny attached spoon into the shimmering contents. Extracting a small, unstable mound, she inhaled the delicate crystals and reloaded, placing the next dose under Agent Falin's nostrils. The sensual thrill seemed to levitate the flakes of powder into his nasal passage, and the icy numbness cauterized his critical thinking. Farah ingested again, sliding her hand deep into Agent Falin's pocket as he took another hit. Their petting escalated in intimacy, and they wet-kissed for the first time. Then, flush and flustered, Agent Falin pushed the door open with his shoulder and pulled Farah out with him before further incriminating himself.

Samantha, having just emerged from the ladies room, caught sight of Duke's sexual activity in the lounge and grabbed the door before it could be closed. She blurted, "Duke!" before slamming it shut.

Emerging from the equipment closet a moment later, Remy heard Duke's name and asked, "Where is he?"

"In there," Samantha pointed, "but I think he's busy."

Agent Falin recovered his tongue and agreed. "Yeah, I wouldn't go in there if I were you."

As Remy sized up the three strangers in front of him, and Chodya joined their midst. The peasant dress Donna had loaned her was poorly resituated on her tired body, and the shawl she had borrowed to cover her head scabs only partially did. Looking every bit the victim of sexual abuse, her appearance demanded an explanation.

No one knew each other, but Samantha had the civic sense to ask, "Are you okay?"

Chodya's eyes squinted in the light, and she found it difficult to speak. Curiously, she held a Beyer Dynamic microphone in her right hand as if it were an ice cream cone.

Treating her like an uncooperative child, Remy couldn't get her to let go of the mic without creating a scene. "She's fine, real fine, if y'all know what I mean," he asserted, putting his arm around her possessively. "Some party! Y'all look like yer having your own fun too," he said defensively.

Samantha readjusted her bustier and said, "Well, I guess," unconvincingly.

Chodya's unsettling appearance and odd behavior put a pause in Agent Falin's passion, and he felt the call of duty again. "You might need some first aid for those cuts," he noted, indicating her scalp.

Chodya straightened her shawl but couldn't find her voice as she mime-talked into the disconnected mic.

Well your motor's running and your hands are weak,
Your mouth's wide open but you still can't speak.
Up around the corner where it's very dark,
There's a thousand places where we could park,
We've been living in a Cracked House yeah,
But that don't mean that it's gonna fall.
We've been living in a Cracked House yeah,
But I don't want no trouble,

I don't want no trouble at all,
No trouble at all.

Remy had forgotten her name, so he said, "Come on, sugar, let's get you something to drink," as if all was well.

Chodya, looking half crazed and semiconscious, smiled meekly as Remy led her away by the hand.

Samantha was skeptical but said, "I've got find my husband," and followed them.

Farah, who had seen her share of aftermath, said, "No telling what got into *her*," squeezing her own agenda back into Agent Falin's hand. "I'm ready to go, aren't you?"

Agent Falin's tour of Southeast Asia had landed him in compromising situations before, and the sight of a victim had sobered him up. "Yeah, I'm ready." He one-armed Farah. "I could use a little fresh air."

"Maybe that guy in the lounge was one of the guys you're looking for," Farah whispered as they went toward the door.

"No shit," Agent Falin agreed, "but we can talk about it – most of it – tomorrow. Your sister's place far from here?"

"Ten-minute walk."

"I could use some exercise."

"Just what I had in mind."

The crisp, after-midnight air hurried their steps, and occasionally holding hands like naughty teens, they walked briskly to Sasha's pad in a huge home on Spruce Street that had been converted into apartments.

With electricity restored, Dennis powered the console back up to check its condition. He was relieved that the sonic interference was gone, and when he turned it off again a few minutes later, the energy of the party began to peter out organically. Walter's interest in anything technical ended when Samantha, full of pent-up female energy, told him it was time to leave. Cynthia, who had become fascinated with Simone and his consorts, accepted their invitation to join them back at the hotel, and with no one listening, Jon's band decided to stop playing and pack up. Donna was with them when Chodya found her.

"You look awful!" Donna gasped.

Chodya mumbled incoherently into the microphone she refused to let go of.

"What's the matter? Are you hurt? Talk to me!"

"I, I feel strange," she finally said.

Donna saw that her clothes had been put on without the aid of a mirror. "Did you … ? With who?"

Chodya looked around, didn't see Remy, and shrugged. A wry smile curled her lips.

Donna smiled and said, "You slut!" as a compliment. "Welcome back!"

"Thanks," Chodya said a bit more audibly. "I'm hungry. Anything left to eat?"

Donna put together a small plate of whatever looked edible and gave it to her. Suddenly ravenous, Chodya grounded her psyche with food.

With the aid of his considerable stash, Duke's playdate in the back lounge lasted much longer than was natural. When he came out to go to the bathroom and check on the party at 4:00 a.m., almost everyone was gone. The detritus of Halloween high jinks littered every corner of the studio, but he was too far gone to care. He thanked everyone for coming, and after ushering the last of the strangers out, he and Remy returned to lounge to share some leftover wine and cheese with their extremely compliant guest. The three of them were still there the next day when Diane opened up to assess the damage.

CHAPTER 42

Agent Walker's date also lasted well into Sunday morning, so by the time Officer McKnight picked him up and they made it into the office, he was still one more cup of coffee away from recovered. The Steamboat weather was a sunny, forty degrees, with sun melt underway, and Officer McKnight, having enjoyed an early bed and his own pillow, took the lead until Agent Walker was fully alert. It didn't take long.

Officer McKnight unlocked his office in the basement of the municipal building. "I heard from your brother last night," he said, rearranging the desktop papers while the coffee pot hissed.

Agent Walker peered out the sidewalk-level awning window. "Really? How's he doing? Why'd he call you?"

"He was looking for you; said he tried to call you yesterday but no one was really sure where you were. Sugar and milk?"

"Thanks. So how'd he find me?"

"I asked him that. I guess he called your dad, and your dad made some calls, and someone told him you were up here. I think it was Farah's mother."

The mention of Farah helped focus Agent Walker on their mission. He took a sip of caffeine. "You hear anything from her or Agent Falin?"

"Not yet, but your brother wanted you to call him – said it was important. I tried to get him to tell me, but all he would say is that he thinks he might have some information about the smugglers everyone is looking for."

"That's Wedge, always trying to make himself feel important."

"Little brothers are like that. He said to call him at home or at the station as soon as you get the message."

"Let's do it now."

A deputy answered the call. "Granby County Police Station. How may I help you?"

"This is Officer Greg McKnight from the Steamboat Springs Customs Office. May I please speak with Officer Wedge Walker?"

"No, sir. Officer Walker went home a few hours ago. Can someone else help you?"

"No thanks, I'll call him at home." Officer McKnight dialed the number he had been given and handed to phone to Agent Walker.

Wedge Walker answered half asleep, but when he heard his brother on the line, it woke him up the rest of the way. "Hey, Mr. Big Shot, where the hell you been? I've been trying to get a hold of you for two days."

"I'm in Steamboat, Wedge, but I guess you already figured that out. McKnight told me you think you might know something."

"That's what he told you? What an asshole! Why are you and your federal buddies always putting us locals down? I track you down to give you the best lead you've had in weeks, and all you can say is you think I might know something?"

"Slow down, Wedge. Nobody's putting you down. We all appreciate the job you guys do. You're our eyes and ears." Agent Walker rolled his eyes at Officer McKnight as he continued to mollify his hotheaded brother. "We're all in this together, brother. What've you got?"

"Well, it sure ain't another stupid alien story."

"That's a relief. No dead cows around?"

"None that I know of, but we did have some very interesting overnight guests this weekend."

"Tell me more."

"I heard a plane come in real late Friday; you know I've been on the night shift since you-know-who got elected sheriff."

"Dad told me."

"Anyways, I figured something fishy was up cause why else would someone try to put down on our soccer field after dark with snow on the ground?"

"Maybe they were lost or in trouble."

"That's why I got in my cruiser and went to see."

"So what was it? Who was it?"

"Let me go take a piss 'cause this may take a minute. I'll be right back."

While he was waiting, Agent Walker asked Officer McKnight to make some calls and see if he could raise Agent Falin.

"When Mother Nature calls," Wedge said as he got back on the line. "So I was saying that I found these two rascals who had landed a little, chopped up high-wing right here in downtown Granby. It was dark, but I could tell they were up to no good."

"So what happened? Did they try to get away?"

Wedge paused to inflate himself. "Well, they might have been thinking about it, but I parked the cruiser so they couldn't get around it. When I shined the service light into their faces, they knew I had 'em."

"What did you do? Arrest them by yourself?"

Wedge flexed his ego. "They gave me some BS story about coming to visit a gal up here, so I tricked them into the back seat, told them I'd give them a ride, and took 'em down to the station instead."

Agent Walker was impressed. "Good work! Where are they now? You got them locked up?"

"Well, I did, but I was the only one on duty that night."

"They got away? Broke out?"

Wedge's tone changed. "Not really, but sort of. They called this friend of theirs, and she came down, and I had to let them go," he admitted sheepishly.

"What? You let them go? Why'd you do that?"

Wedge was silent for a minute before he answered. "Well, you know, remember what happened last year?"

"Yeah, but I didn't think it was your fault."

"It really wasn't, as far as they knew. But they still put it on my record."

"And let me guess, this friend those guys called was going to tell everyone the rest of the story if you didn't cooperate."

"Either I let her cats out, or she lets mine; that's how she put it."

"Women! You really ought to think about settling down, Wedge."

"I know, I know."

"So what did they look like? Who were they? Get any ID?"

"That's why I called you. I think you better look up a Mr. Duke Dunn. He's got some business in Boulder – something to do with music. That's all I know. No idea who the other guy with him was, but he sounded like he was from somewhere down south."

"Thanks, Wedge. That gives us something to go on. Anything else? You get the call letters or know where they were headed?"

"Oh yeah, the call letters – if you can believe them – were easy to remember: AM12BE. It was some kind of homemade, crop-duster-looking thing they were flying so I'm guessing it wasn't registered. They took off heading north, but I wouldn't be surprised if they didn't make it over the mountains in that contraption."

"Thanks for all your help, brother. Now go get some rest. I'll talk to the sheriff next week and see if I can get you off the night shift."

"Thanks, Mr. Big Shot."

Officer McKnight had heard most of the conversation and was ready to talk when Agent Walker got off the phone. "I called around, but no trace of Agent Falin. I checked the Boulder police station, and they suggested trying the Boulderado. I called there too. They said he never checked in, but the woman I spoke with did say it was quite an eventful Halloween party."

"Isn't that where he and Farah were headed?"

"They were supposed to go there, but you know Farah."

"She said her sister was there, and I believe her. What did the Boulderado tell you happened?"

"Well, there was some strange incident in the afternoon. Seems like some sicko cut the finger off an old codger and put it in someone's dessert."

"That's weird. Did they find out who did it?"

"No. The hotel was full of guests, and they went door to door, but they didn't come up with any suspects."

"What else?"

"Well, the detective I spoke with said there'd been a number of reports regarding Native Americans."

Agent Walker's ears always perked up when the subject was mentioned. "What do *they* have to do with anything?"

"No one is sure, certainly not the detective I spoke to. He did seem a bit concerned though. He said people have been seeing Indians around lately."

"Why's that odd? You can't blame them for wanting to get off the reservation once in a while."

"True, it's just that most of the reports weren't about regular Indians – at least that's what he told me."

"Okay, so what are you telling me? What are 'irregular' Indians?"

"Ones that disappear like ghosts."

Officer McKnight's answer was a conversation stopper. Agent Walker loaded the information into his brain and processed it. The connections to what he had seen and heard in Craig, coupled with the clues gleaned from Bobby's crash site investigation were confusing but hard to ignore. "Either this has got to be one of the strangest strings of coincidences I've ever heard about, or the Native Americans around here are up to something," he concluded.

"I thought about that too," Officer McKnight agreed, "but what?"

"Damned if I know. Maybe Agent Falin's come up with something we can hang our hat on. Where the hell is he? He was supposed to check in by noon."

"He's still got five minutes."

The phone rang on cue. Officer McKnight answered. It was Agent Falin on the line. "Where the heck are you?"

"Beautiful downtown Boulder. This place is even nicer than I expected."

"Glad you're enjoying it. Any progress on the investigation, or have you forgotten what you're doing there?"

Agent Falin was surprised to hear Officer McKnight so edgy. He held his finger to his lips and told Farah to be quiet. "Yes, sir. Of course, sir," he said with mock subservience. "Agent Falin calling in on schedule to inform you that I have located and identified a drug dealer."

Officer McKnight put the phone on speaker. "You're now on speaker with Agent Walker and myself. Please repeat what you just said."

Farah sat up in bed and buttoned her flannel shirt. "I'll put the coffee on," she whispered.

"Agent Falin? Where are you? Are you alone? Can you talk freely?"

"Like I said, one suspect identified. Seems like he's a major player too."

"What makes you think so?"

"Well, for one thing, his name."

"What's his name?"

"Duke. Duke Dunn. He owns the big recording studio here."

Agent Walker couldn't believe his luck. "Duke Dunn? Are you sure? How do you know?"

Agent Falin hadn't thought about how he was going to answer that without incriminating himself. "Uh, let's just say there's no doubt. Farah and I were at a party at his studio and – "

"I thought the party was at the hotel?" Officer McKnight noted.

Agent Walker started connecting the dots. "Where is Farah now?" he asked, suspecting the truth.

Agent Falin didn't lie. "She's in the kitchen. Want to talk to her?"

"Whose kitchen? Where are you?"

"Her sister's."

Officer McKnight interrupted. "Duke Dunn? Isn't that the same name your brother just gave us?"

"Yes," Agent Walker said, "but I'd like to know – "

"Listen," Agent Falin continued seriously. "I was there; I saw it with my own eyes. This guy's the real thing. I think we better get the locals involved so we can conduct a search and seizure."

Agent Walker heard him. "Good idea. I'll make some calls if you're that sure. Call back in an hour and I'll tell you what we're doing."

"Over and out."

Farah swiggled back with two mugs, wearing only her flannel shirt and a Cheshire grin. "So Mr. Secret Agent Man, what's the plan?"

"More of same," he said, touching her exposed thigh as he took his coffee. "I haven't had a night like that since I was overseas."

Farah didn't like being compared to previous lovers but accepted the compliment with a twinkle. "So last night wasn't the first time you weren't Mr. Goody Two-Shoes."

"I never snorted coke before, if that's what you're asking."

"Well, maybe now you know why it's so popular."

"Speeding is popular too, but that doesn't make it legal."

"So you're going to arrest yourself?" Farah teased. "Citizen's arrest! Get the handcuffs!"

Agent Falin went along with the joke. "Tie me up! I surrender."

Farah's sister called in from behind the door. "You okay? Can I come in?"

Farah answered, "Sure, I've apprehended the criminal. We're safe now!"

Sasha came into the spare room she had lent them and smiled at her sister's catch. "Well, you better take him down to the station after you change the sheets. My roommate is coming back this afternoon, and I've got to go to work."

"Okay, big sister. I'll see you at the hotel later."

"Just shut the door on the way out. It locks itself."

"I'm really starting to like your family," Agent Falin confided.

"Now don't go soft on me," Farah warned, smiling. "Who's gonna keep us safe from all those bad people who do drugs if you don't?"

Agent Falin couldn't answer that one. He actually felt great; incredibly light, sexually satisfied, and not even close to in the mood for police work. "You feel like going for a drive? Show me around?"

His candor surprised her. "Uh, sure. Maybe we can get breakfast afterward."

"Sounds great. I'm buying."

Farah saw his boyish enthusiasm. "You sure you're okay? Last night kind of blow your mind?"

"I'm fine, really. Something about this place just makes me feel good."

"That's what they all say. It's Chief Niwot's curse. No one ever wants to leave."

After a casual meal at the Fleur Du Lis, Agent Falin called his boss again. Agent Walker had received a third tip naming Duke Dunn as a suspect, this time courtesy of Oswaldo, who had passed the information on through his Colorado contact. The evidence was piling up, so he instructed Agent Falin to meet a team of Boulder officers at the station in thirty minutes. Begrudgingly, Agent Falin left Farah at the hotel and walked over to the main Boulder police station on Canyon Boulevard. A short time later, he was part of the two-car, four-man team that showed up BlueStar Studios with their guns at the ready.

Knowing Duke's history, Diane was not surprised to see the cops at the door and simply buzzed them in. "Good afternoon, Officers, how may I help you?"

The Captain said, "We have a warrant for the arrest of Duke Dunn. Is he here?"

"Yes, he's in back," she said without a trace of loyalty. "Shall I tell him you're here?"

"No thank you. We'll find him ourselves. Which way?"

Diane pointed down the hall. She recognized Agent Falin from the night before but didn't say anything.

The police opened the door to the back lounge without knocking, and were not completely surprised to see a half-naked girl asleep on the couch. Remy was passed out with his head twisted on the arm of the sofa, and Duke, wearing only a buttoned shirt, was seated in a leather armchair across from them. He had a mirror with lines of blow on his lap and was on the phone. He held up his hand to tell the cops that he'd be off in a minute. "Sure thing, cousin, I'll tell them," Duke spoke into the receiver. "They're here now." Duke helped himself to a line in front of the officers. "Toots?" he asked, offering his straw to the startled cops. Then, recognizing Agent Falin, he said, "Another one for you?"

The Captain didn't see Agent Falin cringe, and wasn't sure what to make of Duke's charade, so he simply said, "Duke Dunn, by the authority of the State of Colorado and the County of Boulder I hereby place you under arrest. Please get dressed and come with us."

"Sure thing, Officer," Duke said coolly.

"You come along too," he told the awakened Remy and the party girl.

"What for? What did I do?" the girl asked, redressing. "These two forced me in here. They raped me! Thank you for saving me, Officer!"

One of the detectives recognized her from a previous arrest and whispered in the Captain's ear. After hearing what he had to say, the Captain told her, "Okay, you can go home and get some rest. If you want to press charges, you can come by the station later. But don't go traveling anywhere. We may need you as a witness."

Remy didn't say anything while he got dressed, but he knew from Duke's wink that there was a plan. The cops handcuffed Duke and Remy, and were escorting them down the hall when they met Jon Cells coming in the opposite direction.

Seeing another possible suspect, the Captain asked, "And who might *you* be?"

Jon saw Duke's handcuffs and realized what was happening. "Er, I'm a guitar player. I just came by to get my guitar."

The Captain was skeptical, but Agent Falin said, "That's true. His band played here last night. I saw them."

"We'll need a statement from you," the Captain told Jon. "Agent Falin, please get this man's information and anyone else's you find wandering around here. We'll take these two to the station and see you there in a while."

Duke winked at Jon as the cops ushered Remy and him past.

"Let's go in here," Agent Falin said to Jon as he opened the door to the studio. "This shouldn't take long," he added in a friendly tone. Seated inside, he took out his notepad. "Alright, I already know you call yourself Jon Cells, but what's your real name?"

Jon gave Agent Falin a long look. He didn't remember seeing him at the party, and the idea that a strange cop knew his name was very unsettling. "Uh, my name is Jon Neulin," Jon said, shortening his birth name by a few letters.

Agent Falin recorded the information. "And where do you live?"

"Hotel Boulderado, room 404."

Agent Falin eyed him skeptically. "Look," he said, "I know what you're thinking – why is this cop asking me a bunch of questions? Don't worry, it's just routine. I only know who you are because you've got some very dedicated fans."

This was not a conversation Jon was prepared for. Like most of his associates, he didn't trust the police. He wasn't sure if Agent Falin was being sincere or just trying to soften him up. "Yeah, we're popular, sort of. Who are your friends?"

Agent Falin didn't want to say too much. "I don't know if I'd call them friends, but they did turn me on to your music."

Jon was skeptical. "Thanks, man. What's your name?"

Agent Falin pressed the buddy button. "Agent Todd Falin, US Customs. I really like your music. So you really live at the hotel? Cool."

"Call the hotel and ask for Jon Cells if you don't believe me."

"Okay, I will. How well do you know Duke Dunn? Just a friend or?"

Being connected to Duke, who he had just seen in handcuffs, made Jon felt like he was being interrogated. He got defensive. "I'm a musician, and he owns the recording studio. Anything else you want to know?"

Agent Falin realized he had lost rapport and reverted to cop-speak. "Not right now, but don't leave town. We can get a hold of you at the hotel?"

"Sure thing, whatever," Jon answered, stuffing the power cord to his amp inside it.

The interview over, Agent Falin made a mental note of Jon's face. He jotted the name Cells on his pad, doodled some prison bars over it, and after he had taken a statement from Diane, walked the length of the mall back to the police station on Canyon Boulevard. Duke and Remy were seated in the holding area near the Captain's desk, and Agent Walker was on the phone when he got there.

"Who?" Agent Walker screamed loud enough for Agent Falin to hear him.

"Earl Stanley," the Captain told him, eyeing his prisoners. "He's got clout down here."

Agent Walker was livid. "Remind me, where does he think he's the Earl of?"

"Dunraven, I believe."

"And just where in the hell is that?"

"I'm not sure, somewhere over in England I guess."

"So what's he doing over here? And whose political strings is he pulling?" Agent Walker was furious that his arrestee might be let go. "This is totally wrong, and I'm going to find out who's behind it."

"I'm with you," the Captain agreed, "but we can't hold him without charges."

Agent Falin understood what they were talking about. "Well, what if we have a witness? Is that enough to lock him up for a while?"

The Captain handed the phone to Agent Falin. Agent Walker asked him, "Who's the witness? You?"

Agent Falin realized he had put himself in a spot, but he saw Duke smirk, and that sent him over the edge. "Damn right! And I'll testify. We've got a female witness too."

Duke's smirk turned into a grin. "So are you and your girlfriend going to testify against yourselves too?" he teased Agent Falin.

The Captain's eye for subtlety had buoyed his rise through the ranks, and Agent Falin's blink, combined with the political pressure surrounding Duke's arrest, gave him pause. He removed the prisoners from the area, relocated them out of earshot, and picked up an extension phone. "Is there something else we need to know about this situation?" he asked Agent Falin.

"You saw him doing drugs with your own eyes!" Agent Falin said defensively. "What else is there to know?"

"We saw what we assumed was an illegal substance, but a policeman's testimony doesn't carry as much weight in the courtroom as a citizen's. Do you think whoever was with you would be willing to tell a jury what they saw?"

Agent Walker was listening. "Wasn't Farah with you? We could ask her to testify. Where is she?"

"I don't know where she is; at the hotel, I guess," Agent Falin said.

"Didn't she go to the party with you? She must have seen what you saw. Did you two?" Agent Walker stopped himself from asking a question he didn't want to hear the answer to.

The Captain interrupted the pregnant pause. "So, regarding the prisoners, how do you suggest we handle this?"

"What's their connection to this Stanley guy again?" Agent Walker asked.

"I was told they were distant cousins. The governor's office is sending the state troopers over to pick them up."

Agent Walker knew that the process of applying federal pressure on state bureaucracy would be time consuming. "Tell them the release papers are being prepared, but keep them there while I do some checking. I'll get back to you within the hour." He hung up the phone and asked Officer McKnight what he thought they should do.

"Let's make some calls," Officer McKnight said. "Somebody's got to know something."

No one was in the office on Sunday afternoon, and most officials in Colorado were too interested in the Broncos game to answer their home lines. After debating whether or not it was a good idea to call him, Officer McKnight finally got Jim Temple on the phone.

Jim was surprisingly alert for someone who hadn't slept in thirty-six hours. "No, I haven't heard anything from the good governor," he told Officer McKnight glibly. "Too much money on the slopes to pay attention to Denver politics. Why do you ask?"

"We're following up on some leads regarding an airplane crash. You know police work never takes a day off."

Jim liked being treated like an insider. "Kind of like the ski business. Can't waste fresh snow. What's the latest?"

"They arrested somebody down in Boulder."

"Really? Who?"

Officer McKnight knew it wasn't protocol but floated the name out anyway. "A guy named Duke Dunn. Ever heard of him?"

The silence before Jim's reply said more than his response. "Last name's familiar; isn't he related to the Earl of Dunraven?"

Officer McKnight hadn't put the last names together. "You mean Earl Stanley?"

"Stanley *is* the Earl of Dunraven. He has a big spread in the mountains above Estes Park. You think this Duke guy knows something about the aliens who shot your buddy down?"

"Aliens?"

"Farah said you had some proof – but maybe I'm not supposed to know that."

"Well, you know Farah, she thinks aliens are responsible for everything around here."

Agent Walker could only hear Officer McKnight's side of the conversation and looked perplexed.

Jim pried. "So what do *you* think?"

"I don't know what to think," Officer McKnight admitted. "This early snow, all these tourists; I know it's good for your business, but it sure makes my job harder. I'm not complaining, but between dead cows and aliens in Halloween costumes; all I know for certain is we lost a good man."

"I hear you, friend. Maybe this Duke guy you arrested will be able to tell you something. I've got to go now, but let me know if there's any way I can help. And by the way, I heard our old buddy from Denver had a good time at the party last night. Old dog's still got bite!"

"It's just a hunch," Officer McKnight said after he'd hung up, "but I think Jim knows something he isn't telling."

"Go on," Agent Walker encouraged.

"I told you Jim's got political ambitions. He told me that this guy, Earl Stanley, – he owns that spread up there in Estes Park where they have the landing strip – well Jim let on that he and this Duke character might be related."

"Okay, but what are you saying?"

"I'm not sure, but what if there's a good reason this Earl Stanley doesn't want Duke Dunn in jail?"

Agent Walker put the pieces together. "What if this Stanley character is really the one we're looking for? Agent Dobson seemed like he was headed in the direction of his spread when he went down."

"I wonder how much Jim knows."

"Maybe he's in business with this Stanley guy? You said he has some secret financing."

Officer McKnight lit up at the possibility of solving one of Steamboat's best-kept mysteries. "So you think the Stanley guy is using his private field for smuggling and Jim's on the payroll?"

The truth needed no further explanation.

"The question now is what can we do? We've got to find a way to keep this Duke Dunn guy in Boulder until we can question him. He'll be as good as free once the pols get a hold of him."

"I've got some friends down in Boulder. What if we tell them Duke is part of a murder investigation? Doesn't that change the rules?"

"Murder's always got local jurisdiction."

"But who are we claiming got killed?"

"Agent Dobson! We'll claim it wasn't an accident; maybe it wasn't. He was a great pilot who knew the terrain. Maybe someone, I don't know, the Stanley guy or one of his secret buddies, shot Agent Dobson down."

"It certainly could have happened that way."

"Can't say for sure it didn't."

"Go ahead and call your Boulder friends. We need to get to the bottom of this. We owe it to Agent Dobson."

"I wish I could get a hold of Bobby. He's known Jim his whole life. Never know what else we might find out," Officer McKnight said as he dialed.

CHAPTER 43

The sound of Stanley's cowboy boots on the stone floor woke Nima up, and she rolled over in bed when he came back in the room. "Where are you going?" she asked sleepily.

"I've got to go into town," Stanley said, looking through his closet for the right jacket.

"Why? Aren't you tired? Come back to bed; I need you."

"I'll try to come back tomorrow."

Nima sat up. "Tomorrow? Why? Where are you going?"

Fully dressed, Stanley stood on the other side of the room as he spoke to her. "I've got some business to attend to in Denver. You stay here and take care of the house."

Nima was not happy being talked to like a servant and pouted.

"There's a little something to perk you up in the stash box," he said dispassionately. "I'm leaving the Land Rover here, and you've got Kundun if you need ... company."

Nima collected the covers around her chest against the jealous insinuation.

Buttoning his outside coat, Stanley added, "I'm not expecting anyone, so don't let any strangers in."

The inference was alarming, but she knew there was no use talking to a man in his boots. The wind whistled through the icicles on the eaves, and the whole building shuddered as Stanley slammed the front door. Nima heard Stanley's black Mercedes 450SEL crunching the rocksalt on the driveway and had a chilling premonition.

CHAPTER 44

The state troopers picked up Duke and Remy at the Boulder police station before Agent Walker could stop them, and the arrestees smirked at the Captain as they were driven to the safety of political allies. Stanley was already at the Denver courthouse posting bail by the time they got there. He drove them up to Jim Temple's remote cabin outside Steamboat and planned on leaving them there until they could sneak back to their plane and get out of Colorado. Their nerves fried, all Duke and Remy wanted to do was sleep. Stanley had showed them around the cabin and celebrated their escape with a victory snort when they heard a dog barking. Looking out the window, they saw a bloodhound baying at the back of Stanley's black sedan. A man with the dog was on his walkie-talkie, looking up at the sky.

Stanley heard an airplane when went outside to talk to the stranger. "Can I help you? Are you lost?"

Bobby had his hand on the gun in his pocket when he asked, "Are you Stanley, the Earl of Dunraven?"

Stanley was shocked but said, "Yes, what brings you out this way? Did Mr. Temple ask you to come check on us?"

"Not exactly," Bobby answered.

The dog kept pawing at the trunk of the car, and Stanley didn't want it to scratch the paint, so he opened it, expecting to see nothing but a spare tire. He figured Kundun must have put the old bearskin they used for picnics over it, but had no explanation for how Agent Dobson's battered body, still wearing his torn flight suit, wound up there instead.

Bobby radioed his position to Officer McKnight and Agent Walker before informing Stanley of his rights.

EPILOGUE

Farah got tired of waiting for Agent Falin to return to the hotel, and her afternoon stroll through the mall led her all the way to the foothills on the western end of Pearl Street. Wind chimes on the porches of almost every house sung in the daily breeze that cascaded through the canyons. The smell of burning pine, descending from warm cabins, made her miss her own place in Steamboat, and she wondered if her new relationship would change her plans to return there.

Agent Falin, smitten by both Niwot's curse and Farah's charm, was so disinterested with the political tug-of-war going on in the police station that he stepped outside and let his heart wander. Boulder Creek, a lively stream teeming with large, rounded granite rocks that inspired its name, gurgled past the courthouse complex. Putting his hands in his pockets, Agent Falin remembered the knife that he put in there. He couldn't feel it and hoped it had fallen out at Farah's sister's apartment in case he needed it for evidence. Temporarily fulfilled, he second-guessed his career choice for the first time in his life and thought about the colossal waste of time and energy his government expended punishing people for having a good time.

The Satsang Diner never opened that Sunday. Nancy, who had gone home exhausted and drunk herself to into a wine stupor, spent the afternoon nursing her hangover and talking to family members in New York about getting divorced and moving back home. Joel tried to call her, but she hung up as soon as she heard his voice. Seeing him upset, Crystal stuck a joint in his mouth and made him feel needed.

After leaving the BlueStar party at 3:00 a.m., Roddy and Rosella slept in their car near the river at Eben G Fine Park until a van with four children who had been pent up in church that morning parked next to them. The kids burst out of the sliding side door like explosive confetti, running and taunting each other while screaming with glee. Their terrier mutt barked furiously as it chased them and the soccer ball through the rocky field, and the six-year-old girl who discovered Hipolito asleep beneath a giant cottonwood shrieked because she thought he was dead.

Samantha Hardaway brought the cordless phone to her husband, who had returned to his shop as soon as his wife had let him out of the conjugal bed.

"Professor?"

Walter recognized his brother Edward's voice. "Yes, Professor. Get some snow up there?"

"We did yesterday. You?"

"Nothing but frost down here. How've you been?"

"That's an interesting question."

"It is?"

"Yes, things have been a bit odd up here lately. Ever since that DEA plane went down."

Walter hadn't heard about it.

"The search party guy stayed with me, and I tried to help him. This phone you helped me rig works great."

"You're welcome; not too interesting though."

"Maybe you did something only you and your government buddies know about, but ever since I got that phone, I've been hearing things that, I don't know, are a little scary. I've been meaning to talk to you about it."

Walter stopped soldering. "Hearing things? Like what?"

"Something that sounds like machines talking to each other." Edward made whistling noises that sounded like injured canaries. "Oohhrree oohhrree."

"Maybe it's interference. Is the system working well? I can hear you clearly. Have you checked the antenna?"

"Yes, the phone works great, and so does the radio; that's the weird thing."

"What is?"

"It seems like I'm able to get all kinds of bands that I never could before."

"Sounds like a good problem. Hear anything from Down Under lately?"

Edward paused to consider the question. "Well, maybe, sort of."

"You couldn't understand what they were saying? Maybe they were talking in another language."

"That's exactly what I was thinking, but I didn't call to tell you that."

"No? Why then?"

"I went to check the dish, and there was something strange on it. I don't know if it was attached or how it got there. It's like it fell out of the sky and just got stuck there. It's a really odd looking piece of metal. Kind of shiny and dull at the same time."

"Send me a picture. Is that all?"

"Well, no."

"What then?" Walter's older brother had always been a bit eccentric.

"Well, there's this pilot who crashed. He's supposed to be dead, but I saw him walking around. My neighbor and the DEA guy saw him too."

"Oh no! Not you too! You're not going to tell me about dead cows now, are you?" Walter knew his brother was going to start talking about aliens, how they modified his phone equipment so they could talk to the mothership, and how they were responsible for everything he couldn't explain with his PhD in anthropology. "Really, Edward, I think you've been up there long enough. I can make a few calls and try to get you your university job back. You sound a little freaked out. Maybe you should drink some herb tea and take your tin hat off."

The chambermaid who cleaned his room once a week was the one who discovered Mr. Lawry dead in his chair on Sunday afternoon. Jack didn't bother looking for any evidence of foul play because he had been waiting for Mr. Lawry to die for years, so he phoned the police and locked the door until the coroner arrived. No one was curious enough about the body of an old man who had lived too long to order an autopsy, and the coroner assumed the nasty gash on his scalp was where he'd bumped his head. Chief Niwot, having finally avenged the murderous acts committed by Corporal Lawry's grandfather during the Sand Creek Massacre, retreated to the ethers with a piece of Mr. Lawry's scalp.

Tenzin and Kundun hadn't slept at all, but that didn't diminish their efforts to cleanse the monastery. Their training had prepared them for the hardships of harsh climates, minimal diet, and prolonged isolation, and the urgency of restoring the temple's auric health required them to tap into the stamina they had developed over a lifetime of dedication to Buddhist practices. With the help of their acolytes, they swept the floors and washed all the surfaces where phantom feet had tread. Kundun carried their biggest ritual incense burner from room to room, repeating the purification mantras as the heavy metal cage swung from its chain and covered him in smoke. Tenzin lit the candles at the foot of Buddha's altar, then sat deep in meditation, reconnecting the monastery to the purpose of its existence.

Gyalpo wasn't able to help until late Sunday afternoon, and most of the basic rituals had been observed by then, so he set about the task of identifying and collecting everything in the temple the tulpas had come in contact with. There were too many items of clothing, kitchenware, and tools to burn inside, so a funeral pyre was constructed out near the barns. While his helpers gathered and arranged the dry logs, Gyalpo searched the stable where the first tulpa had lived before it became Niwot's possession. It was hard to know the origin of the feathers that littered the ground because the building had once housed chickens, but poking through the leftover hay, moist dirt, and yak feces with a stick, he found a lost sandal and dropped it into a garbage sack. Assuming there was another shoe waiting to be discovered, Gyalpo dug further. His thrusting hit something solid buried in the dirt, so he forced his poker against it, trying to dig it up, and on the second jab, heard it pop. The probe slid inside something hollow, and the object was still attached when he brought it to the surface. Niwot's broken gourd drum was added to the fire that burned well into the evening.

Chodya was still asleep on Donna's living room sofa when the Sunday phone call from Donna's mother woke her up. Each pulse of the striated ring rankled her exposed nerves, and by the time Mrs. Garfinkle gave up trying to reach her daughter, Chodya was fully awake.

Having missed the call, Donna stumbled into the room in her house robe. "Shit. That must've been my mother. Why didn't you answer it?" she asked before realizing the answer. "How'd you sleep?" she asked more sympathetically.

"Pretty well, considering." Chodya felt the scabs on her scalp. "Are they bleeding?"

Donna came closer to inspect and put her hand on Chodya's shoulder. "Not too much. We just need a few more Band-Aids."

Chodya held her friend's hand. "Thank you so much. I don't know what I would have done without you."

Donna sat down beside her. "You look better than I thought. Do you want to tell me what happened?"

Chodya's face darkened for a moment as she squeezed a tear. "It was awful – but wonderful in a way."

Donna held her hand. "Are you through being a Buddhist?"

Chodya looked surprised. "No, why would you say that?"

"Don't you remember what you said?"

"Sort of. Maybe you should tell me. I think I was pretty out of it."

"They found you in the equipment closet. Remember that?"

"Vaguely. I was … ." The recollection of what happened flushed through her head. "Oh my god! Who *was* that guy?" She put her hands between her legs to feel for damage and winced at the bruises.

"I don't know. They said he left as soon as they opened the door."

"Who opened the door? How much did they see?"

"I don't know, but they said most of your clothes were on, if that's what you mean. You didn't want to let go of the silly microphone for the longest time. What were you doing with it? It kind of freaked us out."

"I, I don't remember," she lied and turned redder. Struggling, she tried to reprise her mantra but had lost her inner voice. Frustrated, she tried harder until she ran out of breath and looked helpless. Finally, she burst out crying. "Chodya's dead!"

Donna wasn't surprised. "Then so is Doh-na! Welcome back, Trudy. Let's celebrate! I'm in the mood for eggs over-easy and some bacon."

After retrieving his instrument from the studio, Jon went to his rehearsal hall to make some noise. His bandmates weren't there, so he used the time to try out some new ideas on his guitar. The D string run that ended with a barred A on the second fret was straight country, and he knew he had a winner chorus as the lick bounced off a first position E. The long-tone melody was as close as he ever got to crooning.

Wild dreams in July.
Try baby, try try try.
Wild dreams in July.

While he was working on verse lyrics, he heard a knock on the door and went to open it.

"'Bout time you heard me," Dennis said. He had on his brimmed beret and was in a particularly good mood. "Nice riff. Play that chorus again."

Happy for the compliment, Jon obliged, and when he sang the lyrics, Dennis joined in with the exact harmony Jon had heard in his head. He was surprised at the smooth, clarion tone of Dennis's voice, and they both heard something special about the vocal combination.

Dennis saw the old console in the other room. "I came over to hook that up, but maybe you want to make some music instead?"

Jon remembered how much he liked what Dennis had done on synthesizer. "Sure man, just plug in."

Manning the synthesizer, Dennis recreated the surging ground swells and gravelly bass lines that Jon had found so inspiring, and by the time they stopped jamming an hour later, it was clear they weren't finished.

Spiritualized Glossary

Spiritualized Characters

Agent Mark Dobson – missing Customs Bureau officer
Agent Todd Falin – Customs Bureau officer
Agent William Walker – chief of Colorado Customs Bureau
Benzi Mogul – music business impresario
Jack Aikens – Boulderado hotel manager
Chief Niwot – Native American chief and ghost
Chodya (Trudy) – aspiring Buddhist nun
Crystal – waitress at Buddhist restaurant
Cynthia – BlueStar Studio receptionist
Demario – Oswaldo's muscle
Dennis – BlueStar Studio engineer
Diane – BlueStar Studio receptionist
Donna (Do nah) Garfinkle – baker, Jon Cells' girlfriend
Edward Hardaway (the Professor) – mountain recluse, Walter's brother
Farah – ski instructor, Sasha's sister
Officer McKnight – Steamboat Springs law enforcer
Gyalpo – Buddhist monk, sorcerer
Hipolito – skinner, musician
Jampo – cook at Buddhist restaurant
Janice Reading – mountain hippie

Jim Temple – Steamboat Springs ski basin operator
Joel – married to Nancy
Jon Cells – musician
Josh Carter – rancher
Ken Ken – Buddhist from New York
Kundun – Buddhist monk, driver
Lama Yeshe – head of Buddhist monastery
Duke Dunn – studio owner, pilot, smuggler
Marco – musician
Marsha Freedman – LA talent manager
Marty Freedman – LA talent manager
Mavis – waitress at Boulderado
Miko – Simone's girlfriend
Mr. Lawry – Boulderado's resident octogenarian
Nancy – owner of Satsang Diner
Nima – Stanley's consort
Niwot's Brave – Native American ghost
Officer Wedge Walker– – Granby cop, Agent Walker's brother
Oswaldo Benitez – Mexican businessman, airplane customizer
Patrick – talent manager, Benzi's second in command
Red Cloud – Native American chief
Remy Lambert – Duke's Mississippi homeboy
Roddy – musician, Rosella's boyfriend
Rosella – singer, waitress
Samantha – Walter's wife
Sandy – health food salesman
Sarquette – Miko's friend
Simone LeFete – Boulderado shopkeeper
Stanley, Earl of Dunraven – Colorado power broker
Sasha – waitress at Boulderado, Farah's sister
Tara – waitress at Buddhist restaurant
Tenzin – Buddhist monk, dishwasher
Tom Carter – rancher, Craig airport manager
Walter Hardaway (the Professor) – electronics engineer

Buddhist words

Bindu – latent energy in the first chakra
Bodhisattva – one who strives to free all beings from the birth and death cycle
Bodhichitta – the desire to realize enlightenment for the sake of others
Bon – ancient religion of Tibet
Chakra – energy center within human body
Chod – purification ritual
Damaru – ritual, handheld drum
Dharma – cosmic law and order
Getsulma – female novice monk
Kangling – ceremonial bone flute
Ojas – transmuted bindu energy
Phurba – magic Tibetan dagger
Prana – energy
Pranayama – breath control activity
Pratimoksha – individual liberation
Sangha – spiritual community
Tantra – yogic practice for transmuting sexual energy
Three Jewels – foundation of monastic life: Buddha, Dharma, Sangha
Tupla – a magical being created by ritual meditation
Zafu – meditation cushion

Native American Words

Kinnikinnick – smoke mixture
Paha Sapa – Black Hills of South Dakota, their holy place
Pemmican – meat jerky
Wakan Tanka – the Great Spirit

Name Derivations

Aikens – early Boulder prospector
Chodya – Gujarati slang
Demario – Mexican cow name
Dohna – a female deity
Falin – Irish wolf
Gyalpo – a sorcerer's ghost
Jampo – gentle
Kundun – the presence
Lama Yeshe – wise one
Nima – sun
Sarquette (Serket) – Egyptian goddess of healing stings and bites
Strothers (surname) – early Coloradan
Tara – mother goddess
Tenzin – first name of Dalai Lama
Walker (surname) – early Coloradan

Suggested Reading

Centennial by James Mitchner
Guns, Germs, and Steel by Jared Diamond
Magic and Mystery in Tibet by Alexandra David-Neel
The Heart of Everything There Is by Bob Drury and Tom Clavin
Chief Left Hand by Margaret Coel

VAPORIZED

MANHATTAN, THURSDAY MORNING, APRIL 15TH 1982

It's just my disposition,
To do the things I do.
A man in my position,
Holds some things to be true.

CHAPTER 1

Jon Cells never filed a tax return, so when the noise woke him up that day, he smacked his hand on the bedside table where his alarm clock lived and tried to go back to sleep. The annoying sound didn't stop, and when he realized it was coming from outside, he got up and stuck his head and torso out the apartment window. There were too many vehicles to tell which one was honking, so he yelled at all of them.

"Shut up!" he roared in a hoarse morning voice, straining to be heard over the din. The sidewalk was full of pedestrians but no one looked up. The car alarm stopped by itself, but other cars, jockeying for position as they inched along the crowded street, drowned out the morning calm with angry beeps and tire squeals. Sneezing on exhaust fumes, Jon forced the window shut. The giant neon clock across the street – the one he actually relied on – blinked through his flimsy curtains. He lit a cigarette and re-arranged his hair, trying to come to grips with reality.

Yesterday's clothes were still on the chair, but he picked up the electric guitar lying next to them instead. Sitting naked on the edge of the bed, he cradled the cool, contoured body against his skin and fingered the neck, mindlessly strumming the song he had been working on the night before. G minor to C minor, then back again. The rhythm crept into his right hand and an early morning dream began to re-materialize. In it, he was performing with his band in front of a packed house at Max's Kansas City. They bounced a heavy pocket off the low ceiling and the crowd pulsed provocatively under its suggestive weight. Lyrics squirmed on his tongue like a live oyster. *"Just my disposition, to do the things I do."* He savored the lines a few times before the taste of inspiration stood him up. Holding the body of the guitar against his waist with his right hand, he bent his knees, one at a time, and marched in place to the rhythm. Then the song took on a life of its own. His left hand stayed with G minor on the third fret while his huge right thumb raked down on the strings and snapped the up-strums. A bass line formed from the hammer-ons and lift-offs. *"A man in my position holds some things to be true,"* he rhymed, repeating the lines until they rode the beat. Weaving some single-note figures between the changes, he felt his free-swinging manhood pulse to life, but just as conviction took shape, his ten dollar alarm clock decided to remind him of the time. Frustrated that he couldn't capture his fresh ideas, he knocked the clock off the table, leaned his guitar back on the chair, and picked up his clothes. Slipping on the same slinky shirt he'd been wearing all week, he wriggled bare-ass into skin-tight jeans, kicked the bedroom door shut with the back of his boot, and abandoned songwriting for the day.

438

Over thirty, in a beaten leather jacket and determined to keep his dream alive, Jon cruised past the densely packed import boutiques on Canal Street, his field of vision as much occupied by the demons in his head as with the colorful plastic gargoyles hanging from the eaves. Tousling his hair as he passed fragments of his reflection in the store windows, he glanced furtively to see who might be watching. He wasn't sure if anyone was; but that was only half the problem.

Jon wanted it all: recognition, rationalization, notoriety, compensation, adoration, vindication, and relief from the pressures in his head. He wasn't sure how he was going to achieve "it" – what he called "artistic success" – but he knew he was running out of time. Unsettled and dissatisfied, every clack of his heel on the pavement gave him the comforting illusion that even if he was years behind, he was, at least, still firmly on his way.

His wiry frame was charged with nervous energy as he twisted through shopkeepers' offerings that protruded onto the sidewalk. With pointed boots, he strode around early morning browsers, groggy homeless sleepers, professional dog walkers, and uniformed school children. He avoided eye contact with the young lovers holding hands, didn't acknowledge the head nods of other pedestrians, and steered clear of all contact that might alter his appointment with destiny.

A subliminal soundtrack paced his heels-first tromp. Gibberish, masquerading as words, gurgled between the lyrics he had already settled on.

Just my disposition,
To do the things I do.
A man in my position,
Holds some things to be true.

Moving smoothly across the uneven sidewalks and curbs like a stealthy predator, Jon crossed the side streets as if he had special permission from the traffic gods who regulated the daily migration through the stone canyons. The familiar smells of smoke and coffee eddied around the vortex of his fitful march, and he breathed in the edible vapors deeply enough to satisfy his hunger without breaking stride. People seemed to bounce off his energy field like polarized magnets as he careened through the busy streets of lower Manhattan with the untamed confidence of a distorted whole-tone solo.

Approaching the wide ravine of Broadway, Jon spotted an intriguing ripple in the scattered flock of people ahead of him – a shapely woman walking in the same direction. Almost unconsciously, he accelerated through the sidewalk gauntlet, trying to get closer. But before he could catch up, the woman sashayed across Broadway and the lights changed, leaving him stuck on the other side. Squinting into the bright clouds of the gray morning that silhouetted the buildings, he waited impatiently at the edge of the swirling river of traffic.

While he was waiting, switching his weight from one foot to the other, a middle-aged man edged warily away from him. Jon didn't notice him or the two schoolgirls who were also waiting to cross. The children were too young to understand Jon's kinetic presence, but their bodies reacted, sending one of them stumbling off the curb and into the street. Instinctively, the middle-aged man grabbed her arm and pulled her back to safety just before she was sideswiped by a taxicab.

"Watch where you're going!" the man lashed out at both the taxi and Jon.

Jon barely heard him. He had seen the little girl saved from disaster, but it never crossed his mind that he had anything to do with it. Who was that guy talking to? Jon looked around and wasn't sure.

"Watch where you're going!" the man repeated, pointing an admonishing finger at Jon's face.

Jon squinted down and tightened his lips against gritted teeth. Six foot two, vain, and sometimes mistaken for Robert Plant, his shaggy blond mane and bright blue eyes made him believe he was as important as he felt. His resentment circuits began to charge, but before he could retaliate, caution seized his accuser. The man lowered his arm to the shoulder of the youngster he had rescued, and the girl moved within the aura of his protection. Jon disengaged, and hurried across the street as soon as the lights changed. A few steps behind, the man shepherded the young girls through the intersection and waited until Jon had gone ahead.

The street-corner incident had thrown off Jon's timing, so he slowed down to peek into the buildings, looking for the woman who had caught his eye. He thought he saw her disappear into a corner shop and stopped for a closer look. The bright daylight obscured the store interior, and he had to cup his eyes against the glass to see inside. A man at the overstocked bodega spoke to a customer whose curly hair was cinched in a high ponytail. Jon couldn't see her face, but while he was pressed up against the glass, Sonya Diaz leaned over the counter and kissed her uncle on the cheek as he handed her a small bag. Jon couldn't remember where he had seen her before and crept away before she came out.

Still walking with the schoolgirls a safe distance behind, Agent Ralph Lowell saw the top of Jon's head bobbing through the crowd ahead of them. He accompanied the girls to the gate of their schoolyard, then continued another block to his office building on Varick Street. After showing his badge to the guard, he took the elevator to the second floor and settled into his administrative job at the United States Customs Department.

Detective Todd Falin, who was already at work in the Enforcement Division of the Customs Department one floor up from Agent Lowell, had no idea that Jon Cells was even in New York. The file with his picture in it had been sitting on his desk for a week, but there were so many other files related to the same investigation he hadn't looked through it yet. It had been three years since Detective Falin had even thought about Jon Cells, so when he finally open the file later that morning he was surprised to see Jon's picture on his desk again. The memo from the FBI authorizing the stakeout at Laden Imports didn't mention him, and Detective Falin didn't understand his connection to the case. As he shuffled through the stack of reports and surveillance photos, trying to piece together the relationships between his suspects, he remembered the Colorado bust that had put Jon's cohorts out of business. He never knew if Jon was guilty of anything, because by the time it came to charge somebody, the Justice Department decided to concentrate on bigger targets. Jon had slipped off Detective Falin's radar without even knowing he had been on it – and had no idea that the place he was now working at was under surveillance by the same man.

Ironically, the same bust that had helped Detective Falin earn his promotion to the New York office was also the reason Jon Cells had moved back east. When Duke, Jon's freewheeling Colorado backer, got arrested, Jon bought a box van for his equipment and moved back to New York, hoping to continue his career. After several years in the relative isolation of the Rocky Mountains, he was more than ready to bond with the musical zeitgeist that had migrated from London to Manhattan. His band moved with him, and they fit right in with the post-punk music scene that was starting to turn out national acts. Money was tight, but they rented a loft together and scraped by between gigs. Totally committed, Jon was determined to make a name for himself, and believed he was on the verge of something big. He went midnight bowling with David Byrne and the Talking Heads, visited the eat-out bars and invitation-only clubs with Joey Ramone and other low-life celebrities, shared a love interest with his arch-friend from Boulder, Marc Campbell, and was a regular in the crowd at CBGB's and other clubs where Seymour Stein and other music business tastemakers cultivated talent. Jon's group, Cells, played some shows in and around New York, got a little local radio airplay, and was developing a reputation as a contender before they suffered the critical setback they were still trying to recover from.

A late-night altercation with the manager of a rival band resulted in Jon's arrest for possession of a controlled substance, and the punishment – ninety days of supervised release – required him to, among other things, get a job society approved of. Humbled, his father's contact helped him find work in the warehouse of a perfume factory at the western end of Canal Street. As the singer, songwriter, and leader of the band, Jon's inability to maintain the rock and roll lifestyle caused all their gigs to be cancelled and sent his bandmates scrambling for other opportunities. But Jon felt like they were holding him back and he didn't really miss them. He rented a room in a different apartment and planned on lying low for a few months, cutting himself off, using the parole as an excuse to write, rest, and reinvent himself before restarting his career as a solo artist.

Nearing the perfume factory, the sickeningly sweet smells scented the sidewalk for two blocks in all directions, and he held his breath as he went inside for another day's penance. Surprisingly, despite fifteen years of promoting his outsized artistic visions – often at the expense of his health – he was still ruggedly handsome and exceedingly strong. And although his day job was physically very demanding, it wasn't much of a mental challenge, so he was able to keep his internal soundtrack going most of the time. There were only ten more days to go before the terms of his parole were satisfied and he would be free to come out of hiding, quit his day job, and reassume control of his destiny.